Praise for
Lauraine Snelling

Wake the Dawn

"Snelling (*One Perfect Day*) continues to draw fans with her stellar storytelling skills. This time she offers a look at smalltown medical care in a tale that blends healing, love, and a town's recovery.... Snelling's description of events at the small clinic during the storm is not to be missed."
—*Publishers Weekly*

"Snelling's fast-paced novel has characters who seek help in the wrong places. It takes a raging storm for them to see tha̶ ... ̶m the wh̶

"Lau̶
page̶
Daw̶

Reunion

"Inspired by events in Snelling's own life, *Reunion* is a beautiful story about characters discovering themselves as the foundation of their family comes apart at the seams. Readers may recognize themselves or someone they know within the pages of this book, which belongs on everyone's keeper shelf."

—*RT Book Reviews*

"*Reunion* is a captivating tale that will hook you from the very start.... Fans of Christian fiction will love this touching story."

—**FreshFiction.com**

"Snelling's previous novels (*One Perfect Day*) have been popular with readers, and this one, loosely based on her own life, will be no exception."

—*Publishers Weekly*

On Hummingbird Wings

"Snelling can certainly charm."

—*Publishers Weekly*

One Perfect Day

"Snelling writes about the foibles of human nature with keen insight and sweet honesty."

—**National Church Library Association**

"Snelling's captivating tale will immediately draw readers in. The grief process is accurately portrayed, and readers will be enthralled by the raw emotion of Jenna's and Nora's accounts."

—*Romantic Times Book Reviews*

"...[a] spiritually challenging and emotionally taut story. Fans of Christian women's fiction will enjoy this winning novel."

—*Publishers Weekly*

Heaven Sent Rain

Heaven Sent Rain

A Novel

Lauraine Snelling

New York • Boston • Nashville

Copyright © 2014 by Lauraine Snelling

FaithWords
Hachette Book Group
237 Park Avenue
New York, NY 10017

www.FaithWords.com

Printed in the United States of America

RRD-C

First edition: July 2014
10 9 8 7 6 5 4 3 2 1

FaithWords is a division of Hachette Book Group, Inc.
The FaithWords name and logo are trademarks of Hachette Book
Group, Inc.

The Hachette Speakers Bureau provides a wide range of authors for
speaking events. To find out more, go to
www.HachetteSpeakersBureau.com or call (866) 376-6591.

The publisher is not responsible for websites (or their content) that are
not owned by the publisher.

Library of Congress Cataloging-in-Publication Data
Snelling, Lauraine.
Heaven sent rain : a novel / Lauraine Snelling. -- First edition.
pages cm
ISBN 978-0-89296-913-5 (pbk.) -- ISBN 978-0-89296-912-8 (ebook) 1.
Businesswomen Fiction. 2. Man-woman relationships--Fiction. I. Title.
PS3569.N39H46 2014
813'.54--dc23
2013047315

To my brother Don Clauson and my sister Karen Chafin—both of whom have made me aware of what a great job Mom and Dad did raising their kids.

Heaven Sent Rain

Chapter One

He's there again.

Dinah Taylor wanted to ignore the small boy and his dog huddling outside the Extraburger. She'd thought he was waiting for someone the other day, but what if he was hungry? And today the mist was struggling to keep from turning into rain. If he was waiting for someone, couldn't he wait inside? No, not with a dog.

Surely he wasn't panhandling.

She slowed, trying to decide what to do. *I don't have time for this today.* Without bothering to check her watch, she knew she would be late. What a way to start a Monday.

But what if he is hungry? The thought refused to leave.

Heaving a less than happy sigh, she stopped in front of him. "Have you had breakfast?"

He looked up at her, dark eyes huge in his face, and shook his head, his Royals baseball hat cocked to the side.

"Is someone coming to meet you?" She knew she sounded abrupt. Right now abrupt was the only tone she could muster.

He shook his head again and wrapped an arm around his scruffy-looking dog. His clothes appeared to be clean; he clutched his backpack with the other arm.

"Shouldn't you be in school?"

"It's not time yet."

Dinah Marie Taylor, you cannot leave a small boy out here alone. A small hungry boy.

"If I get you a breakfast sandwich, you'll go on to school?" He nodded. "What about your dog?"

"She walks me to school."

"And then waits?"

"No, she goes home."

So he wasn't homeless at least. He must live near here. "I'll be right back."

"Thank you."

His immediate response caught her by surprise. She stepped up to the counter, ordered breakfast for him and her usual, tall coffee and breakfast sandwich. "Two separate sacks to go, please."

"Yes, ma'am." The tall skinny kid gave her the total and then her change from a twenty.

"You know anything about that boy outside?"

"I know he can't bring his dog in here and won't leave her out there alone."

"Thanks." She picked up the two bags and headed outside. Usually she left by the inner door that led to the atrium. Usually. If this was any indication, today was not going to go as usual. A knot in her stomach tightened. Handing the sack to him, she added, "I bought you cocoa in case you were cold."

"Thank you." He opened the bag and looked in, then up at her. "I like potatoes like this, too."

The winter wind caught the front flap of her white wool coat and tried to jerk it off. "Look, why don't you come inside the building to eat that."

"No thanks. We'll eat on the way to school." He rose to his feet. "Come on, Downmutt."

Had she heard him right? Was that the dog's name? She pulled open the door, then looked over her shoulder. The two were already moving down the sidewalk. *You can't worry about him; you have enough on your plate for today.* Her staccato heels tapped across the marble floor and, thankfully, carried her into an elevator immediately. You'd think that after ten years as president of her own company, Food for Life, she would be used to budget time. After all, it came twice a year. But this one was the biggie, and in three days she had to present it to her board, ready to defend it and herself. At least that was the way she felt. Her mind understood that, but her stomach did its own thing.

After a pause to suck in a supposedly calming breath, she turned the knob on the door and, smile in place, strode into the reception area. "Good morning."

April Benders, receptionist, assistant, secretary, and friend after all these years, smiled up at her. "They're all on your desk." She glanced at the clock. "As of twenty minutes ago. I have a stack of orange slips for you and good morning to you, too."

Dinah knew she was late, which was not like her at all. In fact, she could count on one hand the times she'd been late in all these years.

But then—that boy. What was the story behind him?

"I know, sorry. Did you look the departmental budgets over?"

April shook her head. "Nope, I gave you mine and you know I hate budgets worse than you do."

"Thanks." Dinah strode two doors down to her office on the left. After setting her briefcase and white leather hobo bag on her desk, she hung her coat in the closet and crossed the room to sink into her white leather chair.

Picking up coffee and sandwich, she spun her chair to look out at the winter-bleak park over the roof of the building across the street. Spring in Ohio never came early enough for her. The mist had gathered force and now ran in lazy rivulets down the window. Half the sandwich later, she rewrapped it and, holding her coffee in both hands, studied the sky that might be showing a bit of blue—anytime now. All the while, she forcefully ignored the stack of reports on her desk and the message slips.

The picture of that little boy would not leave her mind, hanging about on the edges, as if waiting to pounce. Had she done the right thing? What else could she have done? Where did he live? Why would anyone name a dog something like that? What was the boy's name? What if he was there tomorrow? The buzz of the intercom spun her back around.

"I've been holding your calls. You want me to continue?"

"Yes. Forever."

A snort answered her remark.

"I'm attacking the return calls now. Give me the rest of the slips later. Thanks."

She spun her chair toward the desk and started in—returning phone calls. An hour later, she sent those that April could respond to, made sure her notes were legible for later, and picked up the top page, their company purpose, a document she reread every Monday. "Food for Life is here to develop and produce supplements that will promote healing and a richer, healthier lifestyle for those in need, particularly those with diabetes." She read it aloud to assist her focus.

And so that's what they were doing. They had a great product about to be released to the public, named Scoparia, a dietary supplement that was providing help for people with debilitating conditions, although "diabetes" wasn't mentioned in the promotional material, of course. Actually, according to the test results, almost miraculous help, but in order to avoid costly review by the FDA, they would call it a "dietary supplement." Therefore it did not need a prescription and was within the legal boundaries that the government inflicted upon businesses. Let those folks who used it tell of the success. The double-blind results were indeed astounding.

She stood and walked around the room, doing calf stretches against one wall. Her white-wool, below-the-calf dress did nothing to impede her movement, but it was a dress. Like all the companies in the building, they had access to the gym in the basement, but today she had to focus on the budgets.

If he didn't have money for breakfast, did he have lunch in his backpack? Was there such a thing as cafeterias in schools any longer? Would the teacher give him money? How did this work?

Why in the world am I stewing about this? I don't even particularly like small children.

She crossed to the kitchen a la break room, poured herself another mug of coffee, and returned to her dungeon. Three days until the board meeting.

By noon she had made her way through a final review of the PR budget. Sticky notes showed where it needed more work. She started on the office budget. That was the easiest. At 12:30 she called April and had her order lunch in. Two out of four budget proposals now in the out basket.

Chapter Two

Y ou said you wouldn't do this anymore!" Dinah wasn't
able to keep the exasperation out of her voice. Didn't
he understand it wasn't safe to sit out here alone?

"I know, but..." The small boy hid his face in his knees,
his thin back curved against the slate wall. The scruffy dog
beside him glared up at her, one lip slightly curled.

He'd promised her he'd go straight to school the second day she'd bought him breakfast. He had the next
day or the day after that, and now here he was, in the
same spot, again. She heaved a sigh. "Have you eaten
yet?"

The grubby hat moved but he didn't look up. The dog
half stood.

She squatted in spite of the wet sidewalk and the way
her white umbrella tried to fly off on its own. "Please,
come have breakfast with me." She deliberately softened
her voice, as her heart demanded.

The bedraggled little boy hopped to his feet. "I remembered the leash." He snapped a tattered old web
leash onto the dog's collar and tied her to the NO PARKING
HERE TO CORNER sign.

"Come on, then."

She held out her hand and he slid his icy one into hers. Why he trusted her was beyond her, but the two of them marched into the warm interior.

"Your usual?" the boney, tattooed boy behind the cash register asked.

"Yes, thank you."

"S'cuse me." The kid let go of her hand and she watched as he walked off toward the restroom. He was an enigma. He'd mentioned a home, and was not filthy and derelict like so many people who lived on the street were forced to be. For a little kid, he was very articulate. Was he a welfare case, buried in the foster system? Nothing about the situation made any sense. Especially unexplainable was her interest. She cared about him.

But he was too much like—She chopped that line of thought clean off. No, she would never go there again. Never!

Just as she picked up their tray, he reappeared at her side, wiping his still-moist hands up and down on his shirt. He led her to the table in the corner by the window, most likely to keep lookout on his dog. She laid out their breakfast—his the child's meal, including the stupid little toy that came with it, her good old breakfast sandwich, and a cardboard box of scrambled eggs for the dog, whose bizarre name she refused to acknowledge. Downmutt? Not that she cared what the dog was called. Animals of any kind had never made it onto her list of favored things. Children hovered near the bottom. Safer that way.

She had started to take a bite when she caught his look of horror. She nodded. Sighing seemed endemic whenever she was around him. She folded her hands, closed her eyes, and waited. She should have left home earlier; now she was running late.

"Thank You, God, for this good food, for sending Jesus to love us. Amen."

She kept from shuddering. Too many memories fought to surface, but they failed to penetrate the steel-lined barrier.

She watched as he dug into his plate. He was that way yesterday, too. They ate inside that day, at this table now that she thought of it, and it was the first time she could really observe him. Someone, probably his mother, had taught him manners. Just like yesterday, his routine was constant and careful—actually, almost cultured. Yesterday, she had learned his name was Jonah. He had chatted about this and that. He claimed he always drew in pencil. Made her wonder if he'd never had crayons, but of course he had; he was in the second grade, or so he said. She had no reason to think he ever lied. He talked about school. Only.

Yesterday's conversation had actually been productive in small ways. He knew she didn't like *Downmutt* and suggested, "How about just plain old Mutt?" and she cheerfully acquiesced. And she was thrilled; his closest friend, and he changed her name just for Dinah. Possibly he didn't like the first name any more than she did, but what if he did?

She poured two creamers into her tall specialty coffee and sipped. Just the way she liked it, not quite searing. Surely the morning would improve now. "So, how is school going?"

"Good. I got a hundred on my spelling."

"Excellent."

"Yesterday was art day. I drew Dow—" He stopped. "Ms. Farrell said it looks just like real."

"Can you show me sometime?"

He nodded and took a drink of his hot chocolate. "I got it here. Thought maybe you'd..." And he reached for his tattered little backpack.

"I'd love to see it."

He handed her a paper with a wrinkled corner. She stared at the pencil drawing of the dog. It all but barked at her. Dumbfounded, she shifted her stare from the paper to the boy across the table. "I know you are good, but this is so real, I..."

He watching her intently, apparently looking for some sort of sign. He whispered. "You sure you like it, then?"

"Yes!" She nodded with her whole body. *Please, Lord, keep me from hurting him.* "I just don't know what to say."

The thought struck her: *Do you know what you just did?*

No, what?

You asked the Lord to help you.

I did not!

You did. The voice was so positive she quit breathing. How could she have?

"Would you like it?" His voice came so soft, so tentative.

"Of course I would like it, but, ah, are you certain?"

A hint of a smile tugged at the side of his mouth. "I drew it for you."

"Doesn't your mother want it?"

"She has plenty." He glanced at the clock. "I need to leave. Can't be late for school."

"May I walk you there?"

"No, I know you're late for work."

She glanced at her watch. "If the boss can't be late for work, who can?"

"Thank you." He slid from the seat, jammed the box of eggs in his backpack, took the tray of trash, and grinned at her. "Thanks for breakfast."

By the time she had her things gathered together, he was out the door.

"Some kid, ain't he?" The cash-register boy was now wielding a cleaning rag.

"Has he been coming here long?"

The kid nodded. "Used to be with his mother. Ain't seen her in a while..." He paused, his wiping stilled. "Long time, actually. Then he quit coming."

"Hm." She started to ask another question, but he had turned to answer someone else. Instead of taking the outside door, she exited via the main lobby in the atrium and strode to the elevator to the fourth floor. Her company had expanded to encompass this entire floor in addition to the lab on the third floor, two expansions in the last year. If she allowed the shock of it all to surface, she'd go catatonic for sure.

She had nearly reached the elevators when an older woman suddenly stepped in front of her. "Are you Dinah Taylor?"

"Yes." Now what?

"My name is Mary Swann and I lied to you." The woman was well put together with nice clothes and an attractive hairstyle.

When confusion reigns, shift blame. "Frankly, Ms. Swann, you seem a lot happier than a liar ought to be."

Indeed, she was beaming. "I was one of the people with Type II diabetes who took part in a study your company did last November. We were asked to try your test product and see how it affected us."

"Scoparia. And you lied about the results?"

"Oh, no! No, no! You see I started using the test product and within a week, I felt much better; in fact, I could control my blood-sugar levels almost without using insulin. Well, my husband has Type II diabetes also, so that's why I lied."

"I don't understand."

"I told the test director that I had lost my supply on a trip, left it in a motel. So she sent me another, of course, right away. That was the lie."

"You doubled the dose?"

"No, my husband started using it. We still do our blood-sugar test daily, of course, but we rarely need insulin anymore, even though the product test has been over for quite a while, and we're back to all the activities we used to enjoy. In fact, we're volunteering at the animal shelter and we're on the litter crew in the park, like we used to do before we lost so much energy."

"Mrs. Swann, I am very happy to hear this!"

The lady grasped Dinah's hands in hers. "Miss Taylor, we cannot thank you enough! Your Scoparia has turned our lives around."

"And you have brightened my day immeasurably. My whole week. The year!"

The lady squeezed Dinah's hands. "Please, keep up the good work!"

"We shall."

And the lady hustled off.

The elevator doors whisked open and Dinah stepped in. But she did not go to her fourth-floor office. She pushed 3 and stepped out into her lab complex. Marcella's door stood open, as it usually did.

She stepped inside. "Good morning, Marcella."

"Good morning, Dinah."

"The double-blind test on Scoparia last November; one of the subjects was a Mary Swann."

Marcella turned to her monitor. "Two Ns?"

"I suppose; I don't know."

"Here she is."

Dinah moved to the side of Marcella's desk to see the screen. "Was she the product or the placebo?"

"The product." Marcella pointed. "And look at her testimonial from the exit interview; it's so effusive we probably can't use it. It's *too* good. In fact, she got two kits; lost one." She sat back and frowned at Dinah. "Do you think she doubled her dose?"

"She gave it to her diabetic husband and he apparently got lasting results just as spectacular as hers. They still feel the effects. You might want to interview her."

"Wow. Yeah."

"Later." Dinah took the stairs up to the fourth floor and her office. Once upon a time she didn't use elevators at all. Must be getting old.

"Morning." *Cheery* and April Benders were synonymous. April had been with her now for nine years, not long after the opening of Food for Life. "I see you got your coffee already."

"I did. Jonah was outside on the wall again."

"In the rain?"

"I know. I wanted to walk him to school, but—you'd think since I am so much bigger than he that if I wanted to walk him to school, I just would." She shook her head, puzzled beyond sensible.

"You got to admit, he's a sweetie." April handed Dinah a stack of messages. "Your stack of orange slips. You need to return the top one immediately if not before."

She nodded. "Thanks. Hold any other calls until I wade through this pile. Coffee after?"

"You might need it after." April sounded grim. So it was one of those days.

Was April ever right. Orange slips. A different chore on each one. Dinah knew those reminders were listed neatly on her computer, too, but somehow tossing the done ones gave her a sense of satisfaction that deleting a line item just could not provide, sort of like slamming a phone receiver is so much more satisfying than swiping your finger across a screen. The orange slips and email took three hours. She remembered what her Gramma Grace once said: "We'd do such dollar things if it weren't for all that nickel stuff." This was nickel stuff—things that mean nothing but you dare not dismiss them.

"Ready for coffee?" April asked.

"I am, and now we need to finalize the plans the team put together for the Scoparia rollout." A dream come true or another "almost" that wouldn't quite measure up? "Had lunch yet?"

"An hour ago. Should I order for you?"

"I still have a chicken wrap in the fridge." Dinah stretched mightily, her years of playing volleyball through college staying with her in the sure need to stretch often. The morning rain had ended and the sun had broken through the clouds, for the first time in several days. The day had brightened so much that Dinah wished she believed in omens.

And she made an executive decision. "Instead of calling another team meeting, I want just the two of us. If we keep it just the two of us for now, do you think the others will feel left out?"

"You're kidding, right? Left out of another meeting? Back off or they'll be kissing your feet."

Dinah smiled. "The others are all under such tight deadlines, I don't want to waste their time. I'm glad we got the budget under control yesterday. I think we have a lot of work yet to do on this launch."

April nodded. "Where?"

"The back conference room; south-facing windows."

"Sun!"

"Absolutely. You bring your stuff and the laptops, I'll bring my lunch and folders." Instead of seeing herself as the captain or the coach of her team, she believed she was the setter, the one who brought out the best in everyone by always having the ball in the right place at the right time. Most of the time, it worked.

She stuck her chicken wrap in the nuke and prepared her coffee in the double-size blue mug emblazoned with the chemical diagram of acetylsalicylic acid. Aspirin. She'd need all that coffee. Maybe the aspirin, too.

When she entered the conference room, April was setting up at the far end, as close to the windows as she could get. "I have it all transferred to these memory sticks. I'm naming the files for this thing by date; and I made some printouts, too, just the way you like it. Randy sent over the charts and graphs, and I know Alyssa is just finishing assembling her report."

"Thank you." Dinah settled to the laptop beside April's. Now to work.

She pulled down the paper on her wrap. Jonah should be getting out of school about now. Did he go straight home? Did his Mutt await him? *There you go again! Get back to business.*

They covered every aspect of the presentation, including what would be displayed in the background.

The catered lunch. Smoked salmon or salmon salad? The caterer wanted smoked Atlantic salmon; okay, they'd go with that.

What was Jonah's diet the rest of the day? *Stop it, Dinah!*

The question-and-answer session. Whom should they plant in the audience to jump-start questioning when it slows up?

Now. The dinner in the evening.

"I still think we should have black-tied the dinner." April ticky-ticked her keyboard.

"The tone is supposed to be casual." Dinah rather wished she didn't obsess so over details, but it was the details that made the event. Any event.

April rolled her eyes. "Well, I won't be surprised if most show up that way. We've been fielding emails and questions for a week."

"It's my party. I refuse."

"I know, but you can't cut off their ties or anything." April came from Arizona, where a well-known restaurateur did just that to any customer who wore a tie into the dining area. It was a great business *schtick*; locals deliberately brought their out-of-town guests just to watch the receptionist whip out her huge shears and clip them off. Half-ties decorated the walls and ceiling.

Leave it to April to lighten the intensity.

"Anything else?"

"Your lunch date tomorrow canceled."

"Good." Lunch under pressure, never a good idea.

Then she got what was likely a very good idea. "You've been really working this thing. May I take you to lunch tomorrow?"

"No, thanks. I'm joining Adam in the school cafeteria. Tomorrow is parent day."

"Sorry, I forgot. Have fun." Sometimes when she thought about how April loved her family, it made her want to rethink her stand on having a family of her own. Almost, but not quite.

End of day. Sufficient unto the day is the evil thereof. She hated that Bible quote. She stopped by the office for her bag, coat, and umbrella. As she tucked her cell in its pocket, the corner of a piece of tablet paper caught her attention. She pulled the drawing from the front pocket of her bag and stared at it again. Mutt. The dog whose former name must not be mentioned. She would have it framed to put on her wall or on her desk here, so she could see it throughout the day. Why? Because it was extraordinary art, a professional-quality drawing by a second-grader. Besides, the pencil went well with the white décor.

She could just hang it somewhere at home, but since she spent most of her time there sleeping or planning, she would enjoy it here the most. Wondering if his mother had covered her refrigerator with her son's work or pinned it to the walls made her wish she knew for sure where he lived. While she had given him her business card and written her cell number on the back, making him promise to call if he needed help, he'd never reciprocated.

Well, for sure she had never had a picture of a dog before.

By choice.

Chapter Three

Success or no, Dinah found big affairs like this barely tolerable.

A few important people—and a lot of people who only thought they were important—milled about. They cruised past the food table and gathered in knots near the beverage bar. They nodded to each other and balanced plates with glasses and laughed too loudly. Kudos to the caterer who laid a lavish table with the requested tropical theme and a centerpiece of coconuts and coconut fronds, hibiscus, and frangipani. In short, your typical product launch a la Food for Life.

To her left, Ms. Cheery, a.k.a. April, wagged her head. "Not nearly as many here as I hoped, and not the big guns. No AP. We won't get far without AP."

Dinah thought there were more than enough strangers in this room. "Should we have scheduled it for a weekend?"

April shook her head. "Even worse. Everyone leaves town."

A smooth baritone: "You can be proud of not only an event like this but also the difference your product will make in people's lives."

Dinah turned to smile at the man stepping in on her right. "Thank you, and I'm always grateful for your support."

One rather bushy eyebrow rose. "Come, come, Dinah. How long have I known you?"

And supported you was what he didn't even infer, but Dinah did. Gratitude for Hal's belief in her from the beginning made her legs shake. She nodded. "Sorry, I guess I get into polite mode for affairs like this and..." She shrugged.

His smile said he understood. She had met Hal Adler at her college graduation when he had stopped her to offer congratulations—and a job. A dream job that anyone else would have created mayhem for, but her reserve had kept her quiet. All she really wanted to do was start her own research business, for want of a better word, now, not years down the road. Her ultimate dream was to discover and produce products to help people become healthier, especially those diagnosed with Type II diabetes. Had he been a venture capitalist, would she have leaped? But wise investors did not take fliers on a dream.

Hal's appearance had always been more that of an absent-minded professor than the power he really was. Tonight he was dressed up only out of regard for her; she understood that. He had changed out his tweed for an actual sport coat and, of all things, a modest, fashionable tie. She'd had no trouble spotting him in the penguin-and-tropical-birds melee.

"You look like a Greek goddess, simple and elegant."

"Thank you, Hal. And you look exceedingly handsome. A tie that's not painted in hideous colors."

He started to laugh and half choked on the drink in his

hand, coughing enough to make the man next to him slap him on the back.

"Sorry."

"No." He hacked a minute and cleared his throat. "No, you are not. We need some talk time and soon."

"I agree. And, Hal, I can't thank you enough."

"Let's say we're even and let it go at that." He nodded at one of his flunkies—*associates*, as he called them. "Later."

Dinah continued around the ballroom, greeting and introducing and counting the minutes until April would allow her to leave. One of the lesser news reporters, a petite blonde with a dissatisfied scowl (the scowl was probably present from birth, but the blondeness definitely was not) requested a photo op. *That's why we're here*, Dinah wanted to retort. But she didn't, of course.

She posed beside her product display, the Scoparia emblem as unique as the product. And she was glad to realize that she did indeed look good while still feeling comfortable. She had finally discovered a woman willing to create and sew the kind of formal clothes she wanted: classic designs with superior draping fabrics. Discomfort to look fashionable was as far from her lexicon as the sun from the earth. How can you walk in shoes like this young woman was wearing?

When the crowd eventually began to thin, she nodded and smiled and thanked and agreed and finally escaped. Cheery joined her as she was donning her white wool coat and retrieved her own.

Dinah shrugged into her coat. "You don't have to leave now, April. You enjoy this kind of thing."

"I promised the kids I wouldn't be late." She nodded to

the doorman, who signaled a cab forward. "I'll drop you." They went through the same routine at every event.

Total exhaustion struck like a viper. Dinah sank into the car seat and let her head fall against the cushion. At least this was over with and now they could continue working on the other projects as well as distribution for Scoparia. The cab pulled to the curb in front of Dinah's condo. Home sweet home. Dinah handed April a twenty and crawled out.

She hung her coat and didn't bother to turn on the lights as she made her way to the bedroom. It was over! She hung her gown and collapsed into bed. She was taking the next day off. In fact, the business was closed to give everyone a chance to recuperate with a three-day weekend before full-speed-ahead on Monday. Not working was mandatory.

She had promised Hal and April she would do the same. Only a promise would keep her from at least Monday-morning quarterbacking. What she would do with the morrow was still not decided. She knew how she was going to finish today. She opened the book she was reading to her place on page 81 and stretched out on her bed, but she fell asleep before she got to page 82.

Jonah and Mutt were ringing her doorbell. She knew it was them because...

Coming awake, she swallowed her pounding heart, so grateful it was a dream. Or was it? Was it night or morning? The clock said *a.m.* She had slept the night through.

She grabbed her robe, tying it as she headed for the ringing door. Checking the peephole, she saw that of course it wasn't Jonah, but a grinning delivery woman hiding behind a basket of white glads, roses, and who knew what else.

Breathing a sigh of relief, Dinah opened the door and gestured the emissary in.

"Hope it's not too early. The instructions were confusing. I hear congratulations are in order."

"Thank you, Minda. How you always manage to know what's going on astounds me." Dinah pointed to the four-foot-square coffee table in front of the sofas. The two requirements for all furniture had started years earlier: white and comfortable. None of that modern-just-admire style.

The lady set down the flower arrangement and stepped back. "Part of my job. Anything else I can get for you?"

"Can't think of anything. The flowers are stunning, as always."

"You enjoy your time off now, you hear?" She grinned and headed out the door. Delivery girl? Hardly. Minda Martin owned C's Floral Shop, and she always made sure Dinah received the best. They went back a long way.

Dinah inhaled the fragrance of roses and stocks, smiling at the baby's breath and yellow-throated gladiolus. Much as she loved fresh flowers, she never bought her own, a holdover from early days when one rose was an extravagance. She plucked out the card and nodded as she read. The same as always. No matter how she had tried, she had never learned who sent her the flowers, but she strongly suspected Hal was behind it. He covered his tracks well.

One of the roses and a sprig of baby's breath in her hand, she ambled into the kitchen. She would keep these separate on the kitchen table. After putting the flowers in a tall ivory bud vase, she started the coffee maker and set out grapefruit, yogurt, half-and-half, and granola. The sun kissing the rose on the table brought on another smile.

No rain. It seemed like it had been moping and raining all winter, but the weather had been just as varied and crazy worldwide. At least they had not been flooded or blizzarded or scorched or blown off the planet.

Allowing herself a leisurely breakfast at home instead of at the Extraburger reminded her: what if Jonah was there and he'd not eaten? A glance at the clock told her he was already in school, hungry or not. Perhaps someone else fed him when she wasn't there. Or perhaps not. That was what she would do today, learn more about Jonah. How, she had no idea, but now was the time. She had put this off far too long.

Two hours later, steeped in total frustration, she was no nearer the goal. There was one elementary school within walking distance of the Extraburger. School records were closed for reasons of privacy, they said. His father's name-sake? No Jonah was listed in any of the apartment houses in all of Eastbrook, let alone the immediate vicinity. All the Ws came up with zero: the who, what, why, when, and where. Wondering how to break into this set her staring out the window.

Should she have him followed? One possibility. Ask him direct questions? He'd not answered any before. She slapped her hands on her desk and returned to pacing, which had not helped previously. Going outside was the last remaining option, short of banging her head against the wall.

Bundled up against the deceptive March weather, she headed for the park. She could wait for him and walk him home from school! Why had that not occurred to her before? For someone supposedly so brilliant, she knew she sometimes lacked common sense. Hands thrust into her pockets, she continued walking, rejoicing in the slivers of green heralding the coming bulbs, the purple-, gold- and violet-streaked crocuses blooming riotously. Her boots tapped out a sharp rhythm counterpointed at times by the thrum of passing tires, a barking dog, and some birdsong she did not recognize.

Sometime later, she realized she had made a complete circle and stopped at the Bagelry. One should always go there early in the morning, not after the lunch crowd. She ordered her usual, the all-seeds bagel with a schmear of lox and cream cheese, with a tall vanilla latte, and settled into a wrought-iron chair outside in the sun. Only one other person braved the chill and smiled at her. Returning the smile, she dug into her bagel, tonguing the cream cheese off her upper lip. After draining the latte, she tossed the papers in the trash and turned into the grocer three doors up. The small mom-and-pop store held on in spite of the mega–shopping centers, all because of their loyal clientele and personal delivery when ordered. The way they catered to their customers made Nordstrom service look patchy. They delivered day or night, 365 days a year. The only time they had even been closed since Dinah moved into the neighborhood was the day of their daughter's funeral.

Dinah had forced herself to go, fighting the memories the service generated. Mrs. Braumeister held her close as they cried together. Dinah never cried. Today she dropped Greek yogurt, honey-blueberry granola, seven-grain bread, romaine, a chicken breast, and pork steak into her basket. She eyed the Swiss chocolate, searching for milk chocolate with hazelnuts.

"I kept one back for you," Mrs. Braumeister said, reaching under the counter when Dinah stopped at the cash register. "I figured you would be by someday soon."

"You spoil me."

"It's the mother in me. Don't you need some half-and-half by now?"

"Thank you." Dinah shook her head as she stopped in front of the dairy case. Surely these people were angels who happened to inhabit earthly bodies. When she hauled her groceries home and put them away a few minutes later, she found a container of applesauce included. She always had applesauce with her pork steaks.

Glancing at the clock, she hurried back down the three flights of stairs, drove to her office to park, then walked the few blocks to the school. Surely she had waited too long; what if she missed him again? She breathed a sigh of relief when she saw the lined-up cars and waiting parents—she'd made it. She leaned against the front fender of an empty SUV and smiled at the man in uniform who strolled up to her.

After a friendly greeting he asked, "Who are you waiting for?"

"Jonah."

"Jonah who?"

"I don't know."

He studied her. "Obviously, you are not his mother."

"No, just a friend."

"I see, and do you have permission to be waiting for him?" His face changed to deadpan.

"Not specifically. We're friends. I just thought I could walk home with him and—"

"His parents' names and address?"

"I don't know."

"Come inside with me, please, and we'll see what we can do." He barked into his radio, "Visitor coming in, code one." The officer led her not to the check-in desk but into a small room off to the side. "Please be seated. May I have your ID?"

"Of course, but…" She dug in her bag and handed him her driver's license.

Two police officers entered. Not campus security. Police. The security man gave them her driver's license and left.

Grimly, one of the two radioed in her name and address and license number.

She looked from face to face. "What's going on here? I just stopped by to walk home with a friend."

The hubbub of school being let out, children laughing and parents calling, penetrated the windowless office. Jonah was leaving now.

She started to rise. "If you will excuse me…"

"Please remain seated, Miss Taylor." It was not a polite request.

"Wait a minute. Why…You think I'm some pervert or stalker or…"

"If you don't mind, we'll ask the questions." However masked in politeness, it was an order.

Jonah's name? Address? If he were a friend, why did she know nothing about him? And she discovered that buying him breakfast was also strongly suspect. It's the opening door perverts use, like candy and help-me-find-my-lost-puppy.

They grilled her for over half an hour, apparently trying to squeeze blood from a turnip. Or information from someone who really, truly, did not know anything. Finally, with a dire warning not to associate with Jonah or appear in the neighborhood of the school, they let her go.

She walked back to her car in a daze. She had parked

in her office space because she had wanted to walk with Jonah. Still numb, she drove home.

The light on her phone was blinking. She tapped the playback. It must have been a wrong number since she heard only a noise, hissing in the background, and a cough. Caller ID said the number was blocked. Between that and the frightening fiasco at the school, a little snake of fury slithered into her consciousness. If she considered it, the snake owned a triangular head and curved fangs.

Her great fear in life—snakes, vipers, to be exact. The others she tolerated. How could a day that had started out so perfectly degenerate into chaos? Her stomach clenched and she forced herself to suck in and slowly exhale deep breaths. She'd learned the skill on the volleyball courts before the player smashed that first ball across the net. Breathe. Count. Breathe again. Relax!

Never was the only time allotted for a panic attack.

She jumped when the phone rang, but breathed again when she saw the caller. Thank the gods for Hal Adler. Sanity to the rescue. "How did you know I needed a friendly call right now?"

"I am prescient? I take it this has not been the perfect day you planned."

"Perhaps that is the problem. I didn't plan anything for today. I was ordered to rest, relax, and no replays."

"And you managed to do that?" Awe softened his voice.

"Mostly. I pretended I was someone else in a far land."

"And then?"

As she recounted her day, he made the appropriate noises until she got to the infuriating session at the school. "You made this up!"

"Hal, you know I don't tell stories. Besides I couldn't have dreamed this up. So now I'm a suspected pervert. They've all but dropped the noose around my neck."

"You want my law team to check into it?"

"What good would that do?"

A brief silence. Then, "And?"

"How did you know there was an *and*?"

"Prescient, I told you."

"An unusual call on my answering machine. I just had a strange reaction to a wrong number—at least that's what I think it is."

"What did they say?"

"Nothing. Some sort of a hissing, a pause, a cough, perhaps something in the background, and a click. The caller ID was blocked."

"Of course."

"Come on, Hal. It was just a wrong number."

"I'll check that one out, just in case. I have sources."

"I should never have told you." Guilt for worrying him made her shake her head. *Tempest in a teapot*, as her gramma used to say. If only her gramma were still alive, she might have some kind of family. A shutter clicked on the memories.

"Did you eat?" asked Father Hen.

"I did and I will and I refuse to worry and so should you." Barely dusk and here she was yawning—a jaw-cracking yawn. "I'm going to fix some supper, read in the tub, and go to bed early."

"What about the weekend?"

"I have no idea."

That night the ringing phone woke her, sort of. Twelve fifteen. "Hello?"

"Can you help me, please? I'm sorry to call." It took a moment for her to realize this wasn't a dream.

"Jonah. What is it, Jonah? Of course I'll help." She leaped out of bed, the phone clamped between shoulder and ear. "What is it?"

"D-down-d…is bleeding and Mommy can't say anything."

"I'll be right there."

"I'll wait on the corner." A sob. "I'm sorry. I need you."

Chapter Four

Running the stairs was far quicker than waiting for the elevator.

Her mind raced faster than her feet. Why didn't he wait at home? Why the corner? Did she know for sure which corner he meant? What was wrong with his mother? Why couldn't she speak? Dinah ran to her car, clicking the door opener as she reached her parking spot. She fumbled with the key in the ignition and, teeth clamped on her lower lip, finally forced the engine to roar to life. Drive carefully! She knew that, but the urge to play hot-rodder in the parking garage almost took over. Jonah! Jonah! Be safe. Even the exit arm took an hour to raise.

The streets were empty at this time of the morning, or middle of the night, take your pick. Knowing that the police had a way of lurking unseen, she kept sucking in deep breaths so she wouldn't be their latest victim. She passed the Extraburger, all her concentration focused on a small boy standing under a street lamp, his dog in his arms.

She swung in front of him and leaned over to throw open the door. "Do you need help?"

He shook his head and climbed in beside her, clutching

his dog close. The dog must have been through a war. She was bloody, dirt-caked, dripping.

"What happened?"

"Don't know. She went out and didn't come back and I went looking for her and I asked Mommy and she didn't answer and I found her and I think she got in a fight and..." He crashed into sobs, clutching his dog to his chest.

"Is your mother all right?"

Jonah nodded. "But she needs to rest, and..." He broke down again.

A vet, we have to find a vet. She reached for her bag to dig out her phone. No bag, no phone. Turning, she scanned the car, sure she must have tossed it in the back seat. No bag. *Go home!* She gunned the motor, careening down High Street. *No cops, no cops. Why can't there be a cop when you need one?* Did a bleeding dog constitute an emergency in police jargon? If one stopped her now, the ticket would be astronomical. *How could I forget my purse? Where did my head go? I never do things like this!* She who was always calm in emergencies had just destroyed her self image. Calling herself all sorts of uncomplimentary names did nothing to slow her speeding heart.

Back in the parking garage, she clicked open the doors and, in the light from the overhead, assessed the damage. Mud and blood covered the front and the arms of Jonah's jacket and now smeared the white leather seat. "Do you think she's in pain?"

"She keeps crying and trying to lick some of the worst spots but a couple of them keep bleeding and she can hardly walk. I don't know what to do." The light caught on his tear-streaked face. "Can you..."

"I can. We'll go up to my place and locate a veterinarian, an animal urgent care. If there even is such a thing." *How can I be thirty-four years old and not know things like this?* "Do you need help carrying her?"

"No, thank you. She doesn't like strangers much." He slid out the door and Mutt put one front paw on either side of his neck and started licking the fresh blood off her leg.

"You think she was in a fight?" She joined him as he came around the rear of her car, clicking the remote lock as they headed for the elevator. She could barely stand to look at the miserable dog. Never pretty anyway, right now she looked like a bit player in a Grade-C zombie movie. "Does your mother know you called me?" She should have asked that when she picked them up.

"I told her." Something niggled at the back of her mind. Why couldn't his mother help? She unlocked her door and, sure enough, there on the table waiting for her lay her leather hobo bag. She snagged the bag and dug out her phone as they crossed to the sofa so he could set his burden down. Good thing Mutt wasn't a bigger dog.

"We'll tell your mom as soon as we know where we're going." She flipped through possible clinics. Only one urgent care seemed anywhere near, so she tapped the screen to get the map. "Maybe you should stay here in case your mother calls."

He stared at her, eyes huge. "I have to stay with D—Mutt. She needs me."

Dinah glanced at the line of muddy footprints from the door to the sofa and the filth that stained the white seat. Ever since she had left that—that place, she had never allowed dirt to gather on anything around her. Now dirt and blood combined to even smell bad. She smothered the horror with an iron hand. This was Jonah. He couldn't help the fix he was in, but she could help him. "I'll get some towels, keep her warm, and…" Without finishing she returned with two white towels and helped him wrap his dog in one. She carried the other out the door and back to the elevator as Jonah followed.

Pretty certain now that the dog was not dying on them, she drove more carefully, following the instructions from the irritating female voice on the GPS. Strange. As long as she'd lived here, she'd never driven out into the 'burbs much. But then she didn't really do much but go to work, go home, crash, and return to the fray. She slowed, not quite trusting the voice that said, "Turn left in five hundred feet." Strip mall. No street in that amount of distance. She missed it. "Recalculating."

"I'll just go around the block," she grumbled at the supercilious tone. A yip from the passenger side robbed her attention and she missed another turn. *Listen to the voice*, she reminded herself. *That's what you pay her for.* The next street was one-way. No wonder she'd not been ordered to turn.

"Is she worse?" She bit her lip.

"Think so. She's shaking so bad. She almost slid off my lap."

Carefully now, she made sure she did exactly as the voice said and in a couple of minutes breathed a sigh of relief. A red neon sign informed them that Miller and Miller Veterinary Clinic waited in the middle of that strip mall, about the last place she would have expected it. She angle-parked in front and ran around the car to help Jonah get out, still clutching Mutt to his chest.

She pushed open the door and warm air gushed out into the night. A smiling young woman greeted them from behind the desk and leaped to her feet when she saw Jonah and Mutt. "I'll get help!" She hit a swinging door near to running.

Instantly a young man in scrubs strode in through another door. "Here we go, little guy. Let me take your dog."

Jonah shook his head. "I can carry her; she doesn't like strangers much."

"Okay. She looks pretty heavy."

"I got her."

The man in scrubs shrugged, nodded to Dinah, and held the door for Jonah.

The girl returned to her desk. "Can I get some information now, or do you need to be with your son?"

Your son! The words stopped her like a glass wall. "Ah, ah…" Go or stay? "I need to be with him— er, he needs me, ah, maybe…"

"Fine, follow me." Clipboard in hand, she hopped to her feet. Her name tag read *Amber*. "This way. What happened to the dog?" She held open those swinging doors.

"I— Ah, we don't know. Found her like this." Dinah followed her into a broad hallway.

Amber ushered Dinah into an examination room dominated by a stainless-steel table attached to a wall and a big man in green scrubs who didn't bother to look up but kept his focus on Mutt and Jonah. Dinah found it odd that he didn't acknowledge her, let alone introduce himself. But she didn't mind. Not yet, at least.

A scrawny young man in scrubs came in pushing a portable X-ray machine. "So, Jonah, what happened to Downmutt?" The vet was so intent upon the dog that the assistant might as well have been in China.

Dinah took the bench seat at the wall and reminded herself to breathe. Clutching her bag in her lap, she watched his big ham hands tenderly unwrap the towel and begin probing, so gently that Mutt did not object.

Jonah fought tears and the tears won, but he answered clearly. "I let her out like always but she didn't come right back. She always runs out and right back. So I went to look for her and I couldn't find her and..." His voice picked up speed. "And I called and I called and I looked for her but she didn't come. She never runs away. I found her hiding behind the Dumpster. She cried and so I found her and..." Jonah paused and hiccupped.

Dinah found herself fighting tears, too. And she reflected bitterly that had she only obeyed the police and cut all contact with this little boy who was none of her responsibility, her life would be so much simpler, more stable. Let the know-it-all police take his call in the middle of the night. Let them handle the mess.

Except he hadn't called them. He'd called her.

"And she was bleeding and crying and I grabbed her and ran home and...and please don't let her die." The last came out as a wail.

"Jonah! Jonah, listen to me." The vet did not look up from his work. "Your dog is not going to die. She is badly hurt, but she is not going to die."

Jonah scrubbed his sleeve across his face. "You sure?"

"Barring complications, I am sure. I might have to keep her here tonight, but she is not going to die."

Mutt waved the tip of her tail and tried to raise her head. Jonah leaned his cheek close so she could kiss him.

Finally the vet noticed that Dinah existed. He stood erect. "Glad you got her here quickly. Thank you. Now I am going to ask one of my associates to help me, and the best way you can help Downmutt is to keep Jonah out in the other room while we take X-rays and start stitching. I will call you if I need to know something else, okay?"

Jonah turned to Dinah. "Okay?"

The vet's brief gaze was disconcerting, though she couldn't say why. She couldn't manage a smile, not now, but she nodded. "Of course. Jonah?" She stood and Jonah slid his hand into hers as they left the room.

She paused. "Do you want to call your mother?"

He shook his head. "She's sleeping. She needs to sleep—when she can."

"I see." Dinah did not see at all, but what could she say? Obviously his mother had trouble sleeping. She must be ill. Could it be drugs or—or... She shook her head. None of that was important right now.

"Dr. Miller will take good care of your dog. He's the best." Amber knelt in front of Jonah. "Can I get you something to eat or drink? I know you must be really tired."

Dinah wanted to hug the young woman. How did she know how to help a little boy?

Jonah shook his head. "But thank you."

"There are some comic books over there on the table, or you can turn on the television."

"'Kay." He looked up at Dinah.

"I'm going to need to fill out some paperwork here, so you make yourself comfortable."

"Can I watch the fish?"

"Of course." She and Amber spoke at the same time.

Dinah caught her breath; never had she seen such a glorious aquarium. A huge saltwater tank half filled a wall. Brilliant yellow damselfish, vivid blue tangs, and a black-and-white-striped fish Dinah did not recognize swam among corals and anemones. Real, live anemones, with charming little clownfish nestled in them. And look! Below the tank, a modest sign identified the fish by name. The striped one was a sergeant major.

Jonah walked over to stand at the glass while Amber handed Dinah a clipboard.

"Thank you." Dinah took the board, crossed to a chair, and sat down. Glancing up, she realized that all the walls were covered in caricatures of all kinds of animals, some framed, some poster style, all in wild colors that made her smile in spite of all that was happening. What a waiting room! "Who's the artist?" she asked without thinking.

"Dr. Miller. He likes to give children a drawing of their pet. Jonah will get one of..." She paused.

"Jonah's dog was named Downmutt, but now we call her just Mutt." The brilliant aquarium, the splendid art—this man loved bold color. And here sat Dinah, awash in white, the plainer the better. What contrast! She stared at the questions on the clipboard. She had no idea how to answer.

Who were his father and mother? What was his address, phone number, age of pet?

She filled in her own information. They thought he was her son: so be it. If she ever had a child, which she didn't plan on, she would like one like Jonah. Where that thought came from, she had no idea. No children, no family, no commitments—no heartache. Yes, she definitely should have listened to those police officers.

She stopped at the line that listed possible care costs. She was supposed to check one? She shook her head and stared at the boy facing the floating magic world. What was going through his mind? Was he crying inside and out? Did he believe the vet when he said Mutt was not going to die? As if cost had anything to do with a small boy's life line.

Signing the final pages and sure she had just completed an FBI investigative form, she rose and handed the clipboard back to Amber.

The round clock behind the desk indicated that half an hour had passed, though it felt like four. Maybe the clock was a caricature, too.

Itching to do something, anything, she stopped behind Jonah and laid her hands on his shoulders. "D-Downmutt is going to be fine."

He looked at her over his shoulder. "I like Mutt better, too. She don't mind. She comes when I call her no matter what I say."

Dinah clamped her teeth together until her jaw screamed. "Thank you."

He reached up and patted her hand.

Sometime later, the man in green came through the door and crossed to them. "Do you want to see her now?"

"Can I?" Jonah brightened.

"Yes. She is pretty sleepy, but I know she needs to see you, too."

How could a man understand a small boy so perfectly? The thought swam by like one of the darting fish as she followed them through the doors. Mutt did indeed wag her tail as she lay on her side in a blanket-lined cage, Jonah height. The boy stroked her head and leaned in for the required kiss. He heaved a sigh and turned to the vet. "Thank you. She looks weird with all those shaved patches. She has stitches, huh?" He paused and studied his dog again. "But she will get better fast?"

"That she will. She might have to stay a couple of days, but only if I think it best. You can come visit her." He glanced to Dinah, who nodded.

"Okay. Can we come back in the morning?"

"Of course."

"Good."

Dr. Miller's pocket buzzed. "In the morning, then. I see I have another patient. If you have any questions, call me." He handed Dinah a business card and extended his hand. "Good to meet you, Ms. Taylor."

She shook hands; his clasp was firm and warm. "And you, Dr. Miller. Thank you. Come on, Jonah." Together they left the clinic and stepped into a lightening world. At least the sky promised sun later.

Once they were buckled into the seat belts, she inserted the key as if it weighed a pound or two. "You want something to eat?"

Jonah grinned at her. "Extraburger isn't open yet."

"No, but we passed a fast-food joint on the way here. Can you make do with that?"

He nodded as if considering carefully. "I guess."

Later, fortified by coffee, hot chocolate, and breakfast sandwiches, they headed toward home.

As they passed the still-dark Extraburger, Jonah asked, "Can I stay with you so I don't wake my mom?"

"What if she were to wake up and see that her little boy never came home?" *And she'd call the police and this time I really would be jailed.* Dinah didn't add that out loud.

"It's okay. I don't want to worry her."

"Jonah, she's your mother and she doesn't know where you are."

"It's okay. I left her a note with your card lying on it. She'll know."

Dinah sighed. "Jonah..."

"Later, okay? When we go see Mutt."

But she didn't know his mother's name, where she lived, or her phone number. Jonah didn't seem likely to tell her now, and after the other day at his school, calling the police seemed a bad idea.

Brushing aside feelings of guilt, she nodded and kept on driving to her parking garage. They made it to the condo, staggered in, and he crossed to the sofa.

"Can I lie down here?"

"Sure. I'll get a quilt." He was already asleep when she returned, having had to dig the quilt out of the back of the linen closet. She wasn't prepared to fix temporary beds for guests.

She paused. The bloody clothes. Filthy enough that she could smell them. She got her white terry robe from behind the bathroom door. "Jonah? *Jonah.* Wake up."

He looked at her.

"Put this robe on. I have to wash your clothes."

"Huh?" He looked down at his shirt front and sat up.

She went into her bedroom to give him some privacy.

When she returned to her sofa he was curled up on it again, already back asleep, wearing her robe. His soiled clothes sat on the coffee table neatly folded.

His shoes on the floor were lined up precisely, toes in toward the sofa.

What kind of child was this?

Chapter Five

Garret Miller dropped his mask on the table. His cup of coffee had grown cold but he downed it anyway. What a night! Good thing the other Miller would handle the morning shift. They were going to have to look into adding more staff, the way things were going lately. He rubbed his eyes with his fingertips and tipped his head back. How easy it would be to fall asleep right here and right now.

"You want me to drive you home?" Jason, who looked about like Garret felt, offered on his way out.

"Thanks, but I can make it." Recently Garret had moved out of his apartment a block from the clinic (if you took the alley) and into a house only a couple of miles away. He craved land around him, real land, not asphalt like the parking lot surrounding the strip mall.

The Saturday morning shoppers had yet to venture out as he swung into the Bagelry drive-through, picked up half a dozen plus one ready to devour with lox and cream cheese, warmed, and headed west. By the time he pulled into his house on one-half acre, he'd downed the bagel, inhaled the coffee, and within minutes was crashed on a king-size bed. That Taylor woman's eyes were the last image he remembered.

Dinah was standing at that magnificent tank in Dr. Miller's waiting room, and when he came in she could not breathe. He left, she took a breath, he returned, she could not. Recognizing it as a ridiculous hallucination was what woke her. Why would she think she couldn't get enough oxygen when that man was around? *That man* was the only way she could refer to him. She knew his name. Garret Miller. But her mind refused to acknowledge that. As a scientist, she knew everything had to have a reason for being. Nothing happened by accident, including lack of oxygen. But the dream world does not operate on scientific principles.

Finally, she realized that Jonah was standing near her bed. Her body gave an involuntary start. She had forgotten she had a guest. How long he'd been waiting there she had no idea. "Are you all right?"

He nodded. "Can we go see Mutt now?"

She glanced at the clock. Nearing ten. "Have you eaten?"

Another nod. "You don't have much here to eat."

She trapped a yawn. "I know. What did you have?"

"Peanut butter crackers."

"How about I fix something a little better?"

"Can I call about Mutt?"

"Of course you may. The number is..."

"I have it."

"Good. Did you call your mother?"

Nods were becoming his chief form of communication. "She said to tell you thank you. I told her we were going to the vet to see Mutt."

"And she was comfortable with that?" Dinah felt instantly wary.

"Sure. She likes you."

"She doesn't know me."

"Sure she does. I told her all about you."

And that was enough? Stopping her head from shaking, she nodded toward the door. "Why don't you go get out the eggs. You like eggs?"

"Yes. Boiled."

"Coming right up."

"I'll start the water boiling." He turned to go.

He seemed young to use the stove, but she didn't know much about kids.

"Good, and there is bread in the refrigerator for toast and maybe we should do sliced bananas. How does that sound?"

"I didn't make coffee."

"You know how to make coffee?" She felt her eyes widen.

"Not with your fancy machine."

"I'll hurry."

As soon as he closed the door behind himself, she threw the covers back and warp-speeded through an abbreviated routine. But as she passed her sofa she suddenly stopped, stunned. Blood and dog hair still stained it. Okay, stains can be removed. Usually. But this was very nearly lifeblood. Blood and grit. The stink, the filth, the foulness of it slammed into her much harder than they had assailed her last night. Her stomach nearly flipped. At times a keen sense of smell was more liability than help.

When she walked into the kitchen, he had the table set, a pot steaming ready for the eggs, and the bananas on the counter. Her rose graced the table still.

"Your flowers are pretty."

"Thank you. I like them, too." While they chatted, she got the coffee maker going and added the eggs to the boiling water, setting her timer for four minutes. "Hard or soft?"

"Not real runny, please."

"What do you want to drink? I don't have any hot chocolate."

"Mommy makes me white coffee."

"Okaaay." She dragged out the word but added another mug to the one by the coffee maker. "Sugar? You want to add your own? So what did the vet say?" How could a child his age seem so grown up?

"The lady said Mutt didn't eat her breakfast."

"Anything else?"

"She feels better. She's wagging her tail. She misses me, the lady said."

"We'll go right away."

His smile was an adequate reward for hurrying on a Saturday morning.

When they got to the clinic, the attendant told Jonah that Mutt was heavily sedated and may not know him.

Mutt knew him. The tail flapped joyfully, the tongue stroked his cheek and nose. And then they left so that the dog could rest.

Garret scrubbed both hands across the mass of curls that drove him nuts. He hadn't gotten nearly enough sleep, as usual. He also *had* to get a haircut, the only way to keep the unruly mass from needing a rake. Totally on habit mode, he fed his animals, then punched the speed dial for the clinic to check on his patients. He smiled when Lucita said a small boy had already arrived to see his dog. That was one thing he did right: hire staff that cared about both animals and owners, especially when the owner was a child.

He glanced at the wall opposite the foot of his bed where four of his studies, for want of a better word, waited to be given away. Could he get the one of last night's visitor done today?

His fingers itched for the Prismacolor markers that he used in his creations. While animals came first, drawing was a close second. If that was what you called what he did. Drawing, painting, sketching—all he cared for was the delight on a child's face when he presented his gift.

A yawn threatened to dislocate his jaw, but there was no use even thinking about going back to sleep; his mind had already hit overdrive and kept on going when his eyes opened. While he shaved, the electric razor on autopilot, he took out a mind file called "comic strip" and played with his latest idea for *The Day I Ran the World*. Since a local newspaper printed the first one six months or so ago, he was now being forced to consider syndication. Who would have thought such a dream come true could happen with something he played with? He'd only sent it in to the *Daily Call* on a dare. Did God have a sense of humor or what?

Heating two bagels in the toaster oven, he hit the start on the coffee machine that brewed one cup at a time and promised perfection. The machine had yet to fail him. Coffee in hand, bagels hot and on a plate, he moseyed into the sun room/studio/aviary and favorite place where his tiger cat and two yellow Labradors lay curled together on the stuffed bed in the sun. Sun was to be coveted in late March in Ohio. They each opened one eye, tails twitched, and they returned to dreamland. So much for loving and attentive pets.

He sat briefly at his easel to sketch in the boy and dog while they were fresh in mind. And Ms. Taylor. That was what she had written on the form. Married? Divorced? Widowed? No ring, but that meant nothing these days. He set the easel with its unfinished sketch off to one side, put his lunch on the wrought-iron table, and sank into the padded lounger. He stayed there long enough to polish off the bagels, drain the coffee, and check his messages.

And stare at the sketch. Why did that woman seem so familiar? Why did he immediately want to get to know her better and at the same time lock the door against her? Some women did that to him. If he could only deal with the animals and the children and not ever the parents, leastways, mothers, life would be perfect.

A perfect wolf whistle came from the macaw cage and another bird shrieked, "Shut up." He never said that unless it was appropriate. The finches and various other little birds flitted about the aviary, their songs providing a soothing balm when he was overtired. Like now. He rested his head against the padding and, eyes slitted, studied the easel with the cat picture he'd been working on a few days ago.

The problem was that the cat draped over the arm of a small girl and the cat was almost as long as the child. He'd wished he'd had a camera for that one, the pair so perfect together. The grin in the drawing showed the child's missing tooth and the bored look on the cat. Getting up, he grabbed a couple of marker pens, added some lines here and there, and stood back, nodding. Now it was right. He ripped it off the easel pad and pinned it to the wall. Ready for delivery.

After feeding the birds, making sure the two macaws, one a hyacinth and the other a scarlet, had fresh fruit and enough toys to entertain themselves, he checked the thermostat, since the sun was warming the room nicely. Then he headed for his SUV. First stop, haircut. Second, birdseed at the pet store, and third, the clinic, of course.

An hour later, his ears again out in the breeze, his back seat full of birdseed, and feeling free of his consternation, he parked behind the clinic and entered by the back door.

Susan Miller, wearing her requisite lab coat and harried look, glanced up from the microscope. "Hope you slept in." She shook her head at his shrug. "I know, going from shift to shift is hard. But I thought you were tired enough, you'd drop." She turned the magnification dial. "Just what I thought."

Garret paid no attention to her muttering. Susan often talked to herself, perhaps because at home she rarely got a word in edgewise with five-year-old twin girls, bookended by brothers.

"How come you're here?"

He shrugged again.

"I know, just don't trust the rest of us to care for your patients correctly."

He snorted and shot her what was supposed to be a scathing glance but instead made her laugh.

"Did you know Dinah Taylor brought a dog in last night?"

His forehead wrinkled. "So?"

"So you don't know who Dinah Taylor is?"

"Should I?" The blue-gray eyes flashed across his memory.

"Garret, Garret, you have to keep up on things."

"Why? We seem to be doing fine with you keeping

up on things and me making sure the ends meet." He knew that would make her laugh. His sister-in-law Susan was the business head behind their partnership, he the idea man. Together they balanced each other's strengths and weaknesses and made a great team. Except when she expected him to keep up with what was going on in Eastbrook. Or anywhere else, for that matter. He figured keeping up on the latest medical research and techniques was far more important. The dichotomy gave them good sparring topics. "All right, I give. Why should I know Dinah Taylor?"

"Her company, Food for Life, had a big rollout party the other night for their latest product. The news said this new whatever might end diabetes forever and anyone can purchase it over the counter."

"Riiight." He studied the charts of the two dogs they had in quarantine. One looked to be easing into full paralysis. Both of them would most likely have to be put down, leaving their owners heartbroken.

"Did you hear me?"

"Of course, you said..." He finally shook his head. "Sorry. Did you check on the scruffy dog who looks like a patchwork quilt with all the stitches I put in her? I think she was savaged by another dog or even two."

Susan rolled her eyes and shook her head. "That's what I am trying to tell you."

Fine, get to the point.

"The dog is doing as well as can be expected. We're keeping her on IVs; tried to get her to eat, which happened when her boy came through the door. I swear you could see the relief on that dog's face. And the little boy, what a charmer."

Garret nodded. "Good."

"Dinah Taylor brought him in."

"So?" *Get to the point.*

"So, Dinah Taylor is not married, and has no son. From what I've read, she only lives for her business."

He shook his head. "I don't get it."

"So where did she get the boy?"

"Who cares? No matter what kind of celebrity she is, we treat the animal, comfort the boy, and do all we can to not gossip." He put a little force into that last.

"Just thought you should know. I never pass anything on, you know that."

He nodded. "Have they left yet?"

"About fifteen minutes ago. He promised his dog—by the way, he seems to have the same talent for thinking of names as you—that he'd come see her this evening. I figure that will make sure the poor critter eats and drinks."

Garret entered the cage room and stopped in front of D's cage. She was up on her belly instead of flat on her side, a good indication. No temp, no other symptoms, according to her chart, so perhaps Jonah could take her home tomorrow. No, tomorrow was Sunday. Monday, then. "You'd like that, wouldn't you, girl?" Her tail whisked from side to side. It was nearly the only part of her without a shaved patch. "Good girl." He checked the rest of his patients, stopped in his office to dispose of a stack of things needing his signature, returned several calls, and poked his head into an exam room where their intern was giving shots one right after another. This was their low-cost-vaccination day, so they shuffled the dogs through production-line style.

He froze at a greeting he heard. She was back. How could he even remember her voice? She'd hardly spoken.

Frantic, he pushed open the first door he came to and there she stood.

"Hello, Doctor." Cool, stiff. Was she like this all the time?

He nodded and immediately shifted his gaze to Jonah. No smile, only fear. "Don't worry, son, D—"

"You can call her Mutt."

"Thank you. Mutt is doing very well. I hear she gobbled her food as soon as you came in the door."

"That's what they said." His grin lit the room. "She is better, huh?"

"She is that." Garret tried to pay polite, though scant, attention to Ms. Taylor, while all his senses screamed for information about her. Scent—something fresh and blooming. Circles under her eyes. Hands slightly shaking. Guarded. A soft and gentle hand on Jonah's shoulder. Maybe she was the boy's aunt or—as if that mattered. Viewed objectively, she was certainly attractive. And here she was wearing white again. The only splash of color was her scarf, a beautiful silk number, probably Japanese, with bright flowers.

Garret, Garret, get a grip. She's the one who will pay the dog's hefty bill. Be polite, even unctuous. The voice beat a tattoo.

He smiled at the boy. "You want to see her again?"

"Can we take her home?"

"I am sorry, Jonah, but to help her get better faster, she needs the IVs, quiet, and we need to be able to check her vitals regularly to make sure nothing changes."

His shoulders slumped. "I figured. Thank you."

"Monday will be the best."

"Not tomorrow?"

"'Fraid not. Come on, let's go see her again. Do you need something?"

"No, I forgot to give her this." He pulled a much-gnawed bone from his pocket.

"I'll wait by the aquarium." The woman watched for Jonah's nod and turned away.

Instantly the air lightened. Garret pushed open the door to the cage room. Now he could breathe unimpeded.

Garret, you dork, this is ridiculous! You outweigh her by a hundred pounds—well, eighty, maybe—and you're scared of her! Yes, scared. She's quiet, probably an introvert, and you're scared of her! What the blazes is the matter?

Then little Jonah grabbed his attention. The boy had both arms in the cage, cooing to his dog, patting her, stroking her. This was not just a family pet; the two were devoted to each other. Utterly devoted. You could read it in their body language, both of them. He checked the antibiotic and fluid in the IV. Good. He checked the diaper mat. Dry.

The kid stepped back and looked up. "Thank you, sir. I'll be okay now 'til this afternoon." He turned and left as Garret stared after him.

What kind of child was this?

Chapter Six

So much had happened in the last forty-eight hours, Dinah thought. The rollout felt as if it had taken place last week.

She stared at the aquarium, the same one as in her dream. One fish darted in and took a bite out of the angel's wings. No, this was a Moorish idol, not an angelfish. The nip was so fast she wasn't sure it had really happened. The idol continued its stately patrol of the front glass, back and forth. How long had she been standing here totally lost in her thoughts? She glanced around to see several people, pets in hand, waiting on the bench seats that lined the wall—a wall bright with his artwork. No matter what she thought of him personally, as if she had any thoughts, since they had barely met, his caricatures captured her interest. At least now that she'd left off studying the fish. She crossed to study a smallish drawing.

She wandered around the room, lost in delight at the whimsy. How could a man who seemed so stern and cold possibly see these things in children and create them for the rest of the world? The two things did not fit, not at all.

But maybe someone else did the artwork and they had the same initials, or…She could not come up with another scenario other than that he paid an artist and put his name on them. That certainly seemed plausible.

Her cell rang, and a most familiar number popped up on the ID. She stepped outside to answer it. "Hi, Hal. I'm back at the vet's so Jonah can visit Mutt."

"I thought you were there earlier."

"We were, we left, we returned. Long story." A sign on a rather unusual house across the street advertised palm reading and other helpful offers. Dr. Miller had managed to choose a less-than-great neighborhood for his thriving practice. Reading the sign beside the office entry, she realized there were two Millers. So he was married? Why did that surprise her? He was good-looking, personable—at least to others if not to her. Perhaps he was even a father, or a father wannabe or…

Hal was asking, "Where did you go?" She forced her attention back to the conversation.

"When?" she asked.

"Just now. You were making no sense whatsoever. I asked you if you've read all the media hysteria."

"No, I haven't. Why?" She frowned.

"Good. Don't."

"Hal, there wasn't anybody there. A couple independent agencies, but not the big guns, like AP. Why would there be a frenzy?"

"There's a lot of negativity out there right now, and we don't want to feed into it. And leave your TV off."

She snorted a response. He knew she never, or at least rarely, watched television.

He continued barking. "Radio, Internet, and do *not* agree to any interviews. So far they are calling me, as we requested in the press release, but someone is going to dig deep enough to find you."

"Oh, I hate this. I'm a chemist, Hal, a researcher. I find new uses for old chemicals. I'm—"

"I know, I know. All food is chemicals. I talk about the tasty fat in a steak and you draw a picture of a long-chain fatty acid. You're a lab worker, Dinah, but you are also a CEO, and you have a blockbuster on your hands here. Not a positive blockbuster, either. That one reporter for the indie is sure the FDA is going to nail you to the wall, and she wants to help them do it. I—"

"Why can't things just go on as usual? Ignore the little indie and perhaps she will go away."

"I won't say I warned you, but..."

"I know. Is there anyone I should stay away from the most?"

He rattled off a stream of nonsense that filled her ear but did not gain entrance to her brain.

"Thanks. I gotta go. Jonah is coming out. Oh, and by the way, you mentioned you had sources to research Jonah's parents. Would you go ahead and see what you can find out about his mother, please?" She clicked off as he was saying *Will do* and shoved her phone into the bottom of her bag.

The last thing she wanted right now was more attention. All these years she had managed to fly under the radar, which was just the way she liked it, but now...As Hal had reminded her more than once, she was going to be forced to face the world at some point. But she wanted to do it on her terms, not in desperation. Yes, the launch of a new product is intended to generate attention and interest, but nice, polite, manageable attention. Not a negative feeding frenzy.

She smiled at Jonah. "Ready?"

Jonah nodded. "She was happy to get her bone." As they walked out to the parking lot, he grinned up at her. "Dr. G makes good pictures, doesn't he?"

"He does."

"He said he would have one for me, of me 'n' Mutt."

"Really?" Good way to get faithful clients.

"But we can't take Mutt home until Monday and please can we come back? Today?" He searched her face.

"If your mother agrees." She clicked open the car doors and slid into the driver's seat. He had the seat belt buckled before she could even remind him. One had to tell him something only one time and that was it. The child was not normal.

"So, we are going to your house now to talk with your mother, right?"

He nodded. "She said so."

Had he hesitated? Why? Was he ashamed of his mother? That thought brought up the idea of substance abuse again. Something was strange here; perhaps Hal would uncover some answers soon.

Jonah showed her where to park about three blocks from the Extraburger and led the way to a second-floor apartment. They climbed the stairs, since he informed that her the elevator did not work again. Shabby but clean would be the best description. Dinah had feared graffiti on the walls, but this seemed more like a place for elderly or longtime clientele.

He slid his key into the lock on 203 and called "We're here" as he pushed the door open.

Dinah breathed a sigh of relief; this was so different from what she'd feared. Aged furniture with no extras. A couple of dog toys and a bookshelf with Jonah's books and a few games. She noticed a picture of a man in a Kansas City uniform of some sort and a family photo, both framed.

"Please come in." The voice sounded weak but welcoming, so Dinah followed Jonah into the bedroom.

The woman propped up in the bed smiled and extended her hand. "Dinah, I am so glad to finally meet you. Please call me Corinne." Hands and voice shook in tandem, but the smile fought to obliterate the effects of whatever disease was ravaging her body.

Questions bubbled and snapped, but Dinah kept her smile in place and, she hoped, the confusion from her eyes. Why all the secrecy? "Thank you for your invitation. I've been wanting to meet you so I can tell you what a fine son you have. Jonah is—"

Jonah interrupted, so unlike his usual behavior. "Mutt...Ah, we decided to call her that instead of the other name."

"Oh, thank You, Lord, I hated that name. Mutt isn't a whole lot better, but it's better." She touched his cheek with her hand where he sat beside her on the edge of the bed. She smiled up at Dinah. "Please be seated so we can visit. Or are you in a hurry?"

"No, not at all." Dinah sat on the straight-backed wooden chair and set her bag on the floor. Pencil drawings papered one wall. "Oh, no wonder Jonah said you didn't mind his giving me his drawing." Her eyes moved from the wall to Jonah; she was sure her mouth made an *O*. "You really did all those?"

"All but one. My dad did that." He pointed to a picture in the center of the wall, the only one that had a kind of frame, in black. The stuffed puppy and the little boy made her smile. "That was your first dog?"

"Uh-huh."

Corinne added, "He named the puppy Droopy. He was three then."

"And you've been drawing ever since?"

Jonah shrugged. "The early ones weren't so hot."

"I wanted to keep them all, but one day the box just disappeared." Corinne cocked an almost nonexistent eyebrow at her son. Jonah did *innocent* well.

Dinah smiled. "I want to frame mine so I can keep it in my office."

Jonah did a boy-type eye roll. "You can have more if you like."

They chatted like old friends for a few more minutes until Corinne flinched as she shifted in the bed.

Dinah rose immediately, certain that the woman was nearing the end of her strength. She asked Jonah, "How about if I come back and pick you up to go see Mutt?"

The boy shrugged. "We can meet at the corner."

"An hour?" She turned to smile at the woman in the bed. "How about if Jonah and I get something for supper and he can bring some back for you when he returns?"

"You don't need to do that."

"I know, but I'd like to, please, if that would be all right." When another mist of pain flashed across the pale face, Dinah picked up her purse. "See you in a while."

Jonah walked her to the door. "Mommy likes you—she knew she would."

"And I like her."

Back on the street, Dinah realized she still didn't have their phone number. Resolving to get it from Jonah, she slid into her car and drove back to her apartment building. So close and yet so far. If only she'd been able to help Corinne and her son before. When she flicked the turn signal for her parking garage, a thought hit her. Whatever made her think that they either wanted or needed her help? What a bigoted idea. She went upstairs in an elevator that worked.

A blinking light on her house phone announced a message. The building manager's voice intoned, "There have been obnoxious people demanding to see you. I refused. Take my beater when you go out again. Beware." The car key had been slid under the door.

Visiting a hospitalized ragtag mongrel. What a way to spend a weekend. When Dinah got home that evening, it was a good thing the day was done, for she certainly was.

Why not working was more tiring than working was beyond her, but it was true. She could spend a whole day perched on a stool at the bench, doing things no one else thought of, and it would seem like a few leisure hours. Like isolating the sulfur compounds in oysters; oh, she loved that one. Everyone from college organic classes on up knew the sulfur was there. But why? She asked why, and learning why was what got her her first major supplement, a food additive that actually worked to enhance hair growth in men and women. It was still one of the company's better sellers. Or the time she decided to explore why cells use beta-carotene, and...

And now she was a slave to budgets and personnel management and all the headaches of heading up a company, however small it might be.

She glanced up at the ding of the phone but ignored it, along with all the other calls piling up on her answering service. She answered her cell, however.

No greetings. Just, "Be glad. A major emergency; *something big enough to take over the news*. You are no longer front and center."

"Thanks, Hal."

"By the way, I hit zero on information on the family."

"When I picked him up this afternoon he had a change of clothes on. I don't know if that's his mom's doing or his. Strange child. So we visited Mutt again." She usually forgot bad dreams immediately, but the one she'd awoken to this morning was still stuck in her head—no oxygen to breathe when that vet entered the room. "And we bought a bucket of fried chicken, I hope his mother can eat some of it. I'm using the building manager's Chevy, by the way. Did you suggest that, or did he come up with the idea?"

"All I said was 'protect her as best you can.' God Himself is keeping the hyenas from your door, but I know you don't want to hear that so I didn't say it, just thought it out loud."

"Right."

"So what does tomorrow look like?"

"We go visit Mutt; she won't eat unless Jonah's there, and his mother's in no condition to take him, but perhaps tomorrow will be different. We bail her out on Monday, so I assume Jonah will go to school late. We've not discussed logistics yet." To forestall more questions, she added, "I already cleared all this with April."

"Then sleep well and turn off your ringers."

"We'll see." She knew perfectly well that he knew she would not do that, in case Jonah needed her. Since when did her life revolve around a small boy and his dog, relegating the biggest success of the year to a distant second place? Life sure did change in an instant. But was it for the best?

Only time would tell.

Chapter Seven

G arret was on the third rendition of Jonah and DM, as
he had come to refer to the dog.

Why could he not get the boy out of his mind?

Or the woman, either. He saw dozens of patients every
day. Yet, since he'd met them, one or the other of those
two had dwelt front and center in his thoughts. For both
of them, it was the eyes he couldn't seem to capture.
Windows into the souls. Old souls. Souls with heavy se-
crets and heavier burdens. *Lord God, what's with this?*
You know I have a stack of stuff to do four feet tall mini-
mum and here I am fixated on a woman who bothers and
intrigues me and a boy who...Pondering did not help.
Drawing did not help.

While Jonah thought he was taking care of his dog,
Garret knew better. DM, alias Mutt, had one purpose in
life—Jonah.

All the while his mind roamed, his hand flew with the
marker pens. Finally! He stood and walked back, always a
good test when painting, drawing, or whatever. Get a new
perspective. He nodded. At last the eyes matched, Jonah's
and Mutt's. The rest was framework.

Haunted. Was that the word he wanted?

He ripped the page off the easel—Jonah and Mutt version three—and pinned it to the wall. Other people would say the first two versions were typically Garret Miller, but this one? Maybe he should give Jonah one of the others and keep this one here. Why? So it could drive him crazy?

Instead of leaving it on the wall until he took it to the clinic, he unpinned it and rolled it up carefully, sliding it into a protective cylinder. He'd post one of the others on a wall at the clinic. Unlike this version, the boy and dog in the first two attempts had ordinary eyes. He only posted the ones he loved seeing on a regular basis.

The clock reminded him that he should consider going to bed. But instead he moved to a drafting table where he worked on his comic strip. In spite of considerable pressure to go daily, he kept to his one strip a week. He did not want to be an artist full time; he was a veterinarian who got a kick out of drawing. Not the other way around.

This was the first he'd had trouble coming up with a concept. Sometimes keeping away from political innuendo was not only difficult but impossible. He stared at the drawing of a howitzer cannon. That was it. "The day I ran the world, I played with guns. Oops. Sorry, God."

Sorry indeed. Playing with guns, with people's lives. But what if? He drew furiously and leaned back, laughing. That worked. He rose and stretched, nodding and smiling all the while. He figured he'd fallen asleep smiling, because too few hours later he woke, still smiling.

"Thank You, Lord God, for this new day. I missed Your glory sighting, but from the look of outside, I wouldn't have seen it anyway." Although sometimes God managed to sneak a fiery peek through a veil of rain.

A whimper and a paw under soulful brown eyes found

his arm. "Good morning, SoandSo. I know you were waiting patiently." He scrubbed his yellow Lab's soft ears with
one hand while rubbing his own eyes with the other. For
some odd reason, his eyes felt not sandy but gravelly. "I
sure hope you put the coffee on, since someone we know
forgot again." The thuds of two tails assured him they
had.

SoandSo and her brother Sam sat glued shoulder to
shoulder, both quivering, ready to explode ahead of him
toward the kitchen. TC, their tiger cat, yawned and
stretched from his place of honor at the foot of the bed,
unrolling her pink tongue and eyeing her best friends as
only a superior feline can.

"I get it. I get it. I…" They froze, waiting for his next
move. "Am." Four front feet padded the rug. "Coming."
As he leaped to his feet, the dogs exploded out the door
and down the hall, in full barking cry. The cat rolled his
eyes and yawned again.

He laughed at the morning ritual. How could one ever
wake up grumpy around here? Garret followed the thundering horde to his kitchen. The birds screamed and
trilled from the aviary.

Humming while the coffee brewed, he filled dog dishes
and opened a tin of real salmon for TC, who was just padding through the doorway. Garret was sure the haughty
feline waited until the scent of an open can wafted his
way. One time Garret had not followed the routine and he
had paid royally. No one knew how to get even like a cat.

All the other residents of the house cared for, he carried his mug of perfect coffee with just the right amount
of half-and-half back up the stairs, and within fifteen minutes he'd showered and done all the prep to dress for
church. His concession to fashion was khakis, a button-

down shirt, extra long, and a needing-to-be-replaced sport coat. His loafers needed polishing.

A wet brush to the newly shorn hair, and he headed for the car, whistling as he went. The animals lined up to say goodbye, so he patted each head and clicked open the garage door as he strode to the SUV. It was Sunday morning, he had his strip done, the picture of Jonah under his arm, and if he had any sense he would make sure he did not go by the clinic on this, his day of rest.

"Good morning, Garret." John Hanson, Bible Study leader extraordinaire, greeted all his class members as they quickly filled the room. It was time for them to move again to a larger location, but the only alternative now was the sanctuary, the problem being how to get people shuffled around and not have to change service times. For some odd reason, the suggestion of changing the later service from ten to ten-thirty caused ire in a lot of worshipers.

Right on the moment, with a military precision that indicated John's background, he stood smiling at the front of the room. "Good morning and welcome to our study. Please turn to Acts, chapter five." Instead of a lot of pages flipping, most of those attending took out their iPads or e-readers and waited expectantly.

"Let us pray."

Garret, iPad in his lap, closed his eyes and exhaled all tension away.

"We are here, our Lord God, to learn of You, so that we can give You honor and glory to Your mighty name. Speak to us as You always do, into our hearts and minds, what we, each one of us, needs to hear today."

The almost-an-hour disappeared, those who had been to the early service staying for a Q-and-A while the others hustled to the sanctuary. Those ushering had left earlier.

Garret bowed his head with the others for Pastor Hagen to pray before his sermon. "Lord, let the words of my mouth and the meditations of my heart be acceptable...."

The eyes grabbed him.

As if she were standing right in front of him.

He flinched, fighting to hear the words of his pastor. "Lord God above, we give You all our thanks and praise. Amen."

A lightning shaft of fear shot through him. Garret exhaled as if sucker punched, afraid to open his eyes. Nothing like this had ever happened to him before. Was he going totally berserk?

"We all suffer from fear."

Garret snapped to attention. There went his pastor again, reading his mind.

"That is why God says repeatedly, "Fear not!" He paused, giving his congregation time to shake their heads. "I know what you're thinking. First, some of you are a bit smug as you tell yourself that you are not afraid of anything. You are so proud that you are not afraid."

Some people began to squirm, Garret one of them.

"I have news for you, two things that I know you will not consider good news." Again a pause. The man was a master at timing. His voice dropped. "God loves you so much that He will show you what fear is so you can be healed."

And the second, surely the second is easier. Garret leaned forward. Surely this could not be so. He was afraid of a woman. A woman he had only just met, who had done nothing to evoke his fear. She was still just a woman.

Admit it, women have always frightened you, some more than others.

Garret slammed the door on that line of thinking and pasted a sort-of smile on his face. He locked his arms over his chest and stared at one of the stained-glass windows. The Shepherd's window. Not a good choice.

He knew he missed a bunch of words; he hoped all the ones that would eat into his protective shield.

"And the second: some of us are so fear-ridden that we are often unable to function. Anxiety attacks, panic, physical ailments, fear causes an adrenaline rush every time, and after a while your body can't do the fight-or-flight any longer and it begins to break down. All of us fall into one camp or the other, so God says fear not."

Having his arms crossed over his chest kept Garret from slithering into a puddle on the floor. *Just get through this. You don't ever have to come back here, you know.*

Where had that come from? How dare he even consider that?

"But God never gives us a command without giving us the tools to carry it out."

Study the hymnal, the collar of the man in front of you, the floor, the scuff on your loafers.

Time must have passed, because he heard Pastor Hagen say, "Let us pray."

He prayed, they sang a hymn, and then came the benediction. "The Lord bless and keep thee."

Right.

A silence stretched for an hour before the organ and the musicians broke into the exit music. Garret stood, sure he was shaking. Were others reeling, or was he the only one?

A woman he'd known for years greeted him in the aisle. "Oh Dr. G, I am so glad to see you. I want to introduce you to my niece, who is visiting." She turned to the woman beside her, who wore the same embarrassed expression he was trying to make sure did not show on his face. How many relatives did this matchmaker have to trot out?

"Hello, Miss Grayson, glad to meet you."

"Dr. G is our resident veterinarian. The two of you have so much in common. Elizabeth just loves animals, too—don't you dear?" She gushed on.

Garret nodded, smiled, acted nice, and wanted to run screaming. "How long will you be in Eastbrook?"

Was that a spark of devilment dancing in her eyes? "I'm thinking of moving here. Auntie Jane has been on a job search for me, and her efforts just might be panning out."

Her gaze skittered away, so he used the opportunity to excuse himself and introduce her to the couple behind him, hoping and praying they would step up. They did. Someone else called his name, he smiled an apology or excuse, and turned away. But not before he caught a glimmer of relief in her gaze, or had he? He continued down the aisle, asking the correct questions and answering others as they moved toward the front door.

Maybe he might call her after all. She seemed personable enough. Did she really love all kinds of animals, or just loveable animals? What if he said he raised snakes and spiders?

Burky called, "Hey, Garret, going to join us for lunch? The Bunch is adjourning to the Cuppa."

Ask her along. Whatever for? Good Lord, what is happening to me? The Bunch usually did go out for lunch, so what was the big deal? "I need to drop something off at the clinic first."

If Susan catches you there, she will order you drawn

and quartered. If Dinah Taylor was there, he would order it himself.

"On second thought, sure." He'd deliver the drawing later. "Anyone need a ride?"

"You might ask that new person over there; she's coming along. I saw you talking with her. Give me a minute." Burky motioned to Garret to wait and went to Elizabeth, who nodded, glanced over at him, and only paused a moment before nodding again.

Once they were in the car, she turned to him. "I'm sorry. Aunt Jane has a tendency to manipulate, but she really has a great heart and wants the best for everyone concerned. I can't convince her that I already have a boyfriend, and—"

Garret busted out laughing. "And we play along to satisfy Auntie and heave a huge sigh of relief that we got her off our backs?"

She chuckled. "Thank you for being so observant. I do hope to move here. Artie is looking for a job here, too, and, God willing, we'll finally be able to get married. Nothing is final yet, but then what in life really is?"

They enjoyed the conversation, and she fit well into the Bunch, made up of an assortment of singles, marrieds, good friends, and acquaintances. The Bunch had a good time no matter who showed. Today when they were gathered in their usual room at the Cuppa, someone commented, "If that wasn't the most powerful sermon he has ever preached, I don't know what is."

"Powerful, right, but he sure raked us over the coals."

"No, he didn't. Like always, he..."

The discussion continued in bits and pieces as the Bunch went through the buffet line, regathered, talked, and, finally, left.

Garret forced himself to make all the appropriate noises, his mind in turmoil. He dropped Miss Grayson off at her auntie's, then locked himself into auto mode. He was almost home when he pulled over to the side of the street because he was shaking too much to drive.

Was this the fight-or-flight Pastor Hagen had talked about, or was something else happening that he had no control over? Was it the Taylor woman, or someone else in the depths of his memories?

He was supposed to be a rational adult. Why was he so screwed up? Or did he know the answer and was just too stubborn to face it?

Chapter Eight

The stains would not come off the sofa. At all.

Dinah had tried every product in the house, gone out for more, and still only managed to turn the mud and blood into a series of large blotches that glared at her from the pristine white. *Give it a rest. It is only a stain, after all. It will come out with something.* The mud prints from the carpet had faded; surely when dry they would be gone completely or easily brushed away.

Even while giving herself good advice, she scrubbed on. She had promised to pick Jonah up at five to go help Mutt eat. Talk about a stubborn dog. At least they could bring her home tomorrow. But could Corinne take care of the dog while Jonah went to school? How did they usually manage? Of course all depended on what kind of care Mutt needed.

Stepping back, Dinah studied the stains. Any better, or was she only making things worse? Maybe the answer was to hire a professional cleaner.

Her intercom bleeped and she answered. Horace, the condo manager. "Miz Dinah, you better not be leaving. There's one of those news vans out on the curb and some blonde lady with a microphone. The hyenas are gathering for the kill."

"She's no lady. I have to take Jonah to the vet soon."

"Mr. Hal, he said stay put."

"But!" Rage reddened her vision. A prisoner in her own home? "Thank you."

"Anything I can do to help?"

"No, not that I know of, other than sic those people on someone else."

"I wish. They're trampling all over the plants, and people who live here get a mic shoved in their face. Not good."

"I'm sorry."

"Not your fault."

And she got an idea. "Streets and sidewalks are public, but your flowers sure aren't. How about calling the police and accusing the whole lot of trespassing? You even have proof."

The manager cackled. "I'll do that." He hung up.

Hitting speed dial, she bypassed polite greetings and burst out, "I've got to pick up Jonah to go see Mutt."

Hal's patient voice: "Dinah..."

"She won't eat if he's not there and that will make him frantic and that will make his mother frantic and—"

"Dinah! Enough!" Hal never raised his voice.

"Sorry." She swallowed hard. "Hal, I'm frustrated. The vultures are out there interviewing people who know nothing whatever, they're so desperate. If it's big news, why didn't they come to the launch?"

Hal snorted. "That's right; I told you not to watch television. Maybe you should have. The press has distorted the picture dangerously. You and all your promotions and ads say it's a dietary supplement that can help people feel better. They're claiming you said it can cure diabetes. They don't even specify type. They're making, or manipulating, their news, Dinah. Sensationalism."

"What happens if the FDA thinks I said that?"

"Right." Hal paused. "Shame I have never met Jonah, or I could pick him up."

She sighed. True. "I'd call, but I don't have his phone number."

"Look on your phone."

"It's blocked."

"Oh. Tell you what. I'll go meet him and tell him who I am, and if he—"

"His dog's real name is Downmutt. Tell him that you are taking him to feed Downmutt and he will go with you. And will you buy something for him to take to his mother for supper, please?" Although they probably still had most of that chicken.

"Yes ma'am. At your service."

"Thank you, Hal." Her throat clogged and all she could do was sniff. "And incidentally, why aren't they bugging you, like we asked? You're the one who always knows the right thing to say."

"I'm not photogenic. Or intriguing. Or the boss of the company that's going to cure the world of diabetes."

She sighed. "How could such a thing get so twisted?"

"Don't worry, Dinah. It will blow over. The press has a very short memory. I'll take care of the dog thing. How you'll get to work tomorrow is another story."

"We're supposed to pick up the dog in the morning."

A sigh from that end. "I see." She thought she heard him mutter "Please, God, get us through this" as she hung up.

Pacing the living room, she called herself all kinds of

names (unjustly; it wasn't she who'd stretched the truth beyond breaking), peered out from a crack in the blinds to watch the mob below. The police had backed them off the property, but they still crowded the sidewalk. Was this what a shark feeding frenzy looked like? Maybe she should just go down there, talk to them, answer what questions she wanted to. Or maybe Hal could set up a time in the morning for a press conference. After all, what could they do but harass her? She had nothing to hide.

And a worse thought struck. If they were so cavalier about the truth, would they listen to what she said? Almost surely not. They would twist her words into whatever they thought would shock and intrigue. She had released a product that could be beneficial. She could see that the unvarnished truth would not be glitzy, sensational, or even newsworthy.

Surely Hal had thought of all this. He of all people understood. They'd discussed it. But his dire predictions dealt primarily with pharmaceutical companies who might feel threatened by her product if it reduced the need for their lucrative drug regimens. The other side of her mind asked gently, *Is Hal known for overstatement or understatement?* Had he ever made a bad judgment call?

Of course he had; no one could live in this world without making mistakes. She just had no immediate recollection of any in the time they'd worked together. Or she'd just never heard about them. There were lots of plausible answers.

She peeked out the window again. Had the crowd thinned a little? Another news van pulled up, this one with a satellite dish on the roof. The side was emblazoned with an ad for the local technical college.

Waiting was worse than anything. Pacing, checking

email, pacing, checking the window, pacing. What was the matter with her? This was insanity.

"Ah, darlin', you need to be prayin'." Her gramma's voice slid around her, warm and comforting like the shawl she sometimes used to snug Dinah to her side. She'd not heard that voice for twenty years, ever since the day Gramma went into a diabetic coma and left. Dinah had sat weeping at her bed. She had quit praying that day. Praying to a God who claimed to be real and wasn't was not only a waste of time but a fantasy that she no longer bought.

The only one to depend upon was herself. Immediately names and faces bombarded her. True, she depended on her whole team. More family than business colleagues, together they had accomplished the miraculous on so many levels. She knew there was no way to repay them but to keep on creating products so that all their jobs were secure.

Snatching up her ringing cell, she saw Hal's number and hit the answer button. "Are you okay?"

"Of course I am okay, and here is a young man who wants to talk with you."

"Dinah?"

Her day brightened instantly. "Hi, Jonah. How is she? Did she eat?"

His grin swam through the ether to her. "We can pick her up after ten in the morning and Mommy said to tell you thank you and she, not Mommy but Mutt, can stand up now and she licked my face and..." He stopped to catch a breath. "And Mr. Hal is really nice. We're getting pizza for supper."

Dinah restrained the groan. She knew Hal did not like pizza; but then he did not have to eat it, just buy it. "You tell him thank you for me, too, please."

"I will, but how will you get past those people? Dr. G has a TV on in the waiting room and we saw on the TV out in front of your building."

"You let Mr. Hal and me worry about that. I will get you to the vet tomorrow."

"Thank you, and D-Mutt thanks you, too. Oh, and Mrs. Miller said to tell you— er, I mean the other Dr. Miller. Dr. G wasn't there but she says he will be in in the morning to sign the papers so we can bring Mutt home."

Dinah felt tired just listening to his enthusiasm. "I'll see you in the morning."

"Here is Mr. Hal."

"He is some boy," Hal said.

"I told you."

"By the way, I have a plan for the morning."

"I thought the crowd had all but left, but then recruits pulled up."

"They'll find something else to do eventually. I'll pick you up at the back entrance about nine forty-five. Jonah's mother said she'll call the school to let them know he'll be out for the day, so never fear."

"And Food for Life?"

"They will all go to work and you won't, at least not until later. The boss can surely be tardy once."

Surely. The prisoner in her own home sighed and hung up.

The next morning all went as Hal had planned. He was not driving his Beemer today. He had a big Ford Something this morning, and Jonah already sat belted into the back seat, grinning widely. She and Jonah walked into the clinic and immediately a dog in back started barking.

"That's Mutt. She knows I'm here."

"You sure?"

He nodded and broke into a smile. "Dr. G, you're here." He ran to the man and threw his arms around him.

"Good morning." He hugged Jonah and did not smile at Dinah; it was a grimace disguised as a smile. She knew the difference. "Miz Taylor."

"Dr. Miller." Why the sudden coolness? "Good morning. Thank you for taking care of Mutt." Manners covered a multitude of misgivings.

"My pleasure." He left off freezing and smiled at Jonah, warm as sunshine.

How'd he do that? She watched as Dr. G pulled a cardboard tube from behind the reception desk and opened it.

"I have your picture done, Jonah. I hope you like it." He unrolled the paper and held it up.

"D-d-Mutt and me." He stared up at the man. "It looks just 'zactly like us." He turned and held the drawing at arm's length. "Look, Dinah!"

"A very good likeness, Jonah." Dinah closed her eyes, but only briefly. There it was again. What had happened to the oxygen in the room?

She'd never been a fan of cartoons or caricature, but the picture of Jonah and Mutt—why was it different? The eyes, that's what it was. How did he draw with such power that she felt she was looking into the child's soul? All with Magic Markers? Well, maybe they were a better brand than that, but still...

Dr. Miller rolled the drawing and slipped it back into the tube. "Let's go get Mutt."

Elated, the little boy bounded off through the double doors.

"I'll wait for you out here." She crossed to the reception desk. "You have the bill ready?"

"I do." The receptionist reached low beside her desk as a printer down there stopped zipping, and laid out the itemized bill. "We had to do a lot to—"

"I understand. The poor dog was near death. Jonah's mother, Jonah, and I all appreciate the care your staff has lavished on Mutt and Jonah both. I understand that you are not usually open on Sundays, and yet you allowed—"

"There is someone here every day, of course, to check the animals and care for them." The receptionist smiled. "And we do whatever is best for our patients. We had one woman whose basset was so hooked up to machines that we couldn't move him, so we let her bring a cot and her sleeping bag. That's probably the only reason her dog made it."

"This includes meds and all she needs?"

"We have written all the instructions here on this page. They are easy, really, and if you'd like, you could set up the appointment for us to take the stitches out. Of course if you have any questions, please call. Here are all our contact numbers." She passed the paper across. "And congratulations on all your accomplishments. Our community is a far better place with your business here."

Dinah felt her cheeks flush as she handed off a credit card. "Actually, our new product does not do nearly what the press is claiming it does. Just a helpful supplement, certainly not a cure. Nowhere close to a cure."

"Oh, I wasn't referring to that. My son plays on a T-ball team and my daughter plays softball. Both are on teams that your company sponsors. The science department at my daughter's middle school is partially financed by a grant from Food for Life. She wants to be a bio-chemist like you." She chuckled and shook her head. "I don't even know what a biochemist does. But the day you

spoke to her class...well let's just say that was a highlight
for her."

Dinah relaxed a little. "I'm glad to give back. And I
failed to mention to the children: If you are a biochemist,
remain a biochemist and work at your bench. Do not, I
repeat, do not, become CEO of a company."

Dinah could feel heat creeping up her neck. So much
for keeping a low profile. She knew Food for Life supported plenty of activities in the Eastbrook area; after
all she approved each one; but this was different. Personal. She changed her tack. "Tell your daughter to keep
in touch with us. As soon as she can work legally, we will
find something for her to do."

The woman's mouth opened. "Thank you. In case you
want to run for governor, you have all our votes."

Dinah chuckled as she was meant to. "I'd like to meet
your daughter one day." She took her card back, signed
the merchant's copy, and slid her billfold back in her hobo
bag. Glancing up at the pictures on the wall, she asked,
"Does he really give each child with a pet a picture he
drew?"

"Children, yes, and sometimes a mother or grandparent.
He draws the line at teenagers."

"Understandably so." Dinah heard Jonah saying thank
you, so she nodded to the woman and looked over to see
Jonah leading Mutt out into the waiting room. The dog
walked slowly and with a pronounced limp, but she was
moving on her own. And she wore a cone. Dinah knew
they put those on dogs to keep them from chewing on
sores or stitches. Never had she seen a dog wear one without looking downcast and self-conscious. The Cone of
Shame. Mutt spotted Dinah and her tail speed increased
from casual wave to wag.

She recognizes me. Why did that jolt her so? Dinah threw a thank-you in the direction of the frosty, brooding doctor and guided Jonah and Mutt out to the waiting car.

As soon as she stepped out of the clinic, she felt the heavy air lift. She'd known people who were uncomfortable socializing, but that didn't seem to be Dr. Miller's issue. She'd also known people who relate well to children but not adults—or vice versa. But with him, it seemed personal. A specific issue with her. If she never went back there it would be too soon, but she knew she would in ten days to get the stitches removed, if not before.

She buzzed Hal. He was surely waiting close by, because the Ford was at the door a minute later. Dinah waited for her charges to get in the back and sank into the passenger seat.

So now what? Take Jonah home and then talk to Hal about the next steps. Brave the hordes? Call the police? Sneak in to work incognito? A Groucho moustache and horn-rimmed glasses, perhaps. This was getting old really quick.

Tomorrow, regardless, she was going to work no matter what. What did real celebrities do in situations like this? Besides hire bodyguards? One thing she knew for sure: She was not going to remain in hiding, trapped by fear. Not in this lifetime.

Chapter Nine

H ere we go." Hal braked gently and turned into a side
street. He pulled the big Ford up to a stop sign.

Dinah leaned forward over the dash and looked down
the cross street, the street running past her condo. She
flopped back into the seat. "The hyenas are still there."

"You have to give them credit for persistence."

She sat erect again. "Hal, this is ridiculous. They're a
bunch of news reporters, not crocodiles. Surely we can
just march through them and ignore them. What more
can they do?" Was this a real threat or something about
mountains and molehills?

"Dinah, they're pros. Masters of ambush. They have all
sorts of tricks you don't know about. They trick you into
saying something, then trim away all your words except
the ones they can turn into a twenty-second sound bite.
The world of journalism has changed."

"Still…"

"And we haven't even heard from the big guns yet. I
expect a volley any day."

"Meaning?"

"There are a lot of possibilities. Buyout offers, injunc-
tions, all manner of legalities."

She looked out the window. Beyond the corner sat a white TV station van with a dish on its roof. "Are we vulnerable?"

"Technically, no. You were good about dotting all your i's and crossing all your t's. But they have all the money they need, even government backing. You know we talked about this so often and, yes, we've been excruciatingly legal, but someone will dig up something. Or possibly make up something, twist something just a bit. Don't be surprised if you read about your childhood in one of the rags."

"But why?" It burst out of her. "All we've done is produce a product that can benefit millions of people."

"Who will no longer be forced to buy as much of the drug companies' highly profitable diabetic drugs and paraphernalia. Come on, Dinah. We've talked about this over and over."

She heaved a sigh. "I know, but I refuse to live in fear and worry and what-if."

"There is only one real protection in all this."

"And that is ... ?"

"Almighty God." He grinned at her. "Thought that would stop you."

Dinah felt like sputtering and ranting about a God that is not real and never takes care of His people and all the other arguments she had perfected through the years. A picture of Gramma reading Bible stories to her did not flit through fast enough, followed by an image of her and Michael when she was swinging him on the tire hung from a huge oak limb. She clamped her teeth against the scream that threatened to blow them all up.

She abandoned the God thing. "I know I've been hiding my head in the sand, but all I wanted was to get Scoparia out there and go back to my lab bench. We may be on to something, the mechanisms involved, and I want to pursue it further. It's not rocket science; it's bioscience, and I'm beginning to see all kinds of lucky little what-ifs. Is that so terrible?"

"Luck. Or a series of continuous miracles. God has blessed you mightily." Her snort made him smile. "Sorry, my friend, truth is truth, and we did not do all of this on our own. No matter how great a team we all are."

Gramma had said that one time, too, in her warm voice, or many times that morphed into one. "You can't outrun God, Chicken Little. His shoulders are plenty broad enough to carry your anger and He will always love you no matter what. Not like those in your life who have let you down so terribly."

Those in her life whom she had loved and lost.

I'm not trying to outrun Him. You can't outrun something that isn't there. All in people's heads. She jerked her mind from such painful introspection and thought again of Jonah, and of taking Mutt in to see his mother. The little dog didn't adore just Jonah; it was obvious she had a heart big enough for the whole family.

The concept of the whole family led to another thought. Who and where was Jonah's father? Shouldn't he know how terribly ill his wife was? But if there had been a divorce—there were so many scenarios and no answers to any of her questions. So why didn't she ask?

She repeated it aloud. "Re: Jonah. When we left him and Mutt out at his place, I was so tempted to just take you upstairs to see his mother. We know so little, but I can't figure out how he manages to sidestep me every time I start to ask questions. It's as if a door slams and he leaves. At least now that I know where they live..."

"You could go visit with her while Jonah is in school."

"I was about to say that."

He pointed and continued driving. "Someone is waiting by your back door, too."

Dinah sighed. "I think we need to just set up a time for a media interview. Or maybe a press conference. Get up, read a statement, and leave."

"We've talked about this." There was a warning note in his voice.

"I know."

He pulled over to the curb. "I could ask Horace to create some kind of distraction at the rear entrance so we can get in."

"I'd rather just go to the office if I'll have to deal with them either way."

Her mind started bumping and bouncing from idea to idea, as it so often did once she made an initial decision. "We'll do a media interview at one p.m."

He scowled at her as he took a right at the intersection. "That's an hour and a half away."

"Right." She pulled out her cell, hit the speed dial, then punched two for April and put it on speaker. "April, we're doing a media interview at one. Send out an announcement, please."

April sputtered something. Her assistant was very good at sputtering; probably some sort of passive resistance when she disagreed and didn't want to say so. But then she said so: "Dinah, you can't! We have too little time, and they're going to say whatever they want to say; this will just feed into their biases."

"I refuse to live like this."

"Run it past Hal first."

"He is right here, actually, and hasn't said a word."

"Of course he hasn't. What good would it do?"

"None. I think deep down you agree, or you would be spouting advice at me." She glanced toward Hal. He looked grim. "We'll be there in about five minutes. Call a meeting so we can prepare a statement, please."

A give-up lurked in her voice. "I have one ready. I figured you would fold soon."

No, she would never get ahead of April. "Good, we'll go over it, then. We'll want everyone, so we'll all be in the loop."

"Will do." Was that a sigh of resignation?

Dinah thumbed the button and dropped her cell back into her bag. "You think she will have a better idea?"

Hal shrugged and turned into the parking garage, ignoring a reporter's shout. "You're not giving us time to set this up properly."

"What setup? A mic is all we need. I will read it, say thank you, and…"

"No questions?"

"I wasn't going to do a Q-and-A. What do you think?"

"I think we might be opening a can of night crawlers. Perhaps we say there will be a private interview at—"

"And they can pick one person? That might keep them busy for a while." She smacked her head against the car-seat back. "All I want to do is keep working. Get production under way and let people begin to reap the benefits." A sigh. "So much for free enterprise in the land of the free and the home of the brave."

April met them at the elevator door. "We're all ready in the small conference room," she said, leading the way down the hall at a firm march. This was no time for extraneous conversation, but she asked. "Is the little boy okay?"

"Yes, and his dog, too."

"Oh, good. I've been praying for him."

"Thank you, I'm sure." This God thing was getting a bit insidious. *Why can't they just live and let live? I don't go preaching my beliefs to them.* But she put a smile on her face when April opened the door and ushered her in.

Discussion dribbled to a halt.

"Okay, let's get right to this." Dinah took her place at the head of the table. "I understand you all have a copy of the proposed spiel." Glancing around the table, she caught all their nods. All of them: April; Hal; Hans Aldrich, the PhD in biochemisty, department of research; Sandy Dennison, their other PhD in biochemistry, who headed up their production department; and Marcella Kitman, MBA, department of marketing/publicity. All of them had been with her since within the first six months of opening the doors to Food for Life, and Randy and Alyssa joined the company not long after that. Their tight-knit little group, whom Dinah felt proud to acknowledge, truly cared about each other. And they cared about the work even more.

"Are there any questions?" Dinah looked up from studying the one sheet and glanced about. No one seemed unduly upset or scowly.

Hans raised a forefinger. "Two questions. One: Where is this going to be held?"

Dinah had no idea, but April was saying, "In the street out in front of the building. That way we'll have the East-brook Police Department right at hand; traffic control, but if anything cuts loose, they're there. I was going to use the big conference room so we could control the sit-uation better, but then they'd be inside and we'd have to get them to leave. That wouldn't be easy."

Hans nodded grimly. "Question two: Do you really think you can pull this off without getting trapped by overanxious reporters?"

"I'll jerk her offstage with my shepherd's crook." Hal stared at them over templed fingertips. "I think that all of you should be her flanking guard."

"Now that's a fancy term for bodyguards," Marcella, at five foot eleven, made them laugh. But they all had learned to stay away from the edge of her tongue when she went into full Irish temper. One had only to witness it once to learn that lesson.

The chuckles lightened the gloom around the table. Dinah knew that they all knew how much she hated things like this. And so much was at stake. This whole mess had already gotten out of control.

Sandy tapped her page. "I suggest we omit that paragraph about the good of the people. If we keep this on a strictly business level—"

"And not let the emotions get involved." Hans finished Sandy's comment and added, "Forget the warm feely stuff and stick to the facts."

"Wait a moment," Marcella chimed in. "Warm feely sells ideas; facts don't. As much as the public thinks they're rational, they aren't. Emotion rules. Same goes for reporters, although I hesitate to call them human. We shouldn't leave it out if we want to make a case that appeals to the people."

April added, "I doubt it matters at this stage. We're just trying to get the hyenas to go away. They aren't going to hear half of what you say anyway; they'll be trying too hard to get a question in."

Dinah frowned. "We are announcing up front that there will be no questions."

Marcella shook her head. "That doesn't deter them. The big problem is, you might get so frustrated you slip and let loose with some tidbit of information we don't want to provide yet. Worse, a misstatement. Once you say the wrong thing, even if you immediately correct it, you can bet your sweet mama it'll get quoted and misquoted. So we stick to the script. Nothing more." She pushed her paper toward the middle of the table. "I move we accept this, we spearhead her out there, she delivers, and we do an immediate about-face and disappear. April will have a repast set out in here, where we will then disconnect the phones and eat, drink, and be merry."

"For tomorrow we shall die?" Leave it to Hans.

"I surely hope not." Why could Marcella not have said something more positive? More definite? Dinah almost winced.

"I second. Especially the eat, drink, and be merry part," said Sandy.

"Opposed?" Dinah looked around for a negative sign, expecting none and getting none. "Carried."

April pressed her lips together a moment, studying the table. Then she asked, "Do we want the Extraburger package to go, pizza, or subs? Or something else?"

Hans grinned. "Braumeister's deli tray. Three of them. To be delivered by Mr. Braumeister so we don't have to show our faces."

"Braumeister's it is. The usual case of soda?"

Among the chorus of uh-huhs, no one said nay, so April stood up and walked out.

Hal left, the others went back to whatever they were doing, and Dinah returned to her office. Was she doing the right thing? Absolutely the wrong thing? Was Hans right and she was no match for overzealous reporters? Hal seemed to think that, too. Why would they think that? She had a normal supply of smarts—an excessive supply in some areas, like chemistry. Surely she could do this.

She couldn't sit still. She walked to her bookshelf, walked to the window to see just as many media jackals as usual out there, walked away. She wore a track in her office rug much like the one at home.

Time didn't just slow down, it stalled. The hour was a week long. She read through the paper a couple of times so she wouldn't stumble.

At five minutes to one, they marched down the stairs and paused behind the double doors opening into the lobby. Dinah glanced out the little side window toward the street doors. As she had feared, a nightmare's worth of reporters and camerapeople were clogging the lobby, pressed against the security desk, standing around over in the Extraburger, milling in the main doorway, and overflowing out into the street.

"I called the police department," April announced. "They're going to clear the area, they said, as soon as we're done. I apologized and told them we had no intention of causing a problem, but some of the reporters might get pushy. The receptionist said, 'Show me one who isn't pushy.' So watch yourselves."

Oh, how Dinah dreaded this! Even though it was, essentially, her idea.

Hal straightened his tie, took a deep breath, and led the procession out into the lobby, parting the doors like the waters of the Red Sea. They flowed forward relatively unimpeded, thanks to the City of Eastbrook officers, wearing determination as a mask. A lectern with a bank of microphones had been set up. Where had that come from? April, Hans, and Marcella pressed in behind her.

Hal stepped up to the lectern. The roomful of chatter quieted. He waited. Then, "With great pride, Food for Life has launched a new product, a product unlike anything now on the market. Obviously"—he waved his arm in an arc—"it is already generating a media frenzy. And yet, few people understand what it really is and how it can change, and *not* change, lives. It is my pleasure to introduce Dr. Dinah Taylor, president and CEO of Food for Life, who can give you the information you want and need. I must ask you to refrain from questions at this time. I repeat: no questions." He stepped aside. "Dr. Taylor."

As if the bank of microphones on the lectern were not enough, the reporters in front of her were holding variously sized mics and iPhones as close as they could get; the ones behind raised mics high and pointed them at her above the others' heads. People with cameras and cell phones were clicking off pictures. And Dinah could not even remember if she had combed her hair recently.

She almost stammered, caught herself in time, squared her shoulders. *You can do this. So do it.* She began to read from her paper, the words exactly as April had written them, exactly as everyone had approved them. She used the voice inflections she had rehearsed so that it didn't sound quite so much like simply reading. But what she had not thought about or rehearsed was how she would make her exit. Should she say anything? Just leave? How suspicious would that look? She came to the end.

"Thank you for your attention." She stepped back. That sure was a superfluous comment.

"Ms. Taylor, has the FDA approved this yet?"

She almost answered with "Approval is not needed for a food additive," and stopped herself just in time. "I'm sorry; no questions, please."

But someone else was shouting, "An Eli Lilly representative claims that—"

Even as a woman directly in front of her barked, "Can you seriously say this thing is not a drug? It would—"

And right behind her, "You did not address the issue of side effects. What si—"

"No questions!" Hal's voice boomed. He seized her by one arm and Hans grabbed the other, and they plowed a path through the solid mass of shouting people, almost dragging her away. Had they not done that, she surely would not have been able to ignore the clamoring questions.

As she stepped through the doorway, Hal paused to turn back. "Tell you what; we'll allow one in-depth interview with Dr. Taylor. Decide amongst yourselves who will represent you. You may all receive more information about that tomorrow." His tone implied that idea of the interview had just occurred to him, just as they'd planned in their meeting.

The doors closed behind them, muting the cacophony but not blocking it completely. What could have been an informative, even joyful, event had turned into a battle zone. Why? It made no sense. It wasn't like she was peddling dope or something. This was a product that would *help* people.

Hal had tried to warn her that there would be plants, people peppered through the crowd to ask provocative and unnecessary questions. These were not just local media people. She'd seen the logos on the mics. ABC, NBC, and CBS, plus Fox, were all out there, and who knew what papers or magazines, along with the big international news agencies—even the Associated Press was finally getting interested in her. Would they be more honest and evenhanded, or were they caught up in sensationalism, too? Had she taken longer than a moment to glance away from her notes, she might not have continued. While she'd never been stagestruck in her life, there was a first time for everything.

Her dream of a nationwide product was now being known nationwide and halfway around the world. If only the world could know the truth.

Chapter Ten

"**D**inah is sure getting into hot water."

Garret looked up to catch a sad, wistful look on Dr. Sue's face. "Why? What?"

She snorted. "She's our client. Do you not ever keep up on what is happening in Eastbrook?"

"I count on you for that." Garret already wished he'd ignored her, but Sue had a way of getting through to him when others failed. Sisters, and, it seemed, sisters-in-law, could be like that. He returned his attention to the paperwork that he hated with such a passion. Even though they did nearly all of it now on computers. This breeder, like a lot of other breeders and pet owners, had insurance coverage on their animals. Another headache. If only he could spend his time on the animals, his research, and drawing, his life would be perfect. They needed someone who spoke insurance-ese.

But now she had introduced the thought of Dinah, breaking his resolve not to think of her—at all.

"Uh-oh, emergency! Marcy hit the button." Sue motioned to the flashing light on the wall by the door.

A knock sounded on the door. "We need both of you. Stat!"

They shared a look of despair and ran out to the examination room.

Animals always lost altercations with cars. The German shepherd lay on the operating table, still on the quilt the people had used to carry him in. Jason was at his head, removing the collar. Good; at least they'd have that blue rabies tag to ID him.

"How bad?"

"Bad."

"How long ago?" While he questioned, Garret checked the comatose animal's eyes—still able to focus—and gums—still mostly pink. Hopefully, no internal bleeding. But the mangled back leg was heartbreaking enough. "Any idea what happened?"

"Dog ran out in front of a car. Driver and passenger threw the quilt over him and when he went still, loaded him in the car, and brought him in."

"Contacts on tags? He sure looks familiar."

"Checking." Jason peered closely to read the worn tags, then read off the info. Amber, beside him, wrote it down and jogged off to the front desk.

Aha! "I think this is Valiant, Tessa's service dog." He closed his eyes, trying to remember her last name. *Tessa. Tessa! Come on, Garret, you've known her for years.*

Sue shaved a spot on the front leg and between her and Jason got the IV started. Betsy, their cage cleaner, came running in. "Amber says you need help."

"Monitor his heart."

The team swung into ER mode. Garret was always rather amazed at how well and how busy they instantly got. *Training pays off. So does paying personnel instead of skimping with volunteers.* Betsy Kellan was sharp as a new razorblade when it came to instantly and effectively diving in.

"You think we can save the leg?" Jason stepped back.

"No idea. Get the X-ray in here."

"Harold is bringing it right now." One of their better investments had been that portable X-ray machine. As if on cue, the double doors swung open with a clunk and Harold shoved the unit up to the table. At age nineteen he was built like a twelve-year-old, and his social graces weren't quite as good as a twelve-year-old's. But he had the machine up and running in seconds. As an electronic wizard he could not be beat.

While they scrubbed up for surgery, Betsy shaved as much of the leg and hip as she could, disinfecting as she moved. Sue set up the anesthesia. As soon as the X-rays showed up on the screen, they started in. Jason broke open a sterile surgical package and laid it out on a sterile tray for Garret. Many human urgent care centers were not as well equipped as they were, and this would be one of the cases that taxed that.

Garret lost track of time, as he always did when facing a monumental challenge. He would fix Valiant. He *would*. Amber called from the doorway, "Mrs. Welles is here. She says do whatever you need to."

Welles. Of course.

Sue asked, "Papers signed?"

"Yes."

Not that they'd given the cost any thought, not when there was a chance of saving this magnificent animal. Besides, Tessa Welles's life depended on this dog. They'd treat him for nothing to help her if they had to. He started at the top and worked down so that he wouldn't miss anything. Sue monitored vitals and anesthesia and assisted him, filling in where she could.

Two hours later, with the leg pinned and plated, bone

fragments removed or laid back in place and glued in, the hip pinned and plated, the dog's heart continued beating strongly.

Garret stepped back, pulling his mask down and wiping his forehead. "He sure has a will to live."

"That's why she calls him Valiant."

"How'd he ever get out on the street?" Together they lifted him over to a gurney to move him to recovery. His eyelids were already twitching. "Coming out. Let's get him in the largest crate. The heater on there?" He knew he was asking unnecessary questions, but rote was in full drive.

With the dog resting as comfortably as possible but still lightly sedated, they moved to the break room, where the coffee pot had been started and sandwiches intended for lunch waited in the refrigerator, since noon had come and gone.

Amber called from the doorway, "You ready to talk with Tessa now?"

"Give us five and show her back to Valiant's cage." Garret poured two mugs of coffee while Sue set out the platter of varied sandwiches. He bowed his head and whispered, "Thank You, Lord. For food and staff and all You have here given us."

Sue said the amen and the whole team helped themselves, all aware this would most likely be their first and last break of the day. Amber entered with an armload of files and plunked them down. "I've put them in chronological order. None are emergencies, so no triage to do. The waiting room is full, but several regular customers opted to rebook; didn't want to wait. Three others left their pets, so there are cages, too."

"Thanks, Amber." Ham and cheese tasted mighty good.

He tried to remember if he had eaten breakfast but then reminded himself he'd picked up a bagel on the way in. Eating while driving had become a habit.

He glanced at the top file. "I'll start with Tessa at Valiant's cage."

"Fill the rooms and we'll go on to the next as quickly as possible," Sue said, then leaned the back of her head against the wall, chewing slowly.

Garret left his lunch mess for Betsy to tidy up and headed for Valiant in the recovery room. Parked near Valiant's cage, Tessa, a wizened little woman in a wheelchair, paraplegic and a longtime client, wore makeup tracks down her cheeks. Ten years earlier a brain-stem stroke had canceled her growing career in real estate. She'd spent the years since then working at rehab far beyond what had been predicted. Self-sufficiency had always been her goal. Valiant was her second service dog.

Garret peeked into the cage. All good. "What happened?"

"I don't know. Valiant never runs—you know that. I was in the bathroom and he used the doggy door like always. When he didn't come back in, I started calling and he didn't come. He had to have jumped a six-foot fence and what possessed him to do that, I have no idea. Unless someone let him out—I don't know. Oh, Dr. Garret, please tell me he will live. He's my best friend, let alone the best dog I've ever had." A freshet coursed down her cheeks, adding to the raccoon affect.

Garret leaned his haunches against the cabinet counter. "I'm sure he's going to make it. Valiant is his name, all right. But that rear right leg is iffy. He might lose it, although we've done all we can to keep that from happening. Even in the best scenario, it'll be some time before he can work."

"No guesses?" She sniffed and dug out a tissue to blow her nose.

"Can you get someone to stay with you?"

She shrugged. "No idea. I depend on him so much."

"He's the one who's going to need help now. Once we put the cast on, he probably won't be able to chew the wounds, so he most likely won't need a cone. He should be crated and let out only briefly and helped outside to do his business. A towel sling in front of his hindquarters is the usual. But you can't do that."

"When he needs me for a change, I can't help him." Tessa fought the tears back. "This dog has always been my other half." She inhaled and exhaled forcibly. "But God will provide. He always has, so why would He stop now?"

She peered into the cage. "Dr. G, he seems awfully, you know, not caring."

"We are keeping him sedated for a couple of days on heavy doses of pain meds. Let the healing begin. You come any time of day, whenever you can."

She sighed heavily. "Looks like I might have to get an electric wheelchair after all. They are horrendously expensive."

"Can you qualify for assistance? A medical prescription?"

She ignored his question because she was watching her dog. "Hey, big dog, you gotta get better." Tears rained down her cheeks but she held her voice steady. "I love you so." She looked up at Garret, her blue eyes shimmering in the reflected light. "Thank you. Can I just sit here awhile?"

"As long as you want."

"You sure he can hear me?"

Garret pointed to the tip of the dog's tail. It moved slowly, but it moved. "Usually dogs in this condition are lights out, no one home. But he responded."

She rolled her lips together, trying to hold back the tears but failing miserably. "I wish I could sit down on the floor beside him." She heaved a sigh. "Life sucks at times, doesn't it?"

"It does."

"Dr. G, can we borrow you for a bit?" The voice from the hallway made him straighten.

"I'll be right back."

But when he finally made it back, she had left. He thumbed the intercom. "Is Tessa in the waiting room?"

"No, a friend came and picked her up. She said she'd call later." Karen's voice. So Amber had gone off duty and Karen had come on.

"Thanks." He heaved a sigh himself and dove back into the fray. Had every client they served decided today was the day to visit the vet?

Even with all of them pushing hard, the last client did not exit until nearly seven.

"Has Tessa called back?" he asked finally.

"No. I left a stack of messages for you, though. Not a big stack, and most of them can wait until tomorrow." Karen smiled apologetically. "All but the two on top. I said you'd get back to them tonight."

"Good, thanks. Have a good evening."

"Right. You, too." Their chief receptionist/office manager waved as she headed to the back, where the employees parked their cars.

"I'll see you in the morning, then?" Sue tipped her head back. "I know, tomorrow is supposed to be my day off, but we have three spays that were moved to tomorrow, so I will do those. I have a feeling you'll spend the night?"

"Most likely. Easier than coming back to check on him, or rather them."

"We don't usually have six in-patients." She gathered her bag and briefcase with her computer in it. "Call me if you need me."

At least they were not open for urgent care tonight. They swapped with a clinic across town so that each of them were closed two nights a week. But while they had the schedule posted front and center on their Web page and on all ads, they still got calls. Even their answering service referred the callers automatically on the closed days. He threatened to get an unlisted personal phone number but, for some reason, never had. If someone needed him that desperately, he wanted to be available.

"You want me to bring you supper?" Ken Steiger, their beanpole walking assistant, asked before he left.

"Naa, I'll have Pizza Castle deliver. But thanks." This most certainly would not be the first night Garret had slept on the cot in the room with a sick animal.

After the others left, he returned the phone calls, one to an elderly lady who treated her shih tzu like fragile china. The caramel-and-white bit of fluff knew how to work his mama. Garret told her what to do in case Baby threw up again and to bring him in in the morning if it continued. Baby often threw up when he got something to eat he shouldn't. But that didn't stop him from snatching.

He left a message on the answering machine for the next caller, closing with "If you feel you need to see a vet tonight..." and gave the contact information for the other clinic. Perhaps they had already taken that recourse, since no one answered.

Restless after doing catch-up work for a couple of hours, he ordered the pizza, ate that, and tried to settle into the cot. Getting up about an hour later, he checked his charges—all were resting well—and went back into the break room for a cup of decaf. He hated decaf, but he knew the leaded would keep him awake for sure.

Why could he not sleep? His charges were all snoozing soundly. He mopped urine for Valiant, who was now incontinent due to the meds, and made sure he was clean and dry. He changed an IV bag and, having run out of things to do, returned to his cot.

Half an hour later, he was back up. He took out his markers and a half-sheet tablet. Jonah's eyes, so full of emotion he didn't have the words to express, kept invading his thoughts. Garret drew and redrew, ripping pages off, doing multiple studies on different sheets.

Why could he not get them right? He had finally done so on the picture he gave to Jonah. Why not again?

He closed his own eyes to draw on memories.

But when he picked up his fine-point pens the eyes turned to blue that one moment could look like a storm-tossed sea. Lake Erie, mid winter when waves crashed great ships onto rocks and wind ripped roofs from houses. Or like a high mountain lake he'd seen on a backpacking trip into the Rockies. That trip had forever stayed front and center in his memories. A sky reflecting blue, clear and pristine so you could see all the way to the bottom where fish swam and rocks shimmered. Or down into her soul.

His pens flew over the paper, making him wish he had something more substantial. Like brushes and canvas. But he worked with what he had—and the papers littering the floor attested to his feverish preoccupation.

The eyes turned canine, warm brown, full of love, darker, distant. Narrowed, warning. Mutt's eyes. Like Jonah, eyes that shared her soul.

He threw away a couple of drained-dry markers and ripped the last page from the pad. He was finished. In more ways than one.

A child's eyes. A dog's eyes. But did he have to draw hers, too?

What was there about Dinah Taylor that would not leave him alone?

Chapter Eleven

Tuesday felt like the first ordinary day Dinah had had in ages. In fact, it felt so normal that when her home phone rang that evening, she picked it up without looking at the caller ID.

"Dinah, this is Corinne, Jonah's mother."

"Well, what a treat. I take it Jonah and Mutt are doing well?"

"They are. She waits to go out until he comes home from school but he no longer lets her go on her own. He keeps her on a leash, not taking any chances. I have something to thank you for: making him change her name. His dad thought the world of his son, but that pup was so rambunctious he was always saying Downmutt and she began answering to that."

"It was such an odd name, I just couldn't imagine saying it. Especially when she seems so well behaved."

"I know. I have a favor to ask. Could you possibly come visit me tomorrow afternoon, say one o'clock or so? I know you are terribly busy, but I would surely appreciate it."

"Of course I'll come. How about if I bring lunch? Is there something special you would like?"

"Oh, a fresh salad with grilled chicken on it. The one down at the Extraburger is so delicious, and I've not had it for a long time."

"I'll get two salads and be there around one." After hanging up, she glanced through her daily calendar. April would just have to move things around, that was all. Nothing looked impossible. She emailed April the information and sat down in her chair, tempted to turn on the television. How she'd been able to resist that was beyond her. Tonight she just didn't care. They would do what they would do and she'd have to deal with it. Easier said than done. Worry and guilt, two first cousins of extreme disquietude, took up residence on either shoulder, chanting their songs of misery.

The next afternoon, she picked up her order at 12:50 and rang the doorbell, right at one. She'd even been able to find parking. Luck was smiling on her today. From inside, Mutt barked, then whimpered.

"Come on in—the door is open." Corinne sounded so feeble.

Dinah pushed open the door to see Mutt sitting, doing her quivering *I am so glad to see you* routine. "Just your friendly delivery service. I brought you a coffee and a tea since I didn't know which you would prefer, and I like either." She tried to figure which hand she could pet the dog with. "Sorry, girl, when I put this down I'll pet you."

"Could we please eat here in the bedroom? It uses up less energy for me that way."

"Of course." Dinah carried in the box and set it on the bed. Then she leaned over to stroke the fluffy ears, one of which stood half up. "You look good, Mutt. Big improvement."

"I was so afraid she would not make it, and Jonah would have been crushed beyond measure."

"He handled the whole thing so well."

"He's like his father, on the stoic side."

Dinah wanted to ask questions about the missing man but instead handed the lunch container to the pale woman, who seemed to almost disappear into the bed. All but her eyes, her haunted, life-filled eyes. Jonah's eyes. For some reason, Dinah had always thought Jonah had his father's.

Corinne lay propped with pillows against the head-board of a single bed while another single bed filled the corner by the window, so the two were almost foot to foot. A chair and a rather scuffed dresser took up the remaining space, with a closet door opposite her bed. Obviously no man lived here, at least not recently. Dinah's earlier assessment had been correct: shabby but clean. How did Corinne manage the housework and taking care of Jonah when she was so weak?

Dinah tried not to bite her tongue, but that might be what it took to curb her curiosity. "You didn't say what kind of salad dressing, so I brought one of each: thousand island, french, blue cheese, and ranch."

"Ranch is perfect." She managed with a bit of difficulty to open the container and pour her dressing.

"Jonah is an amazing artist." Dinah glanced around the room at all the drawings push-pinned to the walls. The contrast between this busy, filled room and Dinah's im-maculate white apartment struck her like a belly punch.

"He is. His papa was, too. He started Jonah drawing just before he had to leave." A shutter dropped over her that warned Dinah not to question, as if she wished she'd not mentioned a man at all.

Perhaps next time Corinne would feel more free to talk. "Do you have friends around here who help you?"

"Oh, yes. Thank God for all the good souls He sends our way." She took another bite of salad, smiling at the flavors. "Trudy next door is a saint of the first order. Her daughter, Claire, comes to clean once a week. Such good friends." A few more bites and she set the salad aside. "Guess I'll have a snack later. Trudy brought over peanut butter cookies because she knows those are Jonah's favorites." She smiled at Dinah. "Thank you for being such a good friend to my Jonah and to me. God will bless you for the love you share."

There it was again. The God thing. "You're welcome. Jonah is easy to love."

"But you went an extra ten miles with Mutt. I will repay you if you tell me how much."

"I don't really know. We have another vet call, you know. Let's talk then." Dinah closed her salad. "I can see you are really tired, and I need to get back to work. Is there anything I can get for you?"

"Thank you, but no. I'll take my afternoon nap before Jonah comes home." She pointed to an envelope on the dresser. "Please, would you take that? In case Jonah needs you."

Dinah started to ask a question, but the woman's eyes were already drifting closed. The envelope was sealed, and Dinah's name was written on the front. On the back a note said *Open only in case of an emergency.*

"I...hope you never have to use it, but just in case." A slight smile. "Bless you."

Dinah gathered up the lunch things, put Corinne's leftover salad in the refrigerator, and threw the trash away.

That night after she got home from the office, she set

the envelope on the granite mantel above the gas log fire-place in the living room. Why not just open it now, just in case? No. It said *emergency*. She would honor that.

And then her thoughts went scattering again. They bounced off the walls of her world, arranged themselves in interesting ways. It was basically that process of wild, creative thinking that had led to success in their diabetes work. Now Hans wanted to start working on autoimmune problems and autism. Not that they were related, but his brain, like hers, skipped wildly. She got out her legal pad and penciled in thoughts and shorthand chemical formu-las.

This was the part of the hunt that intrigued her most. In the 1930s, researchers discovered antibacterial prop-erties in aniline dyes, attached to azo compounds. Even-tually, they realized you didn't need the azo component at all. She took immense pride that her company used that same outside-the-box approach. And look how it paid off—very occasionally, but profitably. Not to the degree that the discovery of antibacterials served humanity, but important in their own ways.

But before all that loomed the infernal interview on Friday. And it was to that interview that she must apply her galloping thoughts. Maybe she could reward herself by coming in on Saturday to putter in the lab. She fired up her laptop and stretched out on her formerly white sofa. She still had to call in a professional cleaner.

She made two lists: what she wanted to tell the reporter and what the reporter thought he, or she, wanted to know. The list of what she wanted to say was easy. But the other list? Of course! She could populate it with as many of the questions as she could recall being fired at her in that hasty press conference. Side effects, for instance, the one reporter had mentioned. Supplements and food additives were not required to undergo the kind of thorough analysis Food for Life had subjected their products to. But should someone suffer ill effects, their reputation would be tarnished enough to cripple and perhaps kill sales.

And of course, how would they feel if their customers got sick or even died? What if Jonah's mother or someone took Dinah's supplements trying to restore her health and instead got worse? Dinah was downright proud of their stringent testing.

She had the rat results; they were pretty impressive. She'd give him that and fudge on the human results, which weren't completely crunched yet. And she would take him on a tour of the facility, introduce him to Hans and Sandy and Marcella. Show him the layout and some of their methods.

The reporters had been complaining about the just-one-person stipulation; they were pushy to the max. Hal and Dinah decided to allow three people—one reporter, a photographer, and a biochem expert or endocrinologist. If this was pandering to them, so be it. Allowing just one reporter was pretty rigid, even though it felt just a tiny bit like revenge for the way they'd acted. And April had the brilliant idea that in exchange, the reporter's questions had to be submitted in advance.

Her mind bounced off in another direction. Should she feed them? Yes. Another couple deli trays from Braumeister's grocery, and she would lavishly hype the store. In fact, Food for Life would throw a feast like the crew had just enjoyed, perhaps with champagne. And all their existing supplements and other products would be arrayed on the table in the corner, strategically illuminated by the track lights overhead.

The phone rang.

She answered with a noncommittal "Hello?"

Jonah's voice. "Will you be eating breakfast at the Extraburger tomorrow?"

"Just like usual. And you're invited."

"Thank you." A pause. "May I buy an extra breakfast tomorrow to go, and bring it to Mommy?"

"Certainly. Do you want me to take it to her and you go on to school, or would you like to take it to her yourself?"

"Take it myself."

"Then we should meet fifteen or twenty minutes early. Think so?"

"Thank you, Dinah. Thank you very much." Jonah hung up.

Dinah smiled.

When they met for breakfast next morning, she noticed that Mutt was on a leash. Good; Jonah was taking no chances. They ate as usual, Jonah sipping his hot chocolate. He told her about a new art project in school and how, now that a substitute teacher had explained long division clearly, he could do the math problems so much better. He had no idea why his regular teacher was not in class this week. All the usual kid stuff, important to the kid but not of much consequence in the fight to keep America safe for democracy. Or to ensure the Cincinnati team would take the pennant. Or—in fact, he seemed quite chatty compared to his usual stoicism. He left with the box of breakfast for Corinne, and Dinah went up to her office.

April seemed pleased with her notes, all of them, and only added a few details here and there. When April was pleased, you could rest assured the material was pretty much complete.

She spent the morning in the lab with Sandy, trying to remove a hydroxyl from a carboxylic acid complex cheaply, *cheaply* being the operative word. It was either that or do email.

By quitting time, they had received all the reporters' questions that they were going to accept. Dinah was pleased that four of her guesses were on the "real" list, and a fifth was a minor variation of their question. She was as prepared as she was probably going to get.

She went to bed early that night in order to be fresh and bright when her torturers showed up the next morning.

At 1:30 a.m. the phone rang.

She was tempted to answer with, "Do you realize what time it is?" Instead, she answered with a polite "Hello?"

"Dinah?" Jonah, his voice quavering slightly. "I don't know what to do." Pause. "Please help me."

Chapter Twelve

Jonah needed her.

Why did he always need her in the middle of the night? She glanced at her bedside clock. Tiny little numbers glowed.

Slipping into sweats, she grabbed her bag and tennies. Emergencies. You rarely had emergencies in research labs. There were times when you suddenly had to act really fast, certainly, and times when things unexpectedly went wrong. Lots of those. But not emergencies like this. How she yearned for the good old days.

Wait; a little bell dinged. *Emergency.* That envelope Corinne gave her, to be opened in an emergency. She dropped it into her bag and headed out the door.

This would have to be about Mutt. Infection, sudden turn of health. The vet did say to bring Mutt back if anything went wrong. She didn't speed, but neither did she dally. Everyone sensible was home in bed, so she had the streets to herself. Why oh why had all *this* come into her life? No parking near their building. Safe or not, she whipped around the block and parked going the other way, half a block away.

Good thing she had on tennis shoes, not heels, although she had been known to run in heels, too. She took the stairs two at a time, reminding herself to breathe. She was not in as good shape as when she'd been playing volleyball, that was for certain.

Jonah met her as she burst through the stairwell door.

"Mommy can't answer me."

"What?" It took a moment for Dinah to register what he'd said.

"Mommy won't wake up and Gramma Trudy's not home. They went somewhere."

They hurried down the hall, but she stopped and took a deep breath before entering the apartment. Jonah tugged at her hand and led her into the bedroom. Corinne was still breathing. Faint and slow, but the covers moved.

"Mommy?" Jonah patted her cheek. "Mommy."

"Take her hand, Jonah. She can probably still hear you even if she can't answer." It was what her gramma had told her back when... But this was Jonah's mother, not him.

Jonah took his mother's hand and held it to his cheek. "She hugged my hand."

"You can talk to her, just like always. She can hear you."

"Dinah is here, Mommy. Grammy Trudy and Claire went to see the new baby, remember?"

Dinah saw slight motion as the woman feebly squeezed his hand.

"Is there a cell phone number for them, Jonah?"

He looked over his shoulder. "No."

Dinah heaved a sigh. Should she call 911? What made her even doubt that? She pulled her phone out of her bag. "I'll call nine-one-one."

"No! Uh, no. Please, no!" Those huge, deep, pained

eyes grabbed hers. "Mommy doesn't want that, she said."
Dinah could see that the hand was gripping his, vibrating.

"We have to. It's the law."

"Mommy's lawyer said I didn't have to. And Mommy said
if there was an emergency to call Grammy Trudy or you."

"But we . . ." Now what?

The envelope. Was this the kind of emergency Corinne
intended? "Excuse me a moment." She dug the envelope
out of her bag and stepped into the brighter light in the
kitchen. She ripped open the envelope with her thumb
and pulled out a single sheet of paper. The handwriting
was a bit shaky but legible and clear.

Dear Dinah,

*If you are reading this, I am either dying or gone
home. Please do not call 911. There is nothing they
can do but put me on machines to prolong a life that
will not recover. My prayer is that I will slip away
with as little fuss as possible. A file in my bottom
dresser drawer has all the legalities, my will, all the
necessary papers. Our lawyer is handling all that. I
gave a letter like this to Trudy too and included your
phone number in it.*

*Dinah, I am not afraid to die. I know I am going
home to be with my Lord and I already know He
is waiting for me. But Jonah will be left behind and
that is the hard part. I prayed for someone to come
into our lives who could love and care for my son.
His father wanted to but he could do nothing but
provide this home for us. Trudy is too old and her
daughter cannot take Jonah either.*

*There is no one else I can ask. There will be some
money for Jonah from the sale of this condo. The*

*deed is in the file. The lawyer will handle that also.
He promised to take care of any other problems, his
number is below.*

*Will you please accept this gift of my heart? I
know you will love him and he already loves you. He
needs you. He is so small yet.*

Dinah dug in her bag for a packet of tissues to mop the
tears raining down her face. She blew her nose and dried
her eyes so she could see clearly. She could hear Jonah
talking to his mother.

*I do not want him to become a ward of the court
and go into fosterage, which is what will happen if
you cannot see your way clear to adopt him. I had
wanted to talk this over with you but it appears we
were not given the time to do that. I cannot thank
you enough for loving Jonah.*

Corinne Morgan

Dinah laid the letter down and stared at the wall,
where a framed painting, more an abstract than a photo-
graphic depiction, hung. The colors were vibrant like the
scarves she wore, full of warmth and happiness, rippled
and blended, seeming to move like a peaceful sea. Never
still but always alive.

"Daddy painted that before he left."

She looked down to see Jonah at her side and Mutt,
too. "He's an amazing artist."

"He taught me to draw."

"Your mommy told me that. She said you're a lot like
him."

She returned to the bedroom, Jonah at her side. Light from the lamp by the bed lent a soft glow.

Jonah leaned against her. "Mommy likes you a whole lot. She said you made friends with me when you didn't have to. Me and Mutt. She really liked that. She said don't look at what people say, look at what they do. She said you would take care of me."

Oh she did, did she. Dinah perched on the edge of the bed and scooped up Corinne's other hand, clasping it in both hers. "Corinne, I've never married, never had kids, never took care of kids. I know nothing about kids. Nothing about giving Jonah what he needs. I don't think—"

The feeble hand squeezed hers.

"Corinne...are you sure I—"

Another feeble squeeze.

Dinah blotted away tears. Why wasn't Jonah weeping?

Peace like a river attendeth my soul. The hymn leaped into Dinah's head unbidden. Gramma Grace's favorite hymn. The smile on Corinne's face, the serenity. How could life leave like this? But it did. It had, all those years before. Then, she'd watched the dearest persons in her world stop breathing and be gone. Michael Junior. Then Gramma Grace.

Please, Corinne, not now! Not while Jonah is watching. Believe me; I know. Not now!

"Mommy?" Jonah was carefully watching his mother's face.

No squeeze. Corinne had joined Michael and Gramma Grace.

Jonah laid the flaccid hand on her abdomen. "Mommy looks happy."

"She does. She—she..." Words disappeared, all of them. Dinah laid the other hand on the body.

"She went to be with Jesus. She explained it all to me so I wouldn't be scared. She said she was going to go soon, but she didn't know exactly when. She said Jesus would take her when He got everything ready. I think He's ready because she didn't squeeze my hand." He looked up at Dinah. "It's now, right? She's happy up there with Jesus now?"

"That's right." *Dinah Marie Taylor, how can you lie like that?* To ease the mind of a small child who just lost his whole world and doesn't even realize it yet. That's how. And she would lie again if need be.

"And now I'm going to live with you."

"Yes. Apparently. Would you like to gather your things?" What else could she say?

There had been nothing she could do then and nothing she could do now.

Rob. Gramma Grace. Corinne Morgan. Good people. So unjust. So cruel.

And a kid. A strange little kid. Corinne had prepared him as well as can be expected, but nobody had bothered to prepare Dinah. Now here he was in her lap, under her wing.

She wasn't even certain she knew how to love. Care, yes. She cared about Hal, about her employees. But love? What was that, exactly?

While he fetched his backpack and plopped it on the bed, she retrieved the brown accordion file from the otherwise empty drawer and carried it out to the kitchen table. She sat. Corinne had left another note, this one taped to the front of the file.

Just follow the instructions, she ordered herself. *You do not have to think.*

Please do not call 911. Take Jonah and Mutt home with you and call this number. My attorney will take care of all the details. He will see to emptying the apartment and bringing you Jonah's things.

She picked up the phone. A man's voice answered on the fifth ring.

"I'm sorry about the hour. My name is Dinah Tay—"

"Corinne died."

"Yes."

"I'll be right there."

"Thank you." She hung up, utterly amazed at how swiftly that exchange had taken place. Dinah shook her head. Surely this was a dream. Surreal. And she would wake up soon.

She leafed briefly through the file, closed it, and laid it on top of her hobo bag so she would not forget it. She returned to the bedroom. Jonah was struggling to stuff some things into a faded duffle bag. She perched on his bed, the duffle between them, to help. "We still have to call nine-one-one. Here. You hold it open, I'll stuff."

"Mommy doesn't want us to." He held the duffle's jaws wide as she forced things into the corners, the ends. Then he let her zip it while he snapped a leash onto Mutt's collar.

The present tense. He was referring to his mother in the present tense. Perhaps that was a key to his peace of mind. Not dead. Transformed. Or temporarily gone. Sorrow was engulfing Dinah, and she hardly knew Corinne. When would sorrow strike this child? All she could think to do was keep him busy.

"No, but the law requires it. We'll wait until the lawyer arrives. He's on his way. He can explain exactly what we should do."

That's it, Dinah. Pass the buck. You who take responsibility for a whole company cannot bear to take the simple, basic responsibility to call 911. What is wrong with you?

"Wait. We need the dog food. I'll get it." He ran out to the kitchen and returned with a nearly empty bag of kibbles for a mature dog. He juggled it into the crook of his arm, hauled his duffle bag off the ground, and nodded. "Wait." He put them all down. "Mutt's dish." He went back to the kitchen and returned with a dog dish greatly in need of washing.

Dinah raised a hand. "Let's stop and regroup here. Take your backpack to the bathroom and get all the stuff you'd take if you were going on a trip. Like you'd be staying overnight in a hotel."

"I never went on a trip. Or stayed in a hotel."

"Oh. Toothbrush, toothpaste. Hairbrush. Comb. Favorite soap or shampoo?"

"I wash my hair with dish soap. Mommy says it does a better job." There it was again, the present tense. He obviously didn't realize...

"Ah. Then bring the dish soap." *Keep stalling, Dinah. Keep him busy until the lawyer gets here.* She carried his duffle, the dog dish, and everything out to the kitchen, putting them down by the table.

He returned with a worn toothbrush sticking out of his backpack's side pocket. He brought the foaming dish soap over from the sink. "It won't fit, I don't think."

"Any grocery bags in the closet?"

He went back, returned with a plastic bag. They put the jug of soap in that.

School. Kids have school stuff. "How about notebooks, school things, homework? Got all that?"

That burned up another few minutes. Too few. He put

his school things into the plastic bag and stacked it beside his duffle.

"How about stuff to draw with? Got all that?"

He nodded. "It's mostly at school. Wait. My extra pencils." He left and presently returned.

"Favorite toys, books?"

"No. Wait. You mean my bear?"

"Sure."

He was headed for the bedroom when the door rattled and burst open.

Dinah jumped and yelped.

A large man, a very large man, with a neck like a tree trunk, entered.

Jonah paused; then said casually, "Hi, Mr. Jensen." He continued to his bedroom.

The man's build matched his deep male voice. "Sorry I startled you, Dr. Taylor. Lars Jensen. We spoke earlier." He extended his hand.

Dinah rose and was rather embarrassed to see that her own hand was shaking. She took his in a business-type grip. "Thank you for hurrying."

The man didn't smile, but he managed to look fairly pleasant anyway. "I was afraid this would happen sometime soon. How is Jonah doing?"

"He is handling this far better than I am."

"Corinne prepared him remarkably well."

Dinah sat down again. "I'm afraid she didn't prepare me. She gave me a letter, but we didn't talk—Couldn't this Grammy Trudy take him?"

He sat also. "Trudy is an elderly neighbor, no blood relation. Her health will not permit her to raise a child this young, and her daughter has a difficult special-needs child and can't take on Jonah as well. We all felt it would not be in Jonah's best interests for her to take him."

"But a total stranger is just fine."

The huge man smiled slightly. "I did a background check on you, Dr. Taylor. You're not a total stranger. Your business acumen is demonstrated by your financial statement, charitable giving, the obvious happiness and confidence of your employees, the mission statement on your company's Website. And they all attest to your strong moral character."

She sighed. "Jonah already mentioned, 'Don't look at what people say, look at what they do.'"

The smile loosened, spread a little. He sat forward, both elbows on the table between them. "One of Corinne's favorite lines, and mine, too. Corinne and I agreed it will be difficult for you in that you would be a single parent with no experience. We're hoping that if you can pilot a company as complex as Food for Life, you can handle this job, too."

"What are my choices?"

"I'm hoping you can take him in temporarily, at least, so that he has a roof over his head. In the longer term, you could at any time tell me that there is no way you can handle a seven-year-old boy and a dog and that I should come and get him immediately. What we hope most of all is that he not fall into the morass of Social Services. He's a gifted child, a very special child, and fosterage in this area is very poor."

"Right now I believe I am in a state of shock and..." And what? She rubbed her forehead with her fingertips. "You are sure all the legalities are satisfied? What if his father..."

"As far as we know, his father died two years ago. Jonah

has no one who will rise up out of the woodwork to claim him."

"And you will now notify, notify..."

"I already have. EMS is on the way."

"Will they try to—bring her back to life?"

"No. Her condition is known and her death was expected at any time. No heroics."

Jonah came out with his backpack on. He picked up Mutt's leash and looked at Dinah.

She studied Jonah a moment, turned, and studied Mr. Jensen.

He grimaced and nodded slightly toward Jonah. "It hasn't sunk in yet. It will."

There was polite knock on the door and a young man in midnight blue shirt and trousers entered. He carried a red duffle.

Jonah shook his head. "Mommy doesn't want them to come. She said."

Dinah tried to smile and failed. "It's the law, Jonah. But Mr. Jensen will take over now. It's all right."

A second technician entered, a young woman, pushing a gurney ahead of her. Jonah scowled. Mr. Jensen followed them into the bedroom. And here came what was probably the medical examiner or someone similar, an older woman, very thin, with a clipboard.

"Mommy doesn't want them to..." Jonah's voice trailed off.

"Mr. Jensen will take care of it. It's okay."

Presently, the lawyer came back to the kitchen. "You can go now. We have it covered."

Dinah understood he was talking about the corpse as well as the situation. She stood up, incredibly weary. "Got everything?"

Jonah nodded and picked up Mutt's leash. They walked to the car, put his things in the trunk, and climbed in. The sky was lighter, not from just the lights of the city. She checked the clock on the dash. Nearly five a.m. She garaged the car and they trundled up to her apartment, the kibble under her arm so that he could negotiate the stairs more easily.

Dinah nearly choked. Today was Friday. The day of *the interview*. The interview that could make or break her whole world. *Don't be overly dramatic*, another side of her intoned. *The world will not stop because of an interview.*

She kept her outer self in check, acting calm. Inside she screamed. *Not fair. Taking a small boy's mother! What kind of a God are You, anyway? What happened to grace and mercy? That's what You say, but that's not what You do! Just leave me alone. And I'll leave You alone. Not fair!*

Chapter Thirteen

Mutt has to go out."

Dinah turned from her computer and stared at Jonah. "I thought you were still sleeping." She hadn't bothered to try. Tired as she was, she had too much going on to let her rest.

"I was, but Mutt has to go out, and I . . ."

Dinah nodded, thinking fast. "Okay, here's what we'll do. We'll go down to the ground floor and out the rear door." All the while she was thinking, What did the other dog owners in this building do? Did dogs need a grassy spot? "Will that work?"

"I guess. That's what we did at home."

"Let me get my keys. By the way, you need a key for the elevator here."

"Don't the stairs work?"

"Sure. But Mutt has a hard time with stairs right now, right?"

He nodded.

"Get your jacket."

He gave her a Jonah version of a rolled-eyes look. "It's by the door."

On the main level, they followed the hall to the rear door and stepped outside. The sun hadn't bothered to come out yet today, because of the rain. And the cold. Winter had returned with a snarl.

Jonah's windbreaker didn't do any more than break the wind. He and Mutt walked a couple of paces, she stepped off the concrete walk, did her business, and hurried back to the door, where Dinah had held it slightly open.

"Is that the only jacket you have?"

"With me."

"You have a heavier one at home, er . . ."

He nodded. "I like this one better."

"How about I buy you another Kansas City Royals jacket that's warmer?"

He shrugged.

Horace Watson stepped out his apartment door. "I see you have a visitor, Ms. Taylor."

"I do. Jonah Morgan, I want you to meet Mr. Watson, our building manager. If you ever need help, he's the one you call." She smiled at the man with a fringe on top.

"I see you like Kansas City Royals."

Jonah nodded. "My daddy liked them best."

"Well, I do, too. You ever been to one of their games?"

A head shake. "I sometimes watch the games on television. Do you really take care of this whole building?"

"I do."

"And the elevator always works?"

Dinah shrugged at the man's questioning look. "It often didn't where he lived before."

"I make sure the elevator always works. You can count on it."

Jonah nodded as he looked up at the man. "Do you have a dog?"

"No, my two cats would be highly incensed."

"You mean they don't like dogs."

"They *really* don't like dogs. They sit in the window and *yeoowl* at any dog who passes by. In fact, if I pet your dog..."

"Her name is Mutt."

Mr. Watson nodded. "If I pet Mutt, my two cats will give me a good sniff test and then hiss."

"Really?"

"Really. Cats are real smart."

Jonah shrugged. "Do you know what time it is?"

"Six fifty-five. Why?"

"I gotta get ready for school. Nice to meet you." Jonah turned toward the elevator and Dinah followed. How was she going to handle this? That led to another question. What would she tell his school? If she was lucky, Corinne would have thought of that, too.

"Jonah, don't you think it would be a good idea to stay home from school today?"

"Why?"

"Well..." *Because your mother died last night and you are living in a new place and nothing is the same.*

"Mommy isn't here to write a note for me."

"But, Jonah." The elevator door slid open.

"Besides, I have a spelling test today."

Homework. She hadn't thought of homework, either. She hadn't thought of a lot of things, all of which seemed to be yammering for attention right now. Perhaps it would be best to let him go on to school, keep life as near normal as possible. *A copout; you just want to get to work.*

"Tell you what. You get ready for school, I'll get ready for work, and we'll eat at the Extraburger."

"Like we do?"

"Yes. However, Mutt will have to stay here. She can't get around well with that cone on her neck."

"By herself?"

Dinah stared from the dog to Jonah. Jonah who hardly slept last night, who was now living in a new place, had a whole new life, and what could she tell him? *Think, Dinah. You are known for your ability to think on your feet, now do so.* They returned to the apartment.

"Well, she can't go to school with you."

He looked around at the white world. "What if she has an accident in the house?"

"Has she ever had an accident?"

"Not since she was little but..." He chewed his bottom lip. "She wasn't hurt before, either."

You should pick him up today. But the last time she did that, things didn't go well. So many things to think about, and she had an interview to prepare for. "You get ready and we'll talk about this on our way to the Extraburger."

Dinah kept the *Don't think* command at the front of her mind as she dressed in a men's-wool-suiting, warm, white three-button jacket with matching slacks. She filled in the neckline with a scarf in hues of violet, magenta, and deep blue. Silver loop earrings and an etched silver bracelet finished the ensemble. She stared in the mirror. She would need to do heavier makeup for the camera, but that would be last minute. She looked pretty bleary. Two-inch heels; she refused to wear trendy shoes after a chiropractor warned her that shoes like those were helping keep bone and muscle people in business.

Jonah waited patiently on the sofa, backpack at his feet and dog halfway in his lap. He kissed the top of her head, promised Mutt he would come back after school, and said sorry she couldn't go along today, but soon. She followed him to the door but didn't try to go out.

Dinah locked the deadbolt behind them and they took the elevator down to the lobby. Dinah wanted to reach out and set Jonah's cap straight, but he always wore the bill sideways and she figured he had a reason. Probably something his dad did. Would he ever talk about his father?

Jonah looked up at her. "Thank you."

"For what?"

"Letting Mutt sleep with me on the sofa last night."

"You are welcome. This weekend we'll get a bed for you."

"We could go to my house and get my bed from there."

"That's true. We could." A blast of wind bit them as they rounded the corner to the Extraburger. At least it hadn't started raining again. *Maybe, should have, what if,* all bombarded her if she allowed herself to think of anything other than the coming interview. Preparing for that kept her mind occupied enough that she could fend off more personal things. Like a little boy and his dog now living with her.

"The usual?" Tattoo asked.

"Yes, please." Dinah paused. "What is your name? As long as we've been coming here I don't even know your name."

"It's Eric, Ms. Dinah." His neck pinked. "Where's your dog, Jonah?"

"She stayed home today."

"Strange to see you without her."

"Some other dogs beat her up and the vet said she should be quiet for a while."

He frowned. "She gonna be okay?"

Jonah nodded.

"Glad to hear that. I'll bring your order to your table."

"Thank you."

Breakfast as usual. Had last night really happened, or was she still walking around in some dream world? Jonah ate, thanked her, and left as usual. She went upstairs to her offices as usual.

April smiled as she entered. And the usualness ended.

"Jonah's mother died early this morning."

April sucked in air. "I'm so sorry. You didn't get much sleep, did you? How is Jonah? Want to cancel the interview?"

"I was thinking about it, but no. I just want to get it over with."

"So that explains the lawyer's call. A Mr. Jensen." April handed her half a dozen orange slips.

Dinah nodded. Coffee in hand, she headed to her office.

Last night was real. Her lack of sleep was real. The coming interview was going to be on her before she had time to finish her coffee. Too real.

She tapped in the number on an orange slip and hit the speaker. "Mr. Jensen? This is Dinah Taylor. You left me a message."

"Thank you, Dinah. I just want you to know that everything has been taken care of. Corinne did not want to put Jonah through a funeral, but I think it wise if we have a bit of a gathering with their neighbors and some folks from their church. People talking about how much Corinne meant to them."

"I value your judgment, and I agree, Jonah ought to have some sort of closure. But I'd like to run any plans past him first."

"As you wish. We've arranged to have the condo

cleaned and painted and put up for sale. I will have Jonah's things delivered in the next couple of days. If he asks for anything, we will get it to him. All his mother's keepsakes and the pictures on the walls will be boxed in case he wants them someday."

"He was asking about his bed. I don't have a second bedroom." At least until she could get her home office re-arranged for his bed and things. What all did a small boy need?

"I'll see about it."

"And he wanted to go to school today as usual, so I let him. Apparently he has a spelling test."

A brief silence. Then, "Keeping things as normal and routine as possible may be the best policy. My assistant has already informed the school about his mother and that you are *in loco parentis*. She's taking the school some papers with Corinne's signature to confirm it. There shouldn't be any problem."

Well, there was a problem once. I wonder if the police still consider me a pervert. Another rush of panic swept over her briefly. This was all so weirdly weird.

The deep voice spoke gently. "If you have any questions at all, please feel free to call."

"Thank you. Please keep me informed." Staying in professional mode could cover a hundred feelings. Is that what Jonah did, bury his feelings? Stay analytical? Go on as normal? The former normal would never return, not for either of them.

They goodbyed. Silence. She dropped the orange slip in the wastebasket and looked at the next one. Maybe normal and routine was the best for Dinah, too. Keep her occupied, lest she realize the enormity of what had been dumped on her.

April rapped and entered. "They'll be setting up the video equipment, and the interviewers are to arrive at twelve thirty. You don't need to see them until ten minutes before it starts, if you don't want to. No gracious host or any such thing. Hal said to remind you this will probably be an adversarial interview. He says he will be here at noon."

"Sounds good."

April left.

Dinah had just enough spare time to sit down and sprawl out in her chair, shut her eyes, and take a series of deep breaths, exhaling all the tension away. At least that was the way it was supposed to work. This time it didn't, of course.

A gentle rap on the door; "Time," April called softly.

On one more exhale, Dinah opened her eyes. "Makeup time." By habit, Dinah did her own makeup rather than bringing someone in. It was rare that she needed powder and paint; her only public appearances, usually, were product rollouts.

With moments to spare, April and she made their way to the conference room, now set up with five comfortable chairs and a low table with several pots of blooming tulips and daffodils. A display of the company products took over one corner of the room; the lighting could have been adjusted a little better—the right-hand side looked a bit dark.

Two cameras on wheels and one on the photographer's shoulder seemed like overkill to Dinah. The conference table had been shoved back against the wall; only the dents in the carpet from its heavy feet marked where it had stood. This did not at all look like her conference room anymore, and that put her off balance a bit. So did the one reporter's appearance. She was an older woman, toothpick slim, with professional hair and makeup. Watching her, Dinah felt somewhat frumpy. The other woman, the expert, Dinah assumed, was not so obviously manicured for the camera. But she was prim, straight-backed, with a grim, no-nonsense set to her chin and horn-rimmed glasses. Seated casually in the middle chair was a third reporter, an august-looking gentleman with graying sideburns. He, too, was impeccably dressed and made up. A second reporter?

"Oh, there you are." The older woman looked at Dinah. "I was beginning to wonder. You'll sit here." She waved a hand. "Pete and Marty will sit there"—she waved again—"and your moderator can have that chair."

Dinah might as well throw down the gauntlet right away. "I asked for one reporter and subsequently acquiesced to a photographer and expert."

She frowned. "Obviously, your people failed to brief you. Pete and I will be asking the questions. Marty is our expert adviser. I hope you don't try to snow us with a lot of scientific blather; Marty knows biochemistry and physiology better than you do."

Dinah felt her face flush hot, but she let the snub go, for now, and crossed to the woman with the glasses. "Marty. Expert—ah, of course. Martha Harding." She extended her hand for a shake. "I have read your work on fibrocalculous pancreatopathy. Very well researched. I am delighted that you can be with us." She gripped the woman's hand firmly and received a firm grip in response. "Frankly, Dr. Harding, considering the long list of your credentials, you seem quite young."

The woman smiled softly. "So do you, Dr. Taylor."

The slim woman snapped impatiently. "Please sit down, Ms. Taylor. We want to get started here."

Was rearranging her old familiar conference room a ploy on this woman's part to make her feel uncomfortable? Along with the verbal slaps? She could almost think so. On the other hand, it gave the cameras more room to move around. But why should they have to? A hundred thoughts raced around in Dinah's head; sometimes such a scramble of ideas was a blessing, sometimes a curse. But this time they showed her a route to take. *Ignore the professional snub and don't let it rattle you—that's her purpose.*

Her guiding thought had to be, *I am here to help people, to improve their health, and I know my stuff.*

Yes, but they brought an expert.

And then, *But you are an expert, Dinah!*

She bridled her runaway thoughts and hardened her voice. "I am assuming you are Constance Maloney. My associate, April, mentioned your name. You will use the appropriate honorific, Ms. Maloney; it is *Doctor* Taylor; and please keep in mind that you are the guest here."

"Unless it is an earned doctorate, I see no need to—"

Dinah interrupted her, something she rarely did. "Earned doctorates in both physiology and biochemistry, with post-docs at Johns Hopkins and Mayo." She did not sit down. "Apparently you did not read the materials we sent you."

"I read enough of them to know you're a charlatan. But then, that will become clear in the course of the interview."

Hal came bursting in the door. He nowhere near resembled a white knight, but Dinah considered him so. He boomed, "Good, good! I admire a person who can just say up front where she's coming from."

Stuffing down her disgust with *the woman*, Dinah

grinned. "Let me introduce our moderator, Harold
Adler."

He wiggled a finger at the reporter with graying tem-
ples. "You, sir, if you would scoot your chair that way
about a foot and a half...thank you, that's good. Dr. Harding, since you will be our resident expert, where would
you prefer to sit?"

Dinah fought off a smile. Thank you, mentor extraordinaire. Hal had just taken the reins out of Ms. Maloney's
hands, slick as you please. He had already warned Dinah
that as moderator he had to remain neutral and couldn't
protect her, but neutral was good enough. Thank heaven
they were not using the moderator Ms. Maloney had rec-
ommended—in fact, had insisted on.

They settled themselves. The cameraman, a mousy little fellow with unruly hair, fiddled for about ten minutes
adjusting lights and background features. Finally he
picked up his on-the-shoulder camera and nodded.

Hal began, painting this interview as a substitute for
the lack of Q-and-A previously. He introduced everyone
briefly by name and role, and they were off and running.

Ms. Maloney asked the first question on the list they
had given her. Dinah answered.

She asked the second. Good! She was simply going
down the list. Dinah felt a bit more relaxed.

And then Ms. Maloney threw a curve, a loaded question that was not on the list. "Balancing research and development plus cost of production against market price,
what do you think your profit margin will be?"

Hal was nodding slightly. And Dinah realized with a
jolt that Hal had not seen the list of questions. He had
no idea which were good questions and which were stum-
blers, like this one.

Except that Dinah didn't stumble, at least not this time. "Your question is impossible to answer because our research and development is not limited to this one product. So it can't be quantified. As for profit margin, we're keeping it as low as possible, and, I might add, with our backers' approval. Our mission is to get good health to the greatest number of people, and keeping prices low maximizes this." *Take that, you harpy!*

Ms. Maloney snapped back instantly with "Then why not operate at cost?"

Dinah was beginning to feel intensely irritated, and that was not going to serve her purpose. Not at all. "For the same reason you are getting paid to do this interview, Ms. Maloney. You gotta eat."

And Pete Whoever-this-was barked, "If your product is so beneficial, surely some foundation can cover production and make it available at cost, or free. Just how deep does your altruism go, Ms. Taylor?"

Hal had said they might use personal attacks. Here it was. She was about to answer when the harpy—aka Maloney—fired off another funding question.

Hal raised a hand. "You have to wait until the answer is completed before you ask another, Ms. Maloney."

Dinah took a deep breath and composed what she hoped was an adequate answer.

The topic shifted to disease. Dr. Harding seemed quite knowledgeable about diseases, especially in cases where diabetes was a contributing factor. Perhaps they ought to approach the woman to do consulting work for them. They could certainly use her.

She realized her mind was wandering away from the interview, down useless bunny trails, and snapped back to the here and now. Or tried to.

And then someone mentioned *pallor* and Corinne leaped into Dinah's consciousness so suddenly and vividly she froze. Now, of all times—and Jonah at school trying to stay normal while coping with the death of his mother, and the stitched-and-bedraggled Mutt waiting for someone to come let her out...

And her flitting mind, which was so creative and useful when it was going in all directions at once, tripped her, dropped her flat on her face. She misspoke—said the opposite of what she wanted to say. And while she was trying to back up and correct her error, they hammered her with new questions.

Bottom line: Their carefully constructed interview, which had started out so full of promise, with which she so wanted to clarify their purpose and the nature of their product, descended into shambles.

And stayed there.

Chapter Fourteen

We just have to get another vet in here. Garret was up and down all night last night, tonight was his night to do the urgent-care shift, and he had a full day ahead. Totally knackered already and it was only eight a.m. He wandered back to the break room.

"You look about as tired as I feel." Sue was pouring herself a cup of coffee. "Sick kids is about as bad as sick pets. Or maybe worse. The puking is hard to ignore. And so far since midnight I've run two sets of bedclothes through the laundry."

He poured a cup. "Can you ignore it when it's your own kids?"

"Not when they puke in bed." She grimaced and swilled coffee.

He narrowed his eyes. "Are you sure you should be here?"

Sue shrugged. "Allan is doing the day shift at home. He called in sick at work since he was part of the bathroom parade last night. But he says he feels better this morning. Two of the other three are on the mend. Some kind of fast-acting bug that hopefully leaves as quickly as it arrived."

Garret grunted. "I was hoping to leave early and maybe catch a nap at least. Valiant did well through the night, but I think we should keep up with the light sedation for another twenty-four hours."

She nodded. "Jason is on the schedule for tonight. He's coming in at four, I think." Sue glanced over her shoulder at the calendar. "I have tomorrow off with baseball try-outs; Allan will take that while Em and I do the Brownie trip to the Toledo Zoo. Or I'd work tomorrow."

"Maybe moving away from the clinic was not a smart move. I need to run home to feed the livestock, get a shower and back ASAP."

"Then you best go before things get really busy."

"Your first three appointments are here." Amber stuck her head in the door. "Dr. G, Tessa's here. Can she see Valiant?"

"Of course. I'll meet her at his cage."

He stepped out into the hall and Tessa wheeled to a stop next to him. "Good morning, Dr. G. How did he do?"

"Very well. We're going to keep him in about the same state for another twenty-four hours, so don't be worried about him." Garret led the way down the hall and shoved open the cage-room door for her. "What about you? Are you getting along okay?"

"A friend is staying with me for a few days. That gives me time to make whatever arrangements are necessary."

Garret frowned. "Only one person. Older?"

"Yes."

"Then I suggest we keep him here longer than we would need to if you had two people to take care of him. Can you fence off a portion of the kitchen or something to keep him confined? He might still be having an incontinence problem, depending on how long we keep him down. I suggest a roll of red roofing paper to lay over the floor. Protect the floor and easier on him. You just fold it up and toss. You could put down several layers at a time. And a towel or strip of fabric to slip under him in front of his rear legs for assistance when he is walking. Large as he is, a big person would be helpful."

"We will do whatever we need to do. Hey, big boy, sure miss you." She popped the cage door open and leaned forward, stretching her fingers out to touch the tip of his nose. A pink tongue kissed her. "Oh, Valiant, that name sure fits you."

Garret smiled. "That it does. If you have no more questions, I'll be back in a while, but I need to go feed my own herd."

"Thanks."

Garret headed for the back door before someone could grab him. He stopped at the Bagelry, ordering four shots of espresso in his twenty-ounce tall one. He'd be so keyed up he needn't worry about sleep for the rest of the day. It was tonight that caused him concern.

His message unit was flashing when he walked through the door to be greeted by dogs, cat, a raucous parrot crying "Help me, help me!" and the phone ringing. He petted the dogs, let the cat twine around his legs, and yelled "Quiet!" at the parrot. The phone went to the answering machine. A woman's voice caught his attention.

"Hi, this is Elizabeth Grayson, my aunt Jane introduced us at church on Sunday. I have a favor to ask. I need to bring an escort to a company do on Saturday evening. Sorry to be asking on such a late notice, but I guess I am hoping it can work. It won't be a late evening, and I will be eternally in your debt. Sometimes one just

has to still the gossips." She left her number and repeated it.

Saturday night after Friday night on urgent care. Probably not. At the rate he was going, he wouldn't get any
sleep until Sunday. He'd have to stand up in church to
stay awake. Unless it was slow in urgent care. Could he be
so lucky? He'd call her back later.

He fed all his varied housemates, got cleaned up, and
was back in the car in less than an hour, leaving forlorn
friends staring after him. Apologies were not sufficient.
Guilt settled as he drove back to the clinic.

He spoke Elizabeth's number into the built-in car
phone and got an answering machine. "This is Garret. I'm
sorry, Elizabeth, but I have the urgent-care shift tonight
and by Saturday night will be asleep on my feet. Wish I
could help you. Perhaps another time?"

Did he mean it when he said perhaps another time, or
was he being polite? She had said she had a boyfriend.
But then why would she have asked him to—what had she
said? Still the gossips? He was saved from having to answer by a car swerving in front of him so close it almost
clipped his bumper. "You idiot! What were you thinking?"
He'd not even had time to hit the brakes or the horn.
The adrenaline was still rushing when he entered the rear
door of the clinic, so he fit right in. A dog and cat had
gotten loose in the waiting room and tore around it, ter-
rorizing the other animals and infuriating their owners.
The cacophony echoed clear to the back parking lot.

Jason was trying to catch the cat as Garret entered.
Garret stuck out his foot as the dog came racing past, but
instead of blocking him, the little border collie tripped
and went butt-over-tincups and Jason grabbed him, held
him down. The cat, a huge fat Persian, cowered on top

of the air conditioner unit. Garret got hold of the cat and dragged it toward him, until he could seize the scruff of its nape. He announced to the room in general, "This is why cats have to be in a carrier. If someone comes in carrying an unrestrained animal, the animal and owner will be sent back outside."

Jason indeed looked contrite. "Sorry, this one snuck up on me. That Persian sure could leap. I thought it was too fat to be very active."

"They can fool you, all right." Garret made his way around the room, apologizing and setting things to rights again. All the time his mind wanted to play with drawing the mayhem that had ensued. What a poster that would make. Twenty reasons why cats had to be carrier-bound. Even if the carrier had to be wheeled in. Files had gone flying, and Amber had scratches on her arm from when the cat used her as a leaping post to bound up and across the tops of the file cabinets.

"I hope you charge her double or triple," she muttered.

"The thought entered my mind, too." Leaving the others to put the mess to rights, he picked the file off the rack by the door and entered a treatment room.

Things slowed down enough that he could leave at three, promising to be back. He didn't just sleep, he dropped into an abyss. The alarm had to go into its urgent mode to get him up in time to return by seven.

Slow nights were worse than busy ones. He let Jason sleep a couple of hours and then he did the same. They had two phone calls and two drop-ins. Not exactly the kind of night that paid the bills, but the last couple of days had compensated for that.

The regular cage cleaners, Beanpole and his helper, Lenny, showed up at six in the morning. Beanpole, almost six feet tall, weighed maybe a hundred and twenty pounds if he let his hair grow, and his buddy Lenny, a short, dumpy guy from AA, was so far winning his fight with the bottle. Mutt and Jeff. And Mutt made Garret think of that Taylor woman and her charges. He tried to chase the mental image of those eyes back to wherever it came from; it wouldn't chase.

Garret checked Valiant one more time and headed home. The ringing phone dragged him from sleep only an hour later.

"Dr. G!" Beanpole. "Valiant is convulsing."

"Is Sue there?"

"Yes, she said to call you."

"I'll be right there." The panic in his helper's voice jerked Garret from his bed and into clothes. "Please, Lord, please, Lord" was all he could think or say. "Please Lord!" *But he was fine when I left. What brought this on? Help me, Lord. Wisdom needed here. Thank You.*

He broke a few speed limits and ground a few millimeters off his tires screeching to a halt in the back parking lot. He ran to the open door of the cage room. dropped to his knees beside the now comatose animal. "What did you give him?" He nodded as Sue answered. "How long did it last?"

Beanpole was still shaking. "Seemed forever."

"I know, they do, but..."

"Maybe a minute. I wasn't in here when it started."

"Was anyone?" While he questioned, he listened to lungs and heart. Rapid, shallow breathing, heart going at high speed.

"I was in feeding the boarded animals and I came back in here and he was thrashing around and then he went rigid and I thought he died." Beanpole stumbled over his words in his panic.

Sue knelt beside him. "I came in about that time, and he was like he is now. Twitching once in a while. I checked him over, made sure the IV was all right. Amazing that he didn't dislodge that."

"Has Tessa been in this morning?"

"No, not yet."

"Has she ever reported anything like this?"

"Not that I know of, and I think we're the only vets she uses. You think the injury could have caused this?"

"Most likely. We should start easing him off the sedative." He lurched back to his feet.

"I say blood work, see if something is going on. He's running a low-grade temp, but that's not surprising with the trauma." She stood up. "When do you plan to cast him? Or should we?"

"We should. I'm not sure when."

Karen, the Saturday version of Amber, knocked at the closed door. "Tessa's here. Can she come in?"

"Of course."

"I'll see to the next patients." Sue greeted Tessa on her way out.

"I thought this was your day off, Dr. G." Tessa wheeled to a stop beside him. She turned instantly from cheer to concern; he'd thought he was controlling his face, but apparently not. "Did something happen?"

"Yes, Valiant had a seizure. No idea why, but we're looking into it." He shot her what was supposed to be a reassuring smile. But the look she gave him shouted her disbelief.

He asked, "Has he ever had a seizure before?"

"Nope, never. That would end his life as a service dog instantly."

"I know. But it might have been from the injury. Only time will tell."

"I have some things to show you." She dug into her bag and pulled out a torn piece of sweatshirt. "My friend, Gloria, saw this snagged on her side of the fence. And we found this on the back deck." She gestured toward a tool bag in her lap.

He took the sack and peered inside. "Tools? Was someone there to work for you?"

"No, I think someone was there to break in and Valiant chased him off. I have a feeling that someone was in an emergency room somewhere being treated as a dog-bite victim that day." She glared at the tools. "I used the term 'victim' lightly. He obviously did not know a service dog lived in the house. Or maybe he was breaking and entering randomly and this time he made a huge mistake."

"I have a friend over at the ER. I'll call him. Getting to the bottom of this might get real interesting."

"If only it could help Valiant." She choked on his name. "He almost gave his life to protect me." She shook her head, then raised tear-filled eyes to Garret. "You gotta be able to help him."

"What if he can't be your service dog any longer?"

"We'll have to cross that bridge when or if we come to it, won't we?"

"Have you filed a police report yet?"

"No, we just found these this morning. I'd not been out on the patio. But I guess I should, huh?"

"Ask the receptionist out front to call the police for you and tell them you want to report an attempted break-in." Garret smothered a yawn. Did it make any sense to go home and try to sleep, or just keep on here?

He opted for the latter. Kneeling beside Valiant, he

drew a blood sample and left Tessa alone with her dog. Since they closed early on Saturdays, he let the others close up and headed home again, mulling over the new installment in the Valiant chronicles.

Since curiosity was not only a trait of his but a dire need, he dialed Arthur's cell. The two of them attended the same Bible Study on Sunday mornings and had been part of the after-service lunch group for the past three years.

A grumpy voice. "This better be good, I'm supposedly sleeping."

"Sorry, Art. I can call back later. This is Garret."

"I know, I have caller ID. What's up?"

Since Arthur was head nurse at the ER, Garret paused. "I have a story to tell."

"Pertinent to..."

"A question first. Did anyone treat a dog bite a couple days ago?"

"I did. Why?"

Garret told him the story. "Did you check for a rap sheet?"

"About half a mile long, but nothing that cost him any time longer than thirty days. Let me think a minute. His story was that a pit bull ran out of a yard and attacked him when he was just walking down the street. "Took a bunch of stitches, but no real muscle or nerve damage. I'm sure he was shaking hands with delirium tremens as some buddy hustled him out of there."

"I told Tessa, the dog's owner, to file a report. You get an address or contact info?"

"Of course, but it's most likely bogus. I made sure the tetanus shot made him yelp. Not that I'm vindictive or anything. The police will be able to locate him, I'm sure."

He yawned. "Sorry, friend, but I need to get some more shut-eye. I have the midnight shift tonight. Saturday night in the big city. A true adrenaline junkie's picnic."

Garret thanked him and hung up. Too many coincidences. God at work for sure. Now if he would just heal that dog without any hitches. Hadn't the poor beast been through enough?

Chapter Fifteen

The new twin-size bed in Dinah's home office definitely cramped her space. So should she move her office out to the living room or into her bedroom? Pros and cons to either plan kept her dithering. The new chest of drawers, larger than Jonah's old one, would be delivered later in the week. She and Jonah fixed the bed after she washed the bedding, the blue plaid comforter one he picked out. She was fairly certain his choice of blue followed the Royals. She stood in the doorway. A bookcase, he definitely needed a bookcase. A desk?

"Jonah, would having a desk where you could do your homework be a help?"

"Why? What's wrong with this table in the kitchen? Besides, I don't have a lot of homework. I get most of it done at school." He glanced up from the drawing he was working on, Mutt with all her shaving and stitches. In all his pictures, she had one ear up and one flopped half over.

Did second-graders even have homework?

"Mommy always listened to me with math and spelling." He tapped the eraser of his pencil on his front teeth. "I have flashcards." He went back to his drawing.

Dinah moved some of her summer clothes that hung in

the office closet into her own room and laid them on the bed. How could one little boy have so little? She thought of other families she knew. The children had all kinds of toys and computer games and bicycles and skate boards and—she shook her head.

All he had packed in his duffle bag was that stuffed bear. Once it had been a Royals franchise toy, with a snazzy blue Royals vest. Now the vest was faded, one eye and some fur were missing, and its arms were loose, attached by not much more than a thread. He also had his paper, pencils and erasers, a few clothes, a children's Bible. He traveled light.

He set the bear against his pillow and the Bible next to the pillow. The duffle sat on the closet floor, a lonely tribute to his former life now that she had removed the shoe boxes, too. They were stacked in a corner of her bedroom. Looked to be about time to go through her own things and get rid of all she didn't use. She'd been meaning to for some time, but that other closet had made storing things far too easy.

She wandered back into the kitchen. "What would you like for supper?"

He shrugged. "Sometimes me and Mommy had popcorn on Saturday nights and watched a movie on the TV. Mommy and I."

"Do you own any movies?"

He shook his head. "Sometimes people at church gave us movies and we used to get them from the library, but Mommy wouldn't let me go to the library by myself after she got too sick for us to take the bus. We took the bus to church, too."

Church. Would he expect to go to church on Sundays? Tomorrow was Sunday. Perhaps if she didn't mention it.

Mutt went to stand at the door and, when no one paid her any attention, did a two-tone yip.

"Mutt has to go out. I can go by myself."

"I'd rather you didn't after dark."

"It's not all the way dark yet."

She was quickly learning that with Jonah things were either dark or not dark. No gray areas. "You are right, but for now, I need to go with you. Where would you go if you needed help?"

"Mr. Watson. He likes the Royals, too—did you see his hat?"

"He wears that all the time." She figured it was because he didn't like being shiny on top, but to each his own. So why didn't he like Cleveland or Cincinnati teams? For that matter, why did Jonah's father like the Royals if they lived here in west-central Ohio? Mysteries.

Together they went out the door and down the stairs, Dinah letting Jonah lead the way and open the doors. Yes, he could manage.

"Remember that after dark the door here is locked, so you must have the key along."

He pulled the key out of his pocket and held it up. She had forgotten about the key until just now.

"What would you do if you lost the key?"

"And the door was locked and we were outside?"

"Yes."

"We would walk around the building and into the front door and Mr. Watson would say, 'What, did you lose the key already?'"

Dinah about choked. Jonah sounded so much like the manager, even to the slightly Minnesota accent. "You're right. That is most likely what he'd say." She studied him. "How did you learn to do that?"

"Do what?"

"Mimic someone like that?"

He shrugged. "It made Mommy laugh." He pulled open the rear door and he and Mutt walked a little way outside.

Dinah could hear him talking to his dog and within moments they reappeared, he carrying a plastic bag that he dropped in the garbage can by the door. One more thing she'd not considered: cleaning up dog poop. But obviously to Jonah this was part of owning a dog. Were all kids his age this responsible? She knew too many families where this was not the case. Jonah had had to grow up so soon to help take care of his mother.

"We need more dog food tomorrow," he announced after fixing Mutt's supper. "We have enough for breakfast."

"Okay, we'll go find a pet store in the morning."

"After church?"

Stall, Dinah, stall. "Where do you go to church?"

"Since Mommy couldn't go anymore, I went with Grammy Trudy and Claire. We took the bus."

"Do you know the name of the church?"

He frowned. "Something Community Church. I can't remember the whole name."

"How about we skip tomorrow and we'll call Trudy next week and ask her."

He studied her, his dark eyes intent. "You don't go to church?"

She shook her head.

"Then how do you know that Jesus loves you?"

He doesn't. He isn't real. But she couldn't dump her whole life on him. "What would you like for supper? We have tomato soup with grilled cheese sandwiches or macaroni and cheese in the freezer or—"

"No popcorn?"

"Sorry."

"Fried cheese sandwiches with no soup."

"You have a deal. And I think there is ice cream in the freezer, too. I'm not sure."

"How come you don't know?"

"Things get behind other things and I forget to look harder." She had to clamp her teeth on the next thought. Clearly, Jonah and his mother had not had enough groceries at one time not to know everything there was. How long had they been living in that kind of poverty? Would Mr. Jensen have answers to some of her myriad questions?

In the morning they walked to the Bagelry, had breakfast, and stopped by Braumeister's.

Mrs. Braumeister shook Jonah's hand. "Welcome to our neighborhood. We got a grandson about your age. You are eight?"

"Seven. I'm in the second grade."

"So grown up." She glanced up at Dinah, who nodded faintly.

Yes, she would tell Mrs. Braumeister a bit of his background. "Jonah, if you ever need something and Mr. Watson is not available, you can always come here."

Mrs. Braumeister nodded. "You come to us. You always have a place here."

"Can Mutt come, too?" He looked down at his dog.

"Mutt is a funny name, but yes, Mutt can come here, too. In fact, I have some special treats that we keep behind the counter for our very special customers." She brought out a dog biscuit and a red sucker and frowned from one hand to the other. "Now who gets which, do you suppose?" She started to hand the sucker to Mutt but when Jonah laughed, she did, too, and handed him both. "You give to your dog."

By the end of the day, Dinah realized she'd not given the interview or the release of the interview a single thought all day. She and Jonah had gone in the car to a shopping area out beyond the veterinary clinic, where they found dog food, dog treats, a shiny dog dish, a water dish, and a dog bed. At a department store, she bought Jonah a Kansas City Royals winter jacket, two pairs of jeans, a hoodie sweatshirt, a couple of long-sleeved tee shirts, underwear, socks, and two pairs of pajamas.

"Why do I need two?"

"In case I don't get the laundry done?"

"Oh."

They had lunch at the food court at the mall and went to see a movie at the theater, including popcorn. A tub of it.

At bedtime, Jonah snuggled down under the comforter, his new blue comforter. "Thank you for today." Mutt stretched out beside him, only on top of the bedding.

"You are welcome."

"Mutt thanks you, too."

Mutt laid a paw on the back of her hand. Dinah patted the dog and then Jonah's shoulder. "Sleep tight."

"Mommy always listened to my prayers."

"Okay." Dinah waited, then realized he was waiting for her to close her eyes, so she did. *You can at least act like you're praying*, she reminded herself. *It's not like you really are.* But when Jonah asked God to bless Dinah and make her business go well, she had to swallow hard.

"And, please, Jesus, say hi to Mommy for me. I know she is happy with you. Amen."

Dinah blinked several times and sniffed. "Night, Jonah."

In one swift move he threw his arms around her neck and hugged her. "Night."

Her arms automatically clasped him close. "Night, Jonah. And thank you."

He tucked his bear under his arm and rolled over, the other arm thrown over Mutt, who looked up at her as if to say, I will keep him safe during the night. You don't need to worry.

But Dinah did worry. She knew all about grief, and knew one day it would come for Jonah. When it did, would she and this dog be enough to help him through it?

Chapter Sixteen

Even though he'd left instructions to call if there was any change in Valiant, Garret woke, sure something bad was happening. He could feel it. So he made a run to the clinic just before daylight. For a change, he was wrong. At least it seemed that way. They had been turning the dog over several times a day, but it always took two of them, big as he was.

He and Sol, their night guy, turned the dog again, made sure he was clean and dry, the IVs were flowing, his vitals were stable, and he was resting as comfortably as they could make him. But when Garret slid the blood smear under the microscope, white cells dominated the count. That meant infection somewhere in spite of the antibiotics they were giving him. Up the antibiotics or change to something different? What was the best treatment?

Leaving Sol to the early morning chores, Garret went online to UC Davis, the site of the major veterinarian school, hospital, and research center for California. He knew several of the people there, and they would have the latest suggestions on what to do next.

He posted the situation, described the surgery, the treatments, including the seizure, thanked them for their help, and backed out. If he was going to Bible Study and church, he better get a move on. Halfway home, his cell rang.

He pulled over. "Garret."

"Good morning, and let me tell you it is early here. Time difference, you know."

"I'm sure it is, John; thanks for getting right back to me."

John Haycock, Garret remembered, got out and ran every morning at sunrise, probably the reason he was still robust at age sixty-two. "You are aware that this dog will not be allowed to be in the service program any longer?"

"I am, but I guess I kept on hoping."

"I know, hope springs eternal and all that, but his owner can't have false hopes."

"This is her second service dog; she knows the ropes. But I hope they will let her keep him as a pet if we can save him."

"That's iffy. Sorry to be a bearer of such realities on a Sunday morning. But I'm emailing what I think you should try. There's a new antibiotic out designed to nail pesky infections. There are good reports coming through. Preliminary, but it might be worth a try. You might have a superbug on your hands here. You probably can't order it, since it is still experimental, so I'll overnight you some. Keep clinical records on it, is all I ask; we might be able to use him in a clinical study. And I suggest upping the dosage you have him on now, then start him on this as soon as it arrives."

Garret fought to push back the wave of sadness that threatened to swamp him. At times like this he wished he had hung up his vet practice and spent all his waking hours painting and drawing his cartoon strip. "Thanks, John. I appreciate you getting right on this. Valiant is a magnificent animal, and I have a feeling there is more to his story than we know yet."

"Keep me posted."

"I will." They cut the connection and he whipped around the block and back to the clinic, where he added the extra dosage, then told Sol to stay and watch him until Karen came in, promising to return after church. "Call me if anything happens."

"Good morning, Garret. Uh-oh, you look like lack of sleep has been bulldogging you." John Hanson greeted him at the door, like he always did his class.

"You're the second John I've talked to this morning. The first was at UC Davis in California."

"You have a bad patient, or rather sad patient."

"Climbing white count post surgery." Garret scrubbed the palm of his hand over the top of his head.

"There's plenty of hope in our lesson for today."

"Good thing. I could use a major dose right about now." He nodded when John gripped his upper arm. "Thanks." Now he remembered why he did everything he could to make this class every Sunday.

Several members of the class greeted him as he took an offered seat. The room was rapidly filling up. This morning he did not feel like being one of the SROs. They needed a bigger room.

"Hey, Danny, how about if we pushed that wall out and put these two classrooms together?" He thumped on the wall beside them.

"Might be a weight-bearing wall." Danny Stedman, a local contractor, often took on small projects for the church and its members. His work had saved the congregation thousands of dollars.

"So we put in a beam and a post or two?"

"Be expensive."

"Cheaper than a new building at this point." While a major building expansion project was on the dream and drawing boards, it wouldn't help the class now. "We could do it in a week?"

Danny grinned at him. "You do realize you are not one of the most patient people I know."

"Really?" Garret waggled his eyebrows. He turned to greet the person sitting down next to him. "Ah, good morning, Elizabeth."

John took his place at the front of the classroom, where folding chairs now filled every inch of space and still several people already leaned against the back wall. "Good to see all of you. Let's pray."

Garret closed his eyes and *the eyes* stared at him. *Why now?* Thoughts of the star-crossed little Jonah and his Mutt, and most of all the sad, withdrawn Dinah Taylor, kept intruding at the strangest times. Was this a hint from God that he ought to be doing something? If so, the hint was going to have to be a lot more blatant.

"...And hope does not disappoint us because You, oh Lord, are a fountain of hope that never ceases flowing. You are our wellspring, our Lord, our Savior, and this morning and every minute of every day, we thank You and praise Your mighty name. Amen.

"Today I want to remind you that hope is a four-letter word."

That earned him a titter that chuckled around the room.

"It is interesting to me how many of the most powerful words in our Bible are only four letters, or five, like faith. Love, wait, hope, care, bless. Big words are not necessary to describe a big faith or a big life or love or hope. So, the bottom line is, as always..." John glanced around the room.

In unison the class finished the sentence: "what does this mean in my life today?"

"Sounds like a good antidote for depression," someone tossed out.

"Okay, but how?" John looked around the room again, making eye contact with his students. "I know, no pat answers here. But that 'how' is always the stumbling block. How will this change my life right now?"

Again a range of answers, some frivolous and some profound, came from all around the room.

Garret listened with his ears, but he studied that wall with his eyes. Beyond it, a small, one-window room pretty much served as a huge walk-in storage closet. They could stick a bunch of its stuff, like the old folding chairs, into the small, unfinished basement, parcel out the rest to other closets.

"Like the little kids answer every question with 'Jesus' during the children's sermon."

"Amazing how that really is the answer. The one and only answer. Jesus. The all-powerful name Jesus. You put that in your mind every time you catch yourself worrying or getting afraid or confused or doubting." When John smiled, Jesus shone through. That was what Garret had always thought.

And the woman with those sad eyes sprang to mind yet again.

"It is so simple and so hard to do." Everyone groaned right along with him.

"But not impossible. Practice, practice, practice." John's cell time announced the end of class. "Let's pray.

Lord God, son of God, Jesus our redeemer. Remind us always to use Your name. You want us to cry help me Jesus at the first sign of trouble. Please, we beg of You, remind us instantly—before we get into trouble. Amen."

"My word, I think I was just run over by an eighteen-wheeler."

Garret turned to smile at Elizabeth, whom he'd forgotten was even sitting beside him, he was so wrapped up in the class and his thoughts. "I often feel that way. John used to drive heavy equipment in the military before he got promoted beyond that. It shows."

Somehow one would think the service would be anticlimatic after the class, but today God didn't seem to let Garret off the hook. He heard "Trust me" ten times, though Pastor Hagen never said it once.

He joined the Sunday lunch group as always and ended up sitting by Elizabeth again, by her design, or God's—he wasn't sure which. Right now the only thing he was sure of was that he was unsure.

Danny and his wife sat across from them at the table. "I think we ought to get a plan together and submit it to the city planners."

"That's one way to spark a conversation," said Burky from down at the end of the table.

Danny grinned. "We're talking about Garret's idea to take out that wall in the classroom and make the two rooms into one. I checked after class. It's a weight-bearing wall, but two posts and a beam will handle it. There's only Pastor Hagen's office overhead. He's expendable."

Jennifer, the church's accountant, wagged her head. "I hate to be the one to throw water on your fire, but—"

"Try gasoline instead. That's the only way things get done."

"*But* where in the budget is a line that funds a project like this?"

"Spoilsport."

"I know, but someone has to keep their feet on the ground."

"So, we ask for donations."

"From the class? I don't think the class is big enough."

Garret asked, "Ballpark estimate, Danny? What are we looking at here?"

The server arrived with her pad and pencil. She took orders and delivered food, and other conversations picked up the slack. Chatter ebbed as people ate.

Garret finished his eggs and swapped conspiratorial looks with Danny.

Danny announced, "About that wall. I'll submit a plan to the city and our governing board at the same time. If we can fund it, why would the board object?"

"Danny, this is not part of this year's plans." Jennifer didn't seem to mind the water-throwing role. But then bean counters weren't usually dreamers.

"I'll spearhead the funding drive." Garret heard his mouth say the words before he could trap them. *Put your money where your mouth is* was coming true again. Good thing he hadn't hung up his vet card; he might not have the funds from his other life's dream to do things like this.

"And we can all pray about this. We certainly can all see the need." Danny looked at Jennifer. "Putting the plan together is not a firm commitment, you know that. Just the next step. You know, do the next right thing. If God wants this done, He will make sure all the ducks get in a row."

"Or maybe not. Faith is not a four-letter word, but He sure stretches ours plenty of times."

Others chimed in, but the topic was pretty much covered. Garret turned to Elizabeth. "So, how did the event go last night?"

"Got me. I stayed home and loved every minute of it. Auntie Jane and I ordered in pizza and watched two movies. She makes a mean bag of Redenbacher popcorn, too. So thank you for declining. I hope you had a good evening."

"I wouldn't know, but I must have, because I didn't wake up until just before dawn." Even the thought brought on a yawn.

As people were making leaving noises, Garret tapped his water glass to trap their attention. "Okay, you can think on this and pray, of course. But to get Danny's plan going, we need some sort of idea how much would come available. I suggest: Write down what you will be willing to contribute to our classroom expansion. I don't need your name. Just write a number on a piece of paper and hand it to me as we leave."

Even Danny was staring at him.

He raised a hand. "Hey, this is *not* my normal way of doing things. You know that. Just trying to do what I am told. I'm as surprised as you are." He motioned to John. "Who knows what will come of our class today? I hope we have the expenses covered. I know we honor our big God with big dreams. Someone said that recently."

John chuckled, stood, and gave the benediction, followed by "See you next Sunday if not before." They all filed out, laughing and teasing like always. Garret ended up with a fistful of slips of paper.

"Can I give you a ride home?" he asked Elizabeth.

"Thanks, but I have my car here." She paused. "You want to come to supper tonight? Auntie Jane said to ask you."

"She did, did she?"

She shrugged and looked almost bashful. "I con-curred."

"What time?" He couldn't believe he was doing this. He'd planned on—what had he planned on?

"Six be all right?" When he nodded, she walked off with a small wave.

Danny stopped beside him. "Let me know the total, okay?"

"I will."

He usually tried to avoid the clinic on his days off, but he swung by there anyway to check on Valiant. No change.

That afternoon, after spending some time with his furred and feathered housemates, Garret gathered up all the studies he'd done of Dinah, Jonah, and Mutt and pinned them up on the cork wall in his studio. He had sheeted the whole east wall with cork, just for times just like this. The opposite wall faced out onto the garden, with several panels that could be slid open when the weather permitted. He'd seen walls like this in Hawaii, and when he built this house, Danny had put them in for him.

He dug another easel out of the walk-in closet, the sturdy one he used for oils, and laid in a stack of stretched and gessoed canvases. He put up a sixteen-by-twenty but then laid it down and put up a twenty-by-twenty-four. Perhaps if he got her eyes down on canvas, it would get them out of his head. With oils he could keep reworking the painting until he got it right. Straight-on head shot? Or one of Jonah and Mutt? He pulled out another pre-pared canvas, and another easel, and set the two side by side. This way he wouldn't have to wait for the oil paint to dry. He could keep on painting. Who was it said he lacked patience? How silly.

An hour later, with three canvases up on three easels, he had rough-sketched the three studies. A head shot of her, a full study of boy and dog, and a third that he still hadn't settled on. With dogs and cats resting on their beds, he squeezed oils on a paper-lined palette and, with an inch-and-a-half brush, started painting. At some point he switched to palette knives for the background on the head shot.

The dogs' barking jerked his attention to the fact that the timer he'd set for five had been ringing for some time. Right, so he could take care of his menagerie. He'd been totally oblivious.

Call and cancel! I can't do that! The argument raged while he fed and watered, patted and chatted, apologized for leaving yet again, and promised he would not be gone long. As usual, they didn't believe him.

Justifiably so. It was now six o'clock. He ignored the pleading looks and rushed out to the car. He hated being late. He hated leaving his painting even more. *God, this isn't fair.* Was that a faint chuckle or the wind?

Once in the car and out on the street, he glanced down to see that he had cerulean blue paint on his pants along with some burnt umber and various mixed colors. But the clock now read six fifteen and he had about a ten-minute drive. He called to apologize and kept on driving. He also did not have a hostess gift. What kind of guest was he?

One who wished he were still at home in front of the easels, that's what kind of a guest. *Lord, help me keep my mind on the conversation and not back in my studio.*

What *was* it with those eyes?

Chapter Seventeen

Dinah and Jonah slid right through Monday morning like it was already habit, including breakfast at the Extraburger. The last thing Jonah said to her was "You probably need to call my school and…"

"Thanks for the reminder, Jonah, and I'll make sure Mutt gets a potty break."

"Thank you." He left but waved to her again as he walked past the window. She waved back, of course. It was natural somehow.

She took her time finishing her coffee. Sitting here was preferable to whatever awaited her upstairs.

"Good morning." April sounded cheery as ever. She swiveled her chair around, the better to talk to Dinah.

Dinah paused beside her desk. "How did the tryouts go?"

"They both got on the teams they wanted and my dear sweet husband is now coaching Danny's team. Or, rather, assisting coaching, as he said. I did not volunteer to be the team mother, in spite of imploring looks."

"Good for you." Dinah shifted her briefcase to her other hand. "Anything I should know?"

"I've set up a briefing for morning coffee break in the board room."

"Good."

"How is Jonah doing?"

"Remarkably well. Corinne made this all seem so ordinary, that of course she was going to live with Jesus, and of course Jonah would have a new home and, well, here he has a new home." The burn of tears at the back of her nose and throat surprised her. "He's doing better than I am."

April nodded. "Just be prepared for that to change and most likely at the least opportune time." Dinah nodded. "There's a call from Mr. Jensen. Top of your notes there. He seems like such a nice man and so very concerned for Jonah—well, all of this."

"He said he and Corinne had things taken care of, and I guess they did."

"He said to remind you to call the school. He couldn't do that for you."

"Jonah reminded me, too. Did you have to go through all the legal-rights stuff for your kids?"

"Of course. Every parent and babysitter and grandparent and whoever associates with the children has to do the same thing. It's the law now." She thought a moment. "Oh, and this call is just to set up an appointment. You have to do this in person. Allow several hours."

Dinah could feel her eyes widen. "Really?"

"Really, but you won't have to do it every year, just when he changes schools."

Dinah gave her a disbelieving look and headed for her office. So she was still back in the unreal dream world after all.

Today she wore a white cashmere sweater and lined

wool pants with a perfect crease. Her fringed square scarf was more blues than reds and pinks today, and she wore it knotted at one shoulder and draped to a point on the other arm. She might have been wiser to wear a jacket, chilly as it was. Spring had made a brief visit, then succumbed to winter again. Or so it felt. At least Jonah had a warm jacket on.

The conversation with Mr. Jensen was reassuring, like the others had been. He said yes, they would schedule some time together and he would answer as many questions as he could. But when he asked her opinion on a get-together in memory of Corinne, Dinah heaved a sigh.

"I just don't know. It worries me greatly. Jonah is going along as if nothing has happened, so I don't know what would be best for him. Maybe you should ask Grammy Trudy. She's been around him far longer than I have."

"I will do that. Remember, if you need me, I am only a phone call away."

She dialed the school number next and asked whom she needed to talk to regarding becoming Jonah's guardian of record. Five minutes of holds later, which set her to gritting her teeth, she was finally connected to some lady with a title she couldn't quite make out.

"I can make the appointment for you. Can you come in tomorrow?"

"But what if there is a problem today? His mother died and we didn't have time to put this into place."

"I understand. Can you be here in half an hour, and we will try to fit you in."

"Ah, can you be a bit more specific than that? I have a business to run."

"I'm sorry, but today is turning into one of those kinds

of days. Mondays are like that. I'll do what I can to expedite this, but the process has to be followed."

Dinah rolled her eyes. She was already aware of some of *the process*. "I'll be there as soon as I can be."

"I will notify the officer that you are coming. Can you give me your license plate number?"

"Ah—no. I don't know that. How about if I take a taxi?"

"We'll still need your license number."

"I'll call you from my car."

The appointment went downhill from there. She had to wait for the officer to let her into the parking lot. She was third in a line of petitioners waiting in the hall. She had only one piece of picture ID with her, her driver's license. She needed two, and her passport was home in a drawer. Good thing one of her credit cards had a photo.

Finally, finally, she was ushered into an office. A stern, rotund, older woman scowled at her. "Ms. Taylor. Be seated." Icy cold.

Dinah sat. "Jonah's lawyer, Lars Jensen, sent you paperwork over with Corinne Morgan's signature. Corinne knew she was dying when they prepared it."

"I have that paperwork." The ice did not thaw. "Let's just cut to the chase, Ms. Taylor. You are on the school's watch list as a suspected child molester. I cannot in good conscience simply turn a small child over to you."

Fury leaped up and waved flames in her face. "The charges are spurious. They arose when I came by to walk home with Jonah. We are friends. His mother was my friend. Which is why Corinne remanded him to my care."

"Until the matter is thoroughly investigated..."

Dinah could hear her voice rising. She didn't want that; it was happening anyway. "I have a business, Mrs. I-don't-remember-your-name, and I cannot spend idle time sitting in offices. Jonah needs me now, right now, and you have the appropriate papers in hand. They are binding, legal documents. You will clear me to take over my role of *in loco parentis* so that Jonah and I can get on with our lives. It is hard enough on him as is." *And you cannot imagine how hard this is on me.* But she didn't say that.

"Approval does not come automatically just because some lawyer said so. We must review reports of any outstanding warrants and—"

"Must I go to court to force you to honor legal documents?"

"Mrs. Taylor..."

"That is *Doctor* Taylor, and you will please complete the business now."

You could read in her face that the woman was going to keep arguing.

Dinah whipped out her phone. "Let's call Mr. Jensen, the lawyer. You can explain to him why you refuse to honor legal instruments of..."

Scowling, the woman turned to her keyboard and typed furiously. A printer spat out some forms. She retrieved them and splacked them down in front of Dinah. "Sign this."

The forms were upside down. Dinah turned them around, skimmed down through them, four pages of them, and signed and initialed her life away. No matter that she was on a pervert watch list. No matter that she knew absolutely nothing about parenthood or small children or even dogs. As far as the school was concerned, she was now Jonah's surrogate mother.

She walked out to the parking lot furious, still bubbling and snorting like a dragon at bay. Then she remembered:

Mutt. She called April from the car as she backed out of her slot. "I'll be back in a few. I have to run home. The dog needs a potty break."

"I see. Sure." April had a hard time disguising the laughter in her voice. "The boy is coming over here to the office after school, right?"

"Until I can set up babysitting, yes."

"If he is like my kids, he'll be starved."

"Do we have some kid snacks in the cupboard or the freezer?" She stopped behind the red-and-white-striped arm across the road.

"We'll find something."

Slow and stately—not in a dignified way, because you cannot be red-and-white-striped and be dignified—the arm rose and she headed for home.

Still seething, she parked in her stall and jogged upstairs, walked into her condo. "Hey Mutt, sorry. I hope you had your legs crossed." The dog flapped its tail. She looked around briefly, but she could not see or smell any evidence of an accident. She grabbed a plastic bag and they took the elevator down.

There were days, especially when she was working down in the lab, when she could not keep regular hours. Who would take Mutt out or greet Jonah after school when she was struggling with some uncooperative amyloid or carotene derivative until ten at night? Where could Jonah go after school? Today he would come to the office, but that could not become a habit.

The dog did her business, and Dinah breathed a sigh of relief; the pooch deposited quite a large pile, so she must have been holding it awhile. Checking her watch, she saw it was almost three p.m. "You want to come to work with me? See Jonah?"

At her boy's name, Mutt beat a tattoo with her tail and did a couple of doggy jigs. The cone clacked against the curb. She and Dinah returned to the office building, took the elevator up, and walked in. Mutt acted like she did this every day, but when she heard Jonah's voice, the look she gave Dinah said it all.

"Go find Jonah." Dinah unsnapped the leash and Mutt dashed down the hall and into the break room, where laughter and giggles announced the happy reunion.

Turning from the coffee pot, April grinned. "Does your heart good, doesn't it?"

Dinah had to smile, too. "She has a knack for bringing love and laughter with her, that's for sure."

"You've never had a dog, right?"

"Nope." *My mother did not allow animals in the house.* The thought came unbidden, but she would not dignify it by saying it aloud. Coffees in hand, the two headed for her office.

"It's going to be interesting, your pure white home."

"Which reminds me, can you recommend anything that takes blood and mud out of upholstery? They seem sort of indelible."

"Especially once they've set. I can recommend you get a new sofa; that's about all. Or replace the cushions."

Replace the cushions. Why had Dinah not thought of that?

April turned grim. "Hal called. I don't think it's good news. Said he'd be here at four."

"Great. Now what?" Dinah stepped back to check on Jonah briefly in the break room, then went directly to her office. She skimmed her email. Alyssa had attached the Excel files with the latest estimates on when they would have Food for Life's newest darling in health-food stores and on shelves. The original estimate had been May 1, but—there was always that *but*.

Hal rapped on her door at 4:01 and entered, not waiting for an invitation.

She swiveled her chair around to face him. "All right, so what is the problem?"

"I can't decide if it's a problem or a good thing. The interview will go live at 8:00 p.m. on the regional channels and nationwide clips on the ten o'clock news. I doubt it will get much time on the networks. It all depends on what catastrophe happens between now and then."

Dinah ignored the hand strangling her stomach. What difference could this really make? After all, any news was considered good advertising.

Right?

Even if they made her look like a fool by showing her stumbling along, how could that hurt their product? All that was important was getting out news of a new food additive that could help those who needed it.

Right?

To watch it or not to watch it. The query had been running through her head all evening.

She glanced up to find Jonah studying her, a wrinkle between his bushy eyebrows showing his concern.

"I'm sorry, Jonah. Just trying to decide what to do."

"About what?"

"You know the interview I did the other day?"

"Sort of."

"Well, it will be aired on television tonight."

"You don't want to see it?" Sitting on the still-stained couch, he leaned over to rub Mutt's back. She wriggled in delight.

Why did this child have to be so perceptive? "I guess not."

"Then don't watch it. Or . . ." He paused. "You could call Mr. Hal and ask him."

"True." But one of the problems was they'd not been allowed to see the interview in advance. The thought of how she had dropped the ball made her shake. Why had she let them get to her? And was it really as bad as she felt it was? While it was supposed to be shown as taped, the odds on no editing were slim. It all depended on how honorable the producers were. Dinah huffed out a breath. If that was the deciding factor, she was doomed.

Had she had access to the tape, would she have edited it? Good question. Cut out the final ten minutes of the interview. Maybe they'd had camera failure. Could she be so lucky? *Shift gears; this is getting me nowhere.*

"Didn't you say you needed help with flashcards for your math? Go get them, okay?"

He nodded. "If you don't mind." They spent the next half hour reviewing multiplication tables.

Even when Dinah sped up the flashing, he never missed one. "You did really well."

"I like math. It makes sense."

"It does indeed." She glanced at the clock and clicked on the station. If she got too disgusted with it, she could turn it off.

She didn't.

As the closing credits rolled at the end, her cell bleeped.

"Well? Did you watch it?" Hal asked.

"Yes."

"And?"

Dinah shrugged. "Fine up until I totally lost it. Of course they wouldn't edit that out."

"No, they stayed pretty close to the original taping. And, Dinah, you are seeing it as far worse than it was. You did not appear to be falling apart."

"But talk about muddled answers. She had me on the run and she delighted in that." *Thanks for trying to make me feel better, Hal. Water under the bridge and all that. But I know when I messed up royally, and no soothing words can change the fact that I failed to get our message across. Failed miserably.*

"That's part of her job. You did manage eventually to soften her adversarial stance."

Dinah shook her head and wondered inanely why she was shrugging and gesturing in a phone conversation. "Right. Say hello to the tooth fairy for me. And the Easter Bunny is real." Realizing what she'd said, she looked for Jonah, and was relieved to see he was in his room. Did seven-year-olds believe in the Easter Bunny?

"Well, it is done, and I'm sure your phone will be ringing, so just ignore any requests for comments until tomorrow. No matter what you say, someone will try to twist it."

Or add different questions after she'd answered one. And splicing and editing had grown so sophisticated, anything was possible. "So what did you think?"

"I am reasonably pleased. They didn't cut the part about assisting everyday people to regain strength when they're ill, without specifically mentioning Type II diabetes. You got the common-people message across well and didn't ring any FDA drug bells. I think we're pretty well placed. Will we meet the production schedule for a June release?"

"Hopefully the bigger accounts will have product, at

least. If we get it off the ground on schedule, we can re-coup the smaller operating expenses in the next quarter, recover nearly all of it in the next fiscal." Budget. Again. She detested budgets.

Jonah appeared in front of her. "Mutt needs to go out."

She nodded. "Duty calls, Hal. Mutt is standing here with her hind legs crossed. We'll talk later." She clicked her phone shut and slid her feet into clogs.

Jonah protested, "I can go alone."

"I know you can, but I need the exercise, too. The temp is dropping, so you better wear your jacket."

He rolled his eyes but retrieved his jacket from the closet. Since he couldn't reach the bar, he had hooked it over the umbrella rack. Snapping Mutt's leash on, he waited by the door, the dog dancing around him.

She followed him out. "We'll pretend I don't have my keys or anything, okay?"

His shrug said he heard her and he turned to lock the deadbolt from the outside.

They stepped from the elevator into a hallway that was not heated; Dinah hunched into her wool pea coat. Hands in her pockets, she let Jonah open all the doors, take Mutt farther out than usual, and reverse the procedures all the way back up.

Back in the condo, she hung her jacket up. "She seems to be moving a little better. That's good. Looks like we better get some closet hooks for you." One more thing to put on her list for Mr. Watson to do.

"I'm glad we took her cone off."

"If she starts licking her stitches, we'll have to put it on again."

He nodded as he headed for the bathroom. "I know. If it helps, you gotta do it."

She so wished her world were as simple as Jonah's. But then, Jonah's wasn't. Not a bit. She wished hers were simpler. It wasn't. Not a bit.

"Do you think Mutt is getting fat?" Jonah asked when he was tucked in bed for the night.

"I hadn't paid attention. Why, isn't she eating about the same as always?"

"She is, but see?" He patted her belly as she lay stretched out beside him. "Maybe she's not getting enough exercise. Can she walk to school with me like we used to?"

"I'm afraid that won't work. But maybe we can talk to the vet when we take her in to have her stitches out."

"Next Saturday." He yawned. "She needs her toenails trimmed, too. See?" He held up Mutt's paw.

"She hasn't been walking enough outside now to keep them short. Does she need shots or anything?" Dinah sat on the edge of the bed. Her knowledge of dogs was woefully lacking. Her unruly thoughts flipped to Dr. G, as Jonah was calling him. Calling him with these kinds of questions might have been a natural thing to do if he weren't so curt with her. She could probably find all the info she needed on Google anyway. Save both time and money.

Jonah shrugged. "We never took her to the vet before."

"Mm. She smells a little funny, too. We should take her to a groomer."

"She doesn't like getting baths."

"All the more reason to use a groomer. Does Mutt like toys?"

"I guess."

Dinah had figured out that when Jonah answered with "I guess," it usually meant they'd not had the money to buy or do whatever. Or Corinne had not had the energy. "I think another stop at the pet store would be a good idea. Does she play with a ball?"

"We lost it. She likes my socks."

"To chew?"

"No, to carry around." He smiled up at her. "Thank you."

"You're welcome." She wasn't sure what for, but, reaching forward, she smoothed the lock of red-brown hair off his brow. "You ready to say your prayers?"

"Yes. Mommy used to read to me before I went to sleep. We haven't been doing that."

"Do you have a book to read?"

He dug under his pillow and handed her his illustrated Bible. "I like to hear about what Jesus did."

Dinah swallowed. The last thing she wanted to read out of was his Bible. Tomorrow she would order some books, fun kids' books, but for tonight, she flipped to Mark and read the first story she came to. When she finished, she shut the book. "It's getting late." She listened to his prayers and kissed his cheek. "Night."

If you didn't want to read his Bible, why didn't you just tell him no? The reasonable tone of the accuser in her head made her flinch. *You're not his mommy.*

No, she wasn't his mommy, but she was all he had right now, and she would do the best she could. She found one of his socks behind the door to her bathroom. Getting both the dog and the boy some toys might be a good idea. But what?

The next morning on the way to the Extraburger, she asked, "Jonah, did you have some games and books and things?"

He nodded. "Mr. Jensen said they would bring my things over to your house."

"What games do you like to play?"

"Mommy and I played Go Fish and Old Maid. I always won."

"What about Hearts? My gramma and I used to play Hearts."

"Do you like puzzles?" He looked up at her. "I have two, one is new." He pulled open the door for her. "I got it for Christmas but Mommy got too sick and we didn't start it. Do you have a card table? We did the puzzles on a card table that Grammy Trudy loaned us."

Add another thing to the list. They waited in line, turned in their everyday order, and headed for their table. Eric aka Tattoo wasn't working the cash register this morning, so when their number was called, Jonah went up to get the tray.

Her phone vibrated. April. She thumbed the button. "We're downstairs."

"Good. There are a couple of reporters waiting here—just thought I'd warn you."

"Thanks. Do I need to hurry?"

"No, I don't think so. Let them wait."

"Hand them our materials, give them an education. Be there soon."

April chuckled. "*Bon appetit.*"

"Do you need lunch money?" she asked when Jonah set the tray on the table. How had she not thought of that yesterday?

"No, I get free lunch."

Another thing she better talk to the school about. They had her contact information, but so far no one had called her. But then, why would they unless there was a problem? She'd read of mothers being volunteers in class-rooms, attending parent/teacher meetings, being involved, as they like to say. Did they have PTA here like they did when she was in school? How was she going to carve time out of her schedule for all that?

"Jonah, would you like to go to the library sometime?"

"Sure." He scooted over to stand up and sling his backpack on. "You want me to come to your office after school?"

"Yes, please. Have a good day."

He nodded and smiled at her. "I asked Jesus to give you a good day, too."

She watched him go out the door and when he got even with her window, he waved. Her list of questions for Mr. Jensen was growing. Did Jonah have a doctor, a dentist? Who cut his hair? Did she set up an appointment with his teacher or would the teacher call? Had the school told the teacher what had happened? And what was her name? Jonah had mentioned it. *F* something. Foster? Farrell? *Oh yes, Dinah Taylor. Mother of the year. You don't even know your kid's teacher's name.*

She needed to ask Mr. Watson if there were any other children in their building. Did Jonah not have any friends? He never mentioned any. The more she thought about it, the more she was realizing that being a mother, or a guardian, whichever she was before they went before the judge and signed the papers, was taking up more and more of her time. She'd not spent a single evening working at home since Jonah came.

Which, when she thought about it, was only last Thursday night, and today was Tuesday. And if she didn't get up to the office, the workload might just meet her in the hall.

April greeted her with "They were waiting on our

doorstep when I arrived. Three women and a man. I stuck them in the back conference room with coffee and dough-nuts. And Hal says he'll stop by shortly."

"You're the best. Let me put my things away and I'll meet with them in about five minutes."

"Here's your stack. I've put the important ones on top."

"Thanks." Dinah slipped into her office and shut the door without even a click. A bud vase with a pink tea rose surrounded by baby's breath waited in the middle of her desk. There was no card. She punched the button on the intercom. "Who sent the rose?"

"I have no idea. It was on my desk, so I assumed it was for you and put it on yours."

"What made you think it was for me?"

"No one sends me flowers."

She glared at the intercom and shuffled through her orange slips. Nothing that couldn't wait an hour. Tucking her phone into her jacket pocket, she reapplied lipstick and strode down the hall.

None of the four watching her enter the conference room looked familiar. The women were dressed the way media women always dress, and the man did not bother to rise. "Good morning. Thank you for waiting for me." She crossed to the urn to fill her coffee mug, stirred in half-and-half, and chose a raised sugar doughnut. "I assume you saw the interview last evening. Incidentally, I apolo-gize, but I will have to cut this off in thirty minutes. Busy day." She smiled at them and sat down.

Why do so many reporters think they have to be blonde? A young woman with shiny yellow hair opened. "You claim your product can cure diabetes. What kind of proof can you offer for such a grandiose claim?"

"We have never, ever claimed that our product cures

diabetes. The press invented that claim by twisting what we said. It is a food additive, a small part of a complete disease-control regimen."

"But you said—"

"No, we did *not* say." Dinah interrupted her. "Please read the materials. That is what we say. We do provide the testimony of persons in our trials who have been using the product and find that their health is improving."

The male reporter, a rather jaded-looking middle-aged fellow, said, "So if it's nothing but a dietary supplement, why is the FDA coming after you?"

"I have received no notice that they are, but I am sure they will look into everything very carefully. We well-exceed the standard protocols regarding trials, double-blinds, and ingredient analysis. The results are all in open documentation; except the ingredients, of course. Proprietary information. Standard procedures."

"I heard rumors of a buyout."

"Then your ear is closer to the ground than mine. Incidentally, we're not for sale. You have our mission statement in front of you. That's what we do. We will remain independent so as to fulfill the mission." She glanced up to see Hal standing just inside the door at the other end of the room. He raised a thumbs-up. She felt the same.

"So what are your plans for distribution?" The woman at the far end.

"Production is just gearing up. Local release to begin with, and then target both coasts as we build inventory. The same plan we used to distribute Pro Teen, our childhood-obesity supplement. One of our best products. And, again, no claims for cure, but unsolicited testimonials that it helps. We have an extensive distribution system already in place for our other products.

None of which have created the furor this one has, as you can tell."

Two of them at least smiled.

The world-weary-looking man barked, "Why are you so hostile toward the press? Toward the truth? That interview, for example. And right now. That smile on your face fools no one."

Dinah parked her elbows on the table and sipped her coffee, reminding herself to at least look relaxed on the outside. How to phrase this? "Remember a couple years ago when a young man was shot? The press did not run a recent photo of him. They published a photo of the man taken six years earlier, then implied through the photo that the victim was just a cute little bright-eyed twelve-year-old. If the press cherished the truth, I would embrace it."

"But it wasn't falsehood. And the text was accurate."

"Claiming we said Scoparia will cure diabetes is flat-out falsehood. Yes, I am hostile." She checked her watch. "I can take one more question and then I have a stack of work that has been waiting."

"What's this I hear about a little boy coming to live with you?"

How did she know? Dinah smiled sweetly, but her voice was iron hard. "My personal life has nothing to do with our product release, nor is it news." She stood. "Thank you for coming. If you need anything, ask April on the front desk." She turned and left the room.

She heard them scooting chairs, rustling, coming behind her. She ducked aside into the larger conference room and closed the door.

There stood Hal and the staff! They were giving her silent applause, for the reporters had not yet left the building.

"You did a beautiful job." Hal was beaming.

"How did…" She glanced at the video conference monitor behind her, which showed the other empty conference room. "Ah. You watched the whole thing?"

"I set it up before I showed them in there, but left the other monitor off," April said.

Hans moved toward the door. "Our future's at stake here, you know. Besides, it's riveting entertainment. Gotta get back to the bench. I have some hydrocarbons transforming themselves."

"If you get any furfuraldehydes, let me know."

He waved as he left.

Her merry band of employees dispersed, voicing congratulations as they left. Apparently they especially liked the "Yes, I'm hostile" comment.

Hal followed her out and closed the door behind them. "I'm leaving for Atlanta this afternoon. Is there anything you need before I go?"

"How long will you be gone?"

"Two, possibly three, days. Some family business. When do you meet with Jensen?"

She knew there was some dissension going on among several of his family members, but since he never volunteered the information, she never asked. "I don't know. I noticed I have a message from him. And thank you for the rose and the lovely bud vase.

"Don't thank me, I didn't send it."

"Then who did?"

He shrugged. "By the way, I heard rumors that one of the weekly rags is planning an exposé using someone who claims to have become terribly ill, as in life threatening, after using Scoparia."

"And how much are they paying this person?"

"No idea. Just thought you should know."

"Any basis?"

"I'm sure an attorney will be contacting us."

Dinah heaved a sigh. And all she wanted to do was make sick people's lives better. Diabetes was a killer, she knew that well. So why were so many people trying to prevent conquering it?

Chapter Eighteen

Looking back, Garret assessed that the dinner had gone well, and Monday flew by as if chased by rambunctious five-year-olds. Since Susan was on for Monday night, Garret went in early Tuesday to try to catch up on paperwork. And review the list of applications they had received in response to their ads for another veterinarian. Whoever they hired had to like working the night shift in urgent care.

Valiant had been on the new antibiotic since late Monday, so only twelve hours so far. The last blood work had shown the white count still high but no worse. So the other medication had contained the infection, he hoped, and maybe this one would knock it out. They would ease the dog off the sedative today. The pain levels should be manageable with other drugs. They needed to get him up and moving.

Sitting in his office with the door shut and a jug of coffee beside his feet on the desk, Garret flipped through the stack of ten applicants. Three still in school; hadn't they made it clear they needed someone with more than just school experience? One had a letter of referral from an old friend of his. Garret set that one in the to-read-again stack. Another application was from a husband-and-wife team. Could they use two? Only if two came for the price of one. He set that one by to read again, too. By the time his coffee was empty and the bagels digesting, the ten were in three stacks; one didn't even seem worth responding to because the person was a vet tech, not a certified veterinarian.

He refilled his coffee. If he wasn't careful, he'd be popping antacids again. This was all the response they had after a week of advertising in the online veterinarians' newsletter. He put notes on three to set up interviews, on three to send thanks but no thanks, leaving four to think about.

A knock at the door told him the day had officially begun. "Tessa's here."

"Tell her I'll meet her at Valiant's cage."

He laid the stack on Susan's desk—see what she thought—and continued down to the cage room. She was already there, her hand in the open door, stroking her comatose dog. "Good morning, Tessa."

"He's coming out of it, right?"

"Yes. We'll cast him and try to get him on his feet today."

"Did you find out anything about the prowler?"

He smiled. "A man showed up in ER claiming a pit bull ran out and bit him when he was innocently walking down the street. Has a long rap sheet. Did you file the report?"

"I did, and an officer came out and took the tools. Said they'd get back to me if they learned anything." There was a quiet smugness in her voice. "Wouldn't it be interesting if Valiant were able to identify him?"

Garret's mind left the cage room for a moment, trying

to set up scenarios with Valiant fingering the would-be burglar. A police lineup was not out of the question.

She leaned over to stroke Valiant's head. His full tail moved this time and he whined, trying to lift his head. "As a writer friend of mine often says, 'The plot thickens.'"

Garret laid a hand on her shoulder. "Call us if you need anything."

"I will."

He left the room, from the rarified atmosphere of a sweet, disabled lady with her heroic dog to the heavy air of half a dozen sick pets and their owners. Ah, and two routine checkups for this afternoon. You would think with all the work, the time would fly. The whole day dragged.

Finally he had a minute to stop by the lab. "A day without emergencies is like a day without..."

Susan was back, just suiting up. She shrugged into her lab coat. "I read those apps. I agree with your assessment. At least two of the four might be worth interviewing, although, since we can't pay moving costs, that pretty much leaves the California applicant out."

"Not necessarily. She graduated Davis and worked there a year as an intern. She has great references. We should consider her if she can afford to come on her own."

Sue nodded. "She'd find living back here less expensive, too."

"Good thing to remember to add that to the sales pitch if we decide to try her."

They both got back to work.

"Hey, Dr. G," Mrs. Tarbell said as he examined her schnauzer-with-eczema. "I saw your comic strip in yesterday's paper. I get a kick out of them."

"Thank you." Actually he'd forgotten what day it appeared. He'd preferred Sunday, but the paper was still trying different days to see if any got a better response than others. For him, the pleasure was in the creating. At least he was a couple ahead for now.

They put Valiant under again to cast his leg, so that when he became fully alert the cast would be hard, although with today's new quick-drying compounds, that was no longer a problem most of the time. When Garret left for the day at three, Tessa was parked beside her dog again.

A blinking light on the phone greeted him when he arrived home. Three new messages. Why did they all wait until he went out the door?

The first was Mom. "Hi, Garret, just a reminder that dinner is at two on Sunday. I have something I need to talk over with all of you, but this just came up so I do hope you plan to be here. Dad says hello. I say been too long since we've seen you. We love you."

He had the family dinner on his calendar, but once he started the paintings he'd been toying with the idea of not going. Should he call her back and insist on a heads-up on what she wanted to say? Or was it needed? He nodded and hit Erase. Call two: someone selling something. He was on every no-call list known to man. How had that one gotten through? Delete. Call three.

Danny. "I got the estimate prepared and I see you have pledges of three thou. That might cover most of the materials. I need to check further into that. But we have enough information to take it to the board. They meet tomorrow night. We can use volunteers on the finish work, but for the construction I need my crew, or we won't pass inspection. The city meets Thursday night, and I would sure like to have this on their agenda."

So they needed more money. But he'd figured that and hadn't put his contribution in yet. Was it time to ask for more or wait until he saw the final estimate?

By the time he'd finished showering, he still had an hour and a half before he had to be back at the clinic. Time enough to paint.

The ringing phone finally got through to him. He kept studying her eyes as he reached for it, knocking a container of mineral spirits onto the floor. "Yes!"

"Ah, Garret, you were supposed to be here half an hour ago."

"Sue."

"Yes, it is I, and I have to leave. You sound remarkably awake for one sleeping so deep the phone didn't wake him."

"I'm painting. I need to feed here and I'll be there ASAP. You can go on home. Jason can handle it until I get there. Sorry."

"Okay, I'm leaving, but you will be here soon?"

"Yes, I will be there." He flipped the phone shut and stared at the three paintings. The third one was bothering him. Why did he want to put the three of them together? What did he know about Jonah's real family? Why should he care? The kid was all questions, no answers. But those eyes...

Instead of taking the paintings, he took a pad of paper and his markers. Perhaps he could sketch out something he liked. If it wasn't busy.

"Don't fret, Dr. G. All is well." Jason looked up from his position on the cage-room floor next to Valiant as Garret walked in. The dog was no longer on his side but up on his belly, the casted leg angled out beside him. "I think he's embarrassed because he can't make that leg work right.

Will you do another blood draw and see what's happening?"

"Not until the morning. Thirty-six hours on the antibiotic ought to show us something." He nodded at Jason. "You still thinking vet school?"

"If I can get in. Get my bachelor's degree first. I finally resorted to a tutor for the math."

"Wise move. Maintaining high grades in the math and sciences is what keeps medicine from being an easy field to get into. But then all medical programs are difficult. If they weren't, then everyone would be doing it and there goes the quality of the program." He rubbed Valiant's ears one more time. "All the chores are caught up?"

"They are. Being paid to comfort the animals is really a hard gig."

"One way to look at it. You have homework along?"

"I always have homework."

"Then hide in a quiet corner. I'll be in my office."

Garret got a bottle of soda out of the machine and a bag of pretzels from the cupboard and set up his sketch pad.

The rest of the night was slow. Garret worked out several possibles for the third canvas, sketched a new panel for his comic strip, and dozed off for a while. He checked on Valiant.

Occasional showers were still keeping everything outside wet as Sue came in. On time. Garret felt just a tiny twinge of guilt for his own tardiness.

"Did you hear what happened to Dinah?" She shook out her coat and hung it up.

"No. Do you know her personally or something? Why does this bother you so much?" Garret rolled his papers together and snapped a rubber band around them.

"It bothers me because she is trying to help people and

the media are out to crucify her. And she's such a nice person. Quiet, but nice. I just don't get it."

"It sells newspapers, gets ratings, all the same game." He snagged his jacket off the row of pegs on the wall. "Beanpole and Lenny are about done. We got Valiant up on his feet. When Tessa comes in, tell her I think we should keep him a while longer. I'm out of here. See you tomorrow morning."

"At seven?" One of her eyebrows quirked.

"Yes, ma'am. At seven." If he woke early, perhaps he could paint for an hour or two. Or perhaps not. A yawn almost cracked his jaw.

"Go on with you."

Instead of the Bagelry, he decided he needed more protein and stopped at the Extraburger.

"Dr. G!" Jonah, at a table by the window, waved wildly. "Dinah, look who's here! You want to eat breakfast with us, Dr. G?"

"I—ah, umm..."

Dinah Taylor turned from paying the tattooed boy behind the cash register. "I'm sure Dr. Garret does not have time this morning to eat with us, Jonah."

While that was the last thing he wanted to do this morning, the imperious tone of her voice set his teeth on edge. "Why, thank you, Jonah. I'd love to."

He could feel the questions her eyes shot at him. Eyes. Windows on the soul?

He placed his order and stepped back to wait, but the young man said, "I'll bring it out with theirs, sir. No problem." Mr. Helpful. So he walked back to the booth by the corner window.

At least Jonah was bubbly. He scooted against the wall and dragged his backpack onto the floor at his feet, making room for Garret. "How come you're here, Dr. G? Isn't your office a long way away?"

"This is between our office and my house, so I stopped for breakfast. I worked last night."

Dinah slipped into the seat across from them. The feelings she radiated just now were not even close to friendly.

The tattooed fellow plunked a tray between them. "Can I get you anything else?"

Dinah smiled up at him. "Thanks, Eric, but I think that's all. We appreciate your helpfulness." So she was on a cheerful first-name basis with this guy, but she was an iceberg around Garret. Well, he didn't care much for her, either.

The fellow lingered. "How's your dog, Jonah? Is she doing okay?"

"She gets her stitches out on Saturday. Then she'll look better. They shaved her a lot, too, but her hair will grow back. And she doesn't have to wear that cone now." Jonah's chest swelled with pride. "And this here is her doctor. This is Dr. G."

The kid smiled and nodded toward Garret. "Next time you bring her, she gets a special treat if I'm here."

Jonah waited until the man left before announcing, "We do grace."

"Good. So do I." Garret bowed his head.

"Dear Jesus, thank You for our food and for making this a good day for all of us. Give Dinah Your special love. Amen."

Why had he added that? Dinah unwrapped her sandwich while Jonah went through what appeared to be a morning ritual that ended as he carefully laid his napkin on his lap.

Garret asked, "So how is Mutt doing?"

"She's fine. She likes us living with Dinah, and the elevator works all the time. The first couple of days, she went slow." Jonah looked up from his pancakes. "My mommy went to live with Jesus last Friday, and we came to live with Dinah."

Garret stared at him. No visible emotion, almost nonchalance. What the blue blazes was going on with this kid? With both of them, actually. This Dinah Taylor was obviously a close enough friend that she'd taken over Jonah's care, so she should be at least a little sad. But there seemed to be nothing. Was the mother's death sudden? As he thought back, Garret could not remember any evidence whatever of grief and sadness in either of them—apart from the obvious responses to the dog's trauma. "You must miss her terribly."

"Mommy told me all about it, lots of times as she got sick. She said heaven with Jesus is better than here, and when she got there she wouldn't be sick and she would be with my daddy."

"You're his aunt, then—or something?" He shook his head. "Excuse me, that's none of my business."

Jonah barreled on. "Dinah is my best friend. She even took care of Mutt when she needed help. I didn't know what to do and Mommy couldn't help me." He mopped syrup with his pancakes. "So I called Dinah and she came right away."

"I see." He nodded as he finished off his sandwich.

No, he didn't see. This was a weird relationship. Beyond belief, all of them. And he thought *his* relationships were screwed up.

Jonah laid his fork down. "May I get out, please? I got to leave."

Garret stood up and stepped back. Jonah slid out of the

booth dragging his backpack and gathered up his garbage for the trash. "See you Saturday, Dr. G. I pinned your picture up on my wall."

Dinah crumpled her napkin and prepared to leave, too. "I'll go out with you."

"You don't gotta. I'll wave to you." And off he went.

She looked disappointed. "See you this afternoon, Jonah."

She settled back uneasily and picked up her half-empty coffee cup.

The tattoo guy paused at her elbow and gestured with a coffee carafe. "Would you like a refill on that?"

"Ah, sure, why not." She handed him her cup. "Two creams. Thank you, Eric. I appreciate your service."

Outside the window, Jonah smiled and waved to them both, jacked his backpack higher, and disappeared down the street.

"He's a remarkable little boy." Garret slid back into the booth.

"Yes, he is. He smiles every time he looks at your drawing."

Silence. Really heavy silence. *Man up, Garret. You want to say something? Say it.* "Why don't you like me?"

Her mouth dropped open. Her back sagged. She stared dumbfounded a moment. "What makes you...I don't... why..." Extraordinarily heavy silence.

He shrugged. "I don't care, actually, whether you like me or not. I was just curious. You're very open and friendly with others and freeze up when I enter the picture. I was just wondering about the reason. It must be a doozy."

She studied him a long moment, and the starch returned to her spine and jaw. "This is amazing. The reason

I don't like you, Dr. G, is that when you look at me, *you* turn icy. Angry, even. I have been surrounded by enough hostile people lately—I don't need that. You don't like me, so it irritates me. Hostility always irritates me. And since you mention it, I really don't care a bit whether you like me or not."

It was his mouth's turn to drop open.

She scooted out and stood. "I have to get to work. Good day, Dr. G." And she was gone before he could be enough of a gentleman to worm out of the booth and stand up.

He settled back down to finish his coffee. He gazed off down the street where Jonah had disappeared. He gazed at the glass doors leading into the lobby of this office complex, where Dinah had just disappeared.

Where in the world would she get the idea that...How could she?

John said Jesus was the answer to confusion and fear and worry? Well, he was confused—terminally confused—and just now, Jesus wasn't helping.

Chapter Nineteen

She strode into the office, spine straight, shoulders back, teeth gritted. What was it about that man that irritated her so much? Other than his mood that she interpreted as constant hostility toward her. That was a question for another time. Maybe in the next decade or so. If ever.

"What's wrong?" April asked as she came through the door.

"Nothing. Why?" Dinah glanced up, carefully keeping her face washed of expression.

"Dinah, don't try to snow me. Something's bugging you. More reporters?"

"Jonah and I were getting our normal breakfast, when who should appear in line behind us but Dr. Miller, or Dr. G, as Jonah and a lot of his fans call him. The veterinarian."

April's mouth opened. "*That* Dr. Miller?"

"Yeah, why? What do you know about him?"

"He's a celebrity, cartoonist, animal rights activist, artist. He's always on television when they need an animal specialist. His clinic is the one you took Mutt to?"

"MapQuest said it was the closest urgent care open at that time of night. So that's where we went." She wrinkled her face. "So he's full of himself; I guess that's what irritates me, then."

"Where did you get that idea? He's wearing a sign that says *I am famous*?" April snorted.

"The way he acted. He was so kind to Jonah, but I really got the brunt of his whatever. He doesn't like me any more than I like him. So as soon as those stitches are out, we'll find another veterinarian. Although perhaps his wife would be a good one."

"His wife?" April gave her a strange look, clearly confused.

"You know, Miller and Miller Veterinary Clinic."

"Sue Miller is not his wife. She's his partner."

"So they didn't get married. I don't care." Dinah started to leave, but stopped when April sputtered into laughter. "Now what?"

"She is happily married to a very nice man—his brother. I think he introduced them, actually. They all attend the same church I go to. I really like them a lot."

More churchgoers. Was she being surrounded for a reason? No! This was simply a coincidence. Dinah deliberately shrugged. "Whatever. Jonah invited him to sit with us and then told him his life story."

"And you can't handle that very well, can you?" April's voice softened.

Dinah sucked in a deep breath and fought back the sadness that bombarded her every time she thought of Corinne. So much sadness, so many lives screwed up, hers included. "I better go call Mr. Jensen. I didn't get his call returned yesterday. I'm sure there is more to do in this crazy mixed-up new life of mine. I am really not used to having a small boy and a dog around all the time."

"It's a big change, all right. How's your all-white holding up?"

"That's not the problem. It's the space. I really miss my office. I can't close the door and work like I did before. I'm getting behind."

"And you are not used to taking care of anyone but you."

"Right. And in my mind, a boy and a dog need a yard and friends and—" Her purse burst into song. She dug out the cell phone and continued down the hall to her office. "Hello?"

"Ace Delivery Service."

Jonah's things. A fresh wave of grief rushed across her. And how would poor Jonah respond? His most familiar things, evoking memories; it would almost be better if all that simply disappeared. She gave the man her building manager's number, then called Mr. Watson and gave him the message.

She hung up her coat, setting her briefcase on the desk. The rose still looked as fresh as yesterday. Who had sent her this rose? Perhaps she could call Minda and ask if she'd sent a rose up here and then keep pushing her until she gave a hint.

Dinah tapped the intercom for April. "I'm calling Mr. Jensen, so please hold calls."

"Will do. You know you have a meeting with Ms. Hunsaker at ten thirty?"

"Yes, thanks." She pushed in the numbers for Mr. Jensen, all the while searching for her list of the questions she'd been compiling. His assistant put her right through.

His voice sounded jovial. "So, good morning, Dinah.

Thanks for taking time to get back to me. I watched the TV interview and have been keeping up on the print, so I imagine how your time is running away from you. The real question is, how are you and Jonah doing?"

"Better than I expected, I guess. Or maybe not. Still no clear signs of grief. And I didn't realize how self-possessed and independent he is. I keep thinking he is far older than seven."

"That I understand. How is he dealing with his mother's death?"

"Very matter-of-factly. Corinne told him where she was going and what would happen, and it is business as usual. New home, just as Corinne told him, and new all kinds of things. But he reminds Jesus every night to say hi to his mommy for him and says that he misses her. I keep waiting for some kind of grief reaction, but none so far."

"I guess I am as surprised as you are. I see they are delivering his things today. Perhaps opening some of those boxes will trigger a response."

"Are there a lot of boxes?"

"Seven or eight, I think. Gramma Trudy took Corinne's personal clothes and possessions—to give to a thrift shop, as I understand it. So I had the furniture go there also, and the kitchen things. Since you bought him a bed and chest of drawers, those went with the other things."

"Thank you." She caught herself doodling. "May I ask you some rather personal questions?"

"I'll answer what I can."

"Have they always been this poor?"

"No, her husband used to send money for them. He bought the condo."

"That confuses me. Jonah refers to it as an apartment. And it seems quite shabby to be a condo."

"It started as an apartment house. The units went condo about four years ago. Three or four, just after he was deported. He retained me to oversee his family's provision and I got an immigration lawyer on it—friend of mine—but before he could do much, the man died. Corinne got sick about that same time. Went downhill in a hurry. I tried several different ways to contact his extended family, even a private investigator, but never received a response. It was as if he never existed. The money dwindled to the returns on an investment I made for them. These last months used up the principal. When the condo sells, I plan to invest the money for Jonah. Corinne fought fiercely to stay off welfare and keep her son out of the Social Services system."

"I'm confused. Is your interest professional or personal?"

"Both." The voice softened. "Professional when Andre retained me as family counsel, standard lawyer-client relationship. It became personal when Immigration and Customs Enforcement broke into their home in the middle of the night and quite literally dragged Andre out of his bed. A wife and small son? That was unconscionable. And then her illness, which was subsequently diagnosed as terminal. Indignity and ill fortune heaped too high to climb. And the boy...Yes, Ms. Taylor, it's now personal."

There was so much she wanted to know, but her mind was skipping all over.

His firm voice. "Frankly, Ms. Taylor, I had serious reservations. I know we are asking a lot for you to take Jonah and rear him, but, more so, we don't really know anything about you—about the real you, not just the search-engine information about you. But Corinne felt so strongly that God was sending you to take care of her son that I could only go along with her wishes."

Why could she not keep her thoughts under control? "Would a judge grant a single woman guardianship or adoption or whatever we would need to do?" *And why me?* But the last she kept to herself, along with the rest of her questions. This was enough to deal with right now.

"Yes, since all the paperwork is in order. There will be a formal court appearance. The judge will ask if you understand all the ramifications of adopting a little boy and if you are prepared to provide him with a home and care for him until he is grown. Grown in this case meaning the age of eighteen."

"Mr. Jensen, I agreed to this, and as far as I know, I will not change my mind. But what if—I mean—she didn't know me. How could..."

"I understand." She could hear him shuffling papers. "As I said, Corinne believed implicitly that this is God's way of providing for her so much loved son. That's how she could do this."

Again the *how* nearly whacked her. Did she really have any idea what she was getting into? Single parenting. No grandparents or relatives to help her. *Oh, Gramma Grace! Why did you leave me?* What did she know about good parenting based on the way she grew up? Not a lot. Could she learn? Apparently she was going to have to.

Confused? She saw with a jolt how much more she felt than just confusion. Terror. Doubt. Fear. But then there was that ragged little boy with huge, dark eyes and a best friend who was furry and even more ragged. Did he realize how totally his world had been destroyed?

"Here, I have it." Mr. Jensen put his phone on speaker mode. You could tell by the slightly bottom-of-the-barrel echo. "The court calendar. We have a possibility of a hearing before a judge two weeks from tomorrow. That's the

Wednesday after next. Once I know for certain, I will let you know. Jonah will have to be there, too."

Dinah flipped through her own calendar. "I'll mark that Wednesday, then. I was going to ask you, what about Jonah's doctor and dentist? Any specialists?"

"Sorry, I have none of that information. I have his school records here, shots, vaccinations, that kind of thing. I'll send them over to you."

"Did Corinne ever mention her family?"

"No. I asked her more than once, especially when that final diagnosis was made, and she said there was no one."

"And Gramma Trudy and Claire are their only friends?"

"To my knowledge. You will have to ask them. I know they want to know how Jonah is. If you could take him to visit them..."

"As soon as I can find the time. I planned to." Time. Dinah didn't have any time.

His voice purred. "That would be very thoughtful of you. Is there anything else?"

"Not that I know of at the moment. Thank you. Oh, I do have a question for you. How are you being paid to handle all this?"

"Don't you worry about that. It's taken care of."

They hung up.

She sat there staring and pondered his statement. *It's taken care of.* And yet he'd said they had used up all their money. So this was pro bono. He meant what he'd said about personal involvement, then. And, thinking of Jonah, she understood completely.

Chapter Twenty

Why did he get the feeling she had grabbed the first chance available and run?

Garret sipped his cold coffee. How had he happened on this Extraburger, anyway? Obviously it was not his usual stop, but clearly it was Dinah and Jonah's. Rather than taking the bypass like usual, he'd driven through town. If he thought about it, there were no accidents; all was planned by God. His devotions the night before had said to watch for the treasures God had planted in his day. If this was a treasure, he certainly could not see the value of it.

Other than for Jonah. To lose his mother so recently. And his dog got beaten up. And he'd gone to live with someone else. How had he ever met the recluse Dinah Taylor? And why on earth was Garret painting all three of them in oils? So maybe he'd picked up some of their turmoil, things reflected in their eyes that they wouldn't otherwise express. Not to him. It must have awakened the artist in him, that was all. Wasn't it?

He slid out of the booth, dumped his trash, and headed for his car. Sometimes life was just hard to decipher. Was there anything he could do for Jonah? *Lord God, if there is, show me.* He'd see them Saturday. Maybe something would come to him before then.

When he returned to the clinic, he checked on Valiant, who was now standing by himself. "Good for you, big boy." He rubbed the dog's ears. "Sure wish we had better news for Tessa."

At her name, the dog perked up his ears and looked to the door.

"Not yet." He checked the chart by the cage. Morning stats said low-grade temp, all else normal. "You tried walking yet?" He went to the intercom and called for Jason to come help him. He buckled the dog's collar back on and snapped a lead into the ring. Turning at the sound of the door opening, he greeted Jason and told him they were going to walk Valiant.

"I'll get a sheet." They kept lengths of old bedsheets for such a purpose as this, since often a towel just wasn't long enough to use comfortably on a really big dog. When Jason returned, he waited while Garret encouraged Valiant to try to walk out of the cage. The dog moved his front feet and the good back leg, but swayed on the casted one. He looked up at Garret as if asking, What happened?

"Reach in and get the sheet under him." Together they got the dog out of the cage and standing. "Here we go. Give him only enough as a backup." They maneuvered partway around the room and stopped for Valiant to catch his breath.

"He's working hard at it." Jason's brow suggested he was working hard, too.

"I know. Would it be easier if he just let you carry his rear end?" Garret stroked Valiant's head. "Let's do that.

Show him." With Jason half carrying him, they went on around the room. "Set up the portable fence. We'll put him in there."

"You sending him home?"

"I'd like to. See how well her friend does."

Amber stuck her head in the door. "Dr. G, you have a patient in One."

"Okay, thanks. Dog, cat?"

"Nope, cockatiel. Pretty sick."

"Benny isn't eating, huddles in the bottom of his cage," said his owner after their greeting.

Mr. and Mrs. Murphy, older folks; their cockatiel was older, too. Garret had seen the bird before when he'd ripped a toenail out and it wouldn't quit bleeding. "When did this start?"

"He wasn't right yesterday, but overnight..."

Garret picked up the gray bird with orange cheeks and examined him. Benny had tried biting him the other time, but not now. "Got to be an infection of some kind. Most likely digestive tract. I'll give him the initial dose of antibiotics, and then show you how to treat him." He held Benny in the palm of one hand, the little head trapped between his index and middle finger. "This way he can't bite you. The syringes will be prefilled and you just insert the needle in one side of his breast or the other. Then use the eyedropper to give him this pink stuff down his throat." He did both and looked at the older man and woman, who exchanged looks. "You can do it. Wrap him in a towel if it would be easier. I'll warn you, if you don't get the pink stuff down his throat and he shakes his head, you'll both be covered in pink dots."

"We'll manage," the missus said. Her husband paused before nodding.

"Benny should show signs of improvement by tomorrow. Keep his cage covered so he can sleep." Garret patted the man's shoulder. "You'll do fine."

He saw a sick Siamese cat next.

About half an hour later, he watched Tessa's friend helping the dog out the door. Jason trailed them to assist getting Valiant up into the van. They assured him they had a ramp to put in place at home. He would see them again for X-rays in three weeks.

This was one of those no-win situations, but they all agreed on one thing. They would do what was best for Valiant. That was one of the things he admired most about people who depended on service dogs; they put the dog first, no matter how heartbreaking the separation was for the people.

By the end of the day, he realized with relief that he had not given Dinah another thought. Sue came back in at seven. Sometime during the day, Amber had set up job-applicant interview appointments for Monday afternoon. Perhaps they would have help soon. The one in California would be done via a video conference call. Garret and Sue would do the interviews together.

But on the drive home, Dinah invaded his mind. What was it about her that made him want to run the other way? And yet this morning he had agreed to join them for breakfast. He could have said no thanks, but he hadn't.

His menagerie met him at the door, at least the four-footed ones. The full-throated macaw call of "You're late" made him shake his head as he bent to greet those at his feet. At least it wasn't "Shut up" this time. And, yes, the macaw did indeed know the meanings of the rather extensive vocabulary he had acquired. "Shut up" was for any time he disagreed with the macaw in the other cage. Again, he used his words correctly.

Since he had grabbed a sandwich on the way home, Garret fed the others and retreated to his studio. Dogs and cat followed and lined up by his chair.

"Sorry, kids, not tonight. I am going to make some progress on these."

He erased his pencil drawing on the third canvas, drew the boy and his dog in front and a vague female form behind them. He didn't need to know what Jonah's mother looked like; he gave her raw umber hair with a touch of burnt sienna. Not to be confused with blonde. He was going for a feeling, not a likeness, at this point. How would he show love and concern? He drew Jonah kneeling and Mutt with her front feet on his chest. One little boy cared for by two angels. There would be no wings in the painting to denote angels, so what would convey that? He studied the concept. Painting the boy and the dog would be easy. A half-skewed Royals cap, a faded blue jacket. Worn but not ratty. Mutt's ears, one at half mast, one erect, her tail whipping. He wished he had met Jonah's mother. But would that have made a difference?

He left that painting and studied the head shot of Dinah. The eyes were still not right. The jawline, the hair, were easy. He'd not done her mouth yet, either. He'd painted her brilliant fuchsia, purple, and cerulean blue scarf with varying shades of each. The white sweater set it off. Why did she always wear white?

What did it matter to him? He ignored the ringing phone and let it go to the answering machine. "Pick up, Garret. I need to talk with you."

His mother. You do not say "Not now, Mom." He did as

told, laying the brushes carefully aside and sinking down into his chair. Might as well get comfortable; most conversations with his mother were not short.

"So, what's up? I'm coming Sunday. I said I would."

"I know. But since you are the medical one in our family, I wanted to let you know what is going on."

"Going on? Is this what you wanted to talk about Sunday?"

"Yes. Your father insisted I call you." He could hear something different in her voice. *Please, God, don't let her say cancer.*

"Tell him thank you."

"You tell him. He's on the other phone."

"Hi, Dad."

"I told her this could wait until Sunday."

Garret wisely kept his mouth shut. His attention wandered back to the paintings. If he...

"Garret?"

"Yes."

"Well, what do you think?"

Had his attention gone away that long? "I'm sorry, I got distracted. Could you repeat that, please."

Her voice flinted. "I said, the doctor told me that I am diabetic. That is why I've been so tired and out of sorts."

Not cancer. A load he didn't realize he'd been carrying flew out the window. "I was afraid you were going to say something much worse. At least this is treatable. Type II, I assume; adult onset, obviously." He paused. "Does this run in our family?"

"That's what the doctor asked me. Not in my immediate family, but on your dad's side your uncle Walt had it."

"Uncle Walt doesn't count. *Your* relatives."

204 LAURAINE SNELLING

"None." She paused. "I guess it's just the shock of it. I've always been so healthy."

"So what do they say to do?"

"I have to talk with a specialist; I have an appointment for next week. In the meantime, I need to start keeping track of my blood sugar. You know how I hate getting stuck."

"You do what you have to do." Dad chimed in. "Making your finger bleed is no big deal." Dad was into platitudes.

"Not to you, maybe," she snapped back. "It's not your finger."

Garret smiled to himself. "So, have you gone online and looked up treatments, diets, life changes, things like that?" Garret's phone blipped, letting him know another call had come in and switched to the answering machine. "Dad, you can go look it up, can't you?"

"I will. Your mother just wanted to hear your take on it."

"*Don't panic* is first. This isn't life threatening, at least not right now. And with all the new findings and things, I'm sure you'll be able to control it with no problem. Mom, you're made of tough stuff. You have more self-discipline than anyone I know. You'll do fine."

"The doctor said that all of you should have this checked out. They call it the silent killer."

"I thought that was high blood pressure."

"They're both silent, Garret."

Another call blipped in.

"Mom, I need to check these calls in case there is an emergency. Let's talk about this when I see you Sunday."

"Okay. If we learn anything, I'll call you."

He clicked Off and stared at the ceiling, tapping his phone against his chin. He'd heard something lately about a new product. A picture of Dinah Taylor played on the screen of his mind. Wasn't that what her company had come up with, something that could help diabetics? He'd have to look into that. He checked his messages, returned the call to Danny.

Danny sounded enthusiastic. "The board okayed it as long as no finances are needed from the budget. I am ready to submit this to the city planners. Have you done any more on the money end?"

"We have another two thousand dollars, and there are several who said they will pitch in more if we need it."

"Just so I can pay my crew."

"Thanks, Danny. We'll have it covered." He hung up and thought down the list of others he could ask. After all, that room was used for a lot more than their one class. He listened to the other message. That could wait.

But when he went back to his painting, he had trouble concentrating. Nine o'clock. He could paint for another hour. He stood squinting at the third easel. He could fill in background or—he backed up. Sometimes seeing work from a distance helped. He did the same with the other two.

This time of night was not a good time to get involved in a difficult part, like her eyes, or her whole face. The middle easel held the painting of Jonah holding Mutt and she licking his chin. Time to do the dog. He closed his eyes. Where, what, were her markings? More splotchy than delineated. He switched brushes to get more texture. Wiry hair. A smooth coat would be far easier. He'd have to look at her more closely when he took the stitches out. How much brown was there? Her eyes. More problems with eyes.

He painted hair going every which way, knowing he'd put the white and light grays in later.

Soandso and Sam, the sibling yellow Labs, got up stretching and went to stand at the sliding glass door. Clearly they were announcing it was time for an out and then bed. Not that they'd done anything more taxing than sleep, but then dogs were good at that. The cat sat in front of the glassed wall. Unless there was a bird out there or a squirrel, he had no desire to escape. Garret leaned down to pick up TC, who now decided that twining about his legs was more fun than staring out into the dark. As soon as Garret rubbed the cat's neck and chin, his motor started and vibrated the whole relaxed body. Had he been sitting reading, the cat would have been in his lap. Were he on the computer, TC would be sound asleep right beside the keyboard.

TC, Tiger Cat or simply The Cat, depending on how much trouble he was causing, looked up, slightly disdainful. He would take his rightful, God-given spot on the bed. He knew when to ask for cuddling and when to claim it.

The dogs reappeared from the dark, tongues lolling from their run around the perimeter. At least they'd not found something to bark at tonight. The neighbors were not excited when his dogs discovered a strange critter in their yard and tried to let the whole world know.

When he gave in and put his tools away, the dogs raced ahead of him while the cat padded, straight-tailed, alongside. By the time he'd climbed the stairs, he realized he was indeed tired. After reading his devotional for the day and the accompanying Bible verses, he jotted a couple of notes in the notebook he kept beside the bed, checked that all three pets were in their assigned places, and turned out the lights.

Passing through that perfect place for creative thinking, he jerked awake. His mother was diabetic. There could be serious consequences: blindness, kidney failure—what if she were unable to maintain healthy blood sugar levels? And, yes, in this day and age there were a lot of good products to assist, but...it was *his* mother. Mothers weren't supposed to get sick. Well, not dads, either. And he had pretty much blown her off. *God, what is the matter here?* Mighty selfish, huh? He couldn't call now, but he figured he'd better be taking flowers along on Sunday. Why had she called him and not Carolyne? While he was the eldest, his oldest sister was usually the confidante, or Becky, who was his younger sister by two years. But, as Dad said, he was the one with the medical background; even though his training was in the animal field, he had always been interested in all medical issues.

He locked his hands behind his head and stared at the ceiling. While his dad was sixty, his mother hadn't hit that milestone yet. Besides, everyone always said his parents seemed younger than their years.

He rolled over, aware of two sets of front paws on the edge of the bed as the dogs checked to see if he was all right. "Sorry, kids." He stroked the dogs' heads and sent them back to bed. Lying sleepless was not like him. *Lord God, clearly I need Your wisdom here. I can get up and go look things up or I can go to sleep like I need to.*

The animals were not pleased with his decision to go back down to the computer.

An hour later, and much wiser about the disease as it presents in humans, he sent the links to his father and barely made it back up the stairs before his eyes started to close. Now if only he could do something for Jonah.

His eyes popped open. What? What had just gone

through his mind? The child was basically a stranger who was someone else's responsibility.

A child who was going through hell right now. A child without a mom who desperately needed nurturing. Garret was not a nurturer, not a father. But...

But then he drifted off to sleep.

Chapter Twenty-One

"Jonah, are you all right?"

He looked up from picking at his Extraburger pancake. Jonah was normally not a dawdler with food or anything else. His shrug gave her absolutely no information. Other than that he was not acting normally.

"Do you feel sick? Sore throat, tummy ache?"

He shook his head, heaved a sigh, and drank his hot chocolate.

Dinah pasted a smile on her mouth—at least she hoped it was a smile—and changed the subject. "I'm working on the grocery list. What did you like to eat when—" She caught herself. "Well, at your house."

"Mommy made spaghetti."

"Okay, tonight we'll make spaghetti." *I can handle that. Buy a jar of sauce, add hamburger, and cook the spaghetti. Surely I can't mess that up.* Why had she never bothered to learn to cook?

Jonah grabbed his backpack. "Should I come to your office after school again?"

"Yes, please."

"Why can't I go to your house and take care of Mutt? She doesn't like to be alone all the time."

Why couldn't he? Right off the top of her head, she couldn't think of a reason. "I didn't get you a key yet."

"Can you do that today?"

"Tell you what, you come to the office and we'll decide what to do then, okay?"

He nodded, slung his pack over one shoulder, and left. She watched him trudge past the window with no smile and no wave. Something was indeed wrong, but what? *Other than that his whole world had just collapsed. And his mother had died a week or so ago.* The voice sounded more than a little sarcastic.

Dinah gathered up their trash and carried it to the box. Another thing Jonah had or hadn't done. Half his breakfast was still on the plate; only his hot chocolate was empty. Back at their table, she picked up her things and headed upstairs.

"Uh-oh, what happened?" April changed immediately from cheery to concerned.

"Something is wrong with Jonah." Dinah propped her briefcase on April's desk, her bag weighing heavily on her shoulder. The whole morning had gone from normal, whatever that was, to a load far too weighty to be carried.

"He's not sick?"

"He said not." She reiterated all the things she had noticed. "When he walked by the window, he looked like he carried half of Eastbrook on his shoulders."

"Anything unusual that might have triggered a change?"

Dinah shook her head slowly, searching the evening, the morning, the night, whatever. "If something happened, I am not aware of it."

"The best thing is to get him talking. Have you set him up with a grief counselor?"

Dinah frowned. "When I went in to his school Monday—April, that seems so long ago!—they asked for the name of his counselor or psychologist. I said he didn't have any, and they told me to set him up with one, but they weren't allowed to make recommendations. One of the many, many things I haven't done yet. I know. I'll call the lawyer, Jensen. And if he doesn't know any, maybe I could ask around down in the university's psychology department."

Grief counselor. Where was that kind of help when Dinah had needed it so desperately all those years ago? Could grief counseling have made a change in her life? Maybe. Probably not. When God lets you down, you've been let down. Period.

She stood up. "He asked why he can't go be with Mutt after school. I stalled; I said because he doesn't have a key. He's too young to be alone, right?"

April nodded, then grimaced. "I hate to be the bearer of more bad tidings, but have you seen the headlines?"

"Like where?"

"The *Eastbrook Sentinel* for a start." She laid open the front page.

"'FDA Takes a Stand.'" Dinah looked up. "Against us?"

"Or rather against Scoparia."

She picked up the paper and read the opening paragraph.

Ellsworth Botcher, assistant to the chief laboratory investigator for Hostmark Testing Laboratories Inc. of Smithfield, stated in a press conference this morning that the Food and Drug Administration has filed a hold on Food for Life's new supplement, Scoparia, pending a decision on its classification. Mr. Botcher explained that if the product is actually a drug rather than a dietary supplement, approval will be denied pending further hearings. Mr. Botcher further stated that...

Dinah slammed the paper closed. "I guess we knew this was coming. That doesn't really say anything new."

April wagged her head. "I'd think the feds would tell us their decisions first before releasing them to the press."

"April, it's non-news. There's no such decision. Scoparia doesn't meet the criteria for a drug. Some reporter built a story out of nothing." She settled into the other chair by April's desk and read the rest of the story, moving to page ten, back of section one. At least all their facts were straight. So why the innuendo of wrongful conduct? This was really blowing smoke.

Dinah tossed the paper aside. "So, as Hal says, we'll call this free publicity and keep on with what we are doing."

April breathed a sigh of relief. "Oh, I'm so glad you feel that way. Marcella took this as a personal attack."

"I trust she'll change her mind when she thinks it through." Dinah left the paper lying on the desk and went on to her office. She put her things away, checked her coffee. It was lukewarm, so she emptied the cup in the sink. She'd never cared much for lukewarm anything.

By noon she felt like a firefighter, having put out brush fires all morning. As someone so well said, it was the tyranny of the urgent. Her to-do list still waited. She punched April's button. "Order me up some lunch, please—whatever soup they have and half a turkey on rye, toasted."

"I take it you are working over lunch?"

"Yes. I am." How often did April nag her about not taking breaks often enough, and lunch was considered a break? So she added, "On family stuff."

"Oh, good."

Dinah dictated two letters into the machine and returned two more phone calls. Marcella must have calmed down, since she'd not appeared at the door, or called, or texted. Maybe everyone else was on Friday mode, too: get as much done as possible just in case you could leave early on Friday afternoon.

April knocked and entered unbidden, carrying two to-go bags from Braumeister's and a two-liter bottle of ginger ale. She paused, smiling. "I'm an old hand at being mother and you're a newbie. May I help?"

Why burden April with her problems? That thought fled half-formed. "I would be so grateful! Yes."

They settled at the table by the windows, April said grace, and Dinah acted polite. She lifted a lid. "Clam chowder!"

"It's Friday, remember?"

"I know, the fact kind of goes in and out." Dinah took a bite of her sandwich before a spoonful of the creamy chowder. Mrs. Braumeister made the best soups. "Okay, the problem is this: Jonah is seven years old and he cannot stay alone at the condo until I get home from work. From there on I'm in a muddle."

April nodded. "We need the white board, where you draw those goofy diagrams so we can make wise decisions. I suggest that getting Jonah and Mutt back together quickly each day would help a lot. He seems to draw strength from his dog. What about this Gramma Trudy? She might be glad to have Jonah come there."

"Good point. I'll call and talk to her."

"Take Jonah to see her. It might help him right now. A familiar face."

"I know. I told the lawyer I would. But it's right next to his house. Won't that make it worse?"

"Hm. I don't know." April mulled as she chewed. "Does Lincoln Elementary have an after-school program you could sign him up for? Many schools have that now."

"I could call and ask. What do your kids do?"

"You have to remember they are older now, and Joe's mother lives two blocks over. They used to go to her house. Now she takes them to practices or after-school events, if there is something special going on. They are really spoiled, because she always bakes cookies just for them."

Not for the first time, Dinah got another brush of feeling for the value of having family around. That would never happen with her parents, and while Grandma Grace promised to watch out for her from heaven, perhaps that had been wishful thinking, too. She needed a live body now that she had a small boy to take care of.

"Right. My parents aren't into child care." *Not even when we were growing up.* But she didn't say that aloud. "And they live too far from the school." Like three states. She had no white board, so she set up one in her head. In the middle, Jonah plus Mutt. Gramma Trudy in one corner, the school in another; two possible solutions.

"I could hire a nanny to be waiting for him when he returns to my place." Mentally, she wrote *Nanny* in the lower right corner of the board. "If worst comes to worst, do you think it would work for him to go home, get Mutt, and come back here?" She imagined Food for Life in the lower left corner.

"He could. You mentioned once about wanting to keep work and personal separate. That would scotch that."

"True." She jotted herself a real note to order groceries. Why it popped into her head she had no idea, but she was quickly learning that you write these things down instantly. "Would he be a distraction here? Is it fair to him?"

"Dinah, nothing in life is fair for him right now. We do what we must." April stuffed her napkin and containers into a bag.

Dinah scrunched up her napkin and tossed it in. She held April's eye. "Thank you so much. I'll call Gramma Trudy right now."

April bobbed her head. "And I'll call the kids' school. I know their assistant supe well, and she knows what all the area schools offer. Maybe we can even have something in place to tell him when he gets here this afternoon." She tossed the bag in the can on her way out and Dinah returned to her office feeling somewhat buoyed. At least she was doing something.

Gramma Trudy's number. It took Dinah a few minutes to dig it out of her notes. One ringy-dingy. Two. Three. Trudy's daughter Claire's voice explained to Dinah that Trudy was unable to come to the phone right now, but if you would leave a message... Sometimes answering machines could drive one to drink, or swearing, or both. *Oh, relax, Dinah! Trudy will call back as soon as she returns.* She could call Hal, an out she took way too often, but he was still out of town. And he had his own problems.

She kicked off her heels and stood, stretching, bending, turning, stretching, breathing deep, reminding herself that she was no longer a frisky young volleyball player. Maybe it was time she tried yoga. Hands straight-armed against the wall, she stretched her hamstrings. She was not getting enough exercise, that was for sure. She was tighter than a kettle drum. Stretching some more, especially her head side to side, she slid her shoes back on and stood in front of the window. Today would have been a great day for a walk, and she'd not left the building.

Moments after she sat down at her work station, April knocked and entered. "Okay. Here's the info." She plopped a page of notes on Dinah's desk. "Lincoln has an after-school program. You have to sign him up yourself, personally. It lasts until six and he has to be picked up by an approved caregiver; he can't just walk home. They do homework, some crafts, games, music. The program changes with teachers and volunteers who specialize in something. Oh, and art. The way he draws, maybe they can get him to teach it. Some gym time. And adequate supervision."

"Snacks?" The first place Jonah went was the refrigerator or the cupboard. She remembered coming home from school starved, too. She shut that memory down. It did not remain shut. She thought of her mother's stringent food rules; eat to live, not live to eat. Once she'd started going to Gramma Grace's after school, life had been so different. Gramma Grace was not into fasting or austerity, and she used lots of sugar and butter.

"Oops. I forgot to ask that."

"No problem; I can send something with him. Can he go sporadically or does he have to be there every day?"

"Every day. Once you sign up, you are committed without a special permission form."

"Of course. It's pretty rigid, but...it's a backup plan. Thank you, April."

But April was already hurrying out to answer a buzzing phone.

Oh, and a key. She called Mr. Watson and got another answering machine. She told the infernal device that she would need a key for Jonah.

She stretched her neck—again. Checking her list, she called her order in to the grocery store and got put on hold. When Mrs. Braumeister apologized a short time later, what could she say? She gave her order, and said she'd be by to pick it up on her way home. She hoped that would be as soon after three as possible.

If only she could work at home, like she used to. She got a lot done, and could also work out lab problems there. How could she reconfigure her condo, her lovely little perfect-for-one-busy-person-size condo, to maintain privacy for two very different people— and a dog!— and still have a useable workspace?

She pulled up the financial reports she needed to go over, and the next thing she realized was that her clock said four thirty. Why hadn't April called her? She should have set a reminder on her calendar. She slapped her hands on her desk and stood. Her door was closed, no lights flashed on her phone, and she felt like she'd been running on a summer day, she was so thirsty. Grabbing a bottle of water from the small refrigerator in her half-bathroom, she chugged most of it and headed out to see what the others were doing. Surely April would have notified her if Jonah hadn't arrived.

She checked the break room. Empty. April's desk. Vacant. But she heard voices from the conference room. Was that a dog barking? Pushing open the door, she expected to see the television on, but, instead, Mutt came bounding over to greet her.

"You can't do that!" Randy slapped his cards down on the table.

"Can too!" Jonah scooped up the deck.

"Randy, you just haven't played for so long, you forgot the rules." April grinned at Dinah over her shoulder. "You gotta keep these young pups in line."

Jonah was grinning, too. He glanced up at Dinah. "I won!"

Dinah laughed. "So I surmise."

"For the fourth time, he won. He must cheat." Randy reached for a potato chip and dug into the dip. "The ignominy of a seven-year-old boy beating a twenty-seven-year-old computer whiz at Old Maid."

"You didn't win at Go Fish either."

Dinah bent down to ruffle the dog's ears. "And who brought you over?"

"We went and got her. Mr. Watson opened the door for me. He said I should have a key if I'm going to live there."

Great, that was probably where he was when she left the message. "We?"

"I went with him. I needed to get out, too." Randy locked his hands behind his head to stretch. "We should have run." He looked to Jonah. "Can you run?"

Jonah shrugged. "I do at school in gym."

"How far do you think you can go?"

Jonah shrugged again and gathered up the cards.

Why did she feel like she'd just entered another world? And she was the odd one out? And that she had failed Jonah by not...by not—At least he seemed more like himself. Maybe whatever was bothering him this morning had gone away. Maybe she should be grateful she had the kind of staff who stepped in and helped someone else out, without even being asked.

She addressed everyone. "Thank you."

April smiled at her. "You're welcome."

"So, you have plans for the weekend?" Randy asked as they left the room.

"We have to take Mutt to get her stitches out tomorrow morning." Jonah snapped the leash onto her collar.

"That's it?" Randy looked to Dinah.

"I, ah . . ."

"Last Saturday we went shopping and on Sunday we went to a movie. Tonight we are having spaghetti for supper." Jonah spoke so matter-of-factly that it sounded like he always did these things.

April patted Mutt. "You'll look better, dog, when your fur grows back. I have a horde waiting for me to bring pizza, so see you all Monday." She looked to Dinah. "Call me if you need me."

Dinah motioned *Come* and Jonah followed her out.

"We have to pick up our groceries," Dinah said once they were walking down the sidewalk.

"Okay."

"How was school?"

He shrugged.

Was this getting to be a habit? "Do you have homework?"

He shook his head, but he didn't look up at her. Something was still bothering him.

He told Mrs. Braumeister thank you for the sucker and the treat for Mutt, and they headed home, he with his backpack and carrying one plastic sack, Dinah with her beloved hobo bag on her shoulder, briefcase in hand, and two sacks in the other. Why hadn't she had the food delivered? At least the loaf of french bread smelled good.

Mr. Watson met them in the lobby. "Hey, there, Jonah.

I got your key made and put it on a ring, 'specially for you." He handed the key to Jonah and another to Dinah. "I figured you might need an extra, too."

"Thank you."

"Here, let me carry that."

"No, we're fine."

He ignored her and took her two plastic bags and Jonah's. "You should be using their special bags. Don't you have one?"

"I have two, but I forgot to bring them." Today seemed to be a Dinah failure day all around. He handed them back to her when she had the door unlocked.

"I checked to make sure the keys worked."

"Thank you."

"You need anything, you just call."

"I did. I will."

If only she could just kick off her shoes, take a long hot bath, and veg out. Why had she said she would make spaghetti tonight? They could have stopped for pizza. Or ordered something in.

"I'll get my things put away while you feed Mutt, okay?"

Jonah nodded as he hung his jacket on the vacuum-cleaner handle in the closet. She'd forgotten to ask Mr. Watson to put hooks at a boy's level. She was going to have to figure out someplace else to put the vacuum cleaner and mops, too. He took his backpack with him to the kitchen.

Dinah changed her clothes, looked longingly at the bed, and, sliding her feet into scuffs, returned to the kitchen. Mutt was eating and Jonah sat at the table, already drawing.

Dinah turned on the music and got out the frying pan. As she browned the hamburger, she set a pot of water on for the noodles. If Jonah didn't feel like talking, neither did she. But she sensed him watching her as she poured the jar of sauce into the pan.

"Mommy didn't do it like that."

She turned to look over her shoulder. "What do you mean?"

"She didn't use bottled stuff."

"Oh. What did she do?"

"She cooked it all day."

"Oh, really?" She put the lid on, set the pan to simmer, and as soon as the water boiled, added the pasta. "Would you like salad?"

He shook his head, his attention back on the drawing.

After she'd set their plates on the table, sauce on top of the noodles and parmesan cheese sprinkled on top of all, she took the heated bread from the oven and set it on a plate in the middle of the table. Jonah put his drawing things on the chair next to him and studied his plate. He looked up at her, shaking his head.

She sat down and placed her napkin in her lap, then passed him the plate of bread.

He took a slice and waited.

Dinah started to take a bite, but stopped.

"Aren't we going to say grace?"

"Ah, yes, of course." She bowed her head and waited. When nothing happened, she looked up to see him staring at her.

"How come you never say grace?"

"I…ah…"

"Mommy always said grace."

"Sorry, Jonah. Would you please say grace?"

"Come, Lord Jesus, be our guest; let this food to us be blessed. Amen."

"Thank you." *Just to get through this day, that's all I ask.* She took a bite of her spaghetti. Not bad.

Jonah shoved his plate away. "My mommy made good spaghetti! How come you didn't make good spaghetti?" His voice was rising, so unlike him. "How come you...you can't do anything right?" He was yelling now. "That stuff's pukey!" He threw his bread at the plate, bailed off his chair, and tore down the hall to his room. "I hate you. I want my mommy!" The door slammed behind him.

Dinah stared open-mouthed at the spaghetti dribbling off the plate, leaving a trail of sauce behind it.

Chapter Twenty-Two

When she heard Jonah crying in the night, without thinking she slid her feet into scuffs. Wrapping and tying her robe as she made her way down the hall, she fought off a yawn. Listening at the door, she heard a whimper. Dog or boy?

As silently as possible, she opened the door and peeked in.

Mutt looked up from lying lengthwise, her back against Jonah. Her tail brushed his face when she wagged.

It wasn't the dog whimpering. Should she wake him? Bad dreams? He most certainly was entitled to bad dreams after all he'd been through. Mothering instincts that she had no idea lived anywhere inside of her carried her to his side. Automatically, she laid the back of her hand against his cheek. He didn't feel warm, had not complained of feeling sick.

She was the one feeling sick. Her stomach had clenched so often it ached. Along with her neck and shoulders. Glancing around the room, dimly lit by a night-light plugged into the wall by the door, she wished she had brought a chair in here.

"Mommy, Mom-m-y." The agonizing words came through garbled, but she heard them well. Mutt changed directions and, with her head on his shoulder, licked his face, catching a tear that threatened to roll into her boy's ear.

Jonah rolled over, an arm thrown over the dog. He sighed.

Dinah waited and watched for a while, but Jonah seemed more settled now. She returned to her bed and lay on her back, staring at the ceiling. Street lights discovered every crack to steal past the lined drapes, giving enough light that she needn't turn on the lights when she got up in the middle of the night. Not that she'd been a night riser. Once she turned out the light, she turned out the world and slept until the alarm jerked her awake.

Jonah coming into her life had changed that pattern.

A barking dog took the place of the alarm. She leaped out of bed to find Jonah up and dressed.

"Mutt needs to go outside."

Dinah glanced at her watch. 7:00 a.m. "Wait a minute and I'll go with you."

"I can do it. I always did before." This was not a pleading tone, but definitely a challenging one.

"Before" was no longer a pleasant word in Dinah's vocabulary. She heaved a sigh. Give in or stick by her feelings? But he had to be as independent as he could be. "All right." She wasn't sure if she'd agreed only to shut off the voices of indecision in her head, or because this truly was the best thing. She watched him go out to the living room and get his jacket, checking to make sure he had the key. He put the leash on Mutt and they left, the door snicking shut behind them.

The urge to follow him drove Dinah into the kitchen

to start the coffee maker. Should she make breakfast? What did they have to make breakfast with? She should have bought cereal or something. They always ate at the Extraburger. He liked pancakes. Did his mother make pancakes? After the fiasco last night, she hated to ask him what his mommy made for breakfast.

Oh, Corinne, what did you saddle me with? I don't know anything about raising a little boy. The only little boy I ever knew—she forced herself to finish the thought—*was my baby brother. And look what happened there!* She finally managed to slam the door shut on that way of thinking. All memories did was dredge up pain better left at the bottom of the ocean. She'd learned the hard way that that was the only way she could function.

So what could happen to Jonah between here and the back alley where Mutt did her business? Strangers could not get past Mr. Watson, and everyone in the building had been vetted before purchasing their unit. And there were no rentals allowed, according to the building rules.

Still, she breathed a sigh of relief when she heard Jonah's key in the lock. Were all mothers as paranoid as she, or was she worse because she was so new to this game? And since when did she consider herself a mother? But what else was she? A guardian? A—her mind went blank. Once she signed those papers and the judge gave the stamp of approval, Jonah would be her legal son. She, who had always said she would not marry, because she was married to her work, had been thrown to the lions of parenthood. What kind of cosmic joke was this?

"Our appointment is at nine thirty." He hung up the leash.

"Do you want breakfast first?"

That got his attention. He looked up from pouring kibble into Mutt's dish. "Here?"

"Well, we don't have anything to make breakfast from, but if you don't mind the Bagelry...."

"What's the matter with the Extraburger?"

"Nothing. I just thought something different might be better."

"How come you don't have eggs or cereal or even bread for toast?"

"Because I always eat breakfast somewhere else." She poured her coffee and added half-and-half.

"You don't even have hot chocolate." The belligerent tone resumed.

"No, I don't. I forgot to order it yesterday. Look, Jonah, I know this is a whole different life style for you and it is for me, too. We will go to the grocery store today and buy hot chocolate and eggs and whatever else you would like, but that means we'll eat at home more often."

He stared at her. "My mommy liked to cook before she got so sick."

She could see the shutters click into place. So she waited, hoping he would continue. But he set Mutt's dish on the floor and brought her water bowl up to the sink to be filled. He could barely reach the faucet, but managed. "So, what would you like to do?" Oops, bad question. She read his mind as clearly as if he'd said the words aloud.

"I'm sorry, Jonah, but you can't go home. This is your home now." If rage had a color, it was red blazing from his eyes.

"Mommy said she was going to live with Jesus but He would take care of me. You tell Jesus to send her back. I need her more than He does." With that he stormed back to his bedroom and slammed the door. Mutt looked up at her, then down the hall.

"If you are feeling as sucker-punched as I am, we are both in a world of hurt."

The dog whined, looked down at her dish, then, after a look at Dinah, trotted down the hall to scratch at the door.

"Well, at least you have your priorities in order. The boy comes first with you, even before food." Dinah sank into a chair, holding her cup with both hands, hoping she could drink without spilling it. She sipped coffee and stared out the window. The rose drooped. Had she bothered to water it? Tired of everything, so very tired, she picked up the vase and turned it upside down. A little puddle ran out. The cut end of the rosebud was dry. How could she be trusted with the life of a child when she couldn't even remember to water a stinking rosebud? She threw the dead flower in the trash, washed the vase and put it away, and repaired to her bedroom to get dressed for the day. Pulling her white jeans out of the closet, she stared at the paw print on one leg. The second pair was clean, so she threw the first in the hamper and, pulling on ankle boots after the jeans, dug a Scottish fisherman-knit sweater from the drawer. A long-sleeved tee shirt, then the sweater. Perhaps she could forgo the pea coat this way. After all, spring was nearly here, or at least had shown up to visit for a bit.

At eight thirty she rapped on his door. "You ready to leave?"

He opened the door and followed her down the hall, Mutt by his side. When she saw Mutt's empty dish in the kitchen she knew he had made sure she was fed. Trying to ignore the mutinous looks he sent her, she pressed the elevator button for the garage. "If you are hungry, we will have to eat after Mutt gets her stitches out now."

When he shrugged, she wanted to shake him. What had happened to the Jonah who had been living with her for a week now? She really liked that boy, but this one was beyond her comprehension. What had brought about the abrupt change?

Something, obviously. Did she dare ask, or would he answer with more anger?

He stared out the window, Mutt on his lap, for the entire drive over there. When they got to the clinic, he helped his dog out and waited at the door.

Dinah smiled at him, but that boy she didn't know only stared back at her. *I don't have to do this, you know*, she felt like saying, but she knew she did. Have to do it, that is. Once inside, she signed the sheet and wrote down the time.

"There is only one before you, so it won't be long," the receptionist said with a smile.

"Thank you." She went over to sit by Jonah. Mutt sat on his lap, shivering. Was she cold, or did dogs have nerves, too?

Jonah petted her and laid his cheek against the top of her head. "It's okay. Dr. G won't hurt you."

Dinah looked around at the artwork on the walls. She'd planned to go online and learn more about this Dr. G but hadn't gotten around to it. Like so many other things lately. Like trying to reach Gramma Trudy. The lady had not yet returned her call. Maybe she simply didn't look at her answering machine very often.

When Jonah had used push pins to put his drawing on the wall in his room, she had nearly fainted. Pin holes in her pristine, Navajo-white walls. With great force of will, she had remained silent. But look at all these examples for Jonah to copy.

How could a man who was such a jerk around her be the artist behind these delightful drawings? And he'd had the audacity to imply it was *her* fault he didn't like her. How could he have such a thriving practice if he was a jerk all the time? Or was it ego? If she were a betting woman, she'd say ego.

"Ms. Taylor? You want to bring Jonah and Mutt in now?"

No, I want to wait out here. But she nodded instead and waited for Jonah to get a good hold on Mutt.

They were shown into an examining room with a stainless-steel table attached to the wall and a padded bench by the wall by the door. Dinah sat down, but Jonah put Mutt on the floor and leaned beside the door. Drawings of different breeds of dogs almost made her smile. The man did indeed have an eye for caricature. One dog wore a harness and dark glasses. She'd read about Seeing Eye dogs but had never made the effort to learn the breeds. After all, if you're not allowed to have a dog, why bother? And she was beginning to see how deeply her parents' behavior and values had penetrated into her. But what had their values done to Gramma Grace, a woman who knew the world, and little Michael, a child too young to control his own destiny?

She clutched her bag as if it were a lifeline.

When the door opened, Mutt scrambled to get behind Jonah.

"Hi, Jonah, and how is our patient today? Ah, I see she is glad to see me."

Jonah almost smiled. "Hi. Mutt is good. I think her stitches itch."

Dr. G gave Dinah a smile that looked more like a grimace and a polite nod. "Can you lift her up here, or do you want help?"

Dinah put her bag down and half rose, but a look from the good doctor sat her back down.

Jonah shortened the leash, but Mutt still managed to wrap it around his legs as she tried to get out the closed door.

Dr. G squatted down to help, but Mutt lifted the lip on one side of her mouth. "Easy, girl, let's get this taken care of." He looked at Jonah. "Has she ever bitten anyone before?"

Jonah shook his head. "But then she never had to come to a vet before she got in that fight."

"So she doesn't have too good of an opinion of me right now. Here, let me hold the leash and you pick her up and put her on the table. You think you can do that?"

Mutt was sitting on the table before Dinah realized how quickly Dr. G had moved. She asked, "You want me to help hold her?"

"If you could. Or I will call someone else in. Take hold of her like this." And he demonstrated.

She wrapped herself around Mutt.

Jonah glared at her. Here she was trying to help his dog, and he was angry with her.

Within minutes Garret had snipped and tweaked all the stitches out. "There are some stitches inside, but they're made out of string that dissolves away. So they'll disappear without any help." He checked all the spots and patted Mutt, who now almost wagged her tail. "Looks to me like you took very good care of her."

Jonah nodded.

Dinah asked, "Jonah asked me the other day if I

thought Mutt was getting fat. Are we feeding her right?"

Dr. G pinched a bit of skin. "Did we weigh her last time?" He reached for the file and checked. "We did, but let's weigh her again. The scale is down the hall." Jonah wrapped his arms around Mutt and set her on the floor, where she shook as if to get rid of all things medical. Then she walked out the door beside Jonah as if she did this every day.

When they returned, Dr. G jotted something in the chart. "Yes, she has put on a couple pounds, but she isn't fat. See?" He demonstrated more for Jonah than for Dinah. "If it's fat, you won't be able to feel her ribs here. We can." He knelt down and palpated her belly area again. "You know, Jonah, she has never been spayed."

Jonah looked at him blankly.

Garret rose and glanced down at the file folder on the table. He rolled his lips together, then looked at Dinah. "You don't know much about dogs, do you?" It was almost an accusation.

She shook her head. She got almost dizzy and faint. Weight gain. Not spayed…puppies? Puppies! *Good Lord, no! I can't take on puppies! I can't! Not with all this! Not that, too!* She gasped aloud, "Oh, God, no!"

Jonah stared at her. "'Oh, God, no' what! Why did you say 'Oh, God, no'?"

Suddenly frantic, he looked at the vet. "Is she sick? Is she gonna die?"

Dinah tried to stop looking stricken but she couldn't. *Puppies!*

Jonah's eyes grew round. "I don't want her to die!" His voice rose and he stared from the vet to Dinah and back. "Mommy said I was going to be fine and then she dies and now I hafta live with Dinah and I don't want Mutt to die, too!" He shouted again. "No, not die! She can't die!"

"Jonah, stop! Listen." Dinah reached for him, but he spun away.

Dinah tried to follow him. He turned and slammed into her. "No! No!" Arms flailing, he head-butted her.

"Jonah! *Stop!*" The male voice cracked across the room like a close-by thunderclap. "Look what you're doing to Mutt!"

Dinah turned around and saw Mutt cowering in the corner shivering, so obviously terror-stricken that she peed on the floor.

Garret said firmly, "Jonah! Look at me!"

Jonah dropped his arms and did as told. Garret pointed at poor Mutt. "See, you scared her." His voice had gentled and his hand had found its way to Jonah's shoulder.

Jonah flung himself across the space and gathered Mutt into his arms. Still shivering, she licked the tears from his face and tried to clean his ears. "I'm sorry, Mutt! I'm sorry." He cried into her fur.

Dinah stared from the boy to the man, who was kneeling beside Jonah and Mutt now and talking softly. Then he gathered the boy and dog into his arms and held them both. Just held them. Huge hands pressed dog and boy against himself.

Jonah melted against the man, sobbing wildly.

Her stupid outburst had tipped off Jonah's. Dinah closed her eyes and sank back against the wall. Failed again.

She watched the three over there in the corner. Maybe there was more to this man than she had thought. If he could calm this horribly wounded little boy like this, he couldn't be all bad. Grief did strange things to people sometimes, as she well knew. She'd not had a dog to kiss her tears away; instead she had had Gramma Grace. All Jonah had was Mutt and Dinah. And, right now, a man who doctored animals.

How could she possibly ever be or become what Jonah so desperately needed?

Chapter Twenty-Three

Hey, Garret!"
The call stopped him in the hall between the sanctuary and the church kitchen. He turned. "Hey, Gil, good to see you."

Gil stopped right beside him and leaned in. "How's the classroom fund coming along?"

"We need about another three."

"Hundred?"

"Thousand. Got a couple of people still undecided as to their donation amount."

Gil nodded, his shiny bald spot catching the light. "I see. Wife and I talked it over. Two thousand is about the max we can do right now."

Garret clapped him on the upper arm. "Thanks, buddy. You just made my life easier."

Together the two men entered the classroom, where John greeted them before they located seats. Danny stopped beside Garret's shoulder. "I can't believe it, planning board okayed it without any problem. Not sure if they realized all it was or not, but fine by me. If this is God going before us, I'd like Him as a business partner anytime."

"Just ask Him. We're about there on the money. Only about a thousand short for the whole project."

"Good. I have one other job to finish up, so we can start on this first thing Wednesday. Hopefully we can have the beams up and wiring in before the weekend. Won't be too pretty in here, but progress is rarely pretty."

Class was good, but then it was always good.

After class, John stopped him. "You doing the lunch gig today?"

"Sorry. Command performance at my mother's house. You need something?"

"I have to be out of town next week and I wondered if you would take over the class."

"Ah." Garret reminded his mouth to close. "I'm not a Bible teacher, John. In fact I'm not a teacher of any kind."

"Not what I heard."

"That goofy caricature gig for the kids? That's not a Bible study." *And they weren't adults.*

"You told a Bible story using your marker pens and a pad of paper."

"Yeah, but..."

"How about doing the same for the adults? I've had a parent or two mention that idea. I think it would be great."

Garret swallowed. Kids were one thing; he loved entertaining children, but not adults.

"You think on it. I'll call you this evening."

"No pressure or anything, right?"

"Wrong. Big pressure. If this trip were not an emergency, I'd have given you weeks to prepare."

"And have a nervous breakdown."

He argued with God all through the service, but at no point did he hear "Since you really don't want to, you don't have to." Instead, the idea of Abraham and the sacrifice of his son whipped through his mind, turned around, and returned to take up residence. On the way out, he nodded to John. Might as well give up now, for God did not seem to want to let him off the hook. After all, it was only for an hour.

He dropped by home to check on his friends and decided to take the dogs with him. His three-year-old nephew, Peter, loved the doggies. He had the dogs in the car when he remembered the newspaper article he'd seen that morning about Scoparia, some product everyone was talking about that Dinah Taylor's company made. Another trip back into the house to dig out the piece in this Sunday's "Home and Health" section. By the time he got on the road, he was running late. Was this getting to be a habit or something? When his mother said one o'clock, the food would be on the table at one-oh-one.

Scoparia. Dinah Taylor. He couldn't get away from those two, Jonah and Dinah. And Mutt. That beleaguered little boy, stuck with a woman who knew absolutely nothing about either dogs or boys. At all.

So what *did* she know about, if anything? Bigshot CEO, in a position to boss everyone around, and, probably like most CEOs, didn't actually know squat. Was she hired in from outside? Had she come up through the ranks? Had she slept with someone to—*Shut yo mouth, boy! That is totally Unchristian!* Yeah, well, he'd had his education about women CEOs and his fill of them, too. Big trouble, the whole lot of them.

And Jonah's explosion. Garret understood that the extreme pressure on the little guy would blow his cork; in fact, it was a good thing. Let him vent. How often had explosions happened in his day? Did this Dinah woman even understand his need to act out the grief he could not articulate in words? Did she embrace him or yell at him? If the scene in Garret's exam room was any indication, she just stood there with her mouth open. Bigshot CEO indeed.

A CEO that didn't do dogs. Bah.

He'd have to X-ray Mutt to see how far along the puppies were. That would in large part determine their course of action.

And what exactly was this Scoparia? News articles claimed that Food for Life was billing it as a cure. The Food for Life website called it a dietary supplement; it said nothing about a cure for anything, but the papers were saying diabetes. When he looked for sales outlets he found nothing, so it was not out on the shelves yet.

He pulled into the familiar farm driveway and let the dogs out the back.

"Doggies!" Little Peter came bounding off the porch, fell flat on his face, squirmed to his feet, and ran over to Sam. The dog had just lifted his leg beside a tree and couldn't escape the chubby little arms in time. Peter hugged him exuberantly. Soandso, who did not need a tree for anything, scampered off to relieve herself well away from Peter. Good thing his dogs were so good with little kids; with a mother and an uncle who were both veterinarians, Peter had inherited a double dose of love for animals and could get really enthusiastic.

Peter's older brother, Mark, came running out but stopped on the porch when his dad called him from inside.

"Peter, go in and wash your hands. We're eating." Carolyne, who was Peter's aunt and Garret's elder sister, stepped down off the porch. She hugged Garret. "Do you have any idea what this is all about? Mom is acting a little weird and she isn't telling me anything. That's not like her."

"Sort of. Let's see what she has to say." Garret held the door for her as they went inside.

"Dinner is on the table." At fifty-eight, Edith Miller usually looked ten years younger. Today she looked every day of her age. Dark moons under her eyes, along with pale skin, and new lines between her eyebrows, made Garret wonder at the genuineness of her smile. He joined the others as they took their assigned places, his across from Hannah, with Peter and Mark on booster chairs to either side of him. His brother, David, had his hands full, with Sue working at the clinic while he managed their four kids. He was currently trying to convince their twin girls to stay seated at the end of the table.

When Hannah studied him questioningly, he shook his head in answer to her raised eyebrows. Hannah, married to a marine lieutenant stationed overseas for six more months, had no children. She said it gave her more time to be a good auntie.

Garret looked to his dad, Arnet, at the other end of the table. It took a lot to get beyond his calm, and today was obviously not crazy enough to do that. At least not yet.

"Shall we pray?" he said as the hubbub quieted. "Heavenly Father, we thank You for this food and our family. Thank You that we can be together and give us peace. Amen."

The two little boys echoed their grandfather's amen and giggled.

"Sorry, I'm late." Garret's baby sister, Becky, had been

nursing their six-month-old baby girl. "She didn't want to stop." Baby sister? Becky was halfway through her twenties.

"You could have brought her out here." Edith finally stopped bringing out filled serving dishes and sat.

"She'll be asleep in a minute if she isn't already."

Everyone passed the bowls and platters, Garret dishing Peter's plate and Mark's according to the boys' choices. "Lots of mashed 'tatoes. Grammy makes good mashed 'tatoes."

"Grammy makes everything good."

"We have apple pie for dessert," Mark announced.

"But only if you clean your plate," Garret countered.

"No, Grammy said I could have pie no matter what."

Garret looked to his mother. "You said that?"

"Not quite." But it did make her smile. Her grandsons could do no wrong.

After dessert, once the children were camped in front of a video, the dogs lying beside them, Hannah poured another round of coffee.

"All right, what's going on?" She sat down and looked directly at her mother.

"I got some bad news at the doctor's this week." Edith sighed before looking up. She raised her hands. "No, no, not terribly bad, but I'm not happy about it."

Dad chided, "Just tell them, dear. You're making them think it's worse than it is."

"Yes. Yes. They told me that I will have to go on insulin. You know I can't stand shots, let alone stabbing my finger so many times in a day. I just can't do it." A stubborn glint showed in her eyes. "I just won't, that's all."

"So, you are saying you have diabetes." Carolyne stated rather than questioned and looked to Garret, who nodded. "Mom, the great majority of diabetics control their blood sugar with diet. You can—"

"The doctor says I'm too far along. Diet and exercise will help but I'll need insulin too."

Carolyne frowned. "Too far along? Haven't you been getting annual physicals? Blood draws?"

"Why should I go to the doctor? I've been perfectly healthy."

As the others bombarded their mother with questions, Garret sat strangely silent. This sounded much worse than he'd thought. She had been borderline diabetic for years, he knew, but she was active and fairly slim for her age. You don't think about diabetes as a serious issue when the person is not overweight, or a smoker, or sedentary, or...

Or so stubborn? Stubborn was a family trait, that was for sure. And it sounded like stubbornness could cause her worse grief than a disease that was under control. When things had settled down, he laid the newspaper on the table. "Have you read this yet?"

Edith shook her head. "No. Is that today's paper?"

"Yes. The 'Home and Health' section. A new product is being produced right here in Eastbrook and should be on the market fairly soon, called Scoparia."

"Says here it is a dietary supplement, not a medication." Becky looked up from reading the article. "And that in the tests and trials, some people are able to go off insulin." She looked to Garret as she passed the paper to David. "But then it would be a drug."

"The papers have been talking about its effect on diabetics. Nothing in the company's literature or labeling says anything about diabetes. I did some research on it."

"You think it's real?"

"I heard about it, and I heard that the FDA is making

noises about classifying it as a drug." Carolyne shoved the paper aside. "Mom, if the doctor says you need insulin, you need insulin, and you're just going to have to girl up and take it, whether you want to or not."

"Easy for you to say."

"Now, Mother..."

Edith turned on her eldest daughter, her voice loud and gritty. "Don't 'Now, Mother' me! I am healthy, other than this, and if I have to change my diet, all right, I will do that. Another thing I read said it can be controlled with exercise. So I'll exercise more. But shots every day, all day? No!"

"They say diet and exercise reduce the problem; sometimes they're not enough." Arnet spoke softly, but they all knew there was steel under the gentleness.

"According to most medical sources, there is no real cure, just control and maintenance." Garret hated to throw more fuel on the fire. But he knew what diabetes did to dogs. He hated to give that diagnosis to pet owners.

"Well, I didn't invite you all here to order me around. I just wanted to say this once and be done with it." Edith pushed to her feet. "I think I will go do the dishes."

Garret watched her march out of the room. This sure wasn't like their mother; was the disease making her cantankerous, too?

The girls scooped up serving dishes and followed her to the kitchen to help clean up, but there was none of the usual happy chatter amongst the women.

Carolyne stuck her head out the kitchen door. "Garret, I'm sending ham home with you. There's a lot left over. Don't forget and leave without it."

Hannah called, "And sweet potatoes. Lot of them left, too."

Garret sat looking at his father, wagging his head. His mom made mashed potatoes, sometimes sweet potatoes, but not both at once. There had been twice too much food on the table; she'd been cooking excessively, even for her. Nervousness? What other signs of her dread and fear had Garret missed because he wasn't here to spot them? "Mom is usually so level-headed. Were you there when the doctor talked to her?"

"No. Wish I had been." Dad studied his coffee mug.

"I'll call the doctor tomorrow and talk to him. She still with Lucas?"

Dad nodded. "Let me know if you come up with anything."

Everyone found excuses to leave earlier than usual. It was obvious that the dissension made them all uncomfortable. Their mother was not being the mother they knew, and no one voiced any ideas what to do about it.

As he gathered his dogs into the back of the car, Garret got his father aside. "What's she like when we aren't all here?"

"Crying, gets angry, calms down, gets mad again. The closets are all clean and well organized. Even the kitchen drawers. Lot of stuff went to a local thrift store our church helps support. She's some upset now, but she'll be okay." He nodded. And nodded some more. "She'll be okay."

When Garret drove off, he wondered if his father was trying to convince him or himself. Or both.

Two people in two days throwing fits that were out of character. He was sure the other Jonah was the real boy, not the screaming, angry child he'd held in his arms. How to help Jonah? How to help his own mother? And what about Dinah? He'd seen her face yesterday, too.

The fear and confusion had been palpable. Successful business tycoon or not, she was one hurting human. *God, I know You have a plan, but since You put me in the middle of these situations, I'd appreciate at least a clue on how You want me to help; but no matter what, not make things worse.*

And while You are at it, we do need another thousand for the remodel—at least.

Chapter Twenty-Four

"Are we going to church today?"

Dinah blinked in the dimness. Jonah, already dressed, stood beside her bed, Mutt at his side.

"I—ah...Give me a minute to wake up. What time is it?"

"Seven. Mutt had to go out and she was hungry. She likes things the same every day."

Right, little man, and so do you. "Did you eat, too?"

She thought a moment about the profound differences in her kitchen—more specifically, her pantry. They had bought cereal—he picked out a couple of different ones—bananas, grapefruit, and hot chocolate. She'd put in some other staples, like pancake mix and eggs. He said he liked peanut butter, crunchy, so that found its way into the cart. Wisely, she'd been driving; she parked in back of Braumeister's and brought out lots of sacks. Lots of sacks, not the paltry little bag she'd sometimes pick up on the way home. They'd made several trips up, and now the cupboards and refrigerator had food inside.

"No. Are we going to church?"

She pushed herself into a sitting position with her pillows against the headboard. "What church?"

"Gramma Trudy said it was the Eastbrook Community Church and if we want to pick them up or meet them to ride the bus, we will learn the way."

"You called Gramma Trudy already this morning?"

"I called her while Mutt was eating. She gets up early."

This was not the way she'd planned to spend her Sunday, but if it helped Jonah, so be it. "What time is church?"

"Sunday School is at nine and church after that. We caught the bus at eight thirty."

"Would you rather we drive or ride the bus?"

"Gramma Trudy sometimes has a hard time getting on the bus."

"Then you call her back and tell her we will pick her up at eight thirty, and if she and Claire would like, we will go out for lunch after church. How does that sound?"

Jonah smiled at her. Perhaps the nice Jonah was back. Bring up yesterday or not? Letting sleeping dogs lie didn't seem like a bad idea right now.

"Can I have Toasted O's with a banana on?"

"You want me to fix it?" He got that look again, the one that said, *I did this before*. "Sorry. I'll get a shower and get dressed."

"Come on, Mutt, let's go eat."

In the shower, she discovered she was hating herself. She'd not been in church since Gramma Grace died. And she had promised herself and the God she no longer believed in that she would never go to a church again. She would never pray again, nor read His book. It was a pack of lies.

And here she was, getting ready to break her word.

What were her options? She turned the water off and, wrapping a towel around her, stepped out on the mat. She could drop the others off at church—he could go with Gramma Trudy just fine—and return to pick them up. She could let Jonah walk over there and take the bus with them. She could curl up under the covers and refuse to answer. She could—nothing else came to mind.

She stared at the face in the mirror and saw a mouthful of frothy toothpaste. Did Garret go to church? Is that how he knew to wrap Jonah in his arms and hold him? Or had his parents done that for him when he was growing up? Or—she spit out the toothpaste and rinsed her mouth. Somehow she had to get control over her mind this morning or she might just end up in a world of hurt.

She dressed in a cowl-necked off-white cashmere sweater dress and was adding her jewelry when a knock came at her door. "What is it, Jonah?"

"I made you some toast with peanut butter. Do you want banana on it, too? My mommy liked peanut butter toast with banana."

Dinah sucked in a deep breath and stared into the mirror. "Ah, yes, Jonah, I would love that. Thank you." What was going on here?

"I didn't make your coffee because I don't know how to use your coffee maker."

"That's fine. I'll be there as soon as I get my boots on."

"Okay."

She heard him and Mutt go back down the hall. Did she even have time for coffee? She pulled her knee-high off-white leather boots from the closet, rammed her feet in, and zipped them up, forcing herself to hurry. She had toast to eat.

She sat at the table. Jonah dropped his head, closed his

eyes, and mechanically recited grace. She ate her breakfast prepared by a seven-year-old. She was not all that
enthusiastic about peanut butter. And she really disliked
banana on it. Was she condemning her future to peanut
butter, bananas, and church? *I don't think so.* But how to
handle this?

"You be good, now," Jonah told Mutt as he grabbed
his jacket off the vacuum cleaner and slammed the closet
door. She still had not gotten closet hooks.

Mutt wagged her tail and whimpered.

"She likes to ride in the car." Jonah pushed the garage
button on the elevator.

"Do you like to ride in the car? Would you like to go
for a drive this afternoon?"

And if so, where?

"Where?"

She dipped her head. "That's what I was wondering."

"Maybe Gramma Trudy would like that."

"You ask her, okay?" Certainly, Gramma Trudy was a
stranger, but she was not destined to remain a stranger.
Dinah rued her inability to relate well to people she did
not know.

Trudy and Claire were waiting at the curb when Dinah
swung into the loading zone in front of the building.

"This is sure a pleasure," Trudy said as Jonah motioned
her to sit in the front seat.

"Did you have a good visit with your family?" Dinah
watched to make sure the older woman could buckle the
seat belt.

"We did. It was a good break. Sorry I didn't get to call
you back, but we returned late last night." She glanced
over her shoulder at Jonah. "I'm so glad you called me
this morning."

Dinah watched for an opening in traffic. "Sorry he called so early."

"Not to worry. I get up early. These old bones begin to complain if I stay in bed too long."

"I have no idea where we are going."

"That's okay. You take Main south to Washington and turn right. Easier to stay on surface streets than get up on the freeway. It's three, four miles away. The bus takes the long way around."

Dinah followed the instructions and parked as near to the entrance as possible. Since they were a bit early, there was plenty of room. The white clapboard church reminded her of the one Gramma Grace used to go to. Why couldn't it at least have been brick or something else?

Trudy took her arm as they made their way to the side door where Jonah was leading them. Claire had his hand, the two of them talking as they walked.

Gramma Grace shuffled along gamely. "Sorry, I'm a bit slow. Wintertime stoves me up some."

"No problem." Dinah caught herself. She hated the way people used *No problem* as a one-size-fits-all response; and particularly when it took the place of *You're welcome*. Now here she was, doing the same. *Think about something else; you can walk in here without your heart going into overdrive.*

Once inside, Jonah waved goodbye and headed down the stairs.

"He's doing all right, then?" Trudy asked.

"Today he is. Friday night and yesterday were rough."

"Not surprising. Shock often lets up about a week, ten days, and then you feel like you want to rip the world apart." Trudy spoke like someone who'd been down the grief trail before, possibly more than once.

"He was too little to remember a whole lot from before his daddy left, and, since he died far away, and he'd not seen his daddy for a while, that made it easier. Not much, but a little easier. But Corinne has been his whole life."

They paused at the doorway to a classroom.

"You have a choice here," Claire said. "Mom goes to the Bible class and I go to the singles class. What would you prefer?"

I'd prefer to go wait in the car. Dinah paused. "Guess I'll go with you, if that's all right." She looked to Trudy, who patted her arm.

"You do whatever you want. Jonah and I will meet you in the sanctuary."

Dinah made sure her public face was pasted on securely and followed Claire into a classroom, where all the chairs were set in a circle. She bit back a groan. This usually meant discussion, not someone lecturing. *Only an hour— you can do anything for an hour. Then church and then you can take these good people to a restaurant and all will be well.*

Claire leaned over *sotto voce.* "Corinne used to go with Mother but she hasn't been well enough for the last months. We brought Jonah along with us."

"He said you rode the bus but he couldn't remember the full name of the church. He wanted to go last Sunday, too." The two of them took seats and Claire introduced her as her friend Dinah Taylor when others greeted them.

Dinah nodded and smiled and shook hands, all the accoutrements of polite behavior.

"Since you are new here, we won't ask you to take part in the discussion, okay?" Claire leaned close enough to whisper.

Dinah breathed a sigh of relief, especially since she had no idea what the discussion was about.

Of the fifteen people in the circle, most of them took part in the discussion about the upcoming Easter week celebrations in Eastbrook. Dinah tuned it out after realizing Easter was only two weeks away.

She smiled and nodded at those who greeted her when they made their way through the hall to the sanctuary. Jonah and Trudy were waiting for them in the third row from the rear. The organ was already playing, so they took their seats with only a nod, Dinah by Jonah. The quiet was surprising as people filed into the pews with a reverent feel.

Perhaps if she just sat here before the beauty of the stained-glass windows, sunshine bringing the window behind the altar to brilliant life, and let the music fill her ears, she would indeed relax. She felt Jonah beside her and smiled down at him.

Maybe this wouldn't be so bad after all. Surely she could tune out the service, especially the sermon. And then they would be on their way. If this helped Jonah, she could handle it.

Until the choir sang. "On a hill far away, stood an old rugged cross…"

Dinah gritted her teeth, wishing she could plug her ears. How had they ever managed to choose that old, old song to sing today? Gramma Grace used to play it on the piano and sing, tears trickling down her cheeks. "I will cherish that old rugged cross…."

The picture in her mind would not go away. She opened her eyes wide, trying to keep the tears at bay, then bit her bottom lip. *I will not cry. I will not!* Gramma Grace had been wrong, dead wrong; Jesus and all that was all a story. The urge to run made her shift and twitch her feet. She could feel Jonah looking at her. His mother told him the same fairy tale: Jesus loves you. If He indeed loved like they said, why was Gramma Grace gone so young, and, even more to the point, what about Michael? Little boys shouldn't die because a child's parents insisted that Jesus would heal him.

Jesus had ignored the prayers and pleas of those people, and took both of those dearest to her.

She fought her demons through the readings, the sermon, the hymns, and pulled herself back to reality as the blessing rolled out over those gathered. "The Lord bless thee and keep thee. The Lord makes His countenance to shine upon thee and give you His peace."

If they hadn't been trapped by those around them, she would have pushed her way out the door. Anything to get away.

But all she could do was nod and smile and smile and nod and wish Trudy didn't know everyone there and Jonah didn't look so engaging and no one could see her. Finally she was unlocking the doors to her car. Everyone slid in and she could suck in a breath deep enough to unhook the band that let her shoulders drop. This was worse than the horrendous interview. At least no one had asked about Corinne. Or if they did, Trudy fielded the questions to protect Jonah.

"So, where would you like to eat? Well, first of all, what sounds good?" Dinah inserted the key in the ignition, realizing her hand was shaking. "Oh, and this is my treat."

Trudy insisted, "You don't have to do that."

"I know, but I want to."

"We used to like to go to Mom's Kitchen. It's not far

from here." Claire spoke from the back seat. "How does that sound, Mom?"

"Delightful. Jonah, what would you like?"

"Fried chicken."

"Oh, they make good fried chicken."

"Not as good as Mommy did."

Trudy nodded. "I remember your mama's good cooking, before she took sick. She used to bring us cookies and when she cooked something special, she'd share it with us."

"Okay, give me the directions." Another deep breath had settled Dinah even more. How had her defenses of all these years been broached so quickly?

She turned right when they told her, turned left, turned...

And she realized she'd never be able to find this place again. Mom's Kitchen was a little cottage sort of building tucked in behind a hardware store. How had these two ever found it in the first place?

The food was indeed good, well seasoned with the stories Trudy told of her earlier life. And Jonah asked her questions. *I wonder if this is what real family feels like?* The question caught Dinah by surprise. Gramma Trudy and Gramma Grace were cut from the same cloth. Maybe it was not family at all; it was simply their generation.

"What did you want to talk to me about?" Trudy asked later in the meal.

"Can I come to your house after school while Dinah is still working?" Jonah beat her to it.

Dinah nodded. "That's the problem. Not all the time, of course, but—"

"Jonah can come every day. Can I really be so blessed?"

"Well, uh, I mean, I . . ."

Trudy laid her hand on Dinah's. "Please, I have missed Jonah. This would be an old woman's pleasure."

Claire nodded. "The two of them are good for each other."

"Can I go get Mutt and bring her, too?"

Trudy looked at Dinah, then Jonah. "If Dinah says that is all right, then Mutt can come, too."

"She doesn't like to be all alone with no friends for so long."

They finished their meal. Dinah dropped Trudy and Claire off at their building and twisted around to see Jonah. "Would you like to go to a movie?"

"Can we rent a movie and have popcorn at your house?"

"I guess, if you like."

"Mutt can't go to a theater."

"Right." Where could she rent a movie? She'd never signed up for Netflix, nor ordered online. "Do you know what you would like to see?"

He nodded. "If you go that way you can rent movies."

She did and found the place, then motioned him to come with her. "You have to choose."

They ended up with two movies. Dinah did all right with the first, a horse story, but the second was so boring she had to fight to keep her eyes open. She so rarely sat still this long without a stack of work in front of her. When they finished, Jonah brought his drawing pad out to the coffee table. She put some music on, trying to decide what to do. Email. Not in her office, because she no longer had an office, but here in the living room with a small boy and a snoring dog. How would that go?

She'd just gotten all set up when she heard, "I don't want to go to school tomorrow."

"What did you say?" She tore her eyes away from the screen.

"I don't want to go to school tomorrow." Jonah kept on drawing.

"Why not?"

Shrug.

"Are you sick?"

"No. I just don't want to go."

Now what do I do? She stared at the top of his head. *If I keep asking why, he might erupt. I hate to make it worse for him. Is it better to just let his comments lie or—*

"And I don't like lunch there."

"Fine, I'll make you a lunch." *What has come over him? How do I help him? I am an absolute disaster as a mother.* "But you have to go to school. It's the law."

He picked up his drawing things, stuffed them in his backpack, and headed down the hall. Mutt looked up at her, over her shoulder to see where her boy was, then got up, shook, and jumped down to follow him.

If dogs could talk, Mutt had just said a mouthful. What had Dinah done to her boy this time?

When she went in to say prayers with him, he was sound asleep, an arm over Mutt, who thumped her tail. Dinah backed out without waking him. Maybe things would be better in the morning. What a not-perfect end to an already difficult day. At least parts of it.

Surprisingly, she went to sleep right away and woke to the alarm at six thirty. *Just get going*, she told herself. Trepidation tried to strangle her heart.

Jonah wore the ugly-kid look in the morning and kept it on. He put the lunch she made in his backpack.

"You want me to cut up that apple?"

"No."

Dinah went to her bedroom and finished dressing. Right on time, they headed out the door to Extraburger. While the weather looked good, the thundercloud over the child beside her made her shiver.

Why didn't he want to go to school? She could ask him again and get another shrug. He obviously wasn't in a mood to be cooperative. Was moodiness a part of grieving? Probably. And why was she so tongue-tied? In the end she could not think of anything at all to talk about, so they ate in silence.

"Jonah? You go to Trudy's this afternoon, remember."

He grunted and left without a word. She almost followed him to make sure he went to school, but her phone chimed, so she took the call while on the way to her office.

Bringing April up to date, Dinah left a lot of information out. "So, I don't know what to do." *I can't talk about my own feelings, let alone getting Jonah to talk about his. Since when did I become a don't-rock-the-boat woman?*

"Probably not much you can do. I suspect Gramma Trudy will be really good for him."

And then the work week kicked in. Typical Monday-morning problems lay in wait, but Dinah felt like they were wading through rather well. The staff meeting got started and out on time and accomplished the things on the agenda. That alone was cause for rejoicing. Dinah had been back at her desk for a short time when April announced a call on One.

"I think it is the principal at Jonah's school."

Dinah picked up. "This is Dinah Taylor. How may I help you?"

"Ms. Taylor, I hate to be the bearer of bad news, but we

have a situation here with Jonah. How soon can you get here?"

"Situation. What do you mean?"

"Please come as quickly as you can."

"I'm leaving right now." What could be happening? Was Jonah hurt?

Chapter Twenty-Five

Monday morning and Garret could still feel the grieving little boy in his arms.

And Garret's mother, grieving along a different path, but grieving all the same. Grief was hard on those nearby, as well. On Garret.

He walked into the office at his usual time. If he hadn't had to be here for the interviews, he could have gone in later, since he would be running urgent care that night. Faulty planning on his part.

The interviews went as most do—nervous people smiling a lot—with the added twist of Skyping the candidate in California. Garret decided he really did not like Skype, but it certainly was handy; much better than a phone interview.

The ordeal finally ended, and he and Sue took their coffees back into his office.

"So what do you think?" Garret studied Sue. When she didn't leap right in, he prompted her. "Who was your number-one choice, or would it be easier to weed out the noes?"

She shook her head, studying her notes. "I wish we

could hire both of the couple, but since that is out and they didn't seem willing to have only one hired, I'd say our California girl—er, woman."

He nodded. "Julie Crick is my first choice. What if..." His voice trailed off. As his brain went off down a bunny trail.

"You're thinking; that's dangerous, you know." Sue leaned back in her chair.

"What if we offered the couple temp work? The urgent care shift, two, three nights a week. Paid hourly or so much a night."

Sue sat forward, animated. "I like that. And, to carry this one step farther, what if West Side Small Animal Clinic and Stassen Animal Hospital did the same thing? There would be enough hours between the three for both to work full time."

Someone to cover urgent care? A lovely prospect! "I wonder if other clinics have done anything like this. There are companies, agencies, that broker temps for nurses and doctors and office help and engineers—all kinds of positions. Why not vet hospitals, too?" He punched the intercom. "Amber, you got a minute?"

Sue had her laptop up and running. "I'll search. Faster."

Their office manager tapped on the door and entered. "What do you need?"

"Sue's looking up vet temp services."

"There are a couple, but they're located in big cities where there are lots of places needing help, like Los Angeles, New York, Dallas. I didn't find any possibles around here."

Sue and Garret stared at her.

She leaned against the doorjamb. "I just thought about

it earlier today. Something Dr. Whanigan said triggered the idea."

Grinning, Garret reached for his phone and stopped. "Do we agree that we bring Julie here for a visit with the prospect of hiring her and get going on the temp idea immediately?"

"Why do I feel we're standing in the middle of the freeway and a full bank of lights are barreling toward us?" Sue sighed.

Amber stood erect. "Because your business partner is hyperactive. Why don't I call that Los Angeles agency—the New York one will be closed now—and see what I can find out? And don't forget you're on duty tonight, Dr. G. Jason will be on with you."

Garret should go home, feed the horde, and grab a nap, but he was too keyed up for a nap. Too much going on. They made the calls and he walked out to his SUV.

Why did life always come in bunches? Things had been cruising along pretty even—busy, but even. The cartoon strip, his artwork, his profession, his church. Suddenly his mom was ill, he was handling the financing of his church's steamroller building project, a sweet lady was about to lose her beloved service dog, and the clinic was poised to hire one and possibly three new people. Hiring on a new person always forced a period of adjustment for the newbie and hirers both. He wanted peace and quiet and work, and hiring new vets would seriously shake up his world. And on top of it all, a dog and two people with haunting eyes were seizing his interest and taking up way too much time at the easel and in his thoughts.

Like now. Again. Jonah, small, hurting, confused, frightened. Dinah Taylor, the enigmatic CEO hotshot. What had he and she both told each other at that strange breakfast in the Extraburger? "You act like you don't like me." Only they both had said it.

And why shouldn't he be cool toward her? She was frosty toward him. It turned him off, big time. Didn't she realize that? CEOs think they know everything and they're a whiz at human relations. Garret knew all about that; once upon a time, long, long ago, he had married one.

But then there was Jonah. Dinah and he would have to put that tortured child ahead of themselves.

Call her! The voice almost shouted in his mind. Was this the Holy Spirit urging him on, or some weird figment of his imagination? He had to have a reason to call. See how Jonah was doing. That would serve. She'd be at work now. What was the name of her company? He'd left that news article with his mom. Food something? Dinah Taylor.

He tapped into his phone's search engine. Food for Life. There it was. Her office. He told his phone to call the number.

A woman answered, a woman with a soft, pleasant voice.

"This is Dr. Garret Miller, the veterinarian caring for Jonah Morgan's Mutt."

"Dr. Miller! Of course. How can I help you?"

"I'd like to speak to Ms. Taylor, please."

"I'm sorry, she's not available right now. Can I take a message?"

You weren't expecting her to be out. Think fast, brain! "I, uh, we took Mutt's stitches out yesterday and I'm just checking. Checking on Jonah, also. He was uncharacteristically upset."

Hesitation. She took a breath he could hear. "Dinah

told me about Jonah's meltdown Saturday." Another deep breath. "This is totally against protocol, but I'm worried. Jonah's school called a couple minutes ago and asked Dinah to come immediately. They wouldn't tell her what the problem was. I'm afraid it could be another meltdown."

"Which school?"

"Lincoln Elementary."

"I know that one. Thank you. I'll call you if I learn something."

"Oh, but I didn't mean you should—But...thank you, Doctor."

Garret pulled into traffic and took the next right turn. Four of his patients' owners went to Lincoln. Five, with Jonah. He had been the featured speaker at their weekly assemblies a couple times. He crossed Main and took Hawthorn over, the back way to Lincoln, and quicker.

Three city police cars were parked outside the school. Two fifty-five. School should have let out by now, but there were the buses, empty and waiting, lined up along the curb. Crossing guards were in place; no children crossing.

A uniformed guard at the entrance to the parking lot stopped him. "Are you here to pick up a student?"

"No. I'm Dr. Garret Miller, a local veterinarian. I'm here to talk to the principal, Ms. Bickle."

The officer brightened. "I know you; you talked to the kids last spring about rabies. And you do that comic strip."

"That's true." *And please let that make a difference right now.* Sometimes celebrity could be a help.

"Well, I'm sorry, Doctor." And the fellow did in fact

look sorry. "The school is in lockdown. No one enters or leaves."

"Lockdown..."

An officer in a flak vest came around the far corner. Another stepped out the main doors, radio in hand, talking. Two more got out of a police car at the curb near the front entrance and opened the vehicle's doors.

Garret stared. "What in the world is happening?"

"A student smuggled a weapon into the school."

"Weapon...Who would...". He sighed. "I remember a day when the worst thing you could do in class was chew gum."

"Ain't it the truth."

Four of his clients, kids with their pictures on his wall, huddled in there somewhere, locked in their classrooms. What a rotten thing for a kid to have to go through. And somewhere in there, poor little Jonah was cowering under some desk. *Please, God, if You sent me here, open the doors.*

At that moment, the front doors to the school swung open. Two officers came walking smartly out. A woman and child. More officers. Was the whole squad here? All the officers wore those bulky protective vests and riot helmets. The officer nearest the prowl car reached out, grabbed the woman's head, and pushed it down, ducking her physically into the back seat. The child was stuffed in next to her. They had their perps, as they say.

It was Dinah and Jonah.

Furious didn't begin to cover what Dinah was feeling. All this over a small paring knife Jonah had slipped into his backpack to cut up his apple.

"I'm sorry." Jonah stared at his hands.

"I know." *Me, too.* So now Jonah was suspended indefinitely. And arrested. No, not arrested, at least not formally. Detained. By uniformed officers. If that wasn't a good definition of *arrested*...

At least they hadn't handcuffed him.

A seven-year-old boy who until last week had absolutely nothing on his record to show anything but an exemplary student. Well, except last Friday, when he'd gotten into a brief push-and-shove fight. Apparently the class bully snatched a drawing and Jonah grabbed it back.

To quote the principal, and Dinah could almost repeat it verbatim, "I was planning to call you Friday, but I waited to see if problems continued. I know his mother died. We were expecting some kind of normal acting out; it's a way children deal with grief and stress. But the school has a zero-tolerance policy regarding any kind of weapon or anything that even looks like a weapon. I'm sorry, Ms. Taylor. *Zero* tolerance."

How should she, a mommy in disguise, deal with this?

The cruiser drove into the police garage. The door dropped shut behind them. Dinah and Jonah were escorted from the car and led into a room with a long counter on the far end, where they were shown to sit on chairs along a wall.

A brass name tag identified the officer who sat down beside her as Lewiston. "I'm sorry, Ms. Taylor. With all the school incidents happening around the country, everyone is edgy. Zero tolerance."

"Zero tolerance. I keep hearing that. I see." But she did not see. None of this made any kind of sense. Maybe if Jonah was older and the rules had been drilled into his head...

At a counter across the room, another officer was methodically removing everything from Jonah's backpack, apparently inventorying its contents. The invasion of privacy rattled Dinah. Should she speak up, say something about search warrants? She sat mute.

"You understand how alert schools are now." Officer Lewiston was not so much as glancing at Jonah; it was as if the boy were not there. "We take every precaution to prevent serious accidents or violence from happening, of course, and sometimes we have to err on the side of caution."

"Thank you. That part I do understand. What will happen now?"

"You will be given forms to fill out. You will meet with another officer, you will be given an appointment with the judge, and then you can take Jonah home. If he were older he might be facing time in juvie."

Dinah gritted her teeth and forced a polite smile to stay in place. Feeling a small hand sneaking into hers, she looked down. Jonah sat as close to her as he could get, shrunken in on himself, his bottom lip quivering.

She heard the *whoosh* of the door opening and looked up. Dr. Miller strode in like he owned the place. Her heart leaped into her throat. What was he doing here? His smile telegraphed reassurance. A quick flash of his holding Jonah swooped through her mind.

He crossed to her. "I arrived at the school a few minutes ago and—"

Officer Lewiston stood up. "Are you her attorney?"

"No, I—"

"Then I'll have to ask you to wait over there."

"Involved party." Dr. Miller sounded so firm and official that even Dinah believed him.

"Jonah Morgan?" A female uniformed officer called from the counter across the room.

Dinah and Jonah stood up. So did Officer Lewiston. Did he think they would run away or something? *He's just doing his job*, she reminded her clenched jaw. They stepped up to the counter and the clerk asked for her ID. The process had begun.

The woman in uniform slid a clipboard with several sheets of forms across to her. "While you fill these out, I'll see when Sergeant Peters can see you. Things are kind of quiet right now, so it shouldn't be too long."

"Thank you." They returned to their seats.

A woman beckoned Officer Lewiston, so he excused himself and left as they sat back down. Dr. G settled down on the other side of Jonah. Dinah ran down the form. Relationship to the accused. How did she explain that: The judge had not made anything official yet. Complainant. She didn't know. Time of infraction. Surely someone knew; she did not. She filled out what she could and left a lot of blanks.

A woman in a plain gray suit appeared at a hall door. "Ms. Taylor? Jonah Morgan? Sergeant Peters will see you now." The woman raised a hand as Garret approached. "Are you her lawyer?"

"No, ma'am, involved party."

"Then I'll have to request that you remain out here. They shouldn't be long."

Should I have called a lawyer? Of course! She should have called Mr. Jensen immediately. Dinah wished Hal were in town. Since she had just gotten thrown into the parenting pool without any preparation, both Hal's presence and his counsel would have helped stem the threatening flood of tears.

The interview lasted all of fifteen minutes and seemed quite rote and technical. They returned to their chairs in that dingy room. And waited.

A different woman, this one in a pale blue suit, appeared at a different door. "Judge Kittles can see you now."

Again Garret was told to remain behind.

Jonah clung to her hand as if terrified they would jerk him away.

She hoped she smiled down at him. "It's going to be okay, Jonah." But she was afraid neither of them believed her words.

They were ushered into a severe room with no curtains at the windows and directed to two chairs in front of a zip-code-size mahogany desk. Behind it sat Judge Kittles. Jonah tugged his chair slam into Dinah's and sat pressed against her.

Judge Kittles was a woman, but she had a remarkably commanding presence. She wore neither robes nor a fearsome judge face, and she sat at ease, eye level with Dinah. Why a judge now? Why not a court date somewhere in the interminable future? Dinah knew nothing about how this all worked. Her lack of familiarity with the process was almost as bad as the process itself.

Dinah noticed then that judge's chin was lighted. Instead of the traditional blotter, her desktop had a big glass window with, no doubt, a computer monitor below it. She moved a wireless mouse around with her right hand.

The judge studied Jonah a long moment. She looked at Dinah. "He's not been in trouble before, is that correct?"

"That is correct. Except: an hour ago, the school principal told me that there was some sort of skirmish last

Friday. She passed it off as normal acting out. He lost his mother very recently."

The judge nodded. "Let me explain briefly. Quite a few children go through the system, even in a city this small. If the child is a repeat offender—one of our frequent flyers, if you will—we deal with him or her in the usual formal manner: formal charge, arraignment, court date. If it is a child without any prior record who goes afoul of zero tolerance or another standard policy, we try to handle the case quickly and send them back out the door."

"I see." Actually, for once Dinah did see.

The judge looked at Jonah. "So you brought a knife today to protect yourself, right? Possibly to stab the child you argued with last week."

"No, ma'am. I didn't think of that." Jonah's voice was nearly a whisper.

"Then why did you put a knife in your backpack?"

"To cut my apple up and peel it. My mommy always peeled my apples when I took my lunch and I didn't let Dinah do that 'cause, 'cause . . ." His lower lip quivered.

"You didn't want her to peel your apple because . . ." the judge prompted.

Jonah murmured, "Because she doesn't do things right, like my mommy did."

Dinah's heart thumped.

"I see. And your mommy can't do those things for you any longer."

"She went to live with Jesus and I want her to come back, but Dinah said she can't and I know that, but I still want her to."

The judge sat back a bit, nodding, apparently mulling this. "And you were angry at Dinah?"

Jonah nodded, tears meandering down his cheek, one at a time.

"Tell me about this confrontation with your classmate; the principal's notes call it a shoving match. Tell me about that."

Jonah shrugged. "He took my picture so I pushed him away and grabbed it back, but it ripped and I wanted to give it to Dinah 'cause I can't give my pictures to my mommy anymore. I only got half of it back."

"Have you fought with him before? Got into shoving matches?"

"No, ma'am. Mostly he just pokes me with his pencil or something. He does that to lots of kids."

The judge sat there a moment. "Do you have any of your pictures in your backpack now?"

Jonah nodded. "I drew a new one for Dinah."

How had the judge summoned an officer? Dinah heard no bell, saw no motion. The officer simply appeared in the doorway. The judge told him to give Jonah his backpack, then sat back and waited. The fellow hastened out and returned in moments. He handed the backpack to Jonah. The boy clutched it to his chest and watched the judge.

"May I see one of your pictures, please?" The judge's voice seemed softer than it had been before.

Jonah nodded and carefully pulled out a picture. He stood to hand it to her across that vast desk, then took his seat and slid his hand back into Dinah's.

The woman studied the picture, studied Jonah, back to the picture. She pursed her lips. "You are seven years old according to the incident report; is that, right, Jonah?"

He nodded.

"And you did indeed draw this?"

He nodded again.

She looked at Dinah. "Have you seen this?" When Dinah shook her head, she handed the drawing over.

It was another of his magnificent pencil drawings, every detail in place down to the whiskers and every-which-way fur. Mutt sat there, head down, and a tear rolling off her face into a puddle by her paw.

Dinah tipped her head back. *Oh, Jonah. My poor Jonah.* She reached into her bag for a tissue and handed one to Jonah.

The judge took a deep breath and sat back. Again she seemed to be mulling something. Would Jonah be sentenced now or turned loose? How did all this work?

She addressed Jonah. "Young man, taking a sharp knife to school is absolutely wrong. Did they tell you about weapons? What not to bring?"

A very small voice. "Yes, ma'am."

The judge sat silent, looking at him. The silence worked. His voice rose a bit. "It isn't a weapon, though. It's just a knife. For an apple. Weapons are to kill people."

"I understand your point, but it's considered a weapon nonetheless." She turned her eyes to Dinah. "Ms. Taylor, I see a lot of tough kids every day, and I know I am not looking at one now. Have you engaged a grief counselor for him?"

"Not yet. There are so many things I haven't done yet. I'll do so, of course."

"That is one condition of his release. The boy is hurting very badly, Ms. Taylor. You are married?"

"No."

"You have other children?" *Why is this woman prying?*

"No."

"I want to see him again. In the meantime, set up a schedule with a grief counselor."

"Certainly." Dinah should have engaged Mr. Jensen immediately. Another huge mistake. But she had been so rattled.

"And Jonah, no more knives, weapons or not weapons. Understand?"

Jonah nodded as he studied the floor.

Like magic, the officer entered to escort them back out into the waiting area.

Dinah stood, so Jonah stood. She mumbled some sort of words of gratitude or something and hastened out, the picture clutched in her hand.

Garret was still there. He stood. "I'll take you home."

"My car is at the school."

"Fine. We'll pick that up and then I will take you two out for supper. Would that be all right with you, Jonah? I want to hear about what happened."

Jonah smiled and reached for his hand. "Yes."

Dinah nodded. Right now, his act of kindness made her want to turn and run. Before the tidal wave of tears deluged her shore.

Chapter Twenty-Six

Blindsided. Gob-smacked. Splacked between the eyes. A dozen other phrases Dinah had heard to describe how she felt just now rattled in her head. She stared out the windshield of her car at a fuzzy world.

Was it better having Dr. Miller be helpful or not around at all? His appearance at the police station had caught her totally unprepared. When he walked in that door, it brought a breath of—what? Of sanity? Someone caring? Or one more bit of craziness that might just tip her over the edge? After all, every encounter she'd ever had with him irritated her and, obviously, him, too.

But that was before he held Jonah and let him cry.

If she were totally honest with herself, what was she feeling? Relief? Joy? Exquisite joy?

She checked the rearview mirror, saw him and Jonah waiting in the SUV, and decided she better get to moving or he'd be at her door to see if she was all right. Of course she wasn't all right! There wasn't any all right to be had, not that she could see, at least not in the immediate future. The whole incident had terrified her, and if it terrified her, what had it done to Jonah?

She started the car and snapped her seat belt into place. Before Jonah, she'd never realized how many little things she took for granted, like getting home when she felt like it, eating when and if she felt like it, working late or going in early, and getting up on the weekends when she felt like it. Now she couldn't even go running without consulting with someone else.

And now? Jonah would be home for heaven knew how long. Gramma Trudy had said she'd be so happy to have Jonah come be with her after school, but this was different. This was full time.

Dinah pulled into her parking garage. Home sweet home? Hah. Resigned to a world that paid no attention to what she wanted, she locked up and walked to the door with Dr. Miller and Jonah.

"Where's your key, Jonah?"

"On my night stand. I forgot it."

She let them in to find Mutt dancing in circles. She'd not sent anyone to walk the dog. One more whack between the eyes.

"Mutt's gotta go." Jonah snapped her leash on. "Sorry, Mutt, we'll hurry." Out they went.

Dinah closed her eyes and leaned her forehead against the kitchen door. One more thing she should have remembered to do. Near panic had a way of washing the mind slate of anything not immediately connected to the emergency. Poor dog. If she messed in the house, it wasn't her fault.

"Are you okay?" The deep male voice sounded out of place in the stillness of her condo. When Jonah and Mutt left, it was as if both she and the house gave a sigh of relief. The only polite answer was *Of course.* She shrugged instead and turned to give him what she hoped was a confident smile. Instead her lower lip wobbled. If she relaxed the steel bars she had on her emotions, letting loose the deluge, would he take her in his arms like he had Jonah?

That thought made her catch her breath. "Thanks, but yes, I'll manage." Not quite the answer she wanted but better than the alternative.

"He takes Mutt outside?"

"In the back alley." She could feel her eyes widen. "He didn't get his key." She grabbed her bag and dug her keys out. "I'll be right back." By the time she reached the exit door to the stairs, she realized Garret was right beside her. They double-timed down the stairs, but Jonah and Mutt met them halfway up the last flight.

Jonah looked unconcerned. "What?"

"You didn't have your key. I was afraid you locked yourself out."

"I stuck my jacket in the door so it couldn't close all the way."

"Jonah, you are one smart kid." Garret chuckled. "Good thinking."

Dinah made her mouth smile, but she knew it didn't it make to her eyes.

"Where shall we go to eat?" Garret asked.

She wanted to go to bed and pull the covers high. That was where she wanted to go.

Jonah darted up the stairs. "I have to feed Mutt first."

Dinah slogged back up the stairs behind him. She glanced around her living room and realized that a new arrangement of cut flowers graced the coffee table. Might there be a clue this time? No, only the card from Minda with the packets to put in the water to make the flowers last longer. And her signature of Happy Day with a smiley face.

The pink underpetals of the lilies were still tight in buds, but their redolence didn't wait for the flowers to open. Dinah inhaled the rich fragrance.

"They're lovely." Garret was smiling at them.

"They are. If only I knew who sends them."

The smile fell away. "What do you mean?"

"Fresh flowers show up every now and then, sometimes for a special occasion, like the launch. I have no idea who they are from."

"Doesn't the florist know?" He shrugged. "Sorry, dumb question."

"Minda, who owns the shop, won't or can't tell me. She delivers them herself."

"Mutt's taken care of." Jonah planted himself beside them. "Pizza?"

Garret grinned. "Come on. I know this great Italian place on the west side. Pizza, pasta, and standard American burgers." He opened the door for them.

Dinah sighed. "Fine with me. I'm not in the mood for a big supper." She wasn't in the mood for anything. Washed out. Limp. She locked the door behind her and they piled into Dr. Miller's big SUV. It smelled vaguely like dog. She belted in and laid her head back against the headrest, closing her eyes. Behind her Jonah was asking if the restaurant had meatballs.

She should be engaging in witty repartee. Or witless repartee. Something. Anything. "How did you find out where we were?"

"Called your office to see how Mutt and Jonah were doing, and your assistant told me. You came out of the school, so I followed the squad car. I called her back from the police station. She said to tell you not to worry about calling her. She'd have her prayer warriors in action."

Dinah must have shaken her head. Everywhere in her world, she kept running into...

His voice was strong, a voice to match his bulk. "I take it you don't believe in prayer warriors."

"Let's say I don't believe in much of anything and leave it at that, okay?" Somehow she'd already known, or sensed, that he was a believer, like April. One more strike against him. She wasn't sure why she felt that, but her antenna was pretty accurate. *Just don't start preaching to me or I swear I will, I will—do something. And it won't be pleasant.*

The restaurant was everything she had feared—big, bustling, cheerful, with crisp red gingham curtains and a relentlessly happy attitude. All just the opposite of what she felt now.

"Dr. Miller, welcome! Good to see you!" The receptionist snatched up two menus, a child's placemat, and a box of crayons and marched off toward a corner booth. So he was a regular here.

They settled into the booth, Jonah and Dinah facing Dr. Miller. Jonah studied his placemat.

Dr. Miller opened. "You have a very lovely home. But then I am not surprised."

She started to just say thank you but that caught her. "Why? I mean, why are you not surprised?"

"Because everything you do, you do with class. I like your leitmotif; white with splashes of brilliant primary colors. Your condo and your style of dress. It works perfectly."

"Th-thank you." Now what?

He said softly, very conversationally, "Why did you choose that? All the white, I mean."

That is none of your business. But for some reason, the

heavy weariness was robbing her of her usual defenses. How else could she explain why she actually answered his question? "For a while, I wore black. A lot of black. I even found a black lab coat for the lab. Then a close friend said, 'You'll come across to business associates much better if you don't wear black. You'll feel better, too.' So I tried white and liked it. When I bought this condo they asked me what color to repaint the interior and I said white. Easy to decorate."

The server appeared, took drink orders, and left.

Jonah piped up, "Dr. G? Is *ziti* the same as *zit*?"

Dr. Miller laughed, and even Dinah smiled. "It's a macaroni sort of pasta in the shape of a hollow tube, about this long by this wide." He held up fingers to demonstrate.

"Why a hollow tube?"

"So it cooks faster and the sauce you put on it gets inside as well as outside."

"Can I have ziti?"

"Sure thing."

"And meatballs?"

"Yep."

Dinah realized she'd not even looked at the menu. She flopped it open. "What do you recommend?"

Dr. Miller replied, "The house specialties are the clam spaghetti and the lasagne."

The drinks arrived. She felt so numb when she ordered that when the server left she couldn't remember what she'd said. Her dinner was going to come as a complete surprise.

Dr. Garret said, "You had a pretty rough day today, Jonah. Want to tell me about it?"

And Jonah launched into a narrative at once so compelling and so boring that Dinah could not stay focused on it. Her thoughts wove themselves in and out of his monologue. For one thing, she was angry. Despite all the recent publicity about bullying, the school seemed to be doing nothing about that kid in Jonah's class who liked to poke others and grab papers off their desks. Perhaps she should look into private schooling. There were so many things she should look into and do and—her to-do list was becoming book length.

Dinner came. She had ordered the lasagna.

Jonah did his *Come, Lord Jesus* prayer and added his "Tell Mommy hi," then he added more: "Please tell her I'm sorry, I didn't mean to..."

Dinah sniffed and blinked furiously. Was this the straw that would—

Garret struck his fist on the table. "Oh no!"

"What? Are you all right?"

"I'm supposed to be at the clinic in five minutes!" He dug his cell phone out of his chest pocket.

"We can take this to go."

"No. We'll eat here." He paused a moment and told his phone, "I'm sorry, Sue. A lot has been going on. I'll be at least an hour late." He listened, nodding. "Yes, we're fine. I'll be there as soon as I can. Thanks."

He pocketed the phone and smiled at Jonah. "It's all right. We'll go ahead and eat."

He looked at Dinah as he picked up his fork. "You mentioned a black lab coat. You worked in a lab?"

"Biochemist."

"Interesting." He ate quietly a few minutes. "So you hired on at Food for Life as a chemist?"

"I started the company. And I still love the bench work better than administration."

"I know the feeling. I wish my job were just doctor-

ing animals and not all the rest of the hooey that goes
with it."

Even though Garret had showed up at the police station like one of the comic book heroes, she didn't really
know him. And up until today, hadn't really cared for
him—at all, and that was putting it mildly. And now
here he was painting himself as just a regular guy. And
she felt far too drained to assess or reassess the situation.

The lasagne was excellent. Jonah put his ziti away with
enthusiasm, so that must have been good, too. And Dr.
Miller with his clam spaghetti—the sauce was melted butter and lots of chopped clam meat and, no doubt, various
herbs to set it off perfectly. Why had she never even heard
of this place?

Because her life was a big rut and this restaurant was
outside that rut. That was why. Did she want to climb out
of her rut? No. It was comfortable, thank you. She appreciated comfort.

Jonah finished and pushed his plate aside. He explored
inside the crayon box and pulled out blue. He began coloring the outline drawing on his placemat.

Dr. Miller gestured with his fork. "You're coloring everything blue. Why blue?"

Jonah shrugged. "There's no black in the box. It's closest to black. I like pencils better than crayons, but sometimes Mrs. Farrell makes me draw with crayons. I draw
my drawings with pencils. Daddy showed me how to use
hard pencils and soft pencils. I like pencils best."

"I want to see your work. You have excellent fine motor
control."

"Thank you." He studiously applied himself to making
the elephant, the tiger, and an ostrich blue.

Dr. Miller simply handed their server a credit card when she stopped by to ask about dessert. She smiled and left. "Take you back to your place, Ms. Taylor? Do you have to stop at a grocery store or anything first?"

"Home would be lovely. This day has pretty much taken all the air out of my tires."

He smiled, a sort of sad half-smile, or an understanding kind of smile. "I should think so. Jonah, you can take the crayons with you. And your picture."

They drove back to Dinah's condo in silence, except for Jonah's occasional questions. Dinah let Dr. Garret answer him.

He saw them to the elevator and said good night. The cage hummed them upstairs. Dinah opened the door.

Suddenly she realized, "Your backpack. We don't have your backpack."

He stopped, frowned. "I don't remember where it is."

"We'll look for it tomorrow." She headed for her bathroom.

Someone knocked at the door. She heard Jonah answer it. She was going to have to educate Jonah about not opening the door for just anybody. In fact, for a kid as streetwise as he was, you'd think he would know more about safety.

Dr. Garret's voice. He and Jonah were diving instantly into some sort of conversation.

She finished and came hurrying out. Now what? He was supposed to be at work.

Jonah was beaming. He raised his backpack. "It was in Dr. G's car. He just noticed it and brought it up."

"Thank you!" Dinah met the man's eye and he held hers easily. "That was very thoughtful of you. Especially when you're in a hurry to get to the clinic."

He smiled. "Priorities. Jonah just offered to show me some of his work."

"He's very good at it. The one on the refrigerator, for example."

Dr. Miller walked over and studied it. "You did this?"

"Yes sir. I'll get the others."

From her hobo bag, Dinah retrieved the drawing Jonah had shown the judge. "He did this one at school."

The artist who cared for animals wagged his head. "He has amazing talent. Good eye, excellent control. And a master with pencils. Look at the shading on that fur. It looks like fur."

Jonah plopped onto the sofa with a box. Instantly, Dr. Miller settled beside him. She wanted to tell him, *Jonah, the doctor has to get to his clinic.* But she said nothing. Mutt struggled up onto the sofa and laid her head on Jonah's lap, looking at the pictures as if she recognized herself and approved.

"Do you draw anything besides Mutt?"

"Sometimes."

"Have you ever painted?"

"No. I don't like paints much. Or crayons."

The doctor studied him a moment. "I see. You prefer black and white."

Jonah nodded.

Jonah's whole world was black and white; why had Dinah not seen that? Yes or no. This or that. You either do it right or you're wrong. No shades of gray.

Jonah waved a hand toward the boxes still stacked against the wall. "There's more in the boxes. Mommy kept them all."

"Good. Glad she appreciated fine art." He gestured toward the wall. "Jonah's things?"

Dinah grimaced. "I've been meaning to get them moved into his room."

"Let me."

"What? Well, uh..."

"Ms. Taylor. May I call you Dinah?"

"Yes. Garret?"

"Please." He stood up. "You do not have to do everything yourself, Dinah. Please, let me."

She stuttered and shifted her feet and heaved a sigh like a balloon losing all its air. "I don't...of course. If you can take those two larger ones, I'll take the smaller ones." He picked up a large carton and she hurried ahead of him down the hall into what used to be her office and pushed open the louvered doors to the closet. She yanked out the vacuum cleaner and mop and stepped back.

He tucked the box into a back corner. "Jonah. Hey, Jonah? Can you put your clothes on the bed until we get these moved?"

Jonah hopped right to the task.

The whole project took less than five minutes, including putting Jonah's clothes back in. So simple. So easy. A task she'd not gotten around to for days had been completed so swiftly. Not only that, but Dr. Miller—Garret—popped the clothes pole up out of its brackets and rested it across two of the cartons, holding it in place under the weight of boxes above it; Jonah could now hang up his clothes at his level.

The doctor took his leave then, and she locked the door behind him.

She disliked disorder. Those stacked boxes had been disorderly; her living room was back to its neat, orderly, normal state, except, of course, for the stain.

And a hideous, ugly, evil thought struck her: Jonah

needed so much more than she could possibly ever give him. He needed a real mom, not a bumbling, inept one who wasn't even certain how to love him, and he needed a dad. A man. Was she keeping him from what he needed most?

She must give serious consideration to the possibility of turning him over to fosterage so that he could have a real home.

Chapter Twenty-Seven

The scream came again. "No! No!" And garbled.

Dinah sat up. Was it her? Had she been screaming? The dream—was it a dream?

"No, no, I—mean to. No."

She was half way to his door before she realized she was out of bed. Jonah. It was Jonah. She opened his door to see him sitting straight up in bed, Mutt licking his face. Even in the dim light she could see that his eyes weren't focused. She crossed to the bed and sat down gently.

Mutt whimpered.

"Mo-m-m-y." The cry trailed off.

Dinah leaned over and gathered him into her arms, having no idea if this was best or not. "I'm here Jonah, I'm here. You're going to be okay, sweetheart." Her words drifted into mother murmurs as she stroked his back. With his arms clamped around her, he shuddered and whimpered. She laid her cheek on his head and kept on.

She'd done this before. Many years before. With another little boy who often had nightmares with no one else to comfort him. But she knew the difference. This was Jonah. That had been her little brother. But the comfort worked the same.

When Jonah relaxed against her, his breathing changed. It became even, with a hiccup once in a while, as he slept in her arms. Mutt lay stretched beside her thigh, her chin on Dinah's leg, her tail swishing every once in a while.

Her back cramping, Dinah laid him back on his pillow, stroked the hair back off his forehead, kissed him, and patted the dog, who licked her hand. Mothers comforted with whatever came to hand.

Return to her room or stay here? Would she be needed again? Would Jonah remember this in the morning? As far as she knew, he never really woke up. Could this be like sleepwalking?

When she began to shiver, she made her way back to her own bed and crawled under the covers. Getting warm enough to sleep took some time, or maybe her mind did not want to switch off. Which, she didn't know, and she didn't have the energy to puzzle it through.

"Dinah? If I can't go to school today, what am I going to do?"

She sat bolt upright in bed. It was morning.

He was standing there, like usual. "Do you want a peanut butter and banana toast?"

She was going to tell him yes, but she stopped herself. "I don't think so."

"Mommy really liked peanut butter and banana toast."

I am not your mother and never can be. We're going to have to sit down and straighten that out soon. "Jonah, let me get dressed and get going and we'll talk about it."

He shrugged and walked out toward the kitchen.

Her phone sang while she was brushing her teeth. She hit the speaker. "Yeff."

"Dinah?"

"Yeff. Tooffpashte. Minute." She spit and rinsed her mouth. "Sorry. April? You're not in the office already, are you?"

"I came in early. Dinah, be prepared for headlines with photos."

Dinah slipped her brush into the holder. "Maybe I should start subscribing to the paper."

"I have them here. When will you be in?"

"Them? As in plural?" Dinah stared at the mirror, her stomach already tightening. "Give me an hour."

"A short hour, please."

April was usually so efficient and in control; this morning she sounded angry or fearful. Dinah clicked off and headed for the kitchen, zipping up her pullover fleece robe as she went. The condo was chilly. Had she not set the thermostat last night? She checked on her way down the hall. What other normal thing had she neglected in all the turmoil? When she realized she'd flipped the Off switch last night, she turned it on again, set it for day, and entered the kitchen. It was not just her competence as a mother that was eroding rapidly.

Mutt was munching kibble, Jonah was sitting at the table, drawing pad out and pencil in hand.

"What do you want to eat?"

He shrugged. "Banana and peanut butter toast and cereal?"

"Fine with me. You want to get stuff out of the fridge?" She reached into the cupboard for cereal boxes and bowls, set them on the counter, and turned her attention to the coffee maker. Should she bring up what had happened yesterday or not? What about the nightmare? Ask if he remembered? How do you treat a child in a situation like this?

What would her parents have done? Whoa, do not go there. Whatever had brought that idea into her mind? What would Gramma Grace have done? That was no help, either. She had no point of reference to base anything on. Ask April? April was a wise and experienced mom whose kids never got in trouble.

She set her coffee on the table and sat down so Jonah could say grace. This time he kept to the script. She answered the call of the toaster and brought the two pieces back to the table, where Jonah had set the peanut butter. While she spread her toast with butter, she watched him carefully, meticulously cut his banana onto his cereal.

"You want another banana on your toast?"

"I can have two?" His look of amazement jabbed her heart. Bananas were something that could always be purchased, and she could have as many as she wanted. Over and over she was realizing what *poor* meant.

"If you like. Or jam, or plain PB."

"Honey is good, too."

"Sorry, we don't have honey."

"I know, but it is good. Maybe we could buy some honey sometime?" At her nod, he sort of smiled and said, "Jam, then, but I can put it on."

"Yes, you sure can." She set the jar in front of him.

The miserable phone sang again. She didn't recognize the number. "Yes?"

"Dinah, this is Garret. Just checking to see if the two of you are all right. You seemed a little shaky last night."

"We're fine." *Liar.* "Look, can I call you later? April wants me to get to the office ASAP."

"Good. Talk later."

She stared at the phone. He hung up just like that. As if he was glad he didn't have to talk to her. Or was that her wild imagination?

She made it to the office in less than an hour. As per her instructions, Jonah headed back to stay in the break room or watch TV in the conference room. He did not look the happiest, but the ugly face did not appear. He even smiled at April on his way past her desk.

April smiled back at him and turned dead serious again. "The newspapers are on your desk; this sheaf of slips"— she jammed them into Dinah's hand—"is calls for quotes and opinions, of which you have none. Hal says call him on his cell, and there is a message from Mr. Jensen regarding a court appointment for the adoption proceedings. I'll fix coffee and bring it in as soon as I can find a minute. And I want to know about Jonah."

"As to the last, so do I. One more thing to add to that miserable list: What to do about Jonah? I tell you, April, I'm about ready to just pull him out of that school." She waved her sheaf of call slips. "I'll call Mr. Jensen first."

"Good idea."

Her home had been invaded by aliens with two feet and with four. But here in her office, Dinah reigned in her fortress, her place of strength, the place where she could hide out if necessary. She laid her calendar out on her desk. While she had one on the computer along with the rest of the twenty-first-century world, this old-fashioned hands-on calendar helped her plan better. April would transfer her penciled info to the electronic calendar later.

First call.

Mr. Jensen himself answered, not his secretary. "Good

morning to you, too, Dinah. I have some welcome news. The judge to whom your case was assigned is going on vacation to the Virgin Islands."

"That's welcome?"

"They've moved all his cases up to this week. Can you meet me at the courthouse at two o'clock today? Meet with the judge and me and get those papers signed."

"But…" Actually, two o'clock was doable.

"The paperwork is all in place. The process should go smoothly. And quickly, if he's going to get through everything this week."

"What should I bring?"

"Just Jonah. The judge would like to meet him. Standard procedure."

"Okay. He is not in school today, so that won't be a problem." Was she bitter? Are footballs pointy?

There was a sort of grunt at the other end. "I read the papers this morning. I rather wish you had called as the situation was developing."

"Mr. Jensen, I was so confused and dumbstruck, I didn't even think of you until too late. I'm sorry. I'm just not used to this role." *And I am not a fit parent. I must talk to you about that.*

"Let's meet at one forty-five in the coffee kiosk under the stairs."

"I know the place. One forty-five."

Dinah clicked off and picked up the top paper. *Weapon. Criminal. Prominent CEO. Arrest. School threat.* And pictures! A photographer had been on the scene and he or she snapped pictures of that long, long walk from the front doors of the school to the squad car, as she was being stuffed into that back seat. Incriminating pictures. It wouldn't even have to be a photographer. It could be any parent with a cell phone, waiting anxiously to gather up her little cherub.

All innuendo, no truth. Misleading. Could she sue the papers? Probably not. She and Jonah were hardly the first victims to be tried and convicted in the press. She ripped up the messages from the hopeful press without looking at them and punched in Hal's number.

He didn't even say *Hello, how are you*. "Not a good morning there, is it?"

"Not really. When are you coming home?"

"At the airport now. April said you'll be appearing before a judge. About that school incident?"

"No, the adoption. Mr. Jensen and I will be meeting with a Judge Henny at two p.m. with Jonah."

"Henny. Good. Good man, Henny. The bright spot is that there's prominent mention of Scoparia, so we are getting publicity, anyway. Oh, and Dinah? There are rumors that the FDA is about to pounce, so be prepared for that, too."

"Oh sure, and how does one prepare for such, such..." She shook her head. "I am running out of words."

"Columbus, six thirty-nine. Sorry; talking to the check-in woman. You do realize all sorts of special-interest groups will be after you to sue the school district for harassment."

"Why? Jonah clearly broke the rules."

"Trust me. It will happen. Your problem, Dinah, is that you are a very good-looking woman. Photogenic. If you were a hag, the press wouldn't be half as interested. And you and Jonah are great human interest. Poor little orphan boy. Heart tuggers. The press stocks up on human-interest stories to spring on slow news days."

"Lovely." All she wanted to do was work in her nice quiet lab.

"I am confident that this craziness will not affect our profits and may even enhance them. Gate twenty-seven; thank you. Just keep your head low. Gotta run."

Dinah snapped off her cell phone as April walked in the door with two large mugs of coffee and set them on the desk. "Be right back." She returned carrying a platter from Braumeister's with a Swedish or Jewish tea ring; Dinah could not remember which.

"Where's Jonah? He'd probably like a piece of this."

April sat down. "Randy took him along on errands."

As she feared, Jonah was getting in the way, big time. "Doesn't Randy have work to do?"

"He's doing it. Picking up glacial acetic acid and that industrial peroxide you wanted over at Chem-pure, and on the way back he'll get the mail in our post office box."

Dinah sipped her coffee. "Elixir. Thank you. I'm going to have to talk to Trudy today, set something up. Either with her or someone else. This is the problem. He has to stay home from school, but it can't seem like a vacation, either. I mean, there are consequences for his actions. And I have no idea what to do. It seems to me that no matter where I turn in this, I am the one suffering the consequences, not him."

"Welcome to the world of parenting." April sliced herself a wedge. One bite and her eyelids closed in bliss. "However, Jonah loves school, and so not being able to go is punishment for him."

"He didn't want to go yesterday."

"Because of the fight on Friday?"

"Pretty sure that's it. He never said. See, April? I should have set him down and quizzed him. Why not go to school? What was going on? But I was afraid to upset him or something. I simply did not know what was the best thing to do, so I did nothing, and that was the wrong thing, too."

"I'm sure he never thought of a kitchen knife as a weapon; when you think about it, it's natural. Kids play superheroes and use Super Soakers. But they don't think about weapons. Not when they're seven. Forbid a seven-year-old to play with guns and he'll point a stick at his enemy and go bang, bang. And the enemy goes bang, bang back."

Dinah closed her eyes and savored the ring a few moments. Delicious, and a nice counterpoint to her confused and tasteless thoughts. Was this afternoon too late to decide not to take Jonah? No, not as long as she refused to sign the necessary papers. They might give her lots of dirty looks, but that was better than ruining Jonah's life through incompetence.

Her eyes popped open. "Oh, nuts! I told Dr. G I would call him back and I forgot all about it."

"He called you?" April stared at her.

"This morning, checking up on us. Make sure we were doing okay. I told him yes."

April licked her lips. "I don't know if apologies are in order. If they are, I offer them. When I told him you were going over to the school, I thought it was to handle another meltdown, and I let it slip. I didn't think he'd go over there."

"No apology needed. He followed us over to the police station."

"Bet he was a sight for sore eyes."

"Actually, he was a sight for any eyes. I can't believe the relief I felt. I never would have guessed my reaction. And I wish you could have seen poor Jonah, how his face lit up when he saw Dr. G. Hero to the rescue."

"I tell you, that man is...is..." April pressed her lips together.

"Spit it out."

"A gift, that's what." April raised a hand, traffic cop–style. "I know you and he crossed swords from the beginning but he listens—"

Dinah interrupted. "To God? Sure, God talks directly to people, special people. But then you know my views on God, so I won't discuss that part."

"I was going to say, 'He listens to what people need,' but hey, who am I to argue?"

Dinah felt her ears flash warm and hid behind her coffee mug. "I'll call Trudy next."

"One last thing." April was picking up the napkins. "Don't go looking a gift horse in the mouth. I'm speaking of Garret, all right? No matter what you two think of each other, he truly wants to help Jonah. And right now, you need all the help you can get with that boy. From believers or not." She stood up and scooped up Braumeister's empty platter. "You'll need to go get your car, won't you?"

"No, it's in the basement lot. I drove this morning. You said hurry, remember? We're going to go to a store after work and pick out some jigsaw puzzles. And I want to buy a card table somewhere. Oh, and if you would, call Randy, please. Tell him I need Jonah by one-thirty at the very latest. We have to be at the courthouse by one forty-five." *Your employees have far too much to do to be taking care of your personal crisis—make that plural. One thing after another.*

"I will."

"Thank you, I have no idea how I will ever repay any of you for your help and caring."

"Dinah, keep in mind we are more than boss and staff; we are family. And families help each other out."

Mine didn't. No wonder this was all so new and over-whelming. She had no model to work from.

Dinah was no longer counting the things she had to do; now she was counting all the things that had already fallen through the cracks. She had not yet found a grief coun-selor for Jonah. She must not forget again.

She rested her heavy head against the seat back, turn-ing her chair so she could watch treetops out the window. She thumbed the contact list on her phone, found Gramma Trudy—in the Gs, not the Ts.

Why did she feel like she was swimming for the surface for all she was worth and something was trying to drag her under?

Chapter Twenty-Eight

Dinah glanced at Jonah, belted into the seat beside her. "You're being mighty quiet."

He nodded.

"Scared?"

He nodded again and studied the loops on his backpack.

If anyone should be scared it would be she. And she was. From out in the ether or wherever dead people go, Corinne was asking her to sign her life away. Begging her. Going from career woman to single parent with a career was not just a big step but a giant step. She must remain that career woman because so many good people depended on her for their jobs, their own careers. When she allowed herself to think about that, she staggered under the load.

She pulled into the visitor section of the parking garage. They'd be on time to meet Mr. Jensen. For some odd reason, she felt uncomfortable using his first name. An authority thing? Probably.

"You okay?"

Jonah nodded again and unlatched his seat belt. Together they walked across the street and into the City Hall building.

The jovial Mr. Jensen smiled and greeted them and Jonah smiled in return, for the first time in a while. Mr. Jensen ushered them into the building lobby and over to the coffee kiosk under the grand staircase. The building was a part of a courthouse campus where non-courtroom functions were carried out. It smacked of elegance and the nineteenth century.

Mr. Jensen waved toward a little iron sidewalk bistro table near the coffee counter. "Dinah, Judge Henny's assistant says he is running twenty minutes late. What can I get for you?"

"My favorite drink here is their double tall mocha."

"And Jonah? Would you like a drink of any kind? Ice cream?"

"Ice cream?" He brightened.

Mr. Jensen smiled. "Ah. Limited selection; is chocolate all right?"

"Yes, please." Another smile.

He walked over to the counter, so Dinah sat down. Then she got up, scooted Jonah in because these little iron chairs did not scoot well on the marble tile, and sat again.

Mr. Jensen brought the goodies, distributed them, and laid napkins in the middle. He sat. "So you've been here before."

"This is where I have to go for all permits, test clearances, that sort of thing. I find it a pleasant place." She sipped her mocha.

"It is! Now. Jonah. Do you have any questions for me today?"

Dinah watched Jonah's expressive face as questions

chased each other through his mind. She prompted, "You can ask anything you want to, Jonah, it's all right."

"Will I have to live with Dinah always?" Why did he have to phrase it that way?

"Until you are eighteen. She will be your legal guardian."

"She'll be my new mother?"

"No. You have only one mother, the one we all remember fondly. Dinah will take care of you the way a mother would." *Oh, no, she won't, because she can't!* Dinah's head screamed. *She has no idea how to take care of a child.*

"So I am not getting adopted?"

"No. You remain Jonah Morgan, the son of Andre and Corinne Morgan. However! Dinah will have just as much legal authority over you as would a parent. You cannot say, 'I don't have to listen to you; you aren't my mother.' You *do* have to obey her as you would your mother."

How would she balance this new life? She'd thought she had the former life under control, but control had not been even a possibility since this cataclysm. She sipped rich, chocolaty mocha and tried not to think about controlling the future. Future? She could not control the present.

"Dinah? What about you?"

"I need to find a counselor, pediatrician, dentist, barber...that sort of thing."

"I can get some recommendations and email them to you."

Was now the time to say something? "Jonah, if you're done with your ice cream, do you want to go look at those paintings down the hall? I think they have some of animals."

Jonah glanced at Dinah, then stood. "Okay," he said.
Dinah waited until he was out of hearing range. "Frankly,
I have grave reservations."

"Talk to me."

"My parents were, uh, severe. No snuggling, no affec-
tion to speak of. Certainly they loved us and provided well
for us, but it was a…a severe love. Problem? Pray God's
will. Illness? Pray God's will. When I insisted on going
to college, my mother was deeply disappointed. She told
me, 'We are preparing you for heaven, not Harvard.' I had
a younger brother, but he died when I was eight. In short,
I know nothing about nurturing children. And Jonah desperately needs a nurturer."

The expression on Mr. Jensen's face: Shock? Caring?
Amazement? She couldn't tell. He appeared to be deep in
thought for a moment. "When I was doing a background
check on you—that is standard procedure, incidentally, in
any case like this one—I found an exemplary education
CV. Even your senior project in high school was science
of publishable quality."

"You dug up that thing? You really were thorough."

"With Jonah's future at stake, yes. As thorough as possible." He propped his elbows on the little table and
formed his hands into a tent. "And, as you say, I saw no
signs that you were educated about children or prepared
to care for a small child; never babysat, for example, or
took developmental psychology classes in college."

"So if I refuse to take Jonah on, you'll understand."

He smiled and continued as if not hearing her. "The
qualities you do possess, however, are very positive.
You're a control freak, for example." He raised a hand.
"It's obvious in the way, for instance, you hire new employees. You personally interview and vet every one. And

you choose exceedingly well. Your employees are all happy, competent, productive, and fiercely loyal to you. You give them the freedom to be creative and they give you a hundred percent. That is very rare in a company, I daresay almost unheard of in this day and age."

"But they're not children."

"No. Now look at this picture objectively. You read people well. No, you are not a snuggler and nurturer, but you are a very sharp judge of qualities in a person. And listen to your objections just now. They are not selfish. This will alter your lifestyle egregiously; we all recognize that. So do you, I'm sure. But in voicing your misgivings you talked about Jonah's needs, not yours. You put him first."

"But…"

"And you are a splendid scientist. Scientists by nature look at things objectively."

She smirked. "Not always."

"Yes, there is always the human element, the human bias. But they try. You try. You will look at Jonah as objectively as possible to see what would profit him best and act on that. You will instinctively give him what he needs. Snuggling is a learned skill, greatly overrated." Mr. Jensen's phone chimed. He glanced at the text message. "He is ready for us." He stood up, called to Jonah, and motioned toward the elevators.

Dinah made herself smile down at Jonah when he slid his hand into hers. It felt like they were both on their way to the firing squad, not a bright, bluebird-filled forever.

Compared to Judge Henny's chambers, the judge's room in the police station had been cramped, gloomy, and depressingly austere. Everything in this large room smacked of opulence. Its decoration, late nineteenth century, fit its pine paneling well. Tall, narrow windows that reached nearly to the twelve-foot ceiling were softened by monkscloth draperies. Various paintings and diplomas hung from a genuine old-fashioned picture molding near the pressed-tin ceiling. This judge's desk was even larger than Judge Kittle's, but it had no glass surface for viewing a computer monitor. None sat on the desk, either. Perhaps this judge did not believe in computers.

The judge, an older fellow, stood when they entered, but he did not offer to shake hands. He didn't smile, either. And that was strange, for he looked so cheerful and rosy, like a whiskerless Santa Claus, minus the red suit and reindeer. Three chairs were lined up in front of his desk. That firing squad analogy was getting too close for comfort.

Mr. Jensen held a chair for Dinah. She sat. Jonah sat next to her; his feet did not quite reach the floor. Mr. Jensen sat down beyond him. Three crows on a fence.

The judge opened a thick, leather-bound book and began reading a lot of introductory material in legalese, information that Mr. Jensen had already pretty well covered in plain English. He closed the book and sat back.

He looked at her. "Dr Taylor. I've read your company's website and of course your mission statement. Please tell me in your own words what the website does *not* say. About you."

She had not expected such a question. Why would he ask something like that? Could a judge simply pop non sequiturs out of the blue? Apparently; at least Mr. Jensen was not objecting. She stuttered a moment. *Gather your thoughts, Dinah.* She sat back, took a deep breath, loosened her shoulders. "Even when I was in high school, I realized that food is nothing but chemicals. We consume chemicals. Other chemicals in our digestive system process that food and expel what cannot be used. I also saw that chemicals can work with each other or against each other."

She took another deep breath. *Relax, girl.* "I chose bio-chemicals as my career because their interactions fascinate me. I built a company that helps the body's chemicals do good things, you might say. Bolster naturally occurring positive interactions, or suppress naturally occurring negative interactions. I'm sorry if that's vague, but…"

"Not vague at all. I take it, then, that you're a fan of Krebs cycles."

She felt her mouth drop open. Who *was* this man? A judge familiar with biochemistry!

He asked, "Are you a good cook, Dr. Taylor?"

Another bolt from the blue. Totally unhorsed, she stammered, "No. I love creating dietary supplements; the chemical aspects. I don't spend much time with food, per se, as in 'What's for dinner?'" Was that what he wanted to hear, or was he about to kick her out for being a total non-mother? It was another black mark against her nurturing instincts; how many times had she heard that good cooking was a form of nurturing in itself? And suddenly, inanely, she thought of Gramma Grace's chicken pot pie, with fresh vegetables and homemade noodles, and how warmly nurturing that was; especially when Dinah got to roll out and cut the noodle dough.

He studied Jonah. "I understand you got into trouble at school on Monday. Tell me about that."

Now, finally, he was getting on topic. Jonah faltered, then got into the narrative and really rolled, complete with the run-on sentences he spewed when he really got excited.

The judge nodded and asked, "Have you any questions, Jonah?"

He shook his head. "Mr. Jensen answered them. I get to be Jonah Morgan and my mommy is still Corinne. You mean those questions?"

"Yes. Lars?" The judge looked at Mr. Jensen. "Questions? Concerns?"

"I am completely at ease with Corinne's decision. The more I see and hear in this case, the better I think these two will be an excellent match for each other. Jonah will get what he needs to be happy and succeed."

Again Dinah's mouth dropped open. How could he say that after she clearly explained why she was *not* a good candidate for motherhood? No! She'd flunked every one of their nurturing tests. She couldn't even cook. She was not at all what Jonah needed. Mr. Jensen drew a sheaf of papers out of his attaché case as the judge pulled more papers out of his lap drawer.

"No! I can't do this!" She nearly stood up and shouted. "I'm not a mother!"

The judge looked at her, at Lars.

Mr. Jensen said, "She has voiced misgivings. She feels a lack of the ability to nurture."

The judge settled his elbows on his desk and leaned forward a bit. "Dr. Taylor. Jonah does not need a mother. He already has a mother. He needs someone who will look to his best interests and guide him into a productive adulthood. Can you do that?"

She found herself sputtering, stumbling, saying, "Uh...er...but..."

"Please understand, Dr. Taylor, that by completing this legal action, we are placing our full and complete confidence in your ability to raise Jonah well. We do *not* do this lightly. We see many, many cases where children are placed not in the best possible circumstances but in the least objectionable circumstances. Not so here. Here is an extraordinarily talented little boy who needs a bright and creative guardian if he is to grow and soar. To realize the promise in him. You are such a person. We both hope you will not deny the child that promise."

What could she say? The way this man phrased it—she sat back, defeated. Steamrollered was more like it. Were they being truthful, or were they simply trying to get this case over with?

But then she looked at Jonah, saw the worry in his eyes. She forced a smile and he smiled back, relieved.

The judge opened his book again and read off more legalese.

Then he laid out four piles of papers across the front of his desk.

Mr. Jensen laid more papers on the piles. "I have signed and dated these." He turned. "Dinah?" He offered a pen.

Here goes nothing. In every sense of the word. Dinah stood up, accepted the pen numbly, signed where Mr. Jensen pointed. She *never* signed anything without reading it first, but here she was, scribbling her name. The four piles were four copies of one set.

From nowhere, two young women entered. Obviously, Judge Henny had summoned them. Dinah was sorely tempted to run around behind his desk to see where the buzzer was that he tapped, probably with his foot. The women signed on the *witness* lines. "Congratulations, Dr. Taylor!" the blonde pumped her hand. "Congratulations!" The auburn-haired one did also. They left. Easy for them; sign, walk out. They weren't faced with a lifetime job for which they were not prepared.

Jonah had his own papers to sign. He did so obediently in his second-grade scrawl.

The judge signed on many lines. It took him a minute.

Mr. Jensen had paper clips ready. He clipped each set together, left one on the judge's desk, and slipped the other three into his attaché case. While they stood there, the judge read closing sentences from that book.

What had she just done? She didn't even want to think about it. It was done.

Suddenly animated, the judge broke into a wide grin and leaped up. He came hustling around the end of his desk and seized both Dinah's hands in his. "Dr. Taylor, now that the formalities are over I can tell you how glad I am to meet you. My wife and I have been fans of your products for years. We find your pineapple-based digestive aid very useful, especially when we end up at one of those interminable banquets. And your sleep aid, the melatonin extract, works like a charm. And we both admire the way you have built and run your company." He shook her hand, clasping his other over the top of hers. "My wife said to tell you 'God bless you.'"

"Thank you." His sudden transformation from stern to warm floored her. She didn't even need her polite smile. This man was actually genuine.

"And Jonah"— the judge grasped Jonah's small hands also— "I am glad you could come here today. I'm proud to be the one who made your arrangement legal. It is important that you understand what is happening, so ask me when you have a question. You have a great future ahead of you."

Jonah nodded.

The auburn-haired woman came back in with a camera.

"Ah. Over here by the bookcase, I suggest." The judge

piloted Jonah to the corner of the room. The woman arranged them as she obviously had arranged new families many times before. "Smile," she suggested, and she snapped pictures of the judge, Jonah, and Dinah, all smiling together with arms on shoulders.

With goodbyes and handshakes all around, Jonah included, they took their leave. They passed a man and woman with a baby as they walked out.

When they emerged from the elevator, Dinah felt like she'd left a heavy load behind and had picked up another, just as heavy.

"Not your ordinary judge, I know. I was so grateful when I was notified who we would see." Mr. Jensen stopped in the marble-floored foyer. "I'll say goodbye here, as I have some other things to do in this building. Dinah, please call me if there is anything I can do to help you." He shook her hand. "I mean it. I'm sure you have corporate lawyers, but I know a lot of people and possibly sometime I can be of service."

"Thank you. I will keep you in mind."

"And Jonah, you are part of my family, too; I've known you since you were tiny. You call me if you need someone to talk to or whatever. Okay?"

Jonah nodded. "Do you want a picture of Mutt?"

"I would love one."

"I will make you a special one."

"Good."

Back in the car, Dinah felt her shoulders drop and sucked in a deep breath. Breathing deep was a possibility again; the tight bands around her diaphragm were gone. Mostly.

"Are you hungry, Jonah?"

"Can we go let Mutt out first and then eat?"

"We can and we will." She started the car and paid the parking attendant as they drove out. She pulled out into traffic. "I think we need to celebrate."

"Can Dr. G come, too?"

Dinah blinked and swallowed, not once but twice. "Why...I...um...I guess so. Sure."

Blindsided again. Was this going to become a daily event?

Chapter Twenty-Nine

W hy thank you, Jonah. I'd love to join you for supper." Pause. "Okay. Dinah's about six." When
Garret clicked off, he shook his head. Would wonders
never cease? This had to be a God thing. He set the bell
on his phone to remind him at five so he'd have time to
feed his housemates. They wouldn't mind eating a bit
early.

Three easels stood in front of him, and he wasn't making progress on any of them. Each one definitely had a
different feel to it. Dinah's in particular was giving him
trouble. How did one paint "haunted"? Especially when
he only saw it when her guard was down, which didn't
happen often. Perhaps guarded was a good word to use.
He shifted his concentration to Jonah and Mutt. Still
more texture needed. Maybe he should have put some
of the shaved areas and the stitches in. In his mind he
still saw her like that. He glanced to the third one. This
one seemed the most joyful. He returned to painting
two and Mutt's fluffiness. Or lack thereof. She was not
a pretty dog. Wire-haired terrier plus mysterious other
breeds lurked in her gene pool; they did not mix well.

When his phone rang again, he thought to ignore it but checked the caller. Danny. He clicked on Speaker. "What's up?"

"We hit a snag. I knew we'd have to move wiring, but whoever wired this thing in the beginning made some errors. With the concrete slab..."

"Can it be fixed?"

"I had to call in an electrician. This is going to cost more than I figured."

"So what's new—that's the way of remodel projects. We all know that. Just pay it and we'll find the money somewhere. I have a couple of others who have said they'd contribute but I've not gotten back to them."

"I figured that was what we'd do but just wanted to run it by someone else. I'm going to cap it off with a couple six-space outlets and some floor outlets. That way people can use laptops anywhere in that room. It's doubtful that I can make the Easter completion date."

"Would be nice, but not the end of the world."

"See you."

Garret switched to his reminders app and typed in "Check for more funding." Get one thing crossed off and two more jumped on. Good thing he had given up on stewing over things like that a few years ago. Type A people want all their ducks in a row with uniform buttons polished. He still had tendencies toward those behaviors, but, thanks to God's healing, they were growing more seldom. Until he saw someone being abused or picked on.

Jonah came to mind, not that people were picking on him, but life surely was.

He cleaned his brushes and covered his palette.

He arrived at Dinah's building at five till six and hit her

unit number on the pad by the door. Safeguards like that were good for women, especially living alone in the downtown area. Shame Eastbrook had come to that. The times had changed.

Her voice came over the intercom. "Sorry for the delay. I buzzed you."

"Thanks."

When he reached her door, Jonah answered the ding-dong. He swung the door open. "Dinah said to have a seat. She'll be ready in a minute."

"Thanks. So how did your visit with the judge go?"

"He was nice. He gave us lots of papers to sign. I want to make a picture for him. A special one. If judges wore a hat I would put that on his dog."

"If you draw Mutt, how will you make her different?"

"He has round glasses with wire frames. I will draw them on her."

"What if you could paint one of your drawings?"

Jonah studied him. "I don't know how and I don't have paints and brushes. I like pencils good enough."

"I have all kinds of paint and brushes. Would you like to come paint with me? You could meet my dogs, too, and maybe you can draw one of them." Garret flopped onto the sofa, and Jonah and Mutt settled next to him. That gray dirt spot on the middle cushion marred the sofa's crisp, clean look.

"What are their names?"

"Soandso is the female and Sam is her brother. They are yellow Labs, big dogs, and besides the dogs, I have a tiger cat, named TC. He thinks he is king. I used to have a toroiseshell named Wowser. She died an old lady."

"What's a tortoiseshell?" He was now sitting closer to Garret, with one arm around Mutt's neck.

"A type of calico coloring. Did you know that all calico cats are female?"

"I don't know much about cats."

He sensed rather than heard Dinah enter the room. He glanced over his shoulder to see her watching Jonah. Mutt saw her and wagged her tail.

"Would you mind if Jonah came to my house maybe on Saturday and painted with me?"

"If he wants to."

Jonah nodded. "I think I would like that. Can Mutt come, too?"

"Maybe eventually, but how about just you for now?"

"Umm." He stood and turned. "Can Mutt stay here without me?"

Dinah looked surprised. "Of course. She lives here."

"What if she has to go out?"

Dinah kept a straight face; Garret probably could not have. "Then I'll take her out. I can handle that."

Jonah turned back to Garret. "Then I would like to come."

"Good, I'm glad that's settled. Now where shall we eat?"

"Dinah said we're having a celebration."

"So we need to go somewhere nice to celebrate. How about the Homestyle? I heard you like fried chicken and they make great fried chicken."

Dinah joined the conversation. "Where is that?"

"Out by the clinic, about fifteen minutes from here. But they don't take reservations. We'll go somewhere else if the wait is too long." He paused. "You do like fried chicken, don't you? I mean, we can go somewhere else."

"No, that's fine. I'm sure they serve something besides fried chicken." Dinah took her coat out of the closet, but before she could start to put it on, he took it from her and held it. Why did she look so surprised? His mother taught him certain manners; had she not been raised in such a family? His opinion of power women aside, she was tolerable so far. And, he reminded himself, he was doing this for Jonah.

Jonah, however, seemed to be making up for the sullen silence of the last few days. While he sat in the back seat of the SUV, he spoke up. "Dr. G, do you have any kids? Oh. Why do you draw the cartoons of pets? I like it, too. Mine is on my wall. Do you do that for all your patients? Okay. Three? We think Mutt is two or three. Why do you like to paint? What made you start making the colored drawings? I like pencil."

"Is he always like this?" He glanced at Dinah, who was shaking her head.

"Not that I knew. He's making me tired and I'm not the one answering."

"It's okay. Better this than sullen."

She turned, head barely shaking. "You sure?"

Garret kept from laughing by answering another question. If he tried to describe this evening, no one would believe him. He wasn't sure he did himself.

"When will we get there?"

"A few more blocks."

"Do we have to have fried chicken?"

"Not if you don't want to." Garret wondered if they sold adhesive tape or a large cork. What if this is the way painting went? How would he stand it? What had he gotten himself into? They'd do it this Saturday afternoon for two hours and see how it went.

The restaurant tables had white paper coverings and a basket of crayons in the middle. In the basket stood three sharpened pencils. Jonah hadn't even sat down before he reached for the basket.

"Did you know this?" Dinah nodded to the table.

"Clever idea." He nodded and helped Dinah off with her coat, then hung it on the coat hook in the back of the booth seat. Coats hung all down the row. "They cater to families." He motioned her to take the other side, and he slid into the booth by Jonah, who ordered chicken after all, hardly looking up from his drawing.

The orders taken, Garret picked up a red crayon and stroked a few lines.

Dinah sat with her chin on her fists and watched.

He wished he could see into her mind. A brown crayon joined the red lines and circles and a cat began to emerge. The fluffy tail stood straight up, the mouth hissing, back arched. Staring at the dog Jonah was drawing.

Jonah looked at it and giggled. A true little-boy giggle.

Garret handed the boy a blue crayon, pantomiming drawing.

Jonah hesitated, took the crayon, and started making clouds. Then he dropped down on the page and, between the cat and the dog, drew an oval, added a long tail and a circle for a head, whiskers, and tiny ears.

Garret snorted and grinned. With the green crayon he drew a frog, fully extended, hopping just below the clouds, above the other animals.

The waitress arrived with their plates. "I hate to mess up your work here," she said. "You are some artists."

"Dr. G makes lots of drawings." Jonah put his things back in the basket. "That was fun." After grace, he dug into his platter of food, leaving Dinah and Garret to talk.

Now it was Garret's turn to ask questions. Some she sidestepped, like *Where did you grow up?* Every time he got personal, she managed to change the subject. Obviously, she was very good at being the subject of an interview and releasing very limited information. She was also good at controlling the conversation, far more so than he was comfortable with. By inference, though, he deduced that she lived some distance from her parents and was estranged from them. He thought of his own parents, not far away at all, not estranged, and yet how seldom he got out there. A tiny wave of guilt washed across him.

Dinah finished her meal and laid her flatware across her plate. "As good as you are with kids—witness Jonah here—it's a shame you never had any of your own. I remember he asked you this evening."

Garret shrugged. He was going to blow off her comment with some kind of platitude, but then he would be as evasive as she. To prove himself superior in that regard, he answered, "She never wanted any." And inside he froze. He had just spilled a mountain when he intended to tip out a teacup.

And dang it all if she didn't pick up on it instantly. "Divorced?"

"Yes." A tsunami of guilt washed across him. Again.

"I'm done." Jonah pushed his plate back.

What timing! Garret wanted to scoop the kid up and kiss him. He could legitimately change the subject! "Dessert?"

Dinah declined dessert. So did Garret. A seven-year-old does not decline dessert. Smiling, they watched him pick at a one-scoop sundae, scraping spoonful by scant spoonful into his mouth, savoring each bite.

Her cell rang, an intrusion from the outside world.

She answered, staring at Garret without seeing him. "Why are you there so late?" Pause. "Oh." Pause. "Wait!

They passed on that. It's checked off." Pause. Pause. "I'm coming." She muttered a sort of goodbye and stuffed her cell back in her purse. She looked at Garret and this time she saw him. "I'm very sorry. Some problems have turned up at the office, and—"

"It's past seven o'clock. That was April? At your office?"

"Yes. And I must go do something. Can you please drop Jonah and me off there?"

Jonah dropped against the back of his chair and studied the ceiling.

Garret pressed his lips together. "No. Jonah and I will drop you off and go catch a movie."

Instantly the tyke sat erect, grinning.

Garret continued, "Call when you're ready to go home."

"But I don't know when—" She looked at Jonah. Really looked at him. "All right."

Garret couldn't believe it! A difference of opinion with a strong-willed woman.

And he'd won!

She took the stairs up because the elevator was too slow and burst into April's office. "Now what?"

April was wagging her head. "Email from Bill Doolittle. The FDA wants a double-blind study on Scoparia's effectiveness to decide whether it's actually a drug or just an additive."

"That's crazy! Item one, we already did a double-blind, and item two, it's *not* a drug. It's an herb-based dietary supplement. We've said that all along. Absolutely no claims for healing or anything like that. It's how we tested it, how we're marketing it. As a supplement it passes all the tests—tests we didn't even have to make but did any way—and more besides." Dinah's voice was rising with each word and she couldn't control it.

April sighed. "I know that. Here. I printed out the email for you. It's two pages in Helvetica ten." She laid out two sheets of paper for Dinah to read.

Dinah scanned down the post cursorily. *Why now? At this late date?* "April, a study like they're talking about here will take six months to set up and conduct. To repeat a study we've already done. Then submit the results, and they drag their feet another six months. That's a year!" She took a deep breath. "What are our options?"

"You can take them to court."

"Two years minimum before we get a hearing, longer if the offended parties ask for a delay. Who are the parties, anyway? I don't see any hint here. Who put some bug in the FDA's ear?"

"That's why I'm here so late." April sat back. "I thought, someone who's in with the agency. So I did some digging around. Started at four this afternoon and it snowballed. Amazing what Google can provide sometimes. This is interesting. I stumbled onto an independent ad hoc committee being bankrolled by three major drug firms. Drug firms that just happen to supply diabetes drugs and appliances among other things. And the committee spokesman is a sales agent for those companies, so he's in with big pharma and also has contacts with the FDA. Dollars to doughnuts, he's the link."

Dinah felt weak. And horrible. And horribly weak. She flopped into the chair across from April's desk. "Hal said we could expect a hit from the companies that would lose business if Scoparia works. Here it is, bigger than life and twice as ugly. Could you get ahold of him?"

"Not yet. I have some calls in."

Dinah pulled the second sheet off the desk and studied it in better detail. "They really do say we must test it all over again and evaluate its effectiveness as a drug. So if Scoparia is effective, they can call it a drug and refuse to okay it. And if this next study shows that it's not effective, why bother with it at all? April, this is insane." *And there is nothing I can do about it.*

"I probably should have put it aside until tomorrow instead of calling you this late, but I was hoping you and Hal could come up with something and we could hit the ground running in the morning."

Dinah felt physically sick to her stomach, and it was not something one of her products could relieve. This was only the first salvo of a dirty war. And all she wanted to do was help people. She nodded. "Good call. April, you spent all this time on this?"

April shrugged. "This and some, uh, other things." She looked almost guilty. Which was ridiculous; Dinah's mind was playing tricks.

"Well, thank you." Shock, anger, and, yes, sadness. Every delay meant fewer people helped.

"What next?" April asked. She sat back; her chair creaked. Time to get April a new office chair.

Dinah grimaced. "The lawyer today said something about my corporate lawyer. I didn't tell him we don't have one. We hardly ever have a legal matter, especially not enough business to retain someone. Well, now we need one."

"Joe and I don't have a regular lawyer, either. I can't help there."

Dinah tried to think of definite next steps and had to settle for possible ones. "The lawyer handling Jonah's guardianship might know someone in this subject area,

and he said call whenever. And the judge today, Judge
Henny. He told Jonah to call if he had questions; I might
ask his advice, a reference or something. We have to
somehow get this requirement rescinded." She looked at
April. "Thank you for not waiting until Monday. I have to
take Mutt out and—How long is a movie? An hour and a
half?"

"Most. About."

"And it just started. April? Can you give me a ride
home?"

Chapter Thirty

S he likes us!" Sue and Garret high-fived. "And we like
her." From the window they watched Julie Crick slide
into her rental car and leave the back parking lot.

As they turned away, Amber tapped on the door and
entered. "How'd it go?"

Sue was beaming. "We have another vet! We offered
and she accepted. Says our starting salary is a little higher
than California's and she really likes the lower cost of living here. She has student loans to pay off, so this is good
for her financially."

Garret gathered up coffee mugs. "You didn't have
much chance to interact with her, but what's your take?"

"She seems personable. Open. Cheery. She wished me
goodbye by name when she left. So far, I think she'll be a
good fit. When is she coming on?"

"Two weeks. She's gone out looking for an apartment,
flies back to California in three days." Garret left the
mugs in the sink. "What's out there?"

Amber counted off, "Post-spay check, that aging feline
belonging to Mrs. Abercrombie, and four basset pups for
their shots."

"And they are all entertaining the others in the waiting room?"

"They are."

He chuckled. Any basset puppy looks terminally cute just standing still, but these four had a particular gift for romping about looking absolutely hilarious. "Bring 'em on."

Amber sobered. "And Tessa."

Garret felt his good mood evaporate. "Put her in the back exam room. I'll take her first."

Sue nodded. "Good. I don't really want to deal with that. I'll take the pups."

Tessa smiled and greeted him as he entered. He smiled and greeted her.

He wrapped his arms around Valiant and hoisted him onto the exam table. The dog had lost weight during his recovery. He was starting to get it back.

Tessa rolled in closer. "He seems to be getting back to his old self."

"Any seizures? Does he ever stop what he's doing and just stare off into space?" Garret poked and prodded; Valiant showed no signs of discomfort.

"No. And his appetite is normal. More than normal."

Heart and lung action sounded normal, too. Garret peeled Valiant's lips back. "Gums are a healthy pink. Looks like your circulation is back up to snuff, Old Man." He lowered the dog back to the floor. "Take him across the room and back, please."

Tessa did so. The dog's legs worked very stiffly. She parked beside Garret. "He's never going to have full use of his legs, is he." It was a statement, not a question.

"No, I don't think so. In fact, if arthritis sets in—and it often does—it will get worse. Take him to the room beside the cage room, then, the pink place, and I will put a new cast on his leg today; lighter, less bulky. That will help him get around a little better." Garret pulled the wheeled stool over and parked beside her, eye to eye. "When are they coming for him?"

Her eyes filled but did not overflow. "Tomorrow. The director for the service dog agency visited me in person yesterday, Dr. G. He sat down with me and explained it all."

"You already knew they were going to take him back from you."

"Yes. He wasn't telling me anything I didn't know already. Except that he said you called him and begged him to let me keep him. That you sent him all of Valiant's medical records so he could consider it. Thank you so much, Dr. G."

"I didn't think it would work, but it was worth a shot. Their policies are pretty rigid. But when your life depends on your service dog, they have to be."

Beside her, Valiant flopped out on his tummy.

"I know. He says the agency has a black Lab lined up for me. But Valiant..." Her voice trailed off. "And I keep reminding myself that giving up Valiant is best for both of us. He'll have a good home—the director says there's a waiting list of people who want retired service dogs—and I need a dog that's dependable. But..."

"But." Garret gathered her hands into his. "So many buts in life. Bring your new dog by, please. I want to meet him."

She smiled sadly. "I certainly will. Thank you. The pink place. Come, Valiant."

The dog lurched to his feet and fell in beside her. Garret followed them out, watching Valiant move. No, the dog would never walk well again. And the petty thief who'd caused all this would probably get six months or less, if he was even convicted. There was no justice.

They turned aside into the pink place, to apply the new cast. Maybe he should get this room repainted.

By the time lunch came, Garret still felt mopey. He had invested too much emotionally in Tessa and Valiant; it was affecting him more than he would have guessed. Or was it his mom and the changes in her driving him to gloom? And, so far, funding for the church was not happening quickly enough; Danny would be paying people out of his own pocket. Garret didn't want that to happen again; Danny already contributed heavily. Besides, Garret wanted that mess over with. The mess and disorder were depressing. And he still had not completed those three studies of Dinah and her new family.

Dinah. It had been a few days since their celebratory dinner, and he hadn't heard from her. But why should he expect to? Jonah was coming by to paint with him this afternoon. In just a couple weeks, they'd have Julie for backup, and he might be able to cut out early. That would be nice.

He pulled out his phone and instructed, "Call Taylor."

No answer. He glanced at the screen. So no one was home to pick up her landline. She wouldn't be at her office, would she? "Call Dinah."

The receptionist, April, answered.

"This is Garret Miller. Surely you're not working there on Saturday!"

Pause. "Dr. G, my caller ID tells me you're at your clinic. Do I hear the pot calling the kettle black?"

He laughed. "You do. Is Dinah available?"

Another pause. "May I ask you a favor?"

"Certainly."

"Two favors, actually. I have a bit of a problem. Well, actually, a pretty big problem. Could you please pray for me to make the right and best decision?"

"Of course. And God knows the situation, right?"

April giggled, a sort of audible smile. "He does. And Dinah needs extra prayer. Jonah's been having nightmares, so she's not getting enough sleep, and she has her own FDA nightmare to deal with. Say, do you know any good lawyers who handle something like an FDA problem?"

"I'll ask around. I might. If not a friend, a friend of a friend. We have a couple lawyers in our church."

"Thank you. I'll put you through."

Dinah answered and greeted him.

"Barring emergencies, I should be out of here a little early. Is Jonah with you?"

"In the back room watching television. He's been looking forward to this, that's for sure."

"We have not talked yet about Mutt's pregnancy. I'd like to X-ray her to make sure the pregnancy diagnosis is correct and how big any pups are."

"I've been avoiding that whole issue. It's not avoidable, is it?"

"No. I'm afraid it's inexorable."

"Just another cupful in my ocean of things to not avoid. Call when you leave there and I'll have Jonah ready for you."

"Thank you." He thumbed the End Call button and studied the wall. How had she sounded just now? Tired. April said no sleep. Harried. And defeated. This hotshot CEO sounded defeated.

But then the next client was a super feel-good case, a

little Cavalier King Charles spaniel that had accidentally been stepped on. Garret removed the cast today and the dog bounced around the room without a limp, fully recovered. Then Mrs. Porter's Abyssinian cat with an advanced case of mange was growing new hair just fine. Tigger, one of the cutest cocker spaniel puppies known to man, sailed through his shots and checkup with flying colors.

Despite the rough morning, Garret was still smiling when he entered the break room at two. He buzzed Amber. "I can leave now, right?"

"You better get out of here quick, while it's quiet."

He left out the back, calling Dinah as he went.

They were waiting in front of the Extraburger as he pulled to the curb.

"Hi, Dr. G!" Jonah bounced into the back seat.

Dinah stepped back and waved. "Have fun." Her smile did not quite reach her eyes.

"You can come if you like. Have you ever painted?"

"No, but I'm not an artist. Besides, I need to get some work done."

He waved again and pulled out into traffic.

From the back seat, Jonah asked, "You live far away?"

"No, but farther than the clinic. Have you ever drawn a basset hound?"

"No. But I saw one once. They have long ears."

"And short legs."

"How come?"

"They are hunting dogs and can dig or go under brush and trees to get their prey."

"Oh. What are your dogs' names again?"

"Soandso and Sam, the yellow Labs. They're rescue dogs but probably full blooded."

"What's rescue dogs?"

"Rescue is when a dog or cat doesn't have a home, so you take it in. Or a horse. There are farms that rescue horses."

"Like Dinah rescued me?"

Garret paused at the last light in town. "Uh, no. Not like you. You were loved, and you are still loved, and Dinah is taking care of you. You weren't just cast off. Thrown away, like rescued pets."

"Why did someone throw your dogs away?"

"I have no idea. That person made a big mistake, because these are some of the best dogs anywhere. I know they'll be happy to see you."

Happy didn't begin to describe the way they greeted Jonah, yipping and jigging and licking the moment Jonah got out.

"Enough!" Garret finally said as he led the way to his studio. Apparently the dogs didn't think it was enough yet, so he yelled at them and they backed off.

"Where is your cat?"

"He'll come out when he's ready. Cats don't usually welcome company like the dogs do."

"Shut up!"

Jonah's eyes widened. "What was that?"

"You ever see a macaw up close? A macaw is one of the largest of the parrot family; certainly has the longest tail. Come in the sun room and meet them."

"Hello." The hyacinth macaw sidled down his horizontal perch for a better view.

Jonah stared at the huge blue bird. "He talks."

"Hello."

"He won't stop until you answer."

Hesitantly, Jonah said, "Hello."

The bird cocked its head. "Cute."

Jonah giggled. "What's his name?"

"He is Side Car, and the other one who was squawking when we came in is Orinoco. That's why Side Car yells 'Shut up.' He wasn't yelling at us, but at Orinoco."

Jonah looked over at the big flight cage. "More birds?"

"Finches, canaries, and a pair of lovebirds. The lovebirds have a nest again, with three eggs in it."

"How come you have all these birds?"

"I like birds." Garret turned around. "You ready to paint, Sport?"

"Why do you call me Sport when my name is Jonah?"

"Because when I was your age a favorite uncle called me Sport. It's sort of a general name for any guy kid."

"Oh." Jonah followed him into the studio. "Then I guess it's okay."

Garret waved an arm toward the glass wall. "I set up an easel your size and one for me." He had moved the three problematic easels to the far wall and covered them. He was still not sure why he hadn't just left them out.

He settled on his stool and was glad he had guessed the right height for Jonah's seat. "There are many kinds of painting surfaces—Masonite, illustration board for instance. I like gessoed canvas. So let's start with canvas."

Jonah ran his fingers over it. "It really is canvas."

"Yes. With a sort of thin, white plaster painted over it. I thought we'd paint with acrylics today. Another time maybe we'll try watercolors or oils." He picked up a palette from the table between them. "All these paints can be used if you like. And these will be your brushes. You have to clean your brushes well, or they will get hard and not be any good anymore. I'll show you how when we're done for today. What would you like to paint?"

Jonah shrugged. "A picture of Mutt?"

"Mutt is not easy to paint because her hair goes every direction. What if you started with Soandso or Sam? They're only one color and they're short-haired." He nodded to where the two lay by the chair, jaws between their front legs, watching everything the two humans did. "Now, the first step is to draw what you want to paint on the canvas. I have some pictures you can look at, if you want. I do that a lot of times." He pulled open a file drawer and drew out a folder to lay on the table. The pictures were of both dogs in various poses. "How about sitting like this? Use your pencil lightly."

He took a pencil and drew a few lines that quickly became the form of a dog.

Jonah watched him, stared at the picture, then drew, but shook his head and quit.

"Let me show you what I used to use." Garret flicked on his old camera lucida, laid the picture on its bed, and flashed the picture on the wall. "Now you go hold your canvas in the light and I'll make the dog fit. Then you draw around what you see." He moved the black box back until the dogs looked right.

Jonah sketched around the projected image and when he returned to the table, his eyes were dancing. "Could we do that with one of my drawings?"

"Good idea! We could, and we will another time." Garret took an inch-wide brush, dipped it in paint, and started on the background. "Since I am just going to paint the dogs, not with trees and sky and such, I choose a neutral color to start with. 'Neutral' means not sock-you-in-the-eye." He held the palette in one hand and the brush in the other.

Jonah picked up a palette. "Like Side Car and Orinoco

are not neutral." He mimicked Garret's motions, perched at the shorter easel. "Can I put blue in there, too?"

"You sure can. Go ahead."

Jonah dabbed at first, then made bolder strokes, gaining courage as he went. "When can I do the dog?"

"Anytime. I just like to paint the background first. What color will you use for the dog?" Garret stepped back and returned to the easel. "If you want to make a color lighter, you add white to it. If you want to make it darker, you add that gray or the black or sometimes just another deep color, like purple or blue." He mixed the colors on his palette and applied samples to a paper.

"So if I take yellow and mix with white it will look more like their color?"

"Yes. And then if you want some darker, you add Payne's gray like this. You can use this to show shadows. Like, see where there is shadow between the front legs and the chest?"

Together they mixed and made samples. Jonah grinned at Garret. "This is fun!"

"Glad you think so. One of the neat things is that if you paint something and you don't like it, you can paint over it until you get it the way you want. And you can make it look three-dimensional this way. Here, let me show you on a box." He quickly drew a box shape showing the front, the top, and the side, then painted the top light, the front medium, and the side dark. "This is how you show shapes and shadows." Using brush and paint, he made a round ball.

Jonah stared at it, picked up his brush, and did the same. "It looks round."

"You did well. Keep plenty of paint on your brush."

Jonah played with the shapes awhile, then turned his

attention to the easel and studied it. He painted the dog a medium yellow. He added dark in the shadowed areas and light on the top of the dog's head. "Ah, no." He looked to Garret. "How can I erase it?"

"What did I say before?"

"Paint over it."

Garret grinned. "Hey, I want something to drink. What would you like?"

"Orange soda?"

"I have that. Wrap your brush in this and we'll go get the drinks."

Jonah followed him out and pointed at the kitchen clock. "It's past five."

"Oh my gosh, I was having so much fun I didn't watch the clock. We better get our brushes cleaned up. We'll have to finish those paintings another time."

"Next Saturday?"

"If you like. Maybe even sooner." He handed Jonah a cold can. "We can drink and clean up at the same time." He dropped his brushes into soapy water. Jonah was good at copying actions. He was also good at understanding why they did what they did. Garret showed him how to hang the brushes to dry.

Jonah took a swig of his drink as he stood in front of his easel. "This is better 'n' crayons."

"Glad you think so. But we might try the colored markers sometime, too."

Garret led Jonah out to the SUV and opened the rear door. "Should we stop for pizza for supper?"

The boy hopped in. "Sure. Can I call Dinah?"

Garret handed him the phone as he got in. "Just say 'Call Dinah.'" He twisted the ignition.

"'Call Dinah.' Hey! It's doing it. That's so cool!" He

chatted a moment, hung up, and handed the phone back over Garret's shoulder. "She says pizza is fine."

When Jonah became quiet after that, Garret looked in the rearview mirror to see if he had fallen asleep. Jonah looked at Garret's reflection looking at him. "Teacher said at Sunday School that if I believe in Jesus, I get to go to heaven. Like Mommy did, huh?"

"Yes, that's what the Bible says."

"Dr. G, I really want to see my Mommy again. I want to be with her."

"Ah, Jonah, how I wish you could be, too."

"When I die I get to be with Mommy, right?"

"That's right. But that will be a long time away."

The kid lapsed back into thought.

Now what to talk about? Garret asked, "What did you do at Grandma Trudy's yesterday?"

"I drew the picture for Judge Henny and started one for Mr. Jensen. And she made cookies, so I helped her." He paused. "But I miss school. How come I have to stay out so long?"

"Sorry, Sport, but those are the rules. Having a knife at school is way against the law."

"I won't do it again."

"Good."

Chapter Thirty-One

This is overkill. *Three* kinds of pizza." Dinah had re-laxed considerably since they had settled themselves at her kitchen table, the pizzas in front of them. She trans-ferred another ham-and-pineapple slice from the box to her plate.

Garret chose an Italian sausage. "In the next couple days, I'd like to X-ray Mutt, see what's going on in there. Very short visit; step in, do it, step out. You don't even have to meet with a vet. Jason or someone can snap the pictures and we'll call you later."

Jonah was still working on his three-cheese special. "Can I see the pictures? Please?"

"This early in her pregnancy; the puppies' bones are not really calcified, and they don't show up well on an X-ray. Little gray blobby things, not real puppies. We could do an ultrasound, but that's very expensive. Not worth the cost. But sure, Sport. If you want to see blobs, I can email the X-rays to Dinah for you."

"She has to be spayed." Dinah lifted her coffee mug, looked in it a moment, and set it down again. "Can you do it now?"

Garret crossed over to the coffee maker and brought
the pot. He poured for her and warmed up his. "It depends; another reason for the X-ray. There's a cut-off
point, so to speak, a point when the puppies are too far
advanced in development for the operation to be safe for
the mother. If they're still as small as we think, yes. We
can spay her now. Jonah, if she became pregnant the night
she was chewed up, the puppies are still tiny. But if it
happened before then—Did she ever get away from you
before that night?"

"Uh-huh."

"When? A long time? Days? Weeks? Can you remember?"

Jonah's forehead puckered. "I'm thinking. Mommy was
really sick one day and Mutt wouldn't come back when
I called her and so I went up to make sure Mommy was
okay and Mutt came when I went back down. I'm sorry."

"Nothing to be sorry about, Sport. You didn't do anything wrong. In fact, you did everything right."

"What's a spade?" Jonah eyed the triple cheese but
lifted out a ham-and-pineapple instead.

"To spay a female dog is to remove her reproductive
organs so that she cannot have puppies." Garret sounded
casual, matter-of-fact.

Jonah narrowed his eyes. "But the puppies that are in
there will be okay, right?"

"No. They are inside the reproductive organs, so they'd
be removed with the reproductive organs."

Here it came, as Dinah feared. Jonah dropped his
pizza; he looked shocked. "But that would kill the puppies!"

Dinah spoke gently. "Well, yes, but..."

"We can't kill her puppies!" Instantly, he teetered on

the verge of another meltdown. How could this little boy flick the switch so instantaneously from calm to out of control?

Dinah said loudly, "Jonah, stop! Listen. If it means that much to you, we won't."

"You can't kill her puppies!"

And Dinah borrowed a page from Garret. "Remember, we don't want to upset Mutt, especially if she's pregnant. We won't do it, Jonah. We won't spay her."

"Promise?" He was yelling.

"Promise." Dinah sank forward, her elbows on her white table and her head in her hands. "Puppies."

Garret's voice soothed the troubled waters further. "Might put it too close to the line anyway. If she's gaining weight noticeably now, it would have started earlier. Are you prepared for a litter of puppies?"

"No. Of course not. How could I ever handle puppies here?"

He grimaced. "I guess puppies and an all-white condo don't go together well."

"You see what happened to my sofa in there." She felt near tears. "Puppies."

"Your kitchen is small, but you have enough room here to put up a collapsible fence. They sell them at the pet supply places. It would be for about ten weeks, until you can wean them and find them new homes."

"But we'll keep the puppies!" Jonah nearly shouted. "We can't give her children away. Her children would all lose their mommy!"

Garret looked at Dinah and Dinah looked at Garret, an *aha!* moment. *Think, Dinah!*

Garret spoke first. "Ever hear of 'Don't count your chickens before they're hatched'? Well, that's what we're doing. We don't know how many puppies there are, and we don't even know if she has any. The time to think about these things is after the puppies are born; if there really are puppies in her and she's not just getting fat from lack of exercise."

The silence lay heavy. Another grotesque thought jumped into Dinah's mind. Jonah obviously understood that babies came from inside mommies, at least in regard to dogs. But sooner or later his education in such things was going to have to be expanded. And it was his brand-new guardian who would have to do the expanding. This time she could not fall back on the nice sterile considerations of the biochemistry of reproduction. It was going to get rough.

Then Garret and Jonah got deep into a conversation about holidays, and Easter in eight days.

So far, she had kept forgetting about getting an Easter basket for Jonah. And jelly beans and a chocolate bunny and all. She remembered her own Easter baskets when she was a child. No chocolate bunnies. Only solid chocolate crosses, usually with a lily molded into them. No chicks. When she was twelve she'd petitioned her parents for marshmallow Peeps. She pointed out that chicks symbolize new birth—in fact, symbolize the resurrection—and to bolster her point, she went through a *Young's Analytical Concordance* to find all the scriptural references to chicks. None specifically supported her thesis, and no marshmallow Peeps ever appeared in her basket. Kind-hearted playmates shared theirs, but it wasn't the same thing.

Garret finished his coffee. "Almost seven. I have to go on call tonight. Urgent care. So I must leave. I would like to take you both along to Palm Sunday services tomorrow at our church. We do it up big—do the whole Easter week up big. Will you come?"

"Can we?" Jonah brightened. "Dinah, can we go?"

She had had enough trouble sitting through the church service with Grandma Trudy. But a fancy, self-proclaimed *big* service? "Thank you, but I don't think so." She glanced at Jonah's crestfallen face. "If you wish, both of you, Jonah may go. I think he'd love to go."

The boy glowed instantly.

Garret smiled. "Ready at ten tomorrow?"

"Sure!" Apparently, that settled that. Garret took his leave and Jonah went off to read before bedtime.

Puppies. She sighed to the depths of her soul.

The next morning Garret rang the bell at just before ten and Dinah buzzed him up.

"Sure you don't want to go along?" Just by standing in her living room doorway Garret seemed to fill the room.

Dinah smiled. "I appreciate the invitation, but I'm fine here. Thanks."

Jonah came out of the bedroom beaming as if he'd just won a million dollars. He spread his arms. "Look. My Sunday clothes are new and they're not too big. I don't have to grow into anything."

Dinah laughed. "And you look like a million dollars, too."

"Be right back." Jonah snatched Mutt's leash off the hook by the back door and went out with his dog.

Dinah explained, "I could take Mutt out while you two go on to church, but for some reason, it's very important to Jonah that he take her out. So...well..."

"If it's important to a kid, it's important."

She nodded.

Silence.

He broke it. "Thanks for letting me take Jonah."

"No problem. He's delighted to go."

"Are you certain you'd prefer to stay home? We have a special Palm Sunday service that I think you'd like."

"No, really. Thank you anyway."

Long silence.

She was the hostess, he the guest. She really ought to fill the thundering silence, but she couldn't think of anything.

The silence was broken without her help as Mutt and Jonah burst in through the door.

Jonah hung up the leash. "We can go now." All bubbly, he jogged out the front door.

Palm Sunday. When she was small, how Dinah had loved Palm Sunday. The story of a donkey colt carrying Jesus into Jerusalem. The prospect of a whole lot of chocolate and jelly beans seven days from then; the so-long-ago past and the too-long-to-wait-for future.

An Easter basket. While Jonah was off with Garret, she would get him an Easter basket. This was the perfect time. But where? She was not a shopper. She tried a couple likely stores at random and finally found one with a large selection of both baskets and candy.

She could purchase a basket already trimmed, or she could purchase a naked one, so to speak. She chose a large, graceful, pretty, bare-naked one. She picked out the shredded grass. Three packages; two didn't look like they'd do it. And she paused, surprised by her feelings. This was fun! This was just plain delightful! She would not have guessed.

Now for the candy. Anything but crosses. Here was a dark chocolate rabbit that was almost too big for the basket. Almost doesn't count; she laid it in her cart. Soft yellow marshmallow Peeps, the large box of them. Jelly beans, of course. Some mint patties. Peanut butter cups. Gummy bears. How she used to love gummy bears. She was going to take a bag of M&M's, but no. They would just get lost in the grass. Some other time.

She surveyed the cart. There was too much candy here; it would not all fit in the basket. She chose a smaller untrimmed basket, a chocolate setting hen, and two more bags of grass. She would decorate both and give one to Grandma Trudy.

Eggs! Easter had to have colored eggs. She chose an egg-dyeing kit. She would have to ask Garret about paints that would be safe for use on eggshells. Those two artists would surely want to paint pictures on some of the eggs. Wait. Here was a colored-marker kit that promised safe ingredients. Into the cart it went.

She purchased four dozen eggs. Fortunately, she read the instructions on the dye kit before leaving the store and picked up a bottle of white vinegar. Did an opened bottle of vinegar last from one Easter to the next? She had no idea. It didn't matter.

And doughnuts. The baker was putting out trays of fresh doughnuts. Her particular favorites were maple bars, but she also boxed up some chocolates and some plains, for when the churchgoers returned.

She checked out, loaded the car, and arrived back home fifteen minutes before she could expect Garret and Jonah. She left the doughnuts on the table, separated out the eggs, dyes, and vinegar, and carefully tucked the rest under the sink behind cleaning supplies. Then she made herself a cup of coffee and sat down at the table. That heady rush of delight was still there, still making her heart sing. This new guardianship posed enormous tasks, enormous responsibilities, enormous woes. But, she realized for the first time, it also offered enormous joys.

Joy. Had she ever truly tasted joy? Rarely. Fleeting occasions. This occasion, putting together an Easter basket, would no doubt be fleeting, too. She would savor it.

She thought about all the places she had looked for joy. The church in which she grew up had bought an old bus and painted it white. Then in huge letters they named it "JOY BUS." It was supposed to transport grown-ups who were otherwise housebound or did not drive. Most of all, it would bring in all the little children who otherwise could not attend Sunday School, whose parents for whatever reason did not go to church. There the children would learn about Jesus, accept Him, and bask in the joy of salvation ever after. Church membership dwindled. The remaining members could no longer afford the bus. No one else would buy it. The last she knew, it was rusting away amidst a tangle of brambles behind someone's barn. So much for joy.

Even before first grade, Dinah had recited the words her parents told her to say, inviting Jesus into her heart. Had He ever accepted her invitation? Dinah had no idea, but she didn't feel any joy in the whole situation. Being a Christian was too dire, too rigid, too demanding to allow joy a seat at the table. And when the only bright spots in her life died, joy departed forever.

She was the only girl in her small high school who excelled in math and science, but in rural Ohio, math and science were neither encouraged nor discouraged. No joy there. When she forwent marriage and family to earn her PhD in physiological chemistry, her parents disowned her. Girls could become nurses or teachers, maybe, until marriage. Then they were to serve their husband and children for the rest of their lives. That was how it was done. No joy there.

And now these burdens of a child, a dog (puppies! sigh), a company being harassed, a comfortable lifestyle being destroyed—what little happiness she had felt was under attack on all sides.

Mutt leaped up out of a sound sleep and ran to the door barking. The door burst open. Jonah bounded in waving a palm frond. The whole frond. In Dinah's church one palm frond served everyone in the congregation, each of whom had been allowed a single coarse, scratchy leaflet. Garret entered behind him.

Jonah crowed, "They even had a real donkey! We got to ride on him. They are really uncomfortable, Dinah. Really bony. It was so cool!"

Dinah realized she was watching unbridled joy. And her heart ached with—with envy! She envied a seven-year-old tortured, storm-tossed orphan.

Garret laid a hand on Jonah's shoulder. "Got a job for you, Sport. Take Mutt here down to the bus stop and wait for Grandma Trudy to get home. You can give her your palm frond, like we talked about."

"Yeah!" Jonah leashed up his dog and disappeared out the door.

Dinah stood up. "I detect a whirlwind just went through. May I get you a cup of coffee? And here are some fresh doughnuts." She opened the box on the table.

"Thank you. Sure." He sat down across from her chair. "Maple bars!" He pulled a white paper napkin from the holder on the table. "I have the day off. I was hoping Jonah might come to my house so we can finish the paintings we started. And you are welcome, too, of course."

"Don't kitties ever get sick on Palm Sunday?"

He grinned, an engaging, infectious grin. Obviously, he was just as ebullient in his own way as Jonah was. "Jason is holding down the fort today. He is Jewish. He gets Saturday off and doesn't mind working Sundays. Reformed Jew, he says, because sometimes he works Saturdays when we need him. We're hiring on some more help soon, and then we won't need him at all on Saturday."

"What is the difference between a Jew and a Reformed Jew?" Dinah poured.

"Not sure. I really should read up on that."

She settled into her chair and plucked a maple bar and a napkin.

Dinah Marie Taylor, you did not become a major-league entrepreneur by being timid. This is an excellent opportunity. Do it! "I think it's interesting that I thought you were freezing me out and you thought I was freezing you out. I still say you were treating me like ice when you were warm to everyone else."

"I apologize. I didn't know you."

She was momentarily distracted not by his apology but by the size of his hands. They were burly. How could they perform such delicate surgeries? "And I apologize, too. I didn't know you, either. Which brings me to my next question. This sounds very obsessive-compulsive of me, but I want to know more about you."

Garret sobered, nodding. "I hear you. In this day and age, you can't be too careful."

"I don't mean...like that." Now how should she proceed?

"You mean more than what's on the Websites."

"I guess. And, please believe me, I trust you or I would not have allowed Jonah to go to your place. I mean, well, just more about you. You became very sober, in fact dark, when I asked if you had kids. I thought it was an innocent question."

He pondered the maple-smeared stub, all that remained of his maple bar, popped it into his mouth, and chose another. "No, it wasn't a bad question. It just hit me wrong. Sorry. As I said, I was married once."

"I'm sorry, is this too personal?"

"No, it's just..." He stared at the table a moment. "I was still in school and she was a middle-management drone in a department store. She put me through school; we lived on her salary. She worked her way up through the ranks and ended near the top of the management heap. When I graduated I worked for other vets awhile, and she was making twice what I did. More. Then I started this practice and made even less at first. Most of us—Sue, Amber, myself, the core people—have been with the clinic since the beginning."

"Almost all of my employees have been with me from the start, too. They *are* the company." Should she have another maple bar? Oh, why not. She took the next-to-last one.

"Exactly! The company takes care of us and we take care of the company."

Dinah found herself nodding. They thought alike on that subject, at least.

"My sisters could see it better than I could. They claimed my wife was too controlling. A manipulator. Gloria ran me pretty much like she ran her job; she was the CEO. Boss. And I was the peon. I still insist that when I was just getting started, that was what I needed. Keep me focused. You may have noticed I tend to bounce off walls."

Dinah grinned. But what was making her happiest was

that he was finally opening up to her, becoming real, and it had nothing to do with walls.

"Sue says the clinic people were watching me change from cheerful and outgoing to sober and passive. Sue says Gloria's power—I guess *power* is the word I want—started to wear me down, robbed me of my exuberance, to use her words."

Dinah's head was wagging. "Are you saying she wore the pants and you became subservient?"

Garret smiled. "Subservient! That's the word. So one day an old friend of mine from Australia came to visit. He's a psychologist. A good one. He was our houseguest for a week while he attended a seminar series. Saw the way we interacted, of course. Just before he left, he took me aside. I still remember that his first words were, 'Now, look, mate. I know this isn't my business, but I have to say this.' And he laid out in plain English what he saw happening."

"Did you believe him? Usually, a person refuses to believe criticism."

"You're right, but it got me thinking. So I asked around the clinic what they thought and got an earful. That's when I started watching myself more objectively, you might say."

"You figured out what she was doing to you and divorced her?"

"I wish it were that simple. By now she was a senior vice president in the main office. Probably aiming for the presidency, and she might get it, too. The big thorn was children. She didn't want them. I did; it was the only thing I wanted from life. She didn't want to hamper her upward climb, she said, but she was making enough money that she could have hired a full-time nanny. Shucks; hire a whole staff."

"I see. Being denied the one thing you wanted; that's so sad."

He shrugged. "We just sort of drifted apart. Money means everything to her. I don't care about it much. She doesn't like pets; they're dirty. She wanted me to sell the clinic and move to Chicago. Lots of little points; a pitchfork with many tines." He shrugged. "Finally, it fell apart."

"Surely you know that more than half of marriages these days end in divorce."

His voice rose. "I don't care how many marriages fail. This was *my* marriage. I let her down. I let God down. I made promises and didn't keep them. I didn't take control and spend the time on our relationship that it needed. I let the big bad powerful woman cow me. And now it's too late." He hopped to his feet and went to the sink to wash off his sticky fingers.

Dinah just sat, trying not to look too stunned, as wave after wave of realization washed over her. He was angry, maybe even fearful of powerful women. Naturally he would see Dinah as a strong, determined woman who built a successful company, maybe even in a strange way fear her. Was that too overblown? Probably. But any way you looked at it, he was emotionally crippled. If only he could see the reality, what the rest of the world sees. *If only.* The saddest words in the world.

And with a shocking jolt, Dinah extended that thought: *I, too, am emotionally crippled. Am I seeing the reality, what the rest of the world sees? Is there hope for him?*

Is there hope for me?

Chapter Thirty-Two

Monday morning, nothing seemed more appealing than to burrow back into bed, pull the covers over her head, and hope Jonah and Mutt would keep on sleeping. That no one from work would call to see where she was. Actually she wished the whole world would go away and leave her alone.

While sanity knew her company would survive a six-month-or-more hiatus on Scoparia, feelings of rage and fear about the forces trying to kill the product could not be ignored. Low down. High handed. Everything in the middle.

And poor Marcella. It was not her fault, but she was so ripped up. Dinah had talked with her for over an hour last week, trying to get her to see that she had done her job correctly. Marcella was supposed to submit the documentation; she had done so clearly and adequately. But Marcella was still upset. Irrationally upset. On top of all that, something was bothering April, but when Dinah asked, she said she wasn't ready to talk about it yet. That meant it had to be serious, and that made sure that Dinah's imagination took off and dreamed up all kinds of horrible things, like cancer and divorce and—

She crawled from the bed as silently as possible, not able to tolerate the crazy mind attack she was suffering from. After pulling on her robe, she opened her door to find Mutt sitting there looking up at her, her head cocked as if asking a question.

"If you need to go out, which I'm sure you do, I am not dressed for that. Let me get some sweats on, okay?" Mutt followed her into the bedroom as if not trusting her to stay up, or do what she'd said.

Feet in sheepskin slippers, she grabbed a jacket and out they went. She was halfway down the stairs when she remembered her key. Huffing a sigh, she kept on going. She'd have to do a Jonah and put her jacket in the door. That was better than having to trek around the building and come in the front. That would be mortifying.

Outside, jacket in the door, she let Mutt lead. The dog sniffed and nosed before finally doing her business and trotting back to the door. "You'd think spring could manage to stay around, wouldn't you?"

Mutt looked over her shoulder but kept on going.

Jonah met them at the door. "She all right?"

"Yes, just wanted to go out and I thought you might sleep in."

"Why? I have to get ready to go to Grandma Trudy's." He headed for the kitchen. "Come on, Mutt."

Dinah stared after them. *You could have said thank you.*

Her phone sang while she was dressing for work.

"Dinah, this is Trudy. I'm sorry, but I think Jonah better not come here today. I have been hacking and miserable. I don't want him to catch this."

"I hope you feel better right away. Can I bring you anything?"

"No, Claire made a drugstore run, so we're stocked up on cold stuff. I know this gives you more pressure. I so love to have him come."

They hung up and Dinah glared at the face in the mirror. This was just getting worse by the moment.

When she told Jonah, his lower lip stuck out far enough for a bird perch.

She felt even poutier than he. "Look, I'm sorry."

"Why can't I stay here? Mutt and me will be okay. We won't go out but for her to potty. I promise."

"You're just too young, Jonah. Leaving you here alone is against the law."

"Mr. Watson could come check on me."

Dinah shook her head, reminding herself not to get rattled. "Maybe Grandma Trudy will be better by tomorrow."

He slumped down in his chair, arms locked across his chest. "I hate your office. I want my mommy to come back."

"Sorry Jonah, but I can't do much about either. Get your coat and backpack. We leave in five minutes. We're too late for Extraburger now."

"I ate cereal. Can Mutt come?"

"No, Mutt cannot come. Move it." She got her coat out and gathered her briefcase and bag. "Now, Jonah."

"I can't find my hat."

"I'm sorry, but we have to leave. I have a conference call in twenty minutes. *Now*, Jonah!" The urge to snatch him by the jacket collar and push him ahead of her made her take a step back. Instead she snatched up his backpack. He snatched it back and humped it over his shoulder by one strap as they left. He slouched in the corner of the elevator, as far from her as he could get, arms locked again over his chest.

He had been so happy yesterday when Garret was here. The contrast was just another reminder of how inept she was.

Dinah tried to think of something to say, but her mind had gone into freefall, screaming accusations at her. *You can't be a mother. Temper, temper. Failure. Poor kid. You are downright mean.*

By the time they reached the office door, she could hardly drag herself through it.

"Uh-oh, what's up?" April stared from one to the other.

"Trudy caught a cold so Jonah can't go there and—"

"I can stay with Mutt."

"Not when you're seven. Guess you'll have to visit us again," April said brightly.

He glared at her and stomped down the hall to the break room, slamming the door behind him.

"Wow, the kid has a temper after all." She looked to Dinah. "Don't worry, he'll get over it. Give him some time."

"I really need to get him into counseling. Mr. Jensen sent me a list, but I have no idea how to go about finding which one is most competent. I called a few that had good online reviews, but they didn't have availability for a new patient for months." Dinah set her too-heavy briefcase on the desk.

April handed her the inevitable sheaf of orange slips. "Your duty calls. May I call around for you, see what I can find?"

"April, that would be wonderful. You know I'm totally at sea on this. Besides, I have that conference call in five minutes."

"No, you don't. They postponed. Called a couple of minutes ago. But you really need to talk with Marcella some more. She's still pretty upset, talking about quitting." April shook her head. "This is sure a sorry Monday. Did you have breakfast?"

"No. I was awake from four or so on. When I finally couldn't stand the mind and the bed any longer, I tried to be careful but Mutt met me at the door. I can't even have a cup of coffee in the morning by myself."

"I hear you. Mothers feel that way a lot. Welcome to your new life."

Dinah thought of checking on Jonah, but when she heard the television on in the board room, she entered her office instead. Today the rose on her desk stirred up another pool of resentment. She grabbed the bud vase and marched back to April's desk.

"Look. Too much of my life is unknown or out of control already. Please don't put any more flowers on my desk unless we know who they came from. Or on my coffee table at home, either!"

"They are meant to cheer you and thank you."

"So you *do* know where they came from!"

"From all your employees. We have the greatest possible work situation here, and we're grateful. We love our work and we love you. All of us. Even the night cleaning woman."

"And so you levy a—"

"Voluntary donations to a jar. Whenever there's enough in it, we get you flowers. You care about us, Dinah, and we care about you, and about what you've given us."

"I don't—I had no idea. I'm sorry I-I meant to thank you." Stunned, she returned to her office. And left the door open.

A minute later she saw Jonah heading down the hall past her office. He must be going to talk to April.

She crossed to her chair and flopped into it. She just wanted a few minutes to herself. But her breastbone was tickling. Something felt off. Jonah had his backpack with him, that was what bothered her. Surely he wouldn't leave after she told him he had to stay here.

"Jonah?" she called.

No answer.

On impulse she left her office. No one at April's desk. She hurried down the hall.

She was relieved to find him in the break room, standing there with his head bowed, his hands in prayer position. "Thank You, Jesus. So please tell Mommy I'm coming to see her and I love her and I love You. Amen." He knelt down, unzipped his backpack, and pulled out Dinah's paring knife.

Why...?

His words and actions suddenly clicked together.

"*NOOOO!*" Dinah didn't think; didn't aim. She lunged forward so wildly she fell into him, knocking the knife from his hand and carrying them both tumbling against the television stand. The stand rocked back as she slammed against it; the TV set fell forward, hitting her shoulder on the way down. The audio blare quit but the crash reverberated.

How could he so casually do this!

How could she fail him so miserably that he would rather be dead than live with her?

The room filled up and echoed with her screaming and Jonah's violent sobbing. No, it wasn't Jonah sobbing; it was she. He was the one screaming. He flailed like a windmill, his little arms and legs surprisingly effective at pummeling her.

Then April was there, shouting at Jonah. Dinah realized she was in a tug-of-war with April, hanging on to Jonah as April was trying to pull him off her. She must let go of him. She could not.

April won the tussle because Dinah's shoulder gave out.

Jonah...Dinah struggled to sitting.

April was sitting on the floor, tightly wrapped around him, holding his arms down, one leg thrown across his legs, arching her head aside because he was trying to head-butt her. She was cooing, speaking quietly. She began to rock back and forth, softly singing to him. Dinah knew the song, too. In her childhood she had sung it so many times. "Jesus loves me, this I know, for the Bible tells me so. Little ones..."

Jonah wailed, "I wanna see Mommy! Don't! I wanna go to Mommy!" Finally, he melted against April, moaned for his mommy a few times, and apparently gave up.

Dinah butt-scooted over to April and held out her arms, drawing Jonah from April's care into hers. She noticed rather abstractly that her own weeping had reduced itself to occasional wrenching sobs. "Oh, Jonah. My poor, poor little Jonah."

April picked up the knife with two fingers. She wagged her head as she laid it behind her.

"April, he needs something now. Right now. Right this minute. Not when some counselor manages to fit in an appointment."

April drew her knees up and draped her arms across them. "I agree. And this is beyond me. I never had anything like this. I don't know..."

"Thank you." It sounded lame, considering the circumstances, but it was all she could say. "Thank you,

April, for being here for me. I don't know what I'd do without you." *Wait. What is this?* She watched April fighting to school her face. "We've worked together and been friends for too long; we know each other, and I can tell you are not being forthright with me now. What is it?"

"This is definitely not the time to discuss this, but there hasn't been a good time."

"*What is it?!*" Dinah was yelling. Even her voice was wildly out of control now.

"I'm sorry, Dinah. Joe has been promoted. He has taken over the company's LA office. I have to resign."

Dinah stared at her. *Not April. This is too much.* She wanted to ask *How can you do this to me?* Instead, she asked, "How long have you known?"

"Three days. With all that's happened, it just never seemed like the right moment to tell you. Certainly this is not the right moment, either."

"April, you can't! You're key! The company can't function without you!"

"I won't leave you in the lurch; I'll train my replacement. Maybe Marcella would be a good one to take over."

"Marcella can't handle things going wrong. And she's not a good people person, like you are. There is no replacement, so don't talk about your replacement."

Her personal life, and now her business life, all in shambles. It was all falling apart, all of it. What was there left?

Jonah was left; that's what was left.

Dinah kissed the top of the tousled little head still cradled in her arms. "Come on, Jonah." She gained her feet and was dismayed by how wobbly she felt. "April, I'm too

upset to drive; I don't trust myself to stay focused in traffic. Will you drive me, please?"

April stood up. "Frankly, I'm pretty upset myself. I'll
ask Randy. He's not babysitting any experiments right
now. Where to?"

"To Garret's."

Chapter Thirty-Three

Randy pulled Dinah's car past the now-familiar front of the Miller clinic and parked in a handicapped space beside their door. He hopped out and opened the back car door for Dinah.

She swung her legs out and stood up. Behind her, Jonah scooted across the seat and climbed out.

Randy dropped her car keys into her hand.

She stared at them, numb. "How will you...Who...? Uh, we're in a handicapped slot." Her mind was skipping about like a cricket on a caffeine jag.

Randy grinned. "No problem. I'll just move the sign."

"But..."

But he was off, jogging out toward the street.

She led Jonah inside by the hand.

Amber was all smiles. "Hey, Jonah! Good to see you! Dr. G is back in the break room. Why don't you go say hello?"

"Okay." Jonah seemed so despondent, so defeated. Dinah felt just as defeated.

Garret was sitting at the table. He looked up from his laptop as they walked in and grinned. "Hello, Sport! Come sit. Can I get you anything?"

Jonah shrugged.

"How about Orange Crush? I'm going to have one. Dinah? What would you like?"

"Uh...Orange Crush is fine." *For pity sake, Dinah, pull yourself together!*

He stuck his head in their fridge, digging out cans. "April called and explained. I'm glad you came by, both of you." He stood erect. "We have doughnuts, Jonah. Want a maple bar?"

"Okay." *How could he act so...normal?* But because he did, both she and Jonah began to relax.

He set out cans and a box of doughnuts. "Let's just cut right to it. Jonah: you were trying to get to heaven, right?" He sat down and plunked paper napkins in front of Jonah and Dinah.

The boy plucked out a maple bar. "I want to see Mommy again."

Garret nodded and chose himself a maple bar, too. "And she's there and you're here. Actually, when you think about it, that was a pretty good idea you had there."

Dinah gasped, "*What?*"

Jonah was nodding. "The judge said a knife is a weapon, so I figured it would work. But Dinah yelled at me and wouldn't let me do it."

"Good thinking. However. There's some stuff you don't know about yet, and that could cause problems."

"Like what?" Jonah bit into his doughnut.

"Let's see. How can I explain this?" Garret leaned forward, both elbows on the table. "You know there's all different kinds of churches. Catholics, Baptists, plain old community churches. And they all trust Jesus, but they believe different things about Him. Some churches say that only God can decide if you live or die, and if you make that decision yourself—that is, if you kill yourself before God wants you to be dead—they say you can't get into heaven."

"Then I wouldn't see Mommy after all."

Dinah felt her mouth fall open.

"Exactly." Garret unpopped Jonah's can and his own. "I have no idea whether they're right or wrong, but if they're right, you sure don't want to take that chance. You don't want to mess up so bad that you never ever get to see your mommy."

Jonah sat there, obviously deep in thought.

Dinah watched them both but said nothing.

Jonah mused, "So maybe Dinah was right about not letting me do it."

"I think so. She's usually right about stuff. Besides, if Mutt is pregnant like we think, she'll need you. You have to housebreak and train the puppies. They don't do it by themselves, you know."

Dinah sat flabbergasted.

"Okay. So I guess I can't go and be with Mommy, huh?"

Garret wagged his head gravely. "Not yet. Not until God wants you to. He knows best. Hey, I just remembered; Amber has to feed the fish. Can you go help her, please?"

"Sure!" Jonah hopped up, his Orange Crush and doughnut forgotten, and hurried out.

Dinah sank forward and propped her elbows on the table, too. "Thank you, Garret. You knew what to do before, quieting that meltdown; you were the only one I could think of now—you know, on short notice." She sort of chuckled; not a happy chuckle at all. "And in a million years I would never have thought of that. You defused the situation brilliantly."

"He was telling me about when his mother was alive. He was the man of the house in every sense of the word. He may miss having all that responsibility; it was his life. Can you give him more responsibility? With Mutt, of course. But other things, too. Not just make-work, either. He'll spot that in a heartbeat. Real responsibility."

"That's a splendid idea." She stopped. "Unfortunately, there's not a whole lot to do in a condo. It's why I moved there. I've never wanted to take the time to mow the lawn and all the stuff that goes with a larger place. I'm happiest in the lab; that's where I wanted to devote my time."

"Creating new products, like Scoparia."

"Like Scoparia." She smiled a sad smile, not a happy one. "Now if only they would let me help people with it."

"April told me. More tests. Apparently the FDA is considering classifying it as drug, and if they do..." He let it hang.

"It's not the FDA yet. Certain companies who stand to lose revenue are pushing it. But we can't wait until it happens. More tests. More data. Say, you don't know anyone with Type II diabetes, do you?"

"I'll sign my mother up."

"Your mother has diabetes?" She studied his face a moment, pulled her phone out of her bag and thumbed the speed dial. "April? Send a supply of Scoparia over here to Garret's office, please. Today. And make sure the full info pamphlet is with it, not just the one-pager." She watched Garret's face. "Yes, he did. You can't imagine how smoothly he got Jonah past it. I think we're safe for the moment. I'll tell you about it later." April and she goodbyed each other and she dropped her phone back in her bag.

"Thank you, Dinah. From what I hear, it might be a lifesaver. So far, she refuses to consider insulin."

"And I can't thank you enough. And, really, I am going to get him professional help, as soon as possible." She had started to rise when a little bell went ding in her head. She sat down again. "Wait. April told you the FDA might cause problems? That's proprietary information. Did she also mention that her husband is transferring?"

"She did. She said—"

Dinah found herself on her feet. Her brain was racing. "That's not information she's supposed to be blabbing all around! I can't believe she'd—"

And now he was on his feet, too. "She needed prayer support. She still does. When she learned she'd be leaving, we sat in her office a long time talking about options and praying. Your world is falling apart—we both see that—and it's tearing her up just as bad as it's tearing you up."

"But she doesn't have a company to tear up! I do! When she leaves it's going to go right down the toilet. And I can't do this mom thing! And I don't want puppies! Or prayer support! I am so sick of hearing about God and prayer and all that fiction!"

He stood there, watching her. How could he make his eyes appear so tender and caring? So he had learned that April was leaving even before Dinah did. Days before! How could they betray her like this? Supposedly they were friends and yet behind her back, they were...so...so...Christian love? Bah!

"Look, Garret, I've heard all the pretty platitudes. I know the lingo. From way younger than Jonah; we went to church every time the doors swung open—Wednesday and Sunday and any other time my mother and father decided we needed sanctifying. I accepted Jesus Christ as my savior when I was five, when I had absolutely no idea what I was saved from or saved for. I did it to please Gramma Grace and because it was expected of me. And don't doubt that April and all those other so-called Christians in my company have been on my case for years."

He watched her. Simply watched her.

She shuddered and covered her face as the universe crashed down upon her.

Now his big, burly arms had wrapped around her, and one big healing hand was pressing her head to his shoulder while the other rubbed her back the way Gramma Grace had when she was so little and so vulnerable.

She struggled for a fraction of a second and gave up. Gave up. No strength, no desire to live or breathe. She gave up. *Dinah Marie Taylor, you were not raised to give up.* She gave up. Melted against him.

His voice purred like one of the cats he treated. "I'll have to show you the paintings of you and Jonah and Mutt that I started. And haven't finished. It's because of the eyes. Your eyes. You have this lovely face, beautiful hair, and your eyes are haunted. I cannot capture the pain, and, without it, the picture isn't you."

She shuddered again. *Haunted.* Yeah, that was a good word.

That hand on her back continued its gentle rub, just like Gramma Grace. "Dinah, it's time you told me why your eyes are haunted. I want to know because I care about you."

Because I care about you. Dinah found herself yearning to believe that. "My little brother, Michael. He slept more than he ought, drank gallons of water. Then his breath began to smell like he was sneaking wine. He was five. Where would he get wine? But they prayed over him

to get rid of the demon alcohol, then took him to a clinic
for a tonic to spiff him up. The nurse there said he had
an advanced form of Type I diabetes; it had been neglected way too long; and needed treatment right away.
Daily insulin shots. They refused. Our minister declared
that if their faith was strong enough, he would be healed.
Jesus would heal him, like He raised the widow's son. My
mother and father believed him. Michael slipped into a
coma and I watched him die. They told me it was because
I hadn't prayed hard enough."

"I'm so sorry."

"Two years later, the only solid pillar in my world died,
Gramma Grace. Dad's mom. Type II diabetes." *Oh,
Gramma Grace! Michael!* She took a deep breath. "So
you tell me: if those were God's will, why would I want to
love and serve a God like that?"

He said nothing, but his arms continued their fortifying
wrap around her.

"No platitudes, Garret? This seems like the perfect
time for a platitude."

"They didn't seek help for your grandmother, either, I
take it. Was this their idea or their pastor's?"

"What are you getting at?"

"John Hanson. Our study leader. You're going to really
like John. He tells this story: This fellow got caught in a
flood. It rose almost to the roof of his house. So here he
sat on his ridgepole. A rowboat came by. 'I'm here to rescue you,' the boatman said.

"'No problem,' said the fellow. 'I am praying to God
and He will rescue me.' Awhile later, a motorboat came
by. Same thing. Then a helicopter. 'No, no, God will rescue me.' The flood topped his roof and he drowned.
When he got to the gates of heaven he was furious. 'You

promised to rescue me and you didn't! What use is faith?' And Saint Peter, he says, 'Hey, man. It's your fault. We sent you two boats and a helicopter.'"

In her deep despair, she almost smiled.

"Not to put too fine a point on it, but to refuse appropriate medicine is like refusing the rescue that God sent. I'm sorry you blame Jesus instead. It wasn't His idea."

"But..." What could she say?

"Jonah tried to go to heaven and God didn't allow it. It wasn't his time to go."

"Then why was it Michael's?" She insisted. "And Gramma Grace's?"

"I have no idea. I'm not God."

Whatever had given her the idea that this man could care for her? This man who had been so hostile toward her in the beginning? Or that she could reciprocate? But why, then, was it that his hug felt so good? And why, when she didn't know what to do, had she come to him? As if things shuffled around into some kind of order. No longer chaos, but order.

She coveted order.

"Dinah? I realize this sounds stupid, but you're not Gloria."

"Gloria?" She tipped her head back to look at him. "Your ex-wife?"

He nodded. "When I first met you—encountered you is probably a better way to put it—you were the perfect picture of a take-charge woman. It took me a long time to get past the past; to realize that you're not the woman I imagined. Please believe me when I say I've come to care for both you and Jonah. You're stuck with me."

Caring. Was that a lesser form of love? Or perhaps an even greater thing than love. *What if caring leads to love?*

The voice came whisper soft, tiptoeing down the corri-
dors of her churning mind.

She stiffened and he loosened his hug a little. "I don't
know what..." All she could do was wag her head. She
understood what hydration did to carboxyl ions, but she
could not understand her own mind. She did understand,
though, that he had helped Jonah when she could not.
And she stood a good chance of helping his mother when
he could not. And there was April, caring so much about
all of them. And. So many *ands*.

So. Life was not the quiet, simple, controlled environ-
ment of the laboratory. It was the big, wide messy world,
and if Dinah would hide from life and refuse to engage
it, apparently life was going to leap out and engage her
whether she wanted it or not.

Do something! The only way to handle all this. Her
mother used to clean closets when life got hard. They had
had the cleanest, neatest closets in the universe. Where
had that thought come from? Another blindside?

His voice rumbled along. "You probably don't agree
with me, but with your company, you have been doing
God's will all along—helping people live better lives. And
saving lives if you can. It's the same job I do."

"I don't—"

"Hey, I read your mission statement. I didn't see anything there about making money. And I remember that
interview on TV. They tried to stick a profit motive on you
and you shook it off. You do what you do to help others.
That's Jesus."

"That interview." So long ago! Ages ago!

"To a bunch of smelly shepherds, God spoke with a
whole skyful of angels. To eastern sages, all he had to do
was shove a star out of place. He speaks to each person

in a way that is unique to each person. Jesus has been by your shoulder the whole time, and He is more than happy to meet you on your terms. I hope you can find each other."

"You said you got past the past. I'm not sure I can."

He loosened the hug more. "Have I mentioned to you that I belong to a really dynamite group of folks who pray for each other?"

Prayer. There is was again. "You seem to have mentioned it."

He was smiling. "We're having a get-together after the Good Friday evening service, to bless our new classroom. I'd like you and Jonah to come with me. Maybe we can all just start over."

She thought she had learned ways to deal with life. And death. And God and Jesus and—memories. So much changed. Her ways did not work. Everything had collapsed, from her faith on out. Now she must pick up the pieces.

She drew a deep breath. "If you want me to come to your group on Good Friday evening, I will do that."

Epilogue

Dinah sat on the sand facing west as the sun drifted ever lower. Garret sat behind her, his knees bent on either side of his new wife. When she leaned back and turned her head to ask him something, he took the opportunity to kiss her cheek.

Earlier in the day, the South Carolina beach in June had been more populated, but apparently everyone had gone to dinner, leaving the beach to Garret and Dinah.

He pointed to the horizon. "See that spot just to the left of straight out there? It should swell just as the sun disk drops below the horizon."

"How do you know for sure?"

"Look at that little tiny cloud above there. It's getting golder."

"Getting golder?" She tipped her head back, just to feel his nearness.

"You didn't marry a grammar and language professor, you know."

"No, I married a cartoonist who makes sick animals well again. Besides, Jonah insisted that we all live in the same house." She narrowed her eyes. "I think it is coming."

"Hear the songs of the waves? And the birds. Even they are saying goodbye to the day." He inhaled and slowly let it out again. "I love this hush." He nuzzled her neck. "And you."

The golden sun dropped away, but not the golden light.

"There it is." Dinah pointed to the gilded spot that hovered with every blink of the eyes. "I caught it."

He wrapped both arms around her shoulders. "Our glimpse of glory. I think God orders the sun to show us a glimpse of His glory, first with the dawn and then like now, the sun setting. We can't handle any more than this, but someday we will see Him face-to-face and we won't have to worry about burning our eyes."

"I love that." Her sigh sang of contentment and peace. "Thank you for insisting we come out here."

"Other than time alone with you, I wanted you to see this. That's why we are honeymooning here."

"Good a reason as any."

"You think Jonah is hungry yet?" They'd left him at the house. The windows of Garret's aunt Sylvia's house up the beach were blazing now with liquid gold. The sky glinted off them, off every bright surface. How splendid!

Marrying Garret meant a whole big family for Jonah, and for Dinah: brother, sisters, nieces, and nephews. Garret's mother was one of the first to buy Scoparia when it finally went on sale. Dinah had offered to give it to her, but she said she wanted to brag about her daughter-in-law at the store.

Mutt came jogging up the beach toward them. With her pups weaned and given away, running up and down the beach was helping her regain her girlish figure.

Dinah used Garret's knees as braces to stand, dusted the sand off the seat of her jeans, and gave him a hand up. The two of them strolled upbeach toward the house, arms around each other, the evening breeze that had just sprung up tickling their necks.

Barefooted, Jonah met them on the deck. "Mom, you got sand on your feet. You gotta brush it off or Aunt Sylvia won't give you supper. She said so."

Dinah smiled first at Jonah and then to Garret. *Mom.* What a title.

Reading Group Guide

Discussion Questions

1. What advice would you give Dinah when Corinne asks her to take her son?

2. Juggling family and career is never easy. If you have had experience here, what have you done to make it work?

3. Who was your favorite character? Why?

4. Losing one's faith when life gets too rough is not unusual. Have you ever experienced this? What did you do? How have you helped someone else through this?

5. What was the central theme in *Heaven Sent Rain*?

6. God has a knack for turning our lives upside down and taking us down a new path. How has He done that in your life? How did you respond?

7. Have you ever had a negative first impression of someone because he or she reminded you of someone

who hurt you in the past? Did your opinion change over time?

8. Have you ever reached out to help a homeless person or someone hungry? What did you do? How did you feel?

Contemporary novels that celebrate love and family by Lauraine Snelling

Wake the Dawn

"Snelling's description of events at the small clinic during the storm is not to be missed."
—*Publishers Weekly*

Physician's assistant Esther Hansen struggles to run an ill-equipped smalltown clinic during a devastating storm. But she is both tested and finds healing when a grieving border patrolman arrives with an abandoned baby.

Reunion

"Inspired by events in Snelling's own life, *Reunion* is a beautiful story."
—*RT Book Reviews*

Kiera Sorenson is shaken when she uncovers the fifty-year-old secret that she was adopted, and soon after her teenaged niece's pregnancy is revealed. Will love be enough to hold the Sorenson family together in spite of these challenging truths?

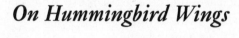

On Hummingbird Wings

"Snelling can certainly charm."
—*Publishers Weekly*

Gillian Ormsby arrives in California to care for her ailing mother with plans to return to New York as quickly as possible. But as her friendship with her mother's neighbor develops into more, Gillian considers trading professional success for a renewed and rewarding sense of family.

One Perfect Day

"[A] spiritually challenging and emotionally taut story. Fans of Christian women's fiction will enjoy this winning novel."

—*Publishers Weekly*

Only days before Christmas, the tragic loss of a child devastates one mother but offers another the miracle she's been praying for. The gift of second chances made bittersweet, can these mothers find hope in knowing that the spirit of each child lives on?

Breaking Free

"Reminding us that love can spring forth from ashes, that life can emerge from death, Lauraine Snelling writes a gripping and powerful novel that will inspire and uplift you."

—Lynne Hinton, author of *The Last Odd Day*

Maggie Roberts gains a renewed sense of purpose through working to keep a horse from being discarded. But her reason for living is threatened when a local businessman offers the horse a permanent home.

Available in trade paperback and eBook formats wherever books are sold.

Historical Fiction From Lauraine Snelling

To see a complete list of Lauraine's books, visit laurainesnelling.com.

Trygve Knutson is a man devoted to his family and his community. He currently has a job on a construction crew, helping to build a future for the town of Blessing, North Dakota. Though he loves his home, he sometimes dreams of other horizons—especially since meeting Miriam Antonio.

Miriam, a student nurse, is in Blessing to get practical training to become an accredited nurse. She hopes to find a position in a Chicago hospital that will enable her to support her siblings and her ailing mother. Eager to return home to a family that needs her, Miriam is surprised to find she likes Blessing very much. In fact, her growing attachment to Trygve has her questioning a future she's always considered set in stone.

When a family emergency calls Miriam home sooner than planned, will she find a way to return? And if not, will it mean losing Trygve—and her chance at love—for good?

To Everything a Season
Song of Blessing #1

◊ BETHANYHOUSE